Jo looked out of the wi[...] to run a list of names thro[...]ing to a beautiful violet from the deep red, and as Jo watched the sun disappear in the horizon a glittering plane caught her eye. It was preparing to land, and, suddenly preoccupied again by her future, Jo imagined packing up her belongings and heading back to the horseshoe-shaped airport with Joanne Hill's passport in her hands. The assistants at check-in would not believe that the slim, beautiful woman in front of them was the same dumpy, ugly girl in the passport photo, and Jo smiled. From the moment she stepped on to the plane and away from Miami it would be the beginning of her new life. Miami had been the making of her, and as Jo remembered the airport's nickname – MIA for Miami International Airport – she knew what she had to be called.

'I'm going to be Mia Blackwood,' Jo said, as she turned back to Gable. 'It has a nice ring to it, don't you think?'

Ilana Fox currently works for the *Sun*, and has previously worked for the *Daily Telegraph*, *Daily Mail*, *Mail on Sunday*, *Evening Standard* and *London Lite*. In her spare time she goes shopping for clothes she doesn't need, sings 80s songs off-key, refuses to read newspapers and fantasises about living in Manhattan. She lives in Wandsworth, south-west London. Visit her website at www.ilanafox.co.uk.

The Making of Mia

ILANA FOX

An Orion paperback

First published in Great Britain in 2007
by Orion
This paperback edition published in 2008
by Orion Books Ltd,
Orion House, 5 Upper Saint Martin's Lane,
London WC2H 9EA

An Hachette Livre UK company

1 3 5 7 9 10 8 6 4 2

A CIP catalogue record for this book
is available from the British Library.

ISBN 978-0-7528-9392-1

Typeset by Deltatype Ltd, Birkenhead, Merseyside

Printed and bound in Great Britain by
Clays Ltd, St Ives plc

The Orion Publishing Group's policy is to use papers that
are natural, renewable and recyclable products and
made from wood grown in sustainable forests. The logging
and manufacturing processes are expected to conform to
the environmental regulations of the country of origin.

www.orionbooks.co.uk

Joshua burst out laughing. '"Secret in your past"? Why the melodrama, darling, and what on earth are you talking about?' Joshua took Mia's hands in his and smiled. 'Did you once make a porn movie in Hollywood when you were helping your brother start his career? Might I have seen it?' Joshua's tone was light, but Mia knew he was worried. He couldn't have a wife with any skeletons in her closet. 'Because I'd rather like to watch you having sex ... especially considering you've been making me wait all this time.'

Mia's green eyes narrowed and her voice turned to ice. 'Don't be stupid,' she snapped, and Joshua stopped laughing as he saw how serious the beautiful woman in front of him was. 'Take a closer look at me, Josh,' she said with slight menace in her tone. 'Don't you remember me? Because after all this time I never forgot you.'

PART ONE

May 2007

Joshua was going to go nuclear, Mia thought, as she sashayed seductively across her living-room to hand him a whisky. As she leant down to pass him the Tiffany cut-crystal tumbler, she caught sight of herself in the darkness of her floor-to-ceiling window. She paused slightly as she once again acknowledged just how beautiful she was. Her long limbs were lightly tanned, her make-up was as fresh as it had been when she'd applied it earlier in the evening, and her cheeks were flushed with anticipation.

Mia smiled softly at Joshua and then walked over to the antique mirror to scrutinise herself properly. Yes, she was stunning, but there was something about her reflection that made her feel uncomfortable: she was too perfect. Mia remembered how she used to look, and rather than disliking the memory of her former appearance, she was haunted by an image of a happier, more carefree girl. As much as she loved her Balenciaga gown, the Cartier garnet and diamond necklace that sparkled against her neck, and her expensive gold-spun highlights, she'd have been happier in jeans and a sloppy T-shirt. She wanted to be herself again.

Across the river Big Ben began to chime midnight, and Mia suppressed a tiny smile. It was so apt. This was the moment when Cinderella turned from the mysterious woman who stole Prince Charming's heart back into the put-upon scullery maid, and Mia was about to do the same.

In the mirror Mia could see Joshua walking over to her with a fond expression on his face, and as she turned round he produced a small Asprey jewellery box and got down on one knee. Mia tried not to look pleased. Joshua really believed that she would accept his proposal and give up running *Gloss* magazine.

'Mia Blackwood,' he announced theatrically in his booming voice, 'will you marry me?'

It was one of those chick-flick moments that Joshua was so keen on, and as if on cue Joshua flipped the lid to the box to expose the largest pink princess-cut diamond Mia had ever seen. She tried not to laugh. She'd always known that Joshua traded in magazine clichés, but this was ridiculously over the top, even for him. His divorce hadn't even come through yet.

'Oh, Josh,' Mia said with a sigh, glancing at the platinum ring with minimal interest. 'What if I told you that at midnight I turn from being the beautiful princess into one of the ugly sisters? Would you still love me then?' Mia scrutinised Joshua's face while keeping hers as emotionless as possible. She sounded like she was in a play, but she knew it fitted the situation perfectly.

Joshua laughed patronisingly, and scooped Mia up into his arms.

'You and your fairy stories,' he said, kissing Mia's nose affectionately. Mia slithered from his grip in a quiet rage and took a deep breath. She was going in for the kill.

'Joshua, I'm serious.' Mia's eyes glinted with steely determination. 'You sit in your gilded office and think you know everyone and everything, but how much do you really know about me? I'm willing to bet you haven't a clue about the secret in my past.'

Acknowledgements

First I'd like to thank my agents — Michael Sissons and Fiona Petheram at PFD — for everything they've done, and for the belief they had in me. I feel very lucky to have such an amazing team of people on my side.

Thank you to my editor Kate Mills for her inspired and patient editing, Genevieve Pegg for holding my hand over email and for her advice, and also to Helen Windrath for ironing out the remains of my strange American grammar. I wouldn't have had as much fun writing this without you. To everyone at Orion, thank you so much.

To my friends and family, I want to thank Ben Harvey and Natasha Moore for reading every word of the very first draft several times. Other notables include Naomi and Abi Stern (best cousins in the world, so proud of both of you), Dad and Magda, and Holly Seddon for just being the best. Also, thank you to: Hannah Weimers, Andre Litwin, Justin Myers, Ewan MacLeod, George Stern, Christian Martin, Lina Sonne, Sophia Wong, Sarah Graham, Claudia Dutson, Helen Nicholson, Stacey Teale, James Seddon, Shaun Terriss, Sean Griffin, Chris Chivrall, Anouska Graham, Jamie Griffin, Pete Picton, Danny Dagan, all the Cobra boys, and my mates at the *Sun* who kept me going — far too many of you to name, but you know who you are. Cheers.

For Harry and Nan Fox.
I love you both very, very much.
I told you I'd do it. So there!

Chapter One

'Joanne Hill!'

Jo had been starting to fall asleep at her desk when she heard her name being barked out in front of the whole class. She groaned inwardly and quickly looked up at her least favourite teacher. It didn't matter if she was daydreaming about running a magazine or was paying as much attention as was humanly possible – Miss Montgomery never failed to sniff out weakness, especially when it came to her. As the teacher shot an icy glare in her direction, some of the more popular girls in the English class began to giggle, and Jo felt her face start to flush. She hated herself for being an easy target, and was aware – for the thousandth time – that her street accent and second-hand, oversized uniform marked her out as someone who didn't quite belong. It didn't matter that she'd been at the exclusive boarding school for seven years – people still relished gossiping about her background, often making up wild rumours when they got bored of the truth. Jo didn't care that her mother lived on a council estate and worked in a call centre, but she hated the others making crude jokes about it on top of everything else.

'Yes, Miss Montgomery?' Jo asked in a quiet voice, hoping that if she stayed calm and measured she'd not draw any more attention to herself. It didn't work. Every eye in the classroom turned towards her, and Jo knew they were scrutinising her double chins and rolls of fat as well as her bright red cheeks and lack of make-up.

'Can you give me an example of brotherly love in *Hamlet*?' Miss Montgomery snapped impatiently, and she raised a perfectly plucked eyebrow.

Jo felt like screaming about how unfair it all was. Even though she normally loved English, she had to admit that she'd not read the play – she'd been up until 4 a.m. on deadline to finish an article for *Saint*, the school magazine, and had completely forgotten about her homework. Jo racked her brain to think of something that could deflect everyone's attention from her and back to the teacher.

'Is it when Hamlet's brother dives in front of a bullet – no, a sword – like a bodyguard, miss?' Jo hesitated, wondering if it really was a good idea to suggest that the seminal moment of a low-budget, made-for-TV film was on par with a Shakespearian play. The roar of laughter from the bitchier girls proved it wasn't, and Jo wanted to slide under her desk and hide. She hadn't meant to be humorous.

'You think you're so funny, don't you, Joanne, but your poor excuse for wit doesn't disguise the fact you've not bothered to do your homework,' Miss Montgomery spat, her dislike for Jo apparent. 'So what were you doing last night that was more important than studying for your A-levels?'

Miss Montgomery began walking around the front of the classroom, and all the girls kept their eyes on her, enjoying the performance. Apparently, before she came to teach at St Christopher's School for Girls in Buckinghamshire, she'd been a journalist on a local paper, clawing her way up the career ladder with her red-lacquered nails until redundancy meant she had to give it up. Teaching and lodging at a private boarding school clearly made more sense financially, but the teacher was still bitter that her career had ended so soon after it had begun, and she hated Jo Hill for her almost naïve determination to succeed in journalism. Miss Montgomery flipped her long auburn hair over her shoulder, and then surveyed the rest of the class with her kohl-rimmed green eyes.

'Well?'

Jo hesitated, not wanting to tell the truth because she couldn't stand it if someone derided her dedication to *Saint*, but not knowing what to say instead. But it was too late – one of the others swooped in for the kill.

'She was eating Mars bars, miss,' Jemima sang out, giving Jo a characteristically bitchy look before smirking at her friends. 'I think Joanne has eschewed formal education in order to beat a world record in the number of chocolate bars she can cram into her face in an hour. If my memory serves me correctly, she ate at least four of them.' Jemima looked smug, and Jo wanted to die. It was true, but she couldn't help it: writing articles for the magazine made her hungry.

'Now, Jems, I don't think that's fair,' added Susie, casually. Jo looked on in surprise – Susie and Jemima were best friends, and Susie had never stuck up for her before.

'It wasn't four bars of chocolate, it was at least forty, and I'm sure Joanne isn't doing this in lieu of her homework. From what I heard she's doing a sponsored eat-a-thon to raise money for impoverished children that walk around in rags. Like she does.'

Jo surreptitiously looked down at her tatty Pop Swatch – one she'd bought with two years' worth of pocket money when she was ten – and worked out how much longer the lesson would last. Despite loving English Literature she hated Miss Montgomery, and she couldn't wait to get to PE – which was unheard of for her.

'Girls,' Miss Montgomery warned, with a hint of amusement in her voice. 'Please can we not discuss Joanne and get back to *Hamlet*. While there is an important lesson to be learnt with regard to Miss Hill's enthusiastic eating habits, you'll be tested on Ophelia's beauty, not Joanne Hill's weight.'

The teacher let the giggles subside and turned back to the whiteboard, starting a soliloquy about Hamlet and Horatio's relationship. Jo tried to take in what was being said, but she felt too numb to concentrate. When she'd passed the scholarship exams at the age of eleven to come to the school she'd never imagined it would be like this.

The day got worse – with Susie hitting a lacrosse ball at her stomach in PE, and her maths teacher making her do algebra in front of the class – but the discrimination shown towards her by teachers and pupils alike didn't affect Jo as much as it used to, and she supposed it was because it was all she'd ever known. Jo wandered up and down the hallowed halls of her boarding school pretending not to notice groups of girls giggling as she walked past, and wondering – for what felt like the billionth time since she'd been at school – what her life would be like if the others stopped being so bitchy.

While the other girls spent break times in the lavatories sweeping MAC blusher on their flawless skin – made possible by pots of Dr Sebagh Breakout Crème sent in bulk from Space NK – Jo sat in the library reading as many books as possible in the hope that they would take her mind off the delicious smells coming from the school's kitchen. She couldn't help it – she was hungry all the time. But even dinner, sometimes, didn't give her that fix like a bag of Maltesers always could.

That evening – after dinner, but before prep – Amelia wanted to make sure Jo was all right. As she walked into the dorm she struggled not to wrinkle her nose; there was a nasty smell coming from the bathroom that was, unfortunately for Jo, at the same end of the room as her bed. Jo glanced up at her friend and smiled weakly. Even if everybody else hated her she must have been doing something right if the most popular – and beautiful – girl at school liked her.

'Are you OK?' Amelia asked, dropping her expensive-looking cardboard shopping bags on to the floor and flopping on to the bed next to Jo.

Jo shook her head, unable to get the words out, as Amelia Gladstone-Denham, with her pretty face, designer clothes from Harvey Nichols and Selfridges, and boyfriends at Eton, Harrow and even Radley, looked concerned.

'I heard about Jemima and Susie being bitches in your English set – you mustn't pay any attention to them. They're just jealous because you got to do that email interview with Justin Timberlake from *NSYNC for *Saint*. They have a massive crush on him.'

Jo let out a wry laugh. 'Ames, that doesn't account for the time they locked me in the chapel in the first year.'

Amelia was silent for a moment. 'Well ... no ... but ... I think they find it weird that you don't even try to fit in any more. Have you ever thought about coming to do your homework with us in the common room instead of spending every evening reading magazines?'

'Yeah, I tried that years ago along with sucking up to everyone but it didn't do any good. We both know the real reason nobody likes me is because of this.' Jo gestured at her body and tried not to feel depressed. Amelia tried to be tactful.

'But it's not because they're being shallow about your weight – it's how we've been raised. It just doesn't do to be overweight in families like ours. And it's not all about good looks, you know,' Amelia said with an air of authority. 'It's about being healthy, too. We go skiing, and sailing, and lots of us have ponies. Why, if I was a stone or two overweight there would be no way I could compete in horse trials at the weekend – old Brownie would never be able to carry me!'

As soon as Amelia spoke both girls pictured Jo – who was at least seven stone heavier than Amelia – climbing on to a horse only to find it collapsing beneath her. It didn't amuse either of them, and Amelia blushed.

'Sorry, Jo.'

Jo gave her a grin. She knew Amelia meant well, even if her words sometimes came out badly.

'What I'm trying to say is that it's all about fitting in, making the most of yourself and being the best you can be. If you just lost a bit of weight, perhaps rinsed your hair to make it darker ...'

'You mean if I tried to look like an overweight Joey from *Dawson's Creek* people would be friends with me?' Jo joked feebly.

Amelia stared at Jo for a second, unable to gauge her mood. Jo took this silence as Amelia not thinking she was taking her advice seriously and rushed to make light of the situation. She didn't want to offend her one true friend. 'I suppose I could try and look like Britney Spears, instead.' Jo stood up and struck a pose. 'What do you think, could I be a sexy singing schoolgirl? Hit me, Susie, one more time ...' Jo sang, before she realised she'd lost a button on her itchy BHS blouse. She quickly crossed her arms over the huge grey bra that showed through the straining gap around her breasts, and pouted.

Amelia laughed. 'This is exactly what I mean! You're fun, and when you let your guard down you're as cool in person as you are in those articles you write for *Saint* ... If you just made a bit more effort with how you look and what you eat ...'

Jo thought about how she'd stopped eating puddings for a week and had gained five pounds in the process. It was a lost cause. 'I do make an effort, but I don't have unlimited pocket money to spend on all those expensive lotions and potions you get. And besides, all the effort in the world wouldn't make much of a difference ... I'm not pretty enough to fit in, I know that.'

'But you have gorgeous green eyes ...' Amelia pleaded, tentatively. She'd had this conversation before, and Jo always shot her down.

'Look, nobody's given me a chance here in seven years, and if I'm brutally honest I'm counting the days until the exams are over and we leave. If I was meant to be friends with everyone it would have happened, and let's face it, Ames, you're the only one who even bothers to speak to me.'

For once Jo let a wave of self-pity wash over her, and she fought not to cry, knowing if she did, like last time, she wouldn't be able to stop. She was stronger than that. She was determined to be.

Amelia could see Jo's eyes shining with tears and she played her trump card. 'Here, this will cheer you up – the new *Cosmopolitan*, just out today. It's got a great piece where they give a girl a make-over ... You should email them and see if they'd do a make-over for you – could be a great chance to make some contacts for when you start your career.'

Jo shook her head, but Amelia dragged her over to the mirror and forced her to look at herself properly. Jo cringed.

Her mousy-brown hair lat flat against her head and limp on her shoulders, and her eyes, set against the frown of her face, were dull. Apart from her wide nostrils, her nose wasn't too bad, as noses went, but her lips were too thin, her eyebrows too thick, and Jo knew that even if she lost some weight she'd be one of those girls who are lost in the crowd. She was average – not ugly, not pretty, just nondescript. Jo wished with all her heart that she was stunningly beautiful like Amelia.

'I bet the beauty department could made you look great in just a couple of hours,' Amelia said, lifting Jo's hair from her shoulders to see what it would look like if it was up. 'And you could pitch them that idea you were telling me about the other night – about how girls should be made-over and PhotoShopped so they look like celebrities, so they don't feel so bad about themselves.'

Jo shook her head, and her hair fell from Amelia's hands. She'd be too terrified to have a magazine make-over – because no matter what they did to her, she'd still be overweight and she'd still be plain old Jo Hill who didn't have class and never would. She refused to look at her reflection any longer – it hurt too much. Jo eyed *Cosmopolitan* longingly, and Amelia got the hint.

'Shall I leave you to fawn all over your magazine, then,' she joked, and after she'd gathered her bags and had gone Jo breathed a sigh of relief – not because she didn't like Amelia's company, but because by picking up the magazine she could finally escape real life and disappear into the glamorous world of models, make-up and fantasising about what it would be like when she was finally an editor of a glossy magazine. She would wear Manolo Blahnik heels, Versace suits and, as well as being thin and beautiful, she would be powerful.

As Jo settled down with the magazine she instinctively ana-lysed it – memorising how to write pithy features and learn-ing what worked on fashion shoots. She opened her bedside drawer and found some Jaffa Cakes, and as she ate her way through the packet she read the top make-up tips from her favourite beauty editors, and worked out what colours she'd use on her eyelids if she were going to a celebrity-packed party. In reality she would never dare use make-up – she believed she was so ugly that a touch of shimmering colour wouldn't make any difference, or worse, would make it look like she actually cared – but when Jo retreated into the glam-orous world of fashion magazines she could pretend she was just like any other girl: carefree, young, pretty and slender.

Because the truth was that Jo was more than just overweight. She was sixteen stone and she was finding that even her extra-large school uniform was straining at the seams.

Jo knew she had to go on a diet – she wasn't stupid – but she couldn't seem to stop herself eating, and even though she hated the rolls of fat that collected sweat under her uniform, she was always hungry. The kind dinner ladies didn't help matters either. Every day they piled more and more food on her plate in the hope of getting her to smile, and even though Amelia frowned at the heaped plates of food, she never said anything about Jo cutting back, not even when the bitchier girls laughed as Jo went up for seconds. She was the one person at school who didn't seem to mind too much that Jo was more than chubby, the one person who could see Jo for who she was: a sweet, fun, bright girl who was driven by ambition and the desire to succeed. But even Amelia couldn't protect her from being the odd one out in a school where everyone had to be perfect.

'Oh, look, there's Jo Hill skipping her homework again so she can be in bed with a magazine, what a surprise!' A nasal voice interrupted her thoughts, and Jo turned to see Dominique and her group of blonde, identikit friends. Dominique had the bed closest to Jo's, and since the first year she'd picked on Jo to make herself feel better about her slightly rounded stomach and large bottom.

'You're never going to lose your virginity if going to bed with a magazine is all you're interested in,' she said cattily, as her friends giggled and nudged each other. 'Men don't like girls who just lie on their backs – they like a bit of movement.'

Jo stared at the girls coolly. 'Not that it's any of your business, but I'm hoping that when I do get a boyfriend he's going to be impressed by the fact that I have ambition and am not an airhead like you.'

Dominique doubled up with fake laughter. 'If you call lying on your back while reading trashy magazines "ambition", then I'm sure you'll find someone to sleep with you. Especially if he can put the magazine over your head before he climbs on top.'

Jo felt her good mood vanish, and she turned towards the wall, desperately trying to ignore the giggles and the slumber-party atmosphere of bedtime that never included her. The magazine fell out of her hands and opened on the editor's letter page, and Jo stared at it, imagining her slimmed-down and made-up face looking back at her in place of the current *Cosmo* editor. One day Dominique – and Jemima and Susie and all the other bitchy girls at school – would be fat from having babies with philandering City bankers, and they would all turn to her magazine for love-life advice. Jo would be thin, stylish and the most revered magazine editor in the UK, and when the girls opened the magazine and saw Jo's beautiful face in prime position on the editor's letter page they'd wish they'd never bullied her at school. She'd show them.

Chapter Two

August 2000

Jo woke with a jolt. The sun was streaming through her thin My Little Pony curtains, and for a minute she didn't know where she was until she realised she could smell burnt toast rather than Dominique's overbearing perfume. She glanced around the bedroom and breathed a sigh of relief: she was at home, and she was never going to have to go back to St Christopher's School for Snobs again. Old posters of Kurt Cobain hung limply from the pale pink walls, and her curtains blocked out the view of the rest of the Peckham council estate. Jo never opened them – they acted as a barrier to the gangs of teenagers outside who taunted her for being 'posh' and fat. Jo often wondered if she was the loneliest person in the world. She didn't feel like she fitted in anywhere.

Today, however, was the start of her brand-new life: A-level results day. Jo couldn't face going back to the school ever again, so Amelia had promised to phone with her results. She couldn't wait – in a few hours she could properly start thinking about how her life was going to be at university, and Jo resolved that today she would start her diet. By the time term started she would not only have lost some of her extra weight, but would be ready to meet new people – the people she would be friends with for the rest of her life. She grinned to herself. The next few years were going to be fantastic.

The phone in the hall began to ring, and Jo was about to

jump out of bed when she heard her mother answer it. As the voice of her hard, brittle mother relaxed into conversation Jo tensed up – why didn't her mother understand how important it was to keep the line free? Jo tried not to panic and hurled herself into the hallway to give Elaine Hill a dirty look. Jo's mum – who was dressed in velour jogging bottoms and a faded Joe Bloggs T-shirt – turned away from her daughter and laughed into the phone, murmuring something distinctly sexual. Jo grimaced. She was on the phone to one of her men-friends then, most probably the one who sometimes gave her money for the final demands piling up by the front door.

Jo stepped into the bathroom, where she pulled off the long shirt that doubled as a pyjama top, and heaved herself into the bath. Suddenly missing the school's top-of-the-range power-showers, Jo made sure the plastic shower attachment was tightly gripped to the bath taps with rubber bands and let the sorry trickle of water wash over her body. As Jo soaped herself she kept her eyes on the flaking enamel of the bath that seemed to get worse every time she washed, and when that became too depressing she squeezed them tight, desperate to think about anything but her looming grades and how she should have forgotten about *Saint* for a month or two while she revised.

In her fantasy Jo became a model in a shower-gel commercial – all leggy with cascading dark hair that shone like glass as the water glossed over it. Jo shook her head, and as her hair touched her back she felt like the girl she knew she was, inside her extra padding. She could be sexy, she could be flirtatious, and she imagined the make-believe cameraman finding her irresistible. As he began to wink at her, Jo turned the other way, flashing her bottom at him while imagining him telling her she was beautiful. Jo began to smile despite her shower starting to run cold, and just as she was working out if the cameraman looked like George Clooney or Russell Crowe in *Gladiator*, her mum's pissed-off voice broke through the daydream.

'Joanne, your posh friend's on the phone for ya.'

For a second Jo was disappointed that she'd turned back into a sad, overweight teenager holding a grubby white shower attachment over her head, but she chose not to let it bother her. It was results time.

'Amelia? Hello, is that you?' The moment she said the words Jo felt stupid, as nobody apart from Amelia ever phoned her. She squirmed under the small threadbare towel that didn't hide her body properly.

'Yah, Jo, hi,' Amelia said perkily down the phone, and in the background Jo could hear squeals of delight coming from her former classmates. Obviously everyone had done well.

'So ...?' Jo was frantic, and couldn't be bothered with small talk. There would be time for that later.

'Three As and a B,' Amelia said proudly, and Jo welled up with pleasure – she was going to Edinburgh! Except ... she had only taken three A-levels. Jo's brow furrowed slightly, and she realised there was silence at the other end of the phone. Suddenly she understood.

'Ames, that's brilliant, well done,' Jo gushed, hoping her disappointment wasn't showing. Amelia deserved good grades. She'd worked hard.

'I know!' Amelia squealed. 'Would have been top of the year but Susie got four As.' Jo's grin faded and anger threatened to spill out. How had Susie – the girl who spent every evening organising her clothes – passed? Had she plagiarised her essays? Jo didn't think Susie was that smart. It was a backhander from her father, most probably. Jo sniffed. Who said money couldn't buy happiness?

'So what about me?' Jo held her breath – she could barely stand it.

Amelia cleared her throat and Jo instantly knew it was bad news.

'Just tell me. It doesn't matter.'

'You got a D in English Lit,' Amelia began, and Jo made a small choking noise. Amelia hurried on, anxious to make Jo feel better.

'But you got a C in General Studies, and a C in History of Art, too.'

Jo was stunned, and she could feel the blood draining from her face.

Amelia rushed on. 'I spoke to Mrs Wickham and she says you can appeal if you want to, but there's not much chance of your grades changing. I think she's a bit annoyed that Bedales beat us in the league table, to be honest. We beat Scabby Abbey again, though ...'

Jo stared blankly at the grubby wood-chip wallpaper. She'd got all Bs in her essays ... and all her teachers – even Miss Montgomery – had predicted top marks for her. Something had gone wrong ... badly wrong. Jo couldn't bear to be on the phone any longer.

'Thanks for letting me know, Ames, I appreciate it,' Jo said as politely as she could, but before she could get off the phone Amelia interrupted her.

'Oh, hang on, Dominique wants a word,' she said, before lowering her voice. 'Maybe she wants to make amends for always being such a cow.'

Jo's heart dropped even further. The last thing she wanted now was to speak to one of her former dorm buddies. Jo forced a bright smile and hoped she'd sound as breezy as possible.

'Domi, hi, how are you?'

There was the slightest pause at the end of the phone before Dominique spoke, and Jo could hear her walking away from the others, her stiletto heels making a hollow clicking noise on the waxed wooden hall floor.

'Very well, thanks, Jo … and it's good to talk to you – I wanted to say goodbye, as we're probably not going to ever see each other again. After all, it's not like we run in the same social circles, is it?'

Jo stopped smiling as soon as she heard the cold tone of Dominique's voice.

'Fine,' Jo said bluntly, all pretence at social niceties gone. 'Goodbye, then.'

Jo was ready to hang up the phone, but Dominique's voice came through the receiver loudly. 'But before we do say goodbye, I was wondering what marks you got,' she said in a nasty tone that implied she knew just how badly Jo had done.

Jo's hand gripped the telephone so hard that her knuckles turned white. She didn't speak.

'Cat got your tongue, Jo? Never mind – the list is up on the wall anyway, and I can see for myself …' Jo imagined Dominique trailing a manicured finger down the list of names, as she let out a tinkling laugh.

'Oh, dear, Joanne,' she said patronisingly. 'Maybe you should have taken my advice after all and actually done a bit of revision! I did tell you that reading all those magazines wasn't going to help your career, and I was right, wasn't I?'

Jo slammed the phone down as hard as she could, but before she could take a few deep breaths and calm down, she spotted her mother staring at her with thinly veiled disgust.

'Well?' she asked impatiently as she started rinsing some dishes in the sink.

Jo shook her head, and refused to meet her mother's eyes.

Elaine Hill snorted and kept on washing up. 'About time you realised you ain't posh like your little friend,' she muttered, and she plunged her hands deeper into the oily suds. 'You can go on the dole and start paying me rent,' she directed at her daughter with a sharp glance and Jo felt sick. She looked at the small kitchen with the peeling 1970s wallpaper and grease-stained oven, and she felt despair quickly consume her. University had been her one chance to escape, but without the grades – or the money – the reality of getting there was impossible. It was a dream, just like everything else good that happened to her.

Jo sat down in the corner of one of her favourite places in Peckham – Frank's Café – and her nose twitched appreciatively as she sniffed the air. Frank's had not changed in years, and its all-day breakfasts were the stuff of local legend. Jo loved it in here; despite St Christopher's trying to rub off her rough edges, she always gravitated back to the café on school holidays. Jo was just sitting down at a small table near the back when Rose – Frank's wife – spotted Jo while serving fried breakfasts to some burly builders reading the *Sun*. Rose's tired face lit up, and she gave Jo a wide grin.

'Frank, Frank!' she called out to her husband, and Frank, the Italian owner, came out of the kitchen wiping his hands on his apron. Frank and Rose were in their late fifties but they loved working in their café, an institution on the high street to those in the know and invisible to those who rushed past on their way to the centre of London in their cheap suits.

'Joanna!' Frank said, grabbing Jo by her shoulders and kissing her on the cheeks. 'How is our little bright spark, eh? Packing her bags for university where she will find another café, no?' Jo grinned at Frank and his wife. They never failed to cheer her up.

'Oh, Frank, I messed up,' Jo began and she played with the salt and pepper mills on the plastic red and white checked tablecloth. 'I didn't get the grades and no university that does my course will take me.'

Frank turned to his wife in mock horror, as Rose, unburdening herself from the plates she was serving, came over.

'Joanna, you are a smart girl, how could this happen?'

Jo shook her head. No words could explain it. She wasn't really sure herself.

'What we will do is this – we give you a good breakfast to fill you up and then you tell us everything, OK?'

Jo looked up at Frank and Rose and felt a wave of appreciation. It felt like it had been a long time since anyone apart from Amelia had been kind to her.

'Thanks, I'd like that, but I'm on a diet. I'll just have a coffee. I don't want to get any fatter, right?' Jo joked sadly.

Rose looked at her husband, who took Jo in hand. 'Today you've had some bad news, so you eat, and then you think. Tomorrow, tomorrow is the day you diet, although I think you are beautiful as you are.'

Jo grinned and nodded, and the couple rushed back into the kitchen while Jo stared despondently at a ring of sticky coffee on the tablecloth and tried to ignore the sounds of Radio 1 coming from behind the counter. She had fucked up, she knew that, but it had never crossed her mind that she might need a back-up plan. Jo had planned to lose weight, go to university, get a brilliant degree, and when she was twenty-one she planned to go to journalism college. A couple of years on she'd be writing for the glossies, and from there it was only a matter of time before she was in charge. Jo planned it so that by the time she was thirty she'd be running a magazine. The only problem was that she wasn't going to get that degree after all. And she had gone from knowing what she was going to do in years to come, to not knowing what she was going to do tomorrow.

Rose brought out a plate of food and a cup of tea for her, and Jo, despite her good intentions to start her life again, gave in to the smell of bacon and the rumblings of her stomach.

The tea was strong, sweet and milky, and as she sipped it she looked at her plate. The eggs had bright yellow yolks, and next to them were golden pieces of fried bread and crispy rashers of bacon with chewy rinds of fat. Soft button mushrooms sat on the side alongside ruby-red cooked tomatoes, glossy baked beans, toast dripping with butter, and plump, juicy sausages – as Jo bit into one she knew she'd be able to clear her plate. Compared to her mother's distinct lack of culinary skills, the food was amazing.

'How is it, Jo?' Rose called out from behind the counter, and Jo, mouth full and eyes shining, nodded in delight. She barely noticed the old ladies on the table opposite looking at her disapprovingly, and didn't register them properly until she was using a crust of toast to mop up the juices on her plate.

'Shouldn't be allowed,' she heard one of them mutter to the other, as they looked up from their tea at her every few minutes. 'She should be ashamed of herself, shovelling food down her throat like that in public. And at her size, too!'

'Someone should stop her – she'll have a heart attack before we know it,' the other one said, tutting, and Jo, who couldn't stand the whispers any longer, stood up and accidentally caught the edge of the table with her hip. The salt mill fell over, and as salt ran on to the tablecloth Jo burst into tears in anger. Rose rushed over and ushered her into the kitchen, where Frank was sitting at a small table smoking a hand-rolled cigarette. He looked up in alarm as he saw Jo's face.

'Joanna, Joanna, what is the matter?' he began, as Jo's tears showed no sign of stopping. 'The breakfast was bad, huh?' he joked, while Rose put another cup of strong, sweet tea in front of Jo and went back to the café. The elderly ladies were self-righteously patting their blue-rinsed curls into place under their plastic headscarves.

'Mum wants me to sign on the dole so I can pay her rent, I have no friends round here, I have no future, and I'm a big fat lump who nobody likes.' Jo's words rushed out, and she sobbed into her hands as Frank stared at her.

'Your mother is not a very nice person, that is right, eh?' Frank began, and when Jo didn't respond he continued. 'For years you come to Frank and Rose with your pocket money to spend on food because your mother doesn't look after you properly, and when you were at that school you were unhappy because the girls didn't understand you. That is correct, yes?'

Jo felt too weary to say anything and nodded, watching a tear splash into her tea.

'And now you don't get the grades you need to better yourself you are upset, yes? You now have to stay with your mother, yes?'

Jo nodded again. She wasn't used to someone trying to understand her.

'So what you need to do is get a job to get away from your mother!'

Jo stopped crying and looked at Frank as if he were mad. 'But who would employ me? I'm fat and ugly and stupid.'

Frank made soothing noises to Jo. 'Yes, you are over-weight, but all the best Italian girls have meat on their bones, with my Rosa a good example. You don't think she is ugly, eh?' Jo shook her head as Frank continued. 'And you are not ugly, you have a bloom that older women want to buy in bottles. Why, if I was a few years younger ...' Frank looked Joanna slowly up and down approvingly.

Jo sniffed. 'But I am stupid. I failed my A-levels.'

Frank disagreed. 'You, Joanna, are not stupid. You have A-levels, you've had a brilliant education. And you have fire, a drive.'

Jo went to argue, but Frank stopped her. 'No, no, let me

finish. You have your dreams, and you have reached a hurdle. People don't give up at these hurdles, and if they can't get over them they go round them to get to their dream.' Frank reached over to Jo and touched her arm. 'Little Joanna, I know you can do this. You are special.'

Rose came back into the kitchen and pulled up a chair, and Frank stepped away from her and moved towards his wife.

'Rosa,' Frank said, looking at her, 'Joanna needs a job, she will start working here tomorrow, yes?'

Rose nodded enthusiastically, and Jo began to weakly protest but the couple refused to let her back down.

'You will be here tomorrow morning at five o'clock, Joanna,' Frank said as Jo blanched at the early start, 'and you will start the rest of your life.'

Frank turned to his wife and grinned, showing her his yellow nicotine-stained teeth. 'Joanna will be like the daughter we never had!'

Life at the café was hard. In the mornings Jo walked to work just as the sun was rising, and she spent hours in the kitchen, signing for the deliveries and preparing food for the early morning rush at six. Counters needed to be wiped down, the floor swept and mopped, and the kitchen had to be sparkling. Jo found that even before the first customers walked into the café she was exhausted. Being at boarding school on a scholarship had been a breeze compared to this.

Slowly, though, Jo began to get used to the hours and slotted into her new working life. The job was physically tough, and her thighs were rubbed raw at the end of the day, but the small amount of pay she earned slowly began to build in her bank account. Suddenly, her life seemed a whole lot better than it had been for years – she had a job, some savings, and while she didn't have friends, most people in the café seemed to accept her for who she was – an overweight, lonely teenager trying to make ends meet. Frank seemed irritated by her, though, glowing red when she stood near him and catching her eye whenever Jo looked towards him. Jo didn't know what she was doing wrong.

'I thought you wanted to be a magazine writer, Joanna,' he said to her one Friday evening, as Jo was tidying up the front counter of the café and he was locking the door.

Jo shrugged, opened the till to bank up the cash, and began to count the notes.

'You have given up on your dream, then, eh?'

Jo looked up at her boss sharply, and then went back to making piles of ten-pound notes, counting and then recounting them until she realised that she'd lost track of her sums. She sighed. 'I've got a plan. I'm going to save up enough to retake my A-levels at the local college and then – when I pass – I'm going to journalism college. I'm going to skip university completely. I think I'm good enough to be able to.'

Frank stared intently at the teenager behind his counter and smiled.

'Jo, it will take you years to save up enough to do that. This is not a good idea, no? And what does this say to Rosa and me? Are you saying that this job is only a means to an end, that our business, that we have built up with love since before you were born, is a meal-ticket until you want out?'

Caught off-guard, Jo didn't understand. 'But I thought you gave me a job so I could find my way? Wasn't that the plan?'

When Frank didn't say anything, Jo suddenly felt as though she was in the wrong, but she didn't know why. 'You know I love working for you and Rosa, Frank, but I want to work on magazines ... it's all I've ever wanted.'

Frank remained silent and Jo felt uncomfortable. But then he smiled.

'Rosa and I have talked, and we have decided we want to train you up to take over running the café. Rosa, she gets tired, but you, you're young, and we love you like you are one of our own.'

Jo felt her heart drop. As much as she liked Frank and Rose, there was no way she wanted to give up her dream of working on magazines to run a greasy spoon.

Frank sat down on a chair and gestured to Joanna to join him, but just as she went for a chair opposite him he reached out for her and pulled her on to his lap. The physical contact of a man jolted Jo, and she froze in shock as she let Frank move her on to him.

'Oh, Joanna, I've watched you grow into a beautiful young woman, but you still have your head in your child-like fantasies. Now, I know it is hard but I think you need to accept that you're not going to be able to go to journalism college.'

Jo began to squirm on Frank's lap and felt uncomfortable. She felt his hot breath on the back of her neck and when Jo tried to stand up she found that Frank's grip was surprisingly strong.

'As you have no father figure in your life, I feel it is my duty to tell you these things. I know it is hard, but I think you accept this as fact, yes? This way, you can settle here and be a proper part of the family. I think you knew deep down this was your best option, and I have also been seeing how you look at your Frank. You like it here, eh?'

Jo tried to use her elbows to push herself from Frank, but it didn't work.

'I've been watching you for years, feeding you food and watching you grow into a ripe, beautiful young woman. Little Joanna, sweet Joanna, I think you want more from me than a job, yes?' Frank's voice was thick with longing as he spoke, and Jo could feel an erection through his apron.

Frank began to stroke Jo's hair, and then his hands moved down to her shoulders, and then her breasts.

The sudden, overt sexual contact jolted Jo, and she moved her body violently in an attempt to get away from Frank's rough hands. 'What do you think you're doing?' she yelped.

Frank turned Jo on his lap and started kissing her to stop her talking. For a moment Jo froze, and she could feel Frank's garlicky, smoke-flavoured tongue force itself into her mouth. With a surge of strength Jo pushed herself off Frank's lap and when she was free she ran to the door. She had forgotten that Frank had already locked it.

'Joanna, little Joanna, you love your Frank, yes?'

Jo was outraged. 'No! Not like that!'

Frank walked towards Jo, undoing his apron and then unzipping his trousers. 'Oh, but I think you do, Joanna,' he said in a whisper, as Jo's eyes darted around the café for the keys to the door. When she spotted them on a hook by the payphone she pushed past Frank, grabbed them, and then fumbled with the lock until the door opened freely.

Jo stared incredulously at Frank with his trousers around his ankles and she realised she could never come back to the café again. A feeling of sad inevitability washed over her, but before Jo could linger on yet another notch in her run of bad luck, the pile of bank notes on the counter caught her eye. With as much courage as she could muster, Jo walked over to them, nervously put them in her pocket, and turned to look at Frank for one final time. His erection had gone limp in his hands, and he no longer looked threatening, but pathetic. Jo threw the door keys at him, and they hit Frank hard on his chest. As he doubled up in pain, Jo pulled the door open and felt fresh air on her face.

'Fuck you, Frank.'

'He actually got his dick out? Are you serious?' Amelia

yelped down the phone in disbelief. 'He offered you a "management" position in his shitty café and then thought you'd want to have sex with him? Are you kidding me?'

Jo bit her lip and tried not to smile. 'Don't make it sound so funny,' she said with a shudder, as she recounted the tale to her best friend and shifted in her seat. Her arm was aching from holding the phone up to her ear, and once again she was grateful that Amelia always phoned her back. At least her mother couldn't yell at her about the phone bill along with everything else.

'Look, you must be feeling pretty lousy, but why don't you come down here for a couple of days?' Amelia stared at her toenails – wet with Chanel polish – and tried not to move her feet. 'The holiday that Daddy promised me for passing my exams is on hold – Granny fell over and broke her hip and Mummy's at home nursing herself with vodka over the price of the hospital bills. I'm dying for a bit of girlie fun.'

'Won't I be in the way of you and Charlie?' Jo asked, feeling awkward. Apart from revelling in Jo's clumsy first kiss with Frank, Amelia's favourite subject at the moment was her new boyfriend, and the various different sexual positions he introduced her to. Every time she started to talk about her love life, Jo felt incredibly uncomfortable. *Gloss* magazine may have provided a detailed guide on how to help him make you come, but Jo felt out of her depth talking about real sex with real people. She smiled to herself: she'd stick to the stuff of trashy novels for now.

Amelia snorted. 'Don't be stupid. Besides, Charlie's bar is having a party and it would be the best time for you to come over. Sounds like you could do with a laugh.'

'But ...' Jo was momentarily floored by the thought of socialising. 'But what would I wear?'

Amelia smiled sneakily as she imagined making Jo over. 'Don't worry about that ... Just leave it to me.'

Chapter   Three

When Amelia pulled into her sweeping circular driveway the next day, Jo's wariness about fitting in intensified. Throughout the train ride from Waterloo to Winchester Jo had lost herself in a new issue of *Marie Claire*, but during the forty-minute drive through the depths of the Hampshire countryside Jo's stomach had filled with butterflies. Now they were outside Amelia's pile she felt sick. She was definitely outside her comfort zone.

The Gladstone-Denham gothic country house was the stuff of people's dreams: it was an imposing tall building with dark grey pillars and intimidating gargoyles, and to Jo it felt like a nightmare, especially when she thought of Amelia's judgemental mother inside. Jo slammed the door of the beat-up Beetle and followed Amelia to the side entrance nervously, looking at the Victorian doorbell that read: 'Servants.' Her palms were damp with sweat.

'We don't use the front door unless we're having dinner parties,' Amelia explained as she entered the house, and Jo tried to look blasé as they walked across the cool grey flagstones into the big kitchen. Amelia's mother was sitting at a scrubbed pine table with the *Daily Mail* in front of her, and as she looked up Jo felt her eyes assessing her. Jo swallowed hard and forced herself to smile. Amelia's mother looked like she was a member of the Royal Family.

'Joanne, isn't it?' Sarah Gladstone-Denham asked politely, and Jo nodded meekly. As Amelia turned on the kettle to make them a cup of tea, Jo struggled with a kitchen chair and ignored Amelia's mother's visible wince as she sat down. Despite Sarah's reservations the fragile pine chair held her weight and Jo fidgeted awkwardly, trying not to stare at the huge rosy pearls round Sarah's neck and the rocks of diamonds and rubies on her impressive engagement ring.

'You have a beautiful home,' Jo said, hastily trying to start a conversation. 'Apart from St Christopher's I don't think I've ever been in such an old building.' An image of her mother's 1960s council flat popped into her mind, and Jo felt even more nervous. The flat was practically the same size as Amelia's kitchen.

Sarah smiled, showing her perfect white teeth, and Jo was reminded of the Cheshire cat. 'Thank you, it's been in the family for two hundred years and we recently renovated it. Now, Amelia tells me you're from London,' she said, glancing at her daughter, who was rummaging around in a bottom cupboard looking for biscuits. Her hipster jeans rode down her bottom as she bent over and Sarah frowned at her black thong on display. 'Do tell, what part of the city do you live in?'

Jo hesitated and glanced at Amelia, who was blithely unaware of her friend's discomfort. 'Oh, just South London, you know, nothing special.'

Sarah straightened her back. 'Battersea?' she asked, enjoying Jo's discomfort. Jo shook her head. 'Wandsworth? Barnes? Putney?'

As Jo began to look miserable, Sarah let out a little laugh and hoped she wasn't being too unsubtle.

'Gosh,' she said innocently as her daughter came to the table with a teapot, cups and saucers. 'Where on earth do you live, then?'

Jo looked at the delicate Wedgwood china cups and saucers and smiled to herself – a real one rather than a forced grin. She'd not seen a set since she'd been at school and they reminded her that she was just as good as her friend – or that she at least knew how to hold a cup and saucer correctly. Fuck it, she thought. She had nothing to be ashamed of. Jo felt amusement bubbling up inside her and wondered what Sarah Double-Barrelled Name would do if she told the truth. Banish her back to the slums, or tell her she was sleeping in the servants' quarters? Jo laughed to herself. Sarah would never be rude to her face. It wouldn't 'do'.

Jo took a sip of tea, quietly cleared her throat and decided it was time that Sarah officially knew her beloved daughter was friends with the working class.

'Officially I live in Peckham,' she said happily, thinking of home with its violence, litter and dirt. 'But really I'm closer to Camberwell, which is great because of the cheap food I can pick up in the Turkish shops.' Sarah looked visibly affronted, as if Jo had just sworn, but she remembered herself and her face returned to what she called 'pleasant'. Amelia struggled to collect herself as she tried not to giggle at her friend's daring.

'James – Amelia's father – believes that some of those big old Victorian mansions may be worth a thing or two in a few years,' Sarah began, struggling to continue the conversation and grasping at something – anything – that could put her back on track. 'Of course, the so-called council would have to get rid of those awful hippies using the places as squats. I blame Tony Blair, personally ...'

Jo didn't say anything and took a gulp of hot tea.

'I expect your parents are quite savvy about things like that,' Sarah continued, thinking, suddenly, that it was quite possible that Jo had rich, bohemian parents who chose to live life in the slums to be subversive. In fact, there had been an article about that in the paper only recently. Sarah's mood brightened considerably as she wondered if she had seen anyone with the surname 'Hill' in one of her society magazines. She vaguely remembered reading about someone in Hampstead called 'Hill-Richards', and she was just about to ask if Jo was related to her when Jo dealt the fatal blow.

'I've never met my father as he beat my mum up when he found out she was pregnant with me, and we live in a flat on a council estate.' Jo's words landed heavily and Sarah's mouth dropped open. She suddenly heard Jo's inner-city accent through the expensive boarding-school polish and felt annoyed. What was Amelia up to with this obese working-class girl? Rebelling, most probably. As the thought of Amelia defying her needled, Sarah excused herself to tend to the rose garden. Jo spotted Sarah giving Amelia a pointed look as she walked out of the kitchen, and Amelia fell about laughing as soon as she left.

'That was brilliant – I've never seen Mummy so put out by anyone before!'

Jo grinned at her friend. 'Was it too much? Was I rude? Perhaps I shouldn't have been so blunt with the truth ...'

'Oh, sod it, Jo.' Amelia stood up and brushed the biscuit crumbs from her flat stomach. 'She bloody well knew you were at school on a scholarship and she knew she wouldn't like the truth but she persisted anyway. Like Daddy says, "Don't ask questions that you don't want to know the answers to."' Amelia frowned as she thought of her father away on his countless 'business trips' and felt a pang of sadness for her mother.

'Anyway, want to see where you'll be laying your pauper's head?'

As Amelia showed her around the house, Jo couldn't believe that people lived like this – Amelia's house was a stately home, like something out of a modern-day fairy-tale. From the sedate hallway they stepped into a luxurious living-room, with deep velvety carpets, heavy swathes of curtains and expensive antique furniture. The dining-room had mounted stag heads on the faded Colefax and Fowler wallpaper, and the table was set with antique silver that glowed yellow. Room after room unfolded – such as the 'Sunday room', the 'library' and the 'nursery' – before Jo was shown the master bathroom, complete with marble floor, Jacuzzi bath and the most high-tech shower Jo had ever seen. She didn't think showers with so many jets existed.

Feeling exhilarated, and slightly sick at the unsubtle wealth, Jo tried not to let her mouth drop open when they came to the guest bedroom from the 'second staircase'.

'And this will be your room,' Amelia said, as she pushed the heavy door open. The four-poster bed was placed so Jo had a view of the vegetable garden and the Hampshire fields beyond, and the en suite – three times the size of Jo's mother's bathroom – came complete with fluffy white towels and Aveda toiletries. Jo didn't know what to say.

'Wow, Ames, this is amazing.'

Amelia shrugged and bounced up and down on the bed, messing up the McCaw Allan sheets. 'It's nice, isn't it? Mummy interior-designs all the rooms in rotation and this was the most recent one. It's pretty new.'

Jo joined her friend on the bed and grinned. 'It's heavenly. I'm so pleased I've come. Thanks for inviting me.'

Amelia smirked and hugged her friend. 'Not a problem. Now, get yourself ready because we're going shopping for that party I was telling you about. I managed to get you on the guest-list at the last minute. Although,' she said with a smug grin, 'if you're the girlfriend of the owner it isn't exactly hard to do.'

Jo felt her smile falter. 'But ...'

'Now, Jo,' Amelia said sternly, 'you have to think

positively. We're going to find you some gorgeous clothes and then we're going to spend the rest of the day pampering ourselves. What do you say?'

Jo wanted to suggest that Amelia was out of her mind, but she didn't dare.

'It sounds great!' she enthused in her perkiest voice, hoping Amelia wouldn't think she was lying. 'Can't wait, super!'

Amelia smiled. 'Then let's hit the shops.'

The first boutique the girls went in was terrible – full of skinny designer clothes that cost a fortune and would have been more suited to models than Jo. Amelia bounced around grabbing clothes off the rails while Jo trailed behind her, looking at the tiny scraps of material and hating herself.

'Aren't you going to try anything on?' Amelia called over to Jo, who was eyeing a black jumper that only went up to a size sixteen – quite a few sizes too small for Jo.

'Not in here I don't think, Ames,' Jo said diplomatically, not wanting to put a downer on the mood. 'Nothing in here's really to my taste, you know?' she remarked with a smile, crossing her fingers behind her back and wondering if Amelia was blind to her weight. 'But you try things on – let's find you an outfit to impress Charlie.'

As Amelia literally skipped into a spacious dressing-room, Jo wondered, awkwardly, where she was supposed to wait. A haughty assistant hovered disapprovingly, and just as Jo decided she'd wait outside the shop, Amelia's thin brown arm appeared from the dressing-room curtain and pulled her in. 'Sit,' she commanded, and as Jo sat down on the flimsy stool she didn't know where to look.

Amelia pulled off her tatty jeans and vest top easily, and Jo tried – but failed – not to drink in Amelia's pert size-eight frame as she looked for a part of the cubicle that wasn't made of mirror. She stared at how the curve of Amelia's tits and hips contrasted with the flat of her stomach and flare of her bottom, and realised that despite her fashion magazines she'd never seen anyone so naked. A tiny ruffled black thong and a flimsy silk bra set off Amelia's lightly tanned skin and Jo, who was wearing large off-white knickers and matching bra, felt terrible. She had no idea that girls of her age looked so sexy and she suddenly felt self-conscious.

'What do you think of this one?' Amelia said as she turned around, pulled off her Lejaby bra, and slipped into a green dress that was slashed down to the stomach – it was identical to the Versace one Jennifer Lopez wore to the Grammys. Jo gulped.

'It's very sexy,' she said, as she noticed the smooth skin of Amelia's taut midriff, and tried not to stare at her nipples poking through the sliver of material at the front.

Amelia stared at herself in the mirror and frowned. 'But is it too obvious?'

'Obvious?'

'You know ... does it make me look too slutty?'

Jo laughed. 'You look like a model. Sensational. You could be a brunette Kate Moss.' If she didn't like Amelia so much, she'd have hated her.

Amelia turned round and stuck her hips out at her reflection. 'I'm too short to be a model,' she said, staring at herself distractedly and then wrinkling her nose. 'Although I suppose I could be a TV presenter, if I wanted to be. They're all tiny in real life, apparently. Cordelia met Cat Deeley from *SMTV* in a bar in town a few weeks ago and couldn't get over how small she was.' Amelia smoothed the top against her flat stomach and sighed. 'Perhaps this dress in hot pink rather than sea green. What do you think?'

As they trailed around the expensive boutiques of Winchester, Jo began to despair. They were never going to find anything to fit her, let alone make her look even half as good as Amelia on a bad day. Amelia watched Jo get more and more downcast, and just as Amelia thought Jo looked suicidal she thought she'd play her trump card.

'Jo,' she began nervously, hoping her friend would be pleased – not annoyed – at what she was about to suggest. 'There's a shop just a bit further down here that may have some clothes that ... you'd like,' she said, tentatively. 'Do you want to try it?'

Jo nodded glumly. It was clear there were no shops around here that would stock anything that would fit her.

'The thing is ... well. This is the shop. What do you think?'

Jo walked around the shop silently, taking in the oversized yet fashionable clothes in amazement. She didn't understand.

'It's a new maternity shop,' Amelia whispered to Jo. 'Don't be angry with me, it's just some things in here will fit you better than others and I thought you might like them.' Amelia's whisper trailed off, and Jo didn't know if she should be pleased at the fact that there were some decent, near-sexy clothes in her size here or if she should walk out, insulted. Just as she thought she couldn't go through with the humiliation of buying clothes for pregnant women, a delicate indigo tunic caught her eye.

'If anyone asks, I'm due in four weeks,' she whispered back to Amelia, and Amelia comically clapped her hands together in glee as Jo picked up the top and began to browse with a smile on her face.

In the changing-room Jo lost the smile.

'I look like an idiot,' she said to Amelia, hating herself for believing, just for a second, that she could look beautiful. 'I should stick to black. I'm safe in black.'

Amelia shook her head. 'You look great, look at yourself.'

Jo stood self-consciously in front of the full-length mirror and tried to hide her bulging stomach behind her hands. The tunic was cleverly cut to show some of her cleavage and then dropped down in subtle pleats over her stomach. A black crocheted shawl covered her bare arms, and the stretchy dark denim jeans (albeit with a maternity pouch that nobody could see) made her legs look slightly longer. If Jo squinted, they could have passed for Diesel.

'I'm not sure ...'

Amelia sighed and sat down on the floor.

'Look, since we've left school you've lost a couple of pounds from your face and it really shows.' Jo looked at her friend in disbelief. 'And as for your clothes, well, those shapeless sacks you wear don't do you justice.' Amelia looked pointedly at Jo's ankle-length faded black skirt and dark grey T-shirt that was bunched up on the floor.

Jo started to open her mouth to protest but Amelia wouldn't let her. Jo could very easily see how Amelia was Sarah Gladstone-Denham's daughter.

'Wear these clothes tonight, let me put some make-up on you, and try looking like a different person just for a few hours. If it all goes wrong – which it won't – nobody will ever see you again anyway, but if it all goes right you can buy me a drink. What do you say?'

Jo stared at her reflection for a long time and then let the faintest smile show on her face. 'Go on, then,' she said with a grin. 'Although if I get mistaken for a drag queen later, you'll be in trouble.'

Chapter Four

Jo and Amelia were sitting in the Beetle outside Gigolo
– Charlie's recently opened bar in the heart of Winchester
– and Jo was on the verge of a panic attack.

'I'm not sure I can do this,' she whispered, as Amelia
applied a final stroke of blusher to Jo's cheeks. Jo moved
her face away from Amelia's hands and stared at the impossibly glamorous people queuing outside the bar. She
felt irrational fear running through her veins. 'Ames, do I
really have to wear all this make-up?' she asked her friend.
'I feel a bit odd with all this stuff on my face ... A bit ...
obvious.'

Jo pulled a mirror from her bag and gazed at herself with
slight horror. Amelia had spent what seemed like hours on
her, blow-drying her hair until it shone, shading blue Dior
cream eyeshadow over her lids, and accenting the curve of
her eyes with heavy black liner. Maybelline Great Lash mascara provided a *femme fatale* look, and a final sweep of Pout
Flush Blush gave the impression of cheekbones. Jo wasn't
sure if she looked sensational or if she resembled a clown,
but she was sure she wasn't fashionable – last month's issue
of *Cosmo* said the natural look was in.

Amelia smiled kindly, but before she said anything Jo
buried her head in her hands.

'It's going to be like school all over again, isn't it?

Everyone is going to take the piss out of me and my make-up and you're going to end up babysitting me.'

Amelia rolled her eyes. 'Don't be stupid,' she said gently. 'You look amazing – like a completely different person … Now, let's go.' Amelia jumped out of the car, hoping that as soon as they were in the bar Jo would stop worrying, but Jo followed her slowly, wobbling on the kitten heels Amelia had made her buy and feeling overdressed and foolish.

The new jeans she'd been so proud of earlier that day suddenly felt too tight, and Jo was sure that her love handles could be seen through her top. She watched the gorgeous girls in the queue pout and stick out their hipbones as they waited to get in, and then felt her heart drop as she realised just how enormous she was in comparison to them. The only way to get through the evening, Jo decided, was to pretend to be an undercover reporter doing a piece on body fascism in England. She wasn't really fat, she told herself, just wearing padding for a magazine assignment.

Amelia confidently led Jo past the staring girls in the queue and, after shooting the burly bouncers a flirtatious grin, led Jo into the dark bar. A barman spotted Amelia and wolf-whistled, but his expression froze slightly when he spotted Jo lumbering behind her. Suddenly everyone stopped talking, and Jo felt herself tense up – she knew they were staring at her, and not in a good way. Amelia took control of the situation and steered Jo to a free table in a roped-off VIP section.

'I'll be back in a sec,' she said, spotting a space at the bar. 'I'm just going to get us some drinks.'

When Jo didn't say anything, Amelia studied her face carefully, and lowered her voice to a whisper. 'Don't worry about what everyone thinks,' she said, grabbing one of Jo's hands and giving it a squeeze.

But Jo did. As soon as Amelia walked away Jo noticed a

pair of skinny girls looking at her curiously. Immediately Jo felt like a rare animal in a cage with no way to escape, and she wished she could run to the ladies' and hide. Instead, she tried to hold in her stomach, and when that failed she crossed her arms over her chest protectively. Amelia swung herself into a seat, and splashed some drinks on to the black leather coasters on top of the table. Her cheeks were glowing.

'So what do you think?'

'I think everyone's staring at me and laughing,' Jo said flatly.

Amelia grinned. 'What? No, what do you think of Gigolo? It's incredible, isn't it? Bet it beats the bars in London.'

Jo forced herself to look around, being careful not to catch anyone's eye. Although she wasn't about to admit that it was the first time she'd been in a bar, she agreed that it was extraordinary. From the outside the doorway looked as though it led into an average Edwardian building, but inside the walls alternated from leopard skin to a deep blue-black that was flecked with glinting pieces of silver. The ceiling had ornate Victorian-style coving painted a luscious gold, and antique chandeliers swooped down over the red velvet chairs. It was an *Alice in Wonderland* fantasy, and Jo suddenly felt as though she had stepped into the glossy pages of a style magazine. In such an alluring setting her make-up felt right, and Jo felt a world of possibilities open up before her. If she could fit into a bar like this, she could fit into the glamorous publishing world – one of designer clothes, fast men and beautiful girls.

'It's astonishing,' she told Amelia, as her eyes flicked across the men brandishing red fifty-pound notes at the bar, the opulent lighting that cast a luxurious glow over everyone, and the expensive diamond-cut glasses. 'I've never seen anything like this!'

Amelia, who was sipping a cocktail, nodded. 'His brother

– who owns most of the pubs and bars in Hampshire – said Charlie could have Gigolo for his twenty-first birthday as long as he lived in the flat upstairs and ran the bar to profit. It's only a matter of time before he makes his name in the scene in London.' She took another slug of her cocktail and grinned a pink, sticky grin. 'Charlie is going to take London by storm, and I'm going to be right by his side.'

Somehow hearing his name mentioned through the big-beat track, Charlie Rutherford sauntered over to their table and sat down next to Amelia. He casually draped his arm around her. 'Hey, babes,' he said, his accent giving away his public-school roots despite his scruffy jeans and blazer combination. 'Been showing off again?'

Amelia punched Charlie jokingly, and swooped in for a kiss. 'Only because I'm so proud of you!' she said, happily. As Amelia kissed her boyfriend, Jo checked him out – he looked rich, like he had never wanted for anything. He had thick, sweeping, dark hair, haughty brown eyes and a body to die for. He was all lean muscle, height and sex appeal.

'Jo, this is Charlie. Charlie, this is Jo, my friend from school.'

Charlie smiled lazily at her. 'Whassup?' he asked stupidly, before composing himself and saying, 'Good to meet you,' despite not meaning it for a second.

Amelia was keen for Jo to feel comfortable as soon as possible, and thought her boyfriend was the man to help achieve it. 'Charlie, want to give her the tour?'

Jo began to protest. 'It's fine, really—' she began, but Amelia interrupted her.

'You should really see the private rooms. *GQ* called them "the jewels in the crown of the best bar outside London",' Amelia parroted like a PR girl. 'They're bloody cool.'

Jo reluctantly followed Charlie through the crowds of people, refusing to take her eyes off the shining black floor.

Charlie made mindless small talk, knowing Jo wouldn't be able to hear him over the sound system pumping out Fatboy Slim, but he was aware that Amelia was watching them and that he needed to give a performance to stay in her good books. As they reached a narrow corridor, Charlie paused.

'Only the regulars know what bit of the walls to press to get into the exclusive spaces. Let me show you one of the main ones.' He casually leant against the wall and pushed an invisible door into a dark room lit with ultra-violet lights. Jo felt a waft of cigarette smoke hit her, and it was a moment before she could get her bearings. As she gazed around the room she saw there was a group of five girls sitting at a mirrored table, and she tried to appear nonchalant when she saw that they were cutting lines of cocaine with a black credit card.

'Fancy some blow?' Charlie asked when he noticed Jo watching them. He gave her a cruel smile. 'As you're a friend of Amelia's I'll let you have the first line for free.'

Jo shook her head, but Charlie laughed in her face. It was a different laugh to the one Jo had seen when he was with Amelia. It was mean.

'You know you want to,' he said, leaning towards her. Jo could smell the alcohol on his breath, and she squirmed slightly. She didn't want to seem rude, but she didn't like Amelia's boyfriend leaning in so close.

'Fat bitches like you are always desperate for coke,' Charlie leered, and his voice was syrupy. 'It's the only thing that stops you eating ... although looking like you do, I imagine you don't get much very often. Go on, Jo-Jo,' he encouraged nastily. 'I bet you'd mainline it if it was sugar.'

A young-looking blonde girl came over to them, and she hung her arms around Charlie's neck while giving Jo a critical once-over. Charlie began to stroke her hair, and Jo could see she was wearing a tiny, flimsy scrap of material that doubled up as a dress. As Charlie's hands moved down past her neck and on to her breasts, Jo didn't know where to look, but as soon as they started kissing passionately, she fled.

Amelia was sitting at their table in the VIP area, and she beamed when she saw Jo approach. She didn't notice that she was out of breath from rushing back to her.

'Isn't Charlie great?' Amelia gushed, and for a second Jo wondered if she was talking about her boyfriend or cocaine.

'He's ... he's certainly a charmer,' Jo said, hesitantly, and that was all Amelia needed to start singing his praises.

'He's amazing – so much cooler than those stupid little boys I used to write love letters to when we were at school. And ...' she said, leaning towards Jo conspiratorially, 'he is incredible in bed. He makes me come every single time. It's unheard of!'

Jo took a sip of her drink.

'And he's just so nice to me,' Amelia continued, blissfully unaware that Jo's face was like thunder. 'He's always giving me free drinks. I joke that he's trying to get me drunk, but he's just such a sweet guy he wouldn't do that. Mummy adores him; she calls him my bit of "rough" even though he went to Eton. You can see why he's one of Winchester's most eligible bachelors – every girl wants to be with him!' she cooed, and Jo downed her drink in one, despite it tasting like cough mixture.

'Do you trust him not to go with them?' she said flatly.

'He doesn't even notice other girls,' Amelia slurred. 'But don't take my word for it, let me go and get him ... Where did you leave him?'

Jo panicked. She didn't want Amelia to go and get Charlie at all, or worse, find him in a compromising situation with another girl, but she was already on her feet and looking around the bar. 'Is he in a private room?' she asked, and Jo shrugged. She hated not telling Amelia the truth, but

Cosmopolitan always said never to get involved in other people's relationships – especially if you suspected one of them to be having an affair.

Amelia teetered on her heels and walked off, and suddenly Jo felt incredibly alone and vulnerable. She was the only person sitting in the VIP area, and it was like she was on a stage, with hundreds of people watching her every move. A particularly loud group of giggling, awkward-looking teenagers who were dressed in practically nothing and had far too much make-up on were strutting around close to her, and every so often one of them would look at Jo and puff her cheeks out. It was worse than school, Jo thought. At least at St Christopher's she knew how to escape.

Gathering all her courage, Jo stood up with as much dignity as she could muster, and moved into the main area of the bar. As she walked past people she could hear them laughing at her, and although she wanted to ask someone where the ladies' was she didn't dare – she was much too shy. Eventually Jo found them – hidden behind a glossy black door that merged seamlessly into the wall – and she took cover in a cubicle just before a couple of girls stumbled in to reapply their make-up.

'So, like, the bastard told me if I refused to work Saturday to help the editorial team meet the deadline he'd sack me!' Jo lifted her head from her hands and stared at the cubicle door.

'And what did you do?' a bored-sounding girl asked.

'What could I do? I worked the Saturday. It was such a fucking pain, but I've only been there for a couple of months and the last thing I need is for everyone to know I got sacked from *Sparkle* magazine.'

Jo held her breath. A girl who worked on a real magazine was only a few feet away, and Jo was desperate to hear what she said next. This girl, Jo thought, could be the person who helped her with her career — if only she stopped being so scared of everyone.

'Don't know why you bother working there anyway,' the girl's friend said. 'It's just a crappy teen magazine.'

'Yeah, true, but it's a foot in the door, isn't it. I don't want to be a secretary all my life, but it's a way in. Today *Sparkle* ... tomorrow *Tatler*. Well, that's the plan.'

Jo's drive for wanting to work on a magazine banished her shyness — she flushed the toilet and approached the sinks. Both of the girls were tall, skinny and blonde, and Jo felt like a frumpy mess standing next to them. They looked like they'd stepped out of *Sex and the City*. She took a deep breath.

'Sorry, I couldn't help but overhear ...' she began meekly. 'But do you work on *Sparkle* magazine?'

The prettier of the two girls looked Jo up and down. 'Yeah,' she said. 'Why?'

Jo beamed. 'I've always wanted to work on a magazine,' she said enthusiastically. 'How did you get to be a secretary there?'

The pretty blonde girl smirked and gave her friend a side-long glance. 'My agency sent me there ...' she began slowly, as if she were considering something. 'You know, you could be a secretary too ... it's really easy.'

Jo's mouth dropped open. 'Do you really think I could?'

'Sure,' the girl said, and Jo was so overwhelmed that she may have found a way into a magazine that she didn't notice the other girl giggling.

'Look, why don't you phone them up? The woman I deal with is Felicity, and she's great. Have you got a pen? I'll give you the number.'

Jo wrote the phone number down carefully on an old receipt, and thanked the girls gratefully as they sauntered out of the toilets. The door slammed behind them, and as

47

soon as they were out of earshot they both fell about with laughter.

'I wish I could see Felicity's face when that fat girl turns up,' the girl said to her friend, who couldn't stop giggling. 'That will teach her for putting me on an assignment where I have to work weekends.'

Luckily Jo didn't hear a word of their conversation, as she was too busy counting her blessings. Who needed A-levels and journalism college when there were other ways to work on a magazine? she thought to herself, with a tiny smile. She carefully tucked the phone number into her bag, and, thinking that the haughty-looking girls in the bar weren't that bad after all, went to find Amelia.

Jo stood in the West End of London looking at the sky. Dark clouds were overhead, masking the afternoon sun. Jo checked her tattered watch and realised she was early for her appointment at the recruitment agency. She pulled at her jacket nervously – she wasn't convinced it was big enough for her, and she also wondered if she had dressed correctly. Jo wasn't so sure she had.

'Think of it as a job interview,' Amelia had advised the week before, when she'd appeared in the morning with a killer hangover. In the cold light of day Jo still felt awkward about having seen Charlie with another girl, and it wasn't until Amelia asked Jo what she planned on wearing to her interview that Jo realised she had to put what she had seen the night before out of her head. Amelia had knocked back an Alka-Seltzer and dragged Jo back to the maternity shop in Winchester – they managed to find a skirt that sat on the knee, along with a simple white blouse and navy jacket. When Jo put it on she felt about thirty, and when she teamed it with black flats and black tights, she felt forty. The whole outfit had cost far more than Jo could afford, but Amelia made her realise it was an investment in her future. Amelia said secretaries in London dressed like this all the time, so Jo thought she should get used to it.

But as Jo watched some secretaries in the West End taking their lunch-breaks, she wasn't convinced Amelia knew what she was talking about after all. Most of the girls looked like models. Many wore tight little blouses and tiny Top Shop mini-skirts that showed off lean, tanned legs, and all of them sashayed around the shops on heels, ranging from killer stilettos to demure kittens and sensible courts. Worst of all was that every single one of them had perfect hair.

Jo ruefully remembered how beautiful her hair had looked after Amelia had been at it with her professional hairdryer, but she resolved to not let her frizzy split ends put her off. She absolutely had to get on this agency's books and she was determined to make them see past her appearance. Felicity – the Sloaney-looking recruitment consultant with an Alice band and twin set – didn't seem so enthusiastic.

'Let's get this straight,' she said, as she sat opposite Jo in an interview room with light blue walls and computers in the corner. 'You've not worked as a secretary before?' Felicity was wondering if the slightly nervous girl in front of her was for real. She didn't want to stare at her body, but she'd never encountered anyone so big before. She didn't know quite how to break it to this girl that when you were a secretary, looks counted for everything. Felicity wondered if she could convince some of her favourite managing directors to take Jo on rather than the slender girls she had on the books. It would be impossible.

'No, I haven't, Jo said slowly, 'but I have only just left school … I went to St Christopher's. In Buckinghamshire.'

Felicity's back straightened somewhat, and Jo was pleased she had gone to a good boarding school after all.

'And you have no plans to go to university?'

Jo shook her head and took a deep breath.

'I was going to, but ...' Jo didn't want to let on that she'd messed up her exams. 'But I'd rather just start working. I think that work experience is as good as going to college.'

When Felicity gave Jo a satisfied little smile she continued. She knew what this woman wanted to hear.

'I know I haven't worked before but I did learn to type at school. Luckily for me St Christopher's was keen – very keen – to make sure all their girls had a well-rounded education. As well as the usual Latin and lacrosse, we also learnt all our computer skills.' Jo let out a little laugh. 'Not that most of the girls at school would need to know how to turn a computer on, considering all the eligible men on their doorsteps.'

Felicity looked at Jo curiously, and Jo could see she was winning her over.

'Why don't we see for ourselves what you learnt at school ... If you could just come this way we'll give you a typing test ...'

Jo aced the test. She breezed through the Microsoft Word, Excel and PowerPoint tests, the telephone-manner test, and excelled at the different filing situations she was put in during the next hour. Like the girl in Gigolo said, it wasn't hard.

'So will you put me on assignment now?' Jo asked eagerly, feeling more confident.

Felicity looked uncomfortable. 'Being a secretary is ... it's more than just being able to do the job, Joanne. You need to look the part too, and I'm not sure by your dress you would be suitable for the majority of our offices.'

Jo felt her heart drop. The whole day suddenly seemed like a waste of time.

'It's my weight, isn't it?' A small tear slid down her cheek, and Jo hated herself for crying.

Felicity nodded.

'But I can do the job, and I'll work really hard, I promise!'

Jo knew she was sounding desperate, but she couldn't help herself. She had been so close to starting out on her dream and suddenly it seemed as though the rolls of fat that had stopped her fitting in at school were going to stand in the way of her career too.

'I'm afraid that our clients won't see it that way.' Felicity looked around the office uncomfortably and lowered her voice. 'Look, I wouldn't normally do this, but I'm going to put you on our books anyway. I'll try to start you on some low-key jobs, and in the meantime you should try to present yourself better – lose some weight and smarten up a bit. You seem like a clever girl, it shouldn't be too hard for you, should it?'

Jo nodded dumbly, and Felicity patted her arm again.

'I'm sure you have some perfectly delightful clothes at home you could wear to the workplace, too. Give me a few days to let our other girls here know we have someone new on the books and I'll telephone you a day in advance when we have some work for you.'

Jo struggled to speak normally – she was delighted that she'd be able to start working for the agency, but when Felicity had told her to lose some weight a flash of white-hot anger had coursed through her.

'Do you think any of those jobs would be on a magazine? Your client list in reception said you supply typists to Garnet Publishing and IMC Magazines.'

'Why yes, we do, but these jobs are like gold-dust and are given to our more experienced girls. But don't you worry. After a few jobs for some of our more blue-collar organisations I'm sure you will be more than ready for them.'

Felicity smiled kindly at Jo and showed her to the door.

'Careful of the rain, dear. Why, don't you have an umbrella?'

Jo wondered what Felicity would have to say if she told her that she didn't have enough money to buy one.

Chapter Five

September 2000

Jo lay on her bed and wished she lived in a remote country cottage miles from anyone. The couple in the flat above – a greasy man with tattoos and a bleached-blonde woman with three-inch dark roots – were arguing again, and the bangs, thumps and screamed swear-words made her uncomfortable. If this was what being in a relationship was like, she thought, she was better off single. She sighed, swung herself out of bed, and walked the three steps to her chest of drawers where she grabbed a Bounty bar from her stash. She crammed half of it into her mouth and felt depressed.

It had been four weeks and the recruitment agency hadn't called.

After three days of euphoria and jumping up and down because she was finally on her way, Jo had begun to feel slightly uneasy. The phone hadn't rung once. When a week had passed Jo had given in and phoned Felicity on the agency's phone number. In a hushed voice Felicity told her that no jobs for newcomers had come in, asked how her diet was going, and said that she'd phone when she had something for her. Jo waited and after three more agonising sitting-by-the-phone weeks she'd rung again. This time the switchboard operator told her that Felicity was unable to take her call, and as Jo watched her tears drop down on her bulging spare tyres she realised it was a lost cause.

To snap herself out of her mood, and to distract herself from the angry yells coming from upstairs, Jo picked up the phone to call Amelia at university. She was halfway through dialling the number when she realised there was no dial tone. Her mother hadn't paid the phone bill again, and, judging by the way she'd started throwing away all the bills rather than saving them for future pay cheques, it seemed she had no intention of getting the line reconnected.

Jo grabbed some coins from her piggy bank and marched down to the phone-box, ignoring the giggles of some schoolgirls who were watching her get out of breath. Jo's hand tightened around her ten-pence pieces – she was going to buy her first mobile as soon as she had some money.

'Ames, it's me. Jo.'

'Jo, hi! How are you?' Amelia settled back in her room at university and carefully held her phone to her ear, making sure it didn't catch on her chandelier earring. 'Have you got a job on a magazine yet?'

Jo could feel herself slump. 'No. That recruitment woman isn't taking my calls, and my phone's been cut off so I can't call her anyway. Can you phone me back?' Jo turned away from the gangs of girls on the other side of the road and tried not to feel overwhelmed at the smell of urine in the phone-box.

'Want to come and stay?' Amelia offered hopefully, after she'd quickly filled her in on how much she'd drunk during Freshers' Week. 'I'm not doing anything really, lectures don't take up much time, and you've not come to see me yet.'

'I haven't got any money, Ames.'

'Well, yes, I know that, but the train fare isn't that expensive ...'

Jo didn't bother to try to explain that she didn't have a trust fund or savings. And that she was down to her last ten pounds.

'I don't know what I'm going to do,' Jo said in a small voice. 'I suppose I'm going to have to go on the dole after all.'

There was silence at the end of the phone as Amelia was lost in thought.

'Look, I have an idea, but I don't know if you're going to like it. Hear me out, OK?'

Jo wondered what Amelia would suggest. Her best friend sometimes seemed so blind to the disadvantages she faced because of her weight that she wouldn't be surprised if she proposed that Jo be a stripper, or a model. Jo knew there was a market for fat-girl porn but it really wasn't something she wanted to get into – it wasn't what she meant when she said she wanted to work 'in magazines'.

'Go on …' Jo said wearily as she crossed her fingers in hope.

'Well, Charlie was saying on the phone that there's a job going at a pub near Bishop's Waltham, that town near my parents' house. It's called the Royal something, I think, and they're looking for a waitress-cum-kitchen hand. The pay is shitty, but it's a live-in job with a room above the bar and free meals.' Amelia was nervous as she heard silence at the end of the phone. She hoped she hadn't insulted Jo. 'Charlie told me about it as a joke in case I "came to my senses and realised I was too dumb for university" – the cheek! – but, well, it could suit you. What do you think?'

'So I'd have to move to the middle of nowhere in Hampshire to do a rubbish job that nobody else wants?'

Amelia felt herself deflating.

'The pub's meant to be really good …' Amelia began, before trailing off. 'They're one of those new ones that does proper food, and they've been in the *Guardian* and everything …'

Jo leant against the phone-box and clutched the receiver so hard her knuckles went white. What would she be leaving?

All her hopes pinned on a phone call that would get her a job filing in a dingy warehouse? At least if she got a job she'd be doing something – and she was desperate to move out of home and away from her mother.

'I'll take it.'

'Seriously? You will? You don't mind me suggesting it?' Amelia let out a sigh of relief.

Jo looked at the group of girls who were all staring at her menacingly, and she realised she couldn't wait to get out of London. 'Just let me know when I start.'

February 2001

Working at The Royal Oak was like being at school again, Jo thought – only with interesting lunch menus and an older clientele more interested in foot-and-mouth disease than *Hollyoaks*. When Jo had started five months earlier she'd been incredibly nervous, but she soon got used to the amused nudges about her weight when she served food to the customers. Jo scrutinised the menu for about a fortnight, and after a while she soon began to be known as the girl who knew as much about the dishes as head chef Michael – from the exact texture of the rabbit and bacon terrine to what the Ryeland lamb had grazed on. David and Dominic – the pub's owners – congratulated themselves on hiring a girl who so obviously enjoyed knowing and eating food, and Jo blossomed with the adrenaline rush that came from living alone and earning a wage.

In the evenings Jo sat in her favourite corner of the bar, feeling her breath catch as she looked up from her notebooks and took in the beauty of the pub. She thought the décor was what it would be like inside Buckingham Palace. All of the furniture was antique and the framed oil paintings cleverly depicted views of the wintry fields on the other side of the country lane. Old letters written to the seventeenth-century owner of the former inn by minor Royals and the aristocracy filled the rest of the wall space, and according to legend, Oliver Cromwell had spent the night there.

Jo had always felt as though London – and school – had stifled her creativity, and as soon as she moved to The Royal Oak she was proved right. Suddenly she found she couldn't stop thinking of feature ideas for magazines, and when she wasn't working, she was sitting in the bar scribbling in her notebooks. Some of the barmen thought Jo was nuts, and asked why she preferred writing to making use of the free drinks The Royal Oak kindly provided to staff, but Jo found she couldn't answer them. Magazines were her obsession, and so far nobody, including Amelia, had ever understood that about her.

'You're either writing your life story or getting something off your chest,' Jo heard a voice comment from the other side of the bar, and she momentarily let her pen hang in the air, giving her hand much-needed relief from the furious scribbling she'd been doing for the past hour.

Jo looked up and realised she was staring into the eyes of the most attractive man she had ever seen. He was tall, had broad shoulders and an athletic frame, and his dark blond hair swept over his eyes. He looked like a cross between Brad Pitt and David Beckham, and as he pushed his fringe from his face and grinned at her, Jo swallowed hard.

The man came over to her table and peered down at Jo's work. He spotted a few tips on 'how to find a boyfriend for Valentine's Day' before she could put her arms over her notebook.

'David told me you're the waitress here, but you're clearly moonlighting as a relationship advisor,' the man said, and he stuck out his hand. 'William Denning. I'm the new bar manager.'

Jo stared at William's hand for a moment and then shyly took it. Every nerve ending felt as though it was on fire, and she felt her face turn red.

'Do you have a name?' William said gently, and Jo bit her lip. He was wearing brown boots, faded blue jeans and a well-fitting dark grey jumper, and his face was slightly ruddy from the cold wind outside. He looked like a model, and Jo wasn't sure she could speak.

'Jo,' she said quietly, and she looked down at the table, unable to look William in the eye again. She was mortified by her physical reaction to the man who was, effectively, her new boss. 'Jo Hill.'

'How long have you been working here, Jo Hill?' William asked her in a light, teasing voice, and Jo forced herself to look William in the eye. His blond hair had flopped back over one of his eyebrows sexily, and when he smiled Jo noticed that his piercing blue eyes crinkled. She wished he would stop smiling – it made him all the more attractive.

'About five months now, I think,' Jo said, hoping she could end the conversation before it really began. She didn't want to make a fool of herself in front of the most perfect man she'd ever seen.

William was twisting his mouth around in a vague sort of bemused grin, and Jo wondered if he was laughing at her. She crossed her arms in front of her chest defensively, caring that she'd left her notebook open and exposed on the table, but desperate to cover the rolls of fat under her breasts.

'I see. And do you enjoy it?' William asked.

Jo tried to smile. 'It's all right.'

William laughed openly. 'You're making me feel like I may have made the wrong decision in coming here,' he said, as he looked at her with interest.

Jo shrugged and couldn't think what to say next. She felt like an inexperienced child and, for lack of knowing what to do or say, she concentrated on holding her stomach in. She looked back down at the table again and felt miserable. As if William would ever fancy me, she thought.

'I hope you don't think me rude, but I promised my father I'd phone him right now ...' Jo murmured, hating herself for lying but desperate to get away from William. 'Perhaps we could catch up tomorrow?'

William shot her an easy, casual grin, and Jo felt her face flush again. She'd never really had a crush on a boy before – apart from the men who did agony-uncle columns in *Honey* and *Gloss*, and they didn't count, not really – and she didn't know what to do, what to say.

'That would be great,' he said, and Jo stood up, suddenly very aware that the last thing she wanted was for William to see her body wobbling as she left. Taking a deep breath Jo shot William one final smile and, carrying her notebook behind her back so that it covered up some of her bottom, she walked stiffly to her bedroom.

March 2001

'So he's tall, dark and handsome?'

Jo put her head against the wall by the telephone and sighed. 'Not only is he tall, *blond* and handsome, he also has a broad chest, footballer legs, these amazing blue eyes and ...'

'And?'

'And the most gorgeous bottom you've ever seen.' Jo's blush burned across her face. She couldn't believe that she would say something like that. What was William doing to her?

'Sounds like someone is in love!' Amelia sang down the phone.

'It's horrible. I don't know what to do – it's been a month and I can't bear it when he looks at me. I blush bright red, can't speak, and most of all I know he's checking me out and thinking how fat and ugly I am.'

'Jo!' Amelia sounded shocked, but Jo knew she wasn't. Not really. 'Is that how you really think of yourself?'

Jo nodded down the phone. Her self-esteem had reached an all-time low when she had failed to be sent on a measily typing job, and she hated herself. Now that William was around, Jo was even more aware of how overweight she was – and she knew that he would never fancy her so long as she was fat.

'You know, I bet if you really put your mind to it you could lose weight,' Amelia said gently.

A million reasons why she couldn't lose weight flooded Jo's mind, but rather than defensively blurting one of them out to Amelia, she thought quietly to herself.

'Do you think I could? Really?' she asked Amelia in a small voice, and Amelia smiled grimly down the phone.

'I don't think it will be easy, but I think if you put your mind to something, you can achieve anything you want.'

Jo flung her newest diet magazine back on to the pile in her bedroom and concentrated very hard on ignoring the rumbling sounds from her stomach. After reading up on the best way to lose weight, Jo had decided to try and drop some excess pounds before attempting to exercise, and after a long and difficult week of cutting out the junk food and fizzy drinks, she had been ecstatic to find she'd lost two pounds. It was the first time she'd actually lost weight, and although she'd not noticed a physical difference, it affected her profoundly. She had over seven stone to lose to reach her ideal weight of nine stone, and although it seemed like a massive figure, Jo knew she had to do it.

Using the diet mags as her benchmark, Jo ate only what was recommended, and submitted herself completely to their advice. She had toast for breakfast, a small sandwich for lunch, and chicken or meat with vegetables in the evening. Jo was starving – and the gorgeous smells that came from Michael's kitchen nearly drove her mad. To supplement her diet, Jo stole cold triple-roasted potatoes from the kitchen, and made herself sandwiches with them when she thought she was going to faint from hunger. The guilt she experienced when she took the last mouthful encouraged her not to do it again, but she couldn't help herself.

Slowly, though, the weight kept on falling off. Jo woke up early, did some stretches, and walked to the local village shop and back as fast as she could under the guise of needing to get the newspapers in for the customers who sat alone nursing their pints of bitter. In the beginning Jo was out of breath and sweaty when she reached the shop, and then again when she got back to the pub, but she soon found she could walk the distance easily. Jo made a point of not buying sweets, chocolate or crisps from the shop and instead bought herself magazines as rewards, using the photographs of slim models to keep her going. She wanted to look like them, and then she wanted to create fashion shoots with them.

Head chef Michael noticed a difference in her. 'Gone off our food, have we?' he asked one lunchtime when Jo had forsaken a pithivier of shredded pigeon with glazed chestnuts for lentil soup and a small slice of bread.

Jo nodded – suddenly food seemed like the enemy, not her faithful friend. As Jo began to eat less and less she realised how eating had been her hobby, how working out what she was going to eat next had kept her entertained. The new Jo Hill swapped her eating addiction for a dieting addiction, but when her weight loss started to plateau she decided it was time to try and exercise. By October she'd lost nearly two stone, and even though all her clothes were looser, she wanted to slim down properly – she wanted to get to a size ten.

At first it was hell, pure hell. Jo didn't warm up enough to begin with and three minutes into a light jog her legs began to ache and seize up. Jo gave up and stretched her legs out properly, and vowed to try again the next day. This time Jo managed to jog – slowly – for ten minutes as a light shower kept her cool. As a result of doing this every evening for a week she lost another three pounds, and a few weeks later Jo caught William staring at her.

'So how are you doing it?'

Jo looked up at William and tried very hard not to blush. Every time they made small talk she felt like she made a fool of herself with her teenage-crush stutters, and she'd started going out of her way to avoid him.

'Sorry . . . how am I doing what?' Jo attempted a casual, carefree grin and tried not to notice just how breathtaking William looked.

'How are you managing to lose all that weight?' William asked her. 'You look terrific.'

Jo immediately felt her blood turn to ice. She hated the thought of William looking at her body and, worse, comparing how she was now to how she'd been a few months earlier. She felt ashamed at how large she'd been.

'I've been working out,' Jo said in a small voice. 'I've been running and watching what I eat.'

William's forehead furrowed slightly. 'But when? You haven't changed your shifts, and you're always writing in your notebooks in the evening . . .'

Jo took a deep breath and desperately hoped she wasn't coming across as shy, or as if she had a crush on him. 'Late at night after closing,' she said. 'When everyone goes to bed I go out and run on the roads.'

'What? In the pitch-black? What if you got hit by a car?'

Jo shrugged and grinned in what she hoped was an off-hand way. 'It hasn't happened yet. And you have to admit it's working.'

William's eyes travelled over Jo's body and despite wanting to cross her arms over her stomach, she pretended she didn't care he was looking at her.

'You know, I go running too – and I'd be happy to help you train if you like ...'

Jo couldn't stand the thought of William seeing her hot, sweaty and red in the face but at the same time she wanted a running partner, she wanted someone to urge her on when her legs burned and she didn't think she could run any more. She wanted to spend some time with him.

'Six o'clock every morning, and then again mid-afternoon,' William said. 'Are you in?'

Jo looked at William, and clocked his broad shoulders, muscled arms and beautiful blue eyes.

'I'm in.'

Chapter Six

‐ ‐ ‐ ‐ ‐ ‐ ‐ ‐ ‐ ‐ ‐ ‐ ‐ ‐ ‐

May 2002

'You've got to keep on going, keep on going, Jo, you can do it!'

Jo thought she was going to die. She was sure of it. Every muscle in her body, despite being hidden by layers of fat, burnt with a hot white heat. Her throat felt sore from the cool breeze and her nose ran, dripping on to her T-shirt, which was soaked with sweat.

She couldn't take much more of this.

William ran behind her with a stopwatch. He was wearing a tight fitted T-shirt, and Jo knew if she turned round she'd see the outline of every single muscle in his torso. 'Come on, it's only fifty more steps to the tree, come on, Jo, come on!'

She couldn't do it, she just couldn't do it, she thought. But Jo knew she couldn't stop either. Focusing her eyes on the dusty track, Jo imagined the tree was made of chocolate. Oh God, she thought, chocolate. If she just kept on going, if her legs didn't give up on her, she would let herself have some Dairy Milk. Her whole body felt as heavy as lead. She wasn't sure if she would ever get to the tree, and just as Jo's body screamed out for mercy she was there.

William stopped beside her as she doubled over in pain, out of breath and feeling like she was going to throw up. 'Nineteen minutes, Jo! You beat your record by nearly six minutes!'

Jo wanted to thump him. She collapsed on the dewy grass and looked up at William, who didn't even seem puffed.

'I am never, ever doing that again.'

William grinned and brushed his blond hair from his eyes. 'Sure you are, and next week we'll beat this time by ten minutes. Just you wait and see.'

William infuriated her, but he was right. They'd been working out for six months, and during that time he was always there by her side. When Jo ate breakfast he was there making sure she ate enough – he persuaded her that porridge with semi-skimmed milk needed to be eaten alongside wholewheat toast with low-sugar peanut butter; that the salad she ate for lunch needed to have lots of grilled chicken and a dressing. He convinced her that she'd lose more fat if she ate enough to give her more energy, thus ensuring she could work out more. If Jo could have had her way she'd have eaten nothing and exercised all day long, but William made sure she ate, and David and Dominic made sure she worked. She had been promoted to serving customers in the bar, with David's reasoning that she looked nice behind it. For the first time in a long while, things were looking up.

On Jo's twentieth birthday, in June, William handed her a birthday card, and she tried desperately hard not to go bright red. William had recently had his hair cut, and somehow his eyes shone an even darker blue because of it. His face was slightly tanned, and he had the healthy complexion of a man who worked outside rather than of someone who ran a bar. He was still dazzling, and Jo longed to touch him.

'I can't believe you remembered,' Jo exclaimed. 'But now you know how old I am, I think it's only fair you tell me your age. You're so old I'd guess about fifty,' she teased.

William laughed. 'I'm twenty-seven,' he said. 'Not that much older than you. But as I am older than you, you need to do as I say ... And I want you to shut your eyes.'

Jo did as she was told, and William brought out a candle-lit chocolate-frosted birthday cake. Before he told her to open her eyes William gazed at her for a long, lingering moment, and realised just how different Jo looked to the girl he'd first met – she was confident, happier and slimmer. Head chef Michael, who'd been watching them, noticed the affection in William's eyes that hadn't been there before, and when Jo opened her eyes and saw the cake they both burst out laughing, as if sharing a private joke.

Michael smiled as he watched Jo blow out the twenty candles William had dotted on the cake. Then he looked at William again, who was staring at Jo with such adoration he wondered why nobody had noticed it before.

August 2002

Jo couldn't believe it.

When she stood in front of the mirror she noticed that her rolls of fat had got smaller, that she had the beginnings of a waist, of cheekbones, of an ass that sat on top of her legs rather than merging into her ample thighs. In her eyes she was still massive – Jo guessed she was a size sixteen – but she had lost loads of weight. Jo grinned to herself. She was definitely on her way, and she phoned Amelia up with her good news.

'So, yeah, I've lost five stone.'

There was silence at the end of the phone.

'Sorry, did you say five stone, Jo?'

'Yup! Five stone! I'm not going to tell you how much I weigh as I have plenty more to lose but I'm getting there. I've got two stone to lose to get to my target weight!'

Amelia looked at the phone first in disbelief, and then in amazement. 'Jo, that's incredible! Well done! Congratulations! I'm so proud of you!'

Jo fell about laughing. 'I'm proud of myself too, but it's been such hard work. I run and cycle every day.'

'Christ, you must be exhausted.'

Jo shook her head happily. 'But that's the thing, I'm not! And the best bit is that I'm no longer going to be hidden in the kitchen and only allowed out to serve meals when the bar is busy. I've been promoted to barmaid.'

Amelia laughed. 'I'm impressed. And what about your plans to actually send one of those articles you've been writing to a magazine?'

Jo paused. 'When I'm at my target weight I'll do it,' she said. 'If a magazine rejects something I've written I'll start comfort-eating again. I just know it. I'll do it in the autumn.' Jo sounded so sincere that she almost believed herself, and as she hung up the phone she resolutely refused to acknowledge the fact that for the moment she could only think of William, and not her career.

Jo looked at the small clock she kept by the side of her bed, and was dismayed to see it was three in the morning. For hours she had been desperately trying to get to sleep, but there was a gentle hum of anticipation in her body that she had never experienced before, and the longer Jo stayed awake, the more intense it got. It was almost as though she was hungry, but she had no appetite, only a craving to be close to William. Jo sighed, and just as she started to imagine William leaning over to kiss her, she heard a crash in his bedroom. Without thinking about what she was wearing or caring about her state of semi-arousal, Jo flung open the door to William's bedroom and stared at the scene with wide eyes.

Although Jo had never been in William's bedroom before, she'd always assumed it was similar to hers. However, William had chosen to paint his walls a deep midnight blue, and his sheets were a clean, crisp white. The room was lit by a few church candles dotted around, and the flickering candlelight settled on William, who was sitting on the wooden floor with his head in his hands. He was surrounded by screwed-up pieces of paper, and he looked utterly miserable.

'William … what's wrong?' Jo asked softly as she padded over to where William was sitting. He looked up at her, taking in her bare feet, her strong legs and the thin cotton T-shirt that barely hid her shape. He focused on Jo's nipples before speaking.

'Writer's block,' William growled, and Jo was momentarily taken aback at the frustration in his face. There was something compellingly masculine about the intense frown that he flung at her, and it made her feel even more exposed as she realised that she wasn't wearing any knickers. William looked up at her again, and Jo quickly knelt down, being careful to make sure that her T-shirt covered her the best it could.

'I didn't know you wrote too,' Jo began softly, and as she spoke she realised that William was wearing nothing but running shorts. His broad chest was tanned, and every muscle in his torso was defined. His arms were strong and muscular, and for a moment Jo longed to touch him. Instead, she continued to gaze luxuriously at his body, but when William caught her staring she lowered her eyes to the floor and blushed faintly.

'I don't like people knowing about my novel,' William said quietly.

Jo took a deep breath and put one of her hands on William's arms. In comparison to his forearm, Jo's hand looked tiny, and she marvelled at just how large William was compared to her.

'If I had a career like that I'd be so proud I wouldn't keep it a secret,' she said, and William let out a little laugh.

'It's not a career yet,' he said, and he caught Jo's eye,

refusing to let her look away. He gazed at her so intensely that Jo felt as though he had power over her, and she shifted on the floor. 'It's very much like you writing in those notebooks every evening ... and not telling a soul what you're up to.'

Jo sighed, stood up and sat on the bed, but as she got comfortable her T-shirt rose higher, so that William could see a tantalising amount of flesh. Jo blushed, pulled her T-shirt down even further, and wondered if she had the guts to climb into William's bed so that she could cover up her modesty. She decided not to risk it, and took a deep breath.

'I want to run the best glossy women's magazine in the country. I want to be thin, and ...' Jo peeked at William and dared herself to say what she was thinking, despite the sexual tension between them. 'And I want to fall in love with someone who loves me.'

William gave her a crooked smile, and immediately Jo was pleased that she had finally confided in him after all the months of mainly only talking about calories and muscle mass.

'So why are you working here and not on some brilliant magazine? You don't seem like the type to give up on something you want.'

Jo shrugged and explained how she'd not got the grades she'd needed in her A-levels.

'But I'm never giving up, you know,' she said. 'Never. I'll find a way to do this, but it has to be the right time. And maybe now – maybe even tonight – isn't the right time for you to write. But when it is right you'll know it, and I think you'll do it well.'

William got up from the floor and joined Jo on the bed. He lay back and gestured to Jo to do the same. She did so uncomfortably but realised that because they had connected over their love of writing, because of the flickering candles, and their closeness on the bed, that this was the most romantic moment of her life.

'You're right, you know. How did you get to be so wise so young?' William said softly, as he shifted from his back on to his side so he could look at Jo closely. Jo held her breath. The heat from his body made her even hotter, and she was sure that William could see the distinct outline of her nipples through her T-shirt.

'When you look like this you have to be smart,' Jo said, trying not to look at William. She focused on the wall behind him, but then, when he didn't speak, she shifted her gaze to his face. Instantly she caught his eye, and she felt her body catch on fire with lust.

William brushed his thumb against Jo's cheek, and she blushed scarlet. 'You mean when you look pretty?' he asked her tenderly, and he gently moved his hand across her face.

'Don't,' Jo said, desperate not to fall apart at the first sign of affection a man had ever shown her. 'Please don't.'

William ignored her and moved his thumb down to her lips.

'Such gorgeous lips,' he said softly, looking into her eyes.

Jo could feel herself melting as he held her gaze, and she couldn't speak, couldn't breathe.

'And such a lovely neck,' he whispered. 'When you wear your hair up I gaze at the curve of your neck all the time. It's extremely sensual, and it distracts me something rotten when I'm supposed to be working.'

Jo stared at William incredulously until she didn't think she could bear it – she thought she was going to explode. Jo looked again at his bare chest and stomach, and she could feel her insides fizzing. Her eyes caught the trail of hair going downwards from his stomach to his shorts, and when she focused on his shorts she could see his rock-hard erection through the thin cotton. She panicked and sat bolt upright.

'I said, don't,' Jo said loudly and the mood was instantly broken. William sat up too, and he looked at Jo in confusion.

'Don't you want this?' he quietly asked her, and he reached out to touch Jo on the back. Jo crossed her arms and felt fear run through her body. What if she tried to kiss him and William was repulsed because she didn't know how to do it? Or what if — worse — he expected sex? The thought of William touching her rolls of fat, even though they were so much smaller, made Jo feel physically ill. As much as she lusted after him she wasn't ready.

'No, I don't. And get your hand off me.' Jo stood up, and even though she was wobbly on her feet she kept her voice as steady as she could. 'I'm going to forget all about tonight, and I hope you do too,' she choked, and she spun on her heel and flung herself into her bedroom.

'Hang on, let me get this straight,' Amelia said, while she tried to keep up with Jo as they walked around Winchester city centre. 'He came on to you in a really nice way and not a seedy way and you said no?'

Jo nodded and walked faster, desperate to get to the next shop. She'd never been able to fit into any of the clothes in normal shops before, and it gave her a thrill to fit into a size sixteen. 'Do we have to talk about it?' Jo said quietly, as she gazed at some shoes in a shop window. 'I mean, you've only just come back for the summer holidays, don't you want to tell me what you got up to in the last few weeks?'

Amelia shook her head. 'Not much to tell, really. If I'd been single I'm sure I'd have pulled a couple of times, but my heart belongs to Charlie.' She gave Jo a sidelong glance. 'You know how it is.'

Jo refused to catch Amelia's eye and they walked into a boutique. Jo was like a child in a sweetshop and gathered up as many clothes as she could carry.

'What about this?' she asked Amelia, when they were in the fitting-rooms. Jo was in some Juicy Couture tracksuit bottoms and a vest top. 'Do I look like I could be a foot-baller's wife?'

Amelia smiled. She was over the moon that Jo could finally dress like the girl she wanted to be. 'You look great,' she said. 'Really good. Honestly, I nearly didn't recognise you when I first saw you.'

Jo looked at herself in the mirror and grinned. She knew she still looked massive compared to her friend, but she was half the girl she used to be. It was a definite improvement.

'You know ...' Amelia began, tentatively, 'maybe now's a good time to start thinking about getting a proper job ...' She paused for a moment, and when Jo didn't react, she continued. 'Did you ever send that piece about courtly love to *Cosmo* like you said you were going to?'

Jo sighed and sat down on the floor amongst the hangers.

'No. And I'm not going to, either. They won't take me on because I have no experience, and they'll probably just nick the feature idea and rewrite it. What's the point?'

Amelia pulled a short dress over her head and sat down on the floor next to Jo. She was just in her underwear and Jo quickly looked at her friend's body – Amelia was tiny compared to her. 'So you're giving up?' Amelia asked gently.

Jo shook her head vehemently and felt determination rush through her. One day she'd have a figure to rival Amelia's – and a career to match. 'No, I'm not giving up. I'm just going to get a magazine job another way.'

Jo was sitting at a table in The Royal Oak, sipping an orange juice. The bar had just shut for the night, and only a few of the staff remained, hurrying about collecting glasses so they could go home. William was behind the bar overseeing every-one, and Jo was aware that he was shooting her confused glances. They'd not spoken for days, and Jo wasn't sure she could bear it for much longer.

71

She looked down at her notebook and reread the article she'd written a month ago titled 'Courtly Love for the Modern Age'. Jo knew it was a crap title, but the article was word perfect – and it explained what to do if an unrequited love was never returned. Jo drew upon all her courage. She was going to act on her own advice and see where it took her.

As the last of the bar staff left the pub, Jo turned to William. 'Can we have a chat?' she asked him nervously. William nodded, and after grabbing a bottle of beer he joined her at the table.

'What are you reading?' he asked her, and Jo explained the basic premise of the article. When she'd finished talking William gave her a sad smile.

'Ironic,' he commented, 'that it's about people having secret feelings for others, because that's how I've felt about you since last winter.'

Jo felt her face turn red and she put her hands to her mouth. 'I had no idea,' she whispered. 'Not until the other night ...'

William rested his head on his hands and assessed her with his icy-blue eyes. Even when he looked miserable, Jo thought, he was still stunning.

'I apologise for that. I misread the signals – I thought you liked me back. Or I hoped you did.' William looked so sad that Jo wanted to wrap her arms around him and comfort him.

'But I do like you!' she exclaimed. 'I'm mad about you!'

William locked Jo's eyes with his. 'So why didn't you want to be with me?' he asked neutrally, and Jo felt her face flush. She looked at her notebook and decided to be honest. She wasn't going to be scared by anything or anyone any more. 'I'm a virgin,' she said quietly. 'And I didn't think you'd like me once I took my clothes off.'

William let out a little laugh. 'Jo,' he said kindly, 'I think

I'd like you with your clothes off most of all.' He reached over to her and held her hands in his. 'I'm crazy about you,' he said, and before Jo knew what was happening he leant over and kissed her.

As William's lips touched hers, Jo's brain raced as she tried to remember the techniques she had read about in magazines. But just as she began to feel nervous William gently opened her mouth with his tongue, and she gave in to the sensation of having him so intimately close to her. Her whole body became hot with desire, and although the kiss was over as quickly as it began, Jo was breathless. It was perfect.

'I promise that we'll take this really slowly. We'll go at whatever pace you're comfortable with.'

William looked so keen and so happy that suddenly Jo felt wretched. She wriggled her hands out of his, and was aware that tears were forming in her eyes.

'Oh, William,' she said, biting her lip and trying not to look at him in case she changed her mind. 'I think we should just be friends.'

William looked confused and then hurt. 'But you said you liked me,' he said, stung.

Jo nodded. 'I did. And I do like you a lot, an awful lot, but I don't think I'm ready to have a relationship.'

William frowned. 'But this isn't just any old relationship – this is you and me. What we have is something special. I …'

Jo looked up and straight into William's eyes. 'What?' she said softly, but he didn't need to finish what he was going to say. Jo knew he loved her.

'Look, Jo …' William ran his hands through his blond hair, and Jo gently placed a finger on his lips to stop him from speaking. His eyes were a pool of deep blue, and Jo felt she could lose herself in them for ever, but she had to be sensible. She took a deep breath and steadied herself.

'I want to be with you – I really do – but until I'm completely happy with myself I don't think it's fair for me to get involved with anyone.'

William shook his head. 'But I'm happy with you,' he said. 'And you look so amazing now compared to how you did before—' he began. Jo interrupted him once again.

'I may be fitter,' she said, taking a deep breath, 'but so far the highlight of my career has been a promotion to barmaid, and I know, deep down, that I'm talented enough to make it on magazines. And now that I'm no longer ... you know ... *large*,' she said, grasping around for any word, 'I've made a decision.'

A tiny crease of anxiety appeared on William's forehead, but Jo was so concerned about getting the words out right that she didn't notice.

'I'm going to move back to London and get a job on a magazine,' she murmured. 'I feel it's my time now. I'll never forget you, and I hope we can be friends but ... if I start a relationship with you I'll only be distracted. And, William, you distract me so much.'

Jo stood up and with as much strength as she could muster she walked out of the bar, away from William, and started packing for her new life.

Chapter Seven

September 2002

Jo was in the recruitment agency waiting for Felicity, who was running ten minutes late. Despite marvelling that her thighs didn't spill over the edges of the chair as they'd done two years before, her foot jangled nervously. Jo didn't normally like confrontation — she was usually too nice and timid to stand up for herself — but today she was fired up. She'd literally just signed the contract on a tiny studio flat near Waterloo, had managed to cart all her stuff from Winchester into it, was dressed more smartly than ever before, and was raring to go. She had a plan, and she was *going* to get a job on a magazine.

Felicity rushed into the room, and after breathlessly offering her apologies she dug out a PowerPoint presentation and launched into an authoritative, robotic spiel about the recruitment agency, its clients and history. Jo tried to listen attentively, but as Felicity droned on she found her mind wandering, and without warning an image of William burst into her head. She allowed herself to linger on the memory of him kissing her, and then, knowing she had to play this meeting perfectly, banished him from her mind. He'd have loved her in this outfit, though, Jo thought sadly as she looked down at herself. She was in sexy spike heels, a pencil skirt that hugged her curvy size-sixteen hips, and a flattering fake-cashmere jumper that accentuated her breasts. She glanced up at Felicity, who was rambling on about her client-list, and smiled. She wasn't surprised that the recruitment consultant didn't recognise her. When she'd dressed that morning she'd barely recognised herself.

'You mentioned you have some magazine publishers as clients ...' Jo leant forward and interrupted Felicity's soliloquy. She was keen to get to the point, and Felicity gave her a cold and impersonal smile. Jo guessed that Felicity was asked this question a lot.

'Absolutely,' Felicity replied. 'Depending on your experience and how long you have been with us, I think I can firmly say that we'd be delighted to send you on assignments like those.'

Jo looked at Felicity in amazement. Was it really that easy for thinner girls? It was time to play her trump card.

'Well, as I've been a secretary for your company for two years, I'd say I'm ready to do one of those assignments now. Wouldn't you?' When Felicity didn't say anything Jo sighed and lowered her voice. 'Felicity, we've met before.'

Felicity let out an embarrassed little laugh. 'Have we? You should have said! I'm sorry, I didn't catch your name ...?'

Jo sat back in her chair and tried not to look smug. 'I'm Joanne Hill and we met the summer before last ...' When Felicity looked none the wiser, Jo felt slight compassion towards the woman. 'Why don't you go and get my file and we can take it from there?'

Minutes later Felicity had returned, smiling uneasily. Jo could tell she was startled.

'Joanne, I didn't recognise you, you look incredible!'

Jo smiled magnanimously but inside she felt sad. Despite losing all that weight she knew she was just an average overweight girl with boring brown hair and a pleasant face. She wasn't 'incredible' at all. Just keep smiling, she thought to herself. Keep smiling and go for the kill.

'Felicity, we both know the reason you didn't send me on a job originally was because of my weight, and that's fine. I've come to terms with it. But I'd like a job now, and I want it to be on a magazine.'

Felicity looked nervous.

'You know, even if you don't send me to a magazine I'm determined enough to get a job on one eventually. And I'm sure they'd be very interested in an exposé of a recruitment agency that has very specific ideas about what secretaries should look like ... you do remember telling me to lose weight, don't you?' Jo kept her voice light and her smile friendly, and all the while she thought of how proud William would be of her. Tiny beads of sweat had appeared underneath Felicity's flawless foundation, and when she attempted to smile Jo noticed she had lipstick on her teeth from chewing her lip. Jo desperately didn't want to feel sorry for her but she couldn't help it.

'We have one job,' Felicity began slowly, 'but it's something we'd normally give to one of our more experienced girls ...' As Felicity caught sight of Jo's deadly stare she hurried to finish her sentence. 'However, due to your ... your change of image, I'd be happy to send you there. Have you ever read *Gloss* magazine?'

Jo didn't know how she was going to contain herself – she was brimming with excitement. Her eyes kept darting around what she could see of the office, drinking in the surroundings, and she could feel delight bubbling up inside her. In her wildest dreams she'd never imagined that the reception area of a magazine office would be so trendy, so stylish. Even the red suede sofa screamed 'designer', and the framed magazine covers behind the Scandinavian-style reception desk added a cool, contemporary edge. The Italian-looking receptionist, however, eyed Jo with barely concealed disdain while shaking out her frosted, glossy hair. She was absolutely beautiful, and Jo tried not to stare at her or her expensive-looking clothes.

'Frieda will see you now,' she said, looking Jo up and down, and letting her eyes linger on a thread dangling from Jo's skirt. Jo tried to not let the girl ruin her excitement at being here, and she wondered if she'd worn the wrong outfit. She'd spent hours the night before working out what to wear, but the receptionist was clad head to toe in black as though she was the girlfriend of a beat poet. Her shiny leather boots set off her tan and showed long, lean legs that were in a tiny black mini-skirt that stopped halfway up her thighs. Despite the last of the summer heat she was wearing a black turtle-neck that clung to her tiny, perky breasts, and when she stood up Jo noticed she had the narrowest hips she had ever seen. Jo envied her and felt dowdy in comparison. Her limp dark skirt, white blouse and navy pumps felt cheap and inappropriate. Jo suddenly regretted spending a hundred pounds on a second-hand sofa for the flat she'd started renting – she could have bought some better clothes instead.

'Go down the hall and turn left.' She eyed Jo up and down again and momentarily ignored a ringing phone. 'That's where the *secretaries* work.'

Jo tried to smile her thanks at the receptionist but she had already taken the call, and as soon as Jo heard her swap her ice tones for honeyed warmth when she said, 'Good morning, *Gloss* magazine,' she felt a shiver run down her back. She still couldn't believe she had a job on a magazine ... and to top it all off it was at *Gloss*, one of her favourites.

'You must be Joanne,' an angular-looking woman said to Jo, snapping her out of her daze with curt tones. She was in her mid-thirties, Jo guessed, and her clothes were cut so well Jo instantly pegged them as Armani. Her hair was carved into a strict dark bob, and the beginnings of laughter lines were sketched on her face. Jo instantly wondered how it was possible that this severe-looking woman ever smiled. 'I'm Frieda. I've been expecting you.'

Jo suddenly felt poor, young and out of her depth, as she quickly glanced around the cramped office and saw five other girls who all looked immaculate and impeccably groomed. Amongst the pot plants and framed magazine covers the typists were all looking at her with brazen interest, and Jo tried not to blush underneath their stares. She turned back to Frieda, who assessed her swiftly.

'I'm going to be your manager for the three months you're here with us. If you have any problems or issues you come straight to me. Now, we need to give you a quick tour of the office.' Frieda looked Jo up and down swiftly and settled on the gape in her blouse that showed a glimpse of her greying bra. 'I'm sure your recruitment consultant would have mentioned it but in case she forgot, we have a dress code here. I'll make sure you get a copy. But in the meantime follow me.'

Frieda walked briskly back through the corridor and past the receptionist who gave her a mocking smile as if Jo was the entertainment. Jo didn't know how to react so she tentatively smiled back and crossed her arms to hide the stretch of fabric straining across her breasts. Jo had thought a size fourteen would fit but clearly not. She must have put on a couple of pounds.

'You've met Rachel, I see,' Frieda said pointedly, as she gave the receptionist a quick nod. 'Rachel deals with all our telephone queries. If you have a telephone call you must immediately put it through to her. It will be a wrong number as all internal calls to the secretary pool come through me first.'

Jo nodded brightly and followed Frieda to a set of double doors.

'It's quite simple to do, really, as your phone can't make any outgoing calls apart from to her, anyway. I'll show you how to do it later but all you need to do is press zero. I'm sure you will be able to remember that?'

Jo smiled blandly – why did everyone patronise secretaries, including other secretaries? – and she looked down at the grey-blue carpet that led to the office. Nothing seemed spectacular any more, and her nerves got the better of her. She wondered if she'd made a mistake. Jo wasn't sure if she was going to be able to bite her tongue in front of this secretarial Nazi, and she didn't see how she'd be able to get headhunted if she was crammed into a small room away from where the action was. Maybe this wasn't the way into the industry that she had hoped it would be.

'This,' said Frieda, interrupting Jo's train of thought, 'is the editorial office of *Gloss* magazine. You're not to speak to anybody in this room, or disturb them.' Frieda often showed new girls this room to make sure they knew their place, and she pushed the doors open with a flourish. Jo drank in the view.

In the large open-plan office sat about twenty slender and beautiful girls who were dressed – like Rachel – in black. The sun streamed through the large windows and bathed them in a glorious gold as though they were blessed. Some of the girls walked industriously around the office, but many were on the telephone, speaking in languid voices and laughing falsely. Several of the girls were peering intently at photographs of models, and one was opening a package of what looked like designer clothes. 'Oh, look!' she heard her say in a breathy, little-girl voice. 'It's a new couture Dior gown – how wonderful of Nicholas to send it. It's darling!'

'To the right is the executive suite,' Frieda said hastily, ignoring the rush of the editorial staff to look at the shimmering turquoise dress and cutting into Jo's reverie. Jo tore her eyes from the glittering sequinned gown and looked towards the executive suite with interest. There was no time for elegant dresses when Jo had to concentrate on filtering into the editorial team. She stood on her tiptoes and caught a glance of an attractive man in a beautiful charcoal suit through a glass-walled office.

'Madeline Turner, who won Editor of the Year last year, sits in the office to the right, and in the end office, the biggest one, is Joshua Garnet.' Frieda looked at Jo knowingly. 'He's taking a keen interest in this magazine at the moment.'

'Do you mean,' Jo began, before Frieda raised her eyebrows at her to lower her voice. She started again. 'Do you mean that Joshua Garnet himself works in this office?'

Frieda led Jo out of the office and shut the door firmly behind them. 'Yes, and you're not to approach him.'

'But I thought all the Garnets – apart from Harold – were silent directors and preferred to take a back seat on their investment,' Jo thought out loud, and Frieda looked at her sharply.

'You seem to know a lot for a twenty-year-old secretary,' Frieda remarked with one eyebrow raised, and Jo remembered that she was here to work as a secretary, and not a wannabe journalist.

She thought quickly. 'Felicity, at the agency, provided me with some background reading. I have a good memory.'

This placated Frieda somewhat. 'Yes, it is unusual for a Garnet to take an interest, but he appears to have a knack for these high-end magazines. He acts as publisher for *Gloss* and several of the other titles but he's paying particular interest to this magazine at the moment. Josh Garnet has a golden touch. Circulation has improved with his input.' Frieda looked at Jo and decided to take pity on her. She looked so young and suburban. 'Circulation is what we call the number of magazines that are sold.'

Jo nodded distractedly – she was still astounded at the news that Joshua Garnet actually worked on the magazine.

All the press coverage she had read about Joshua Garnet when she was at school had said he was a millionaire playboy who spent his evenings in exclusive private members' clubs with blonde models for arm candy. Perhaps, she thought, he had changed his mind about not working and had taken an interest in the family company. The idea that she might actually meet one of the Garnets – and Joshua in particular – gave Jo an exhilarated feeling in her stomach. He was magazine royalty, the JFK of publishing. Frieda spotted the adoration on Jo's face and led her swiftly back to their small office.

'And here, as you have seen, is our office. You'll be assigned copy to type because some of our journalists prefer to handwrite their pieces. You're not to make any amendments apart from spelling and punctuation, and to copy what you are given word for word from the handwritten notes. Do you understand?'

Frieda looked at Jo with a stern expression and Jo smiled back. She was about to start working on a magazine – practically with Joshua Garnet! – and she would do anything she was told.

October 2002

Every morning Jo would stand outside Garnet Tower smiling to herself. Set in the heart of Covent Garden, the shiny dark red skyscraper dominated the skyline, and all the theatres and boutiques of the West End cowered underneath it. Jo would watch the extremely thin and glamorous magazine writers, editors and designers rush into the foyer with an obvious sense of purpose. Then Jo would do the same, flashing her staff pass at the docile security man and squeezing herself into the mirrored lift, taking care not to look at her reflection because the sight of her size-sixteen bottom in comparison to the size-eight girls hurt. *Gloss* was on floor nineteen, directly under *DG* magazine – standing for *Discerning Gentlemen* – and above *Honey*, the most popular teen magazine not just in the UK, but in Europe too. Jo would breathe in the smell of power, domination and money. Garnet Publishing was the largest and most successful magazine company in the UK, and Jo was thrilled to be part of it.

The work, however, bored her to tears. And there was so much of it.

For her first few weeks Jo kept her head down and concentrated on her typing. Her computer was temperamental and it kept on crashing. When Jo paused to try to reboot it, or to read through an article before typing it up, she would catch Frieda frowning at her, and she'd quickly start moving her fingers again, trying to look busy. She was used to hard work, but Frieda expected such exactness that she felt under pressure.

'It has to be perfect, Joanne. Do it again, please. And faster this time too. We do have a deadline to reach.' Frieda said to Jo at least once a day while the other girls smirked, and she found she was working harder than she'd ever done, especially as she wasn't invited to join in the gossip and tea breaks with the other girls. Jo didn't care. Friends were a luxury, but her career was not, and because she'd chosen it over William she was determined to make it. She was going to become a features writer.

The first part of her plan to become a journalist was to look the part. One Saturday, Jo went to Top Shop and out went the smart skirts and blouses and in came Helmut Lang military-style touches, Anna Sui-inspired embroidered skirts, extra-long scarves, slouchy boho bags and longer skirts – anything that was a cheap version of what had been on the catwalk. Jo ignored the fact that most of the clothes she bought were size eighteen because size sixteen was suddenly too tight, and she didn't care that she looked faintly ridiculous because she had a bottom, large tits and ample thighs. She wanted to ooze self-confidence and dressing like a mousy secretary wasn't the way forward. Strictly speaking Jo kept within the Garnet dress code for administrative staff, but she could tell Frieda disapproved of her new outfits. When dressing like she was a journalist didn't cut it with any of the editorial staff she spotted in the foyer, or with Rachel, who still looked straight through her, Jo turned to more drastic measures.

For years Jo's dull medium-brown hair had hung limp from a centre parting. Jo had always trimmed it herself with nail scissors, and it sat just on top of her shoulders, hanging slightly in front of her face to hide how round it was. Her hair had been something she had neglected while she concentrated on getting her weight down, but now she realised that she looked like a hippie from the 1960s and not the hip magazine girl she wanted to become. She suddenly hated her hair as much as the extra weight she had been putting on, and she wanted to get rid of it. She wanted to be fearless.

Despite being broke Jo took herself to a trendy Soho salon that had been namechecked in *Gloss*, and told a junior stylist to give her a cut like Catherine Zeta-Jones had in *Chicago*. When he looked doubtful Jo said that she worked at *Gloss*, and with those magic words he got out the scissors, sat her down, and cut into her hair so the strands fell gently to the floor. In Jo's mind it represented shedding her skin and becoming a butterfly. She wanted to transform herself even if she was having problems losing weight again. She settled back and reread the latest issue of *Gloss*, and felt pride that she was part of the magazine, even in a small way.

When the hairdresser finished Jo looked in the mirror and wanted to cry. She had the newest, sharpest cut, but it looked terrible on her, despite the hairdresser fussing with hairspray and a comb. She had the appearance of a fat Harry Potter from the *Chamber of Secrets* film, and when she got home she found that no amount of lipstick, false eyelashes or blusher made a difference. She quietly made her way into the office next day and studiously avoided everyone's eyes.

'It won't work, you know.'

Jo spun round in her chair and looked at the girl sitting in the corner of the office. Of all the girls in the typing pool, Debbie was the one who made the most jokes about Jo's weight, the one who Jo sometimes caught looking at her with annoyance. She had long, stringy, blonde hair and an engagement ring that she constantly waved in people's faces, although she never mentioned her fiancé or if they'd actually set a date for the wedding. She was second in command to Frieda and she loved the power.

'I don't know what you're talking about.'

Debbie stopped typing and fixed her gaze on Jo. 'Let me guess. You want to be a journalist when you grow up and you think that if you start dressing like them you'll be noticed.' The older girl watched Jo's skin pale underneath her foundation and continued, satisfied, 'It won't work. It won't get you a job on the magazine. It never does.'

Jo bristled. 'What makes you think that's what I'm trying to do? I just fancied a change of image. It's nothing to do with you.'

Debbie waved her hands dismissively. 'Seen it all before, sweetheart. You're just one of a number who have come here with stars in their eyes about being asked to write for the magazine, but you haven't got a chance. They only employ talent, or people who have been here for years and aren't opportunists.' Debbie looked Jo up and down. 'You're on the bottom rung of the typing pool. You're invisible. And you know what, I'm next in line to be asked to join their team. You haven't got a hope in hell.'

Don't react, Jo thought, just don't react. She could feel

her body tensing and she forced a smile. 'It's a good thing you're wrong, then, isn't it?' she said lightly, and she pointedly ignored the stares from the other girls in the office as she engrossed herself in typing up an article about relationships that she knew she could write a hundred times better. Jo lost herself in her work but she heard Debbie sniggering to Katherine. She was going to have a lot of fun proving Debbie and everyone else wrong. She was going to do it.

When changing her image didn't work Jo flung herself into the second stage of her plan. It was all about making herself seen, known, and obviously available. Jo got to work at 8 a.m., a whole hour before the other typists arrived. She'd linger in the canteen over her coffee as she watched the editorial staff limp in with hangovers, and she'd sit near them, listening to their conversations and hearing where they had been the night before. Most of the time the journalists went to events that were invitation only: club openings, book launches and fashion shows. They mingled with famous actors, danced with popstars, and were on first-name terms with all the doormen at the hottest clubs. One cold autumn morning, a girl called Araminta was moaning to the others about a bar that refused to give her entry to the VIP section.

'It was just, like, so unfair,' she whined in her upper-middle-class accent. 'I told the guy at the rope that not only did I write for *Gloss*, but that Kate Moss knows me personally but he wasn't having any of it.'

'So what did you do?' breathed the flame-haired girl who was clearly fascinated that a doorman wouldn't allow one of them past a rope. 'Did you bribe him?'

Araminta shook her long blonde hair in disgust. 'No I did not. But I am boycotting that place, as are all of you. I told him that we are not going back and we're going to spend every evening at Chantez instead. We're never going to write about Bababund again!'

'That will show him, Minty. Oh, well done,' enthused Hannah, *Gloss*'s travel editor. 'As soon as we stop writing about it, Bababund will be dead!'

Jo gulped – Bababund was the hippest, most exclusive bar in Europe at the moment, hotter than the Met Bar or Soho House had ever been. Did the *Gloss* girls really have that much power? When Jo queued up at Chantez the next night with the hope that she'd accidentally on purpose bump into them, it became clear that they did. Jo watched them with envy as they strutted through the queues of gorgeous babes, straight past the velvet rope into the club. She could hear murmurs of jealousy rippling through the queue behind her, but Jo had to begrudgingly admit that the *Gloss* girls knew how to work their status as London's journalistic elite, even if they couldn't write very well. She wondered if she'd ever be part of their gang, if she'd ever be able to swan past the hordes of nobodies because she was that important. Jo looked down at her Miss Selfridge outfit – the skimpiest, sexiest dress she owned – and saw the bulges of flesh through the tight Lycra. She knew that if she didn't look the part she wouldn't have a chance.

Suddenly whispers vibrated through the back of the crowd, and some girls stood on tiptoes to see who was getting out of the long, sleek, black limousine that had smoothly pulled up in front of her. Jo looked on with interest as she spotted a woman get out of the car, and she was trying to pinpoint exactly how she recognised her when there were yells from the ubiquitous photographers whose cameras began to flash. 'Madeline, Madeline, over here!'

Jo gasped. It was Madeline Turner, the editor of *Gloss*. Jo hadn't seen her in person before, and only knew what she looked like from her photograph in the magazine. In the flesh she was gorgeous, with almond-shaped eyes and thick, glossy black hair. She looked like a skinnier version of Bianca Jagger in the 1960s, with flawless skin and impeccable make-up. She was wearing what appeared to be a deep purple couture Miu Miu dress, and the diamonds round her neck picked out the steely glint in her eyes. Madeline gave the photographers a tight little grimace and waited as the chauffeur went to the other side of the car to open the second passenger door.

Joshua Garnet climbed out of his seat and the cameras flashed frantically. In the flesh, Joshua Garnet was absolutely gorgeous, and Jo felt her face flush red as she saw him. He had short, dark brown hair, chocolate-coloured eyes, and his face was tanned from a recent holiday. He wasn't as good-looking as William, Jo thought, but she could see the appeal, could see why Joshua was paparazzi fodder. Unlike Madeline, Joshua had kept his outfit simple; a beautifully cut black suit highlighted his strong shoulders and arms, and his crisp white shirt was open at the neck, allowing a tantalising glimpse of chest hair.

Madeline took Joshua Garnet by his arm, and they stood having their photograph taken as he assessed the crowd coolly. Jo had read in an old copy of *Press Gazette* that the pair had married the year before – which had caused quite a stir – but she didn't think they looked happy or comfortable together. She kept her eyes on Madeline, who, in turn, watched Joshua Garnet irritably as his eyes swept the crowd. He bypassed Jo without even noticing her and then drank in the erect nipples of the freezing, semi-clothed teenagers that were in the queue behind her, flashing them a sexy, easy grin. Madeline locked eyes with Jo for a moment, and then the couple walked into the bar.

'Debbie, have you heard?' A few weeks later Katherine rushed into the small typing office, brimming with excitement and spilling her cup of tea. Debbie stopped typing and looked at her in amusement, but Jo kept on moving her fingers, wondering what the cause of Katherine's flushed face and wide eyes was. A boy, probably – nothing to do with work, and definitely nothing to do with her.

'Joshua Garnet is going to have a new personal assistant because he sacked the last one for being lazy! And they're going to choose someone internally!'

Jo looked up at Katherine with a jolt, and the typing pool went silent as everyone stopped typing and gasped. Debbie's face began to go red.

'Are you joking?' Debbie looked as though she were beside herself. Jo watched her carefully. It was as if she had just been told she'd won the greatest prize on earth, but Jo knew Debbie didn't give a damn about the work and was only excited because she fancied the pants off Garnet.

Katherine shook her head quickly. 'Justine in sales heard it from Edwina in design who heard it from Lizzie in editorial. Garnet needs someone as soon as possible and, rather than advertising, they want to pick a current secretary here. It's an internal promotion!'

Debbie leant forward in her chair and looked excited.

'Technically speaking I have been here the longest,' she said, looking at her freshly painted nails. 'And Joshua *certainly* knows who I am. Do you know if we need to apply, tell them if we're interested?'

Jo looked at Katherine and held her breath.

'I think the assumption is that whoever is asked will want to do it. I mean, he's so divine who wouldn't want to be Joshua Garnet's PA?'

Jo looked down at her half-typed-up article and felt an ache in the pit of her stomach. She knew that if she was Garnet's PA it would mean that she could sit at the desk in front of his office and be part of the editorial team. If she were Garnet's PA, she thought, she would not only have one of the most coveted positions in the company, but a chance to sit in on editorial meetings, the chance to see her name on the *Gloss* masthead. Jo wanted to be Joshua Garnet's PA more than anything, and unlike everyone else, she thought, she didn't give a damn about what he looked like.

Debbie gave Katherine a lazy, slow smile. 'You're right. There's going to be stiff competition for this job, absolutely everyone is going to want it. Do you know when they're making the selection?'

Katherine was practically jumping up and down. 'Today! I think they're going around the office today! Well, that's what Justine said, anyway.'

Debbie suddenly didn't look so sure of herself. She sat bolt upright. 'Today? Are you sure? But I haven't got any make-up on, I'm not wearing my new mini-skirt, and oh!' Debbie looked down at her Elizabeth Duke engagement ring and tore it off with difficulty. 'I can't have Joshie Garnet thinking I wouldn't give him one hundred per cent. Quick, toilets! This is an emergency.' She shot Frieda a quick look. 'Sorry, Frieda. Needs must,' she said, as the others practically ran out of the office to look at themselves in the decent mirrors in the ladies'.

Jo sighed, and started typing up the rest of the article. She hadn't a chance. Even if she was tall, skinny and had Scandinavian cheekbones it wouldn't have made a difference – Debbie would clearly get the job, as she had been here the longest. She had paid her dues, Jo thought with a sniff, and she didn't look too bad when she put lots of make-up on to cover up her spots. But still, wouldn't it be nice if Joshua Garnet walked up to her desk to ask her if she would like to be his PA? He'd stand in front of her and she'd look up at him, taking in his dark hair, broad shoulders and easy charm. He'd tell her how wonderful he thought she was, and mention how he had always admired her from a distance. Why, he would say, he had always known she was talented and this was her chance to shine. He would offer a hand and Jo would get up from her desk and glide to his office with him where he would tell her that he didn't actually need a PA, but a new editor of *Gloss* because Madeline had been struck down with a mystery illness—

'Joanne!' Jo heard Frieda's curt voice through her daydream and she stopped typing to look up at her. Standing in the corner of the office was Madeline Turner, watching her with a strange expression. Frieda turned back to Madeline when she was satisfied Jo was paying attention. 'Sorry about that, Ms Turner, but Joanne does like to get engrossed in her work.'

Jo blushed. She couldn't believe Madeline Turner was in the same room as her. She wondered if she remembered her from the night at Chantez.

'Oh, I see,' she said, her voice sounding polished and cool. 'I'll cut to the chase. Rather than being a typist we'd like Joanne to be Mr Garnet's new personal assistant. The role would involve assisting Mr Garnet on his personal business as well as providing some support to the journalists. We think Joanne would do a good job and would like her to join the team. That is, if she would like to.'

Jo's mouth dropped open. Her daydream had spilt into real life.

'Joanne, would you like the job?' Madeline Turner was almost smiling at her, and rumour had it that Madeline was normally so miserable that she never smiled.

Jo turned to Frieda, whose expression remained blank, and then back to Madeline. 'I'd love it,' she said, praying she would stop blushing. 'I'd absolutely love it.' Was this really happening to her?

Madeline grimaced. 'Then it's all settled. Let's go.'

Jo picked up her handbag and followed Madeline out into the hallway in shock. She couldn't believe it. Not only was she about to meet Joshua Garnet, but she was going to be his right-hand girl. This was the break she'd been waiting for – she'd have to get in touch with William to let him know that her career was on track after all.

Chapter Eight

December 2002

'You mean after all this time you still don't know why you were picked? Oh, that's so sweet.' Debbie was sitting on Jo's desk, casually swinging her long, slender legs, and Jo wondered how she could get rid of her without causing a scene. It was still early – not yet half past eight – but Jo knew Joshua Garnet had a meeting at nine with Madeline Turner and she was worried that he would come in at any minute. She didn't want him to think she was the type that liked to gossip with the other secretaries.

'OK, let me put it another way,' Debbie said, picking up a card Amelia had sent her and reading it idly. 'Why do you think Madeline Turner, a magazine editor who happens to be Joshua's wife, came and picked you herself rather than human resources?'

Jo didn't know whether knocking her off her desk or ignoring her outright would be the better option. 'Look, can you please just go?' she said, trying not to sound annoyed. Both girls could hear the soft murmurs of the editorial staff filtering into the office, and Jo knew that if Frieda found out that Debbie was in the editorial office – let alone the executive suite – there would be hell to pay. Debbie shot her a dirty look but she knew Jo was right.

'It will keep. But have a think about it, won't you?' she said, glancing back at Jo. 'I'll give you a clue. You certainly weren't promoted because of your typing skills.'

Jo watched Debbie swinging her hips in her tight pencil skirt as she strode out of the office, and she put her and her bitchy comments out of her mind. She was just jealous of her promotion, Jo thought with a smile. And who could blame her? Jo had finally arrived – not many girls who wanted to work on magazines began their careers as Joshua Garnet's right-hand girl. And not many of them had his complete trust, either.

Jo had been working for Joshua Garnet – *Mr* Garnet in front of visitors or Joshua when they were alone – for almost two months and despite being exhausted she had loved every minute of it. From the moment she woke, Jo was dedicated to making Joshua's day easier. Her first task was to pick up Joshua's bespoke Savile Row suits from the dry-cleaner's. The Greek owner of the shop marked Jo out as a special customer due to the number of items Joshua sent to them, and he sometimes cleaned some of her blouses free of charge – a kind gesture considering Jo never had time to go to the launderette during the week. From there she would hastily eat a breakfast of two croissants from the canteen, and then, when the private-entry security guard buzzed her to say Joshua had entered Garnet Tower, she would brew him his first cup of coffee with a blend imported especially from America. Sometimes Joshua stopped at her desk to thank her, but most of the time he swept past her in a business-like rush. Jo didn't mind; she respected the lack of small talk, and besides, he was so powerful he didn't need to make pleasantries with anyone.

'Hold all my calls, will you? I have to go through this dummy front cover with Madeline,' Joshua said that morning as he casually walked past Jo's desk, brutally ignoring the piles of circulation reports she'd been reading in a bid to impress him. Madeline Turner was behind him wearing a Gucci shirt and the most amazing snakeskin stilettos Jo had ever seen – and she was deeply envious. Madeline had told her that as a secretary she wasn't allowed to dress provocatively in any way, and Jo had duly obeyed. She was in a crumpled grey striped blouse and a faded black skirt, and she knew she looked like a poor relation compared to all the stunning girls on the magazine.

Jo carefully switched Joshua's phone to voicemail, and contented herself by surreptitiously watching Joshua and Madeline through the glass-fronted office. They were engrossed in conversation, and when Madeline began to gesture, angrily, Jo looked on in fascination, and wondered if they were having a work disagreement or a marital spat. Joshua caught her eye, and then gestured for Jo to come into his office.

'Joanne, you're a *Gloss* reader, aren't you?' Joshua was sitting in his leather Eames chair behind his walnut desk, and he casually put his hands behind his head. He looked ridiculously relaxed in comparison to Madeline, who seemed tense as she sat upright on a chair next to the dummy front pages.

Jo nodded warily.

'See, Madeline? I told you she was. She's young, aspirational and desperate to be told what to wear and what to think,' Joshua remarked with an eyebrow raised at his wife. Jo tried to keep her expression neutral, even though he was mocking her. He was right about the target audience, but wrong that it included her. She wasn't a bimbo, she thought with determination, and she was going to make him see that.

Madeline didn't look happy. 'I'm sure Joanne's a lovely girl but she's not as sassy as our readers, Josh, and you know it.' Madeline turned back to Joshua behind his desk. 'Our readers aren't blank canvasses that will just buy what they're told. They want to be more like an Oxford-educated beauty than a Playboy bunny. They want to be appreciated for their brains as well as their looks. Which is why,' she said, in her perfect cut-glass accent while jabbing at one of the enlarged front covers with a perfectly manicured fingernail, 'this image is completely wrong. The model needs to wear a jacket. To represent her power.'

Joshua smirked. 'And cover up her tits, no doubt. Joanne, which do you prefer?'

Jo looked down at the two mock-ups of the *Gloss* front cover. The model on the front was a corkscrew blonde who looked like a provocative Carrie Bradshaw. A baker-boy hat with navy trim sat jauntily on her head, and her lips were made up with a pale 1960s-style lipstick. Her dress was a peacock blue – the exact same shade as the large letters that spelt the word 'Gloss' at the top of the page. The only difference between the two photographs was that in the second one the model wasn't wearing a short white jacket. Instead her shoulders were bare, and if you looked closely enough you could see the model's dark pink nipples brushing against the blue of the delicate fabric. It was a sharp, sexy, disturbing look. And it was perfect for *Gloss*.

Jo bit her lip and forced herself to concentrate on Joshua rather than on Madeline, who was looking at her Patek Philippe impatiently. 'I like the one without the jacket,' she said, finally, wanting to be honest, and, more importantly, not wishing to piss off Joshua. Madeline sighed, and Jo hoped she wouldn't get into trouble for taking sides.

'Oh, what does she know anyway,' Madeline said to Joshua, who grinned.

'She's the target audience, Madeline, and as you know, we always give them what they want.' He gave Madeline an infuriating smile and then turned to smile at Jo, who basked in his gaze. He agreed with her!

Jo was excused, and for the rest of the day she sat at her desk in a warm glow. Joshua had taken her advice for the front cover instead of Madeline's, and it felt great. She briefly thought about phoning William to tell him, but the idea of speaking to him and actually hearing his voice started to upset her, so she consoled herself by writing a short email to Amelia, who was now in her third year at university. Amelia's reaction was exactly what she'd hoped it would be – happy, impressed and proud of her – but Jo longed for a hug from William. To get him out of her mind she thought about Joshua and Madeline's relationship, and wondered why they appeared to be at war.

A few days later – when Jo overheard the editorial team gossiping in the canteen – the reason for the rift became clear.

'Did you see Mad Madeline's face yesterday when Joshua said we had to pay more attention to features about beauty products?' Araminta said, taking a bite of a sandwich and grinning. 'She looked like she had eaten a lemon!'

'But why did he say that? I don't understand.' Lizzie, one of the fashion editors looked confused. 'We already have fourteen pages of beauty, why do we need more? I thought Madeline wanted us to write more about "fashion culture" or whatever she's calling it, not writing copy about lipstick.'

Araminta looked smug. 'It's all about advertising. If we write favourable reviews of products then the companies will place more adverts. It's all about keeping them sweet.'

A girl called Lucy laughed. 'You have to wonder what Joshua knows about keeping people sweet, because his wife doesn't seem very happy at the moment!'

Araminta grinned, and flicked her long, shiny hair behind her shoulders. 'You have to admit he's a good publisher, though. We must be making money considering the latest Christmas pay rises!'

Jo felt herself blush red. She had issued the payslips on Joshua's behalf a few days earlier, and when she heard the squeals of pleasure she quickly rushed to open her own. Unlike the girls on editorial, Jo hadn't been given an extra penny, and she'd been annoyed – she didn't even get paid for all the overtime she did and her wage barely covered her Central London rent. Jo had spent the rest of the day in a bad mood, and despite telling herself to be grateful that she had a job, that she could, in theory, be out of work or still working in The Royal Oak, it didn't do any good. She was exhausted.

As Jo left the office that evening at nine – her usual time – she wondered how much longer she could face doing demanding twelve-hour days. Jo knew that Joshua's workload was imposing; yet she seemed to do much more than the usual grunt work. Along with typing and filing, Jo organised Joshua's diary with military precision. She arranged meetings, kept the distributed minutes, and ensured that Joshua's housekeeper knew when he would require a home-cooked meal. Jo made sure he was informed of current affairs, arranged tickets to premieres and club openings, and kept a diary of staff birthdays. Jo was so methodical that Joshua's life ran smoothly, but keeping track of her boss's life took up so much of her time that her own personal life dwindled to nothing. There was no time to work out, shop for healthy food or look after herself properly.

Jo knew her personal life was turning into a mess, but part of her didn't care. She loved being so close to the action. The only problem was that the harder she worked, the less time she had to think about how she could start writing for the magazine, and she seemed to be treading water, not moving forward. She wanted to be coming up with ideas and running the magazine with Joshua, and she didn't want to keep on being the quiet chubby girl who made coffee for meetings. She was better than that.

At the weekends Jo slept, daydreamed about being William's girlfriend, and forced herself to prepare ideas for the magazine. As she looked through the notebooks of ideas for articles and features that she had written while she was at school she realised how woefully naïve she had been. Had she really thought that aged sixteen she was ready to take on the industry and bombard the world of journalism? Jo laughed to herself. Her ideas, while creatively brilliant, lacked commercial knowledge, and the sixteen-year-old Jo hadn't realised she needed to work out how to make features about capsule wardrobes make money. Still, she was learning. Journalism college could never have given her the experience of sitting in on a shareholders' meeting while taking minutes, or joining the weekly editorial meetings where she wrote down everyone's ideas.

'We should do a whole feature on how to get boyfriends to dress like the men in *Sex and the City*. You know, like Mr Big in his expensive suits?' Lizzie said in the next editorial meeting excitedly. 'I've seen a hot new model called Rupert who would look great in Ozwald Boateng.'

Jo laughed quietly to herself. It was a shit idea, and Madeline agreed.

'Lizzie, this is a women's magazine. What about your ideas for female fashion?'

Lizzie consulted her notes hurriedly. Jo watched Hannah and Araminta exchange a bitchy look.

'I thought we could go to some obscure European festival, call the piece "Slovakia/Estonia/Romania Rocks", and really go for the heavy bangle look that is just so gipsy hot right now. The models could stand in front of the stages, and they can look all wild and romantic, with their curls blustering in the wind. We could even get one of those Romany caravan things, too. And get some little indie bands to be in the photographs.'

Madeline looked excited. 'Lizzie, that's a fabulous idea. I love it, it will inform our readers about places they've never heard of with bands that they may have done.'

'And it can be done on the cheap, too, as it hardly costs the earth to get to these funny little countries,' Joshua added. 'Well done.'

Lizzie blushed with pleasure, and Jo made a note that Joshua Garnet liked ideas that didn't cost much. It may have seemed obvious considering he was the publisher, but so many of the journalists didn't seem to worry about how much they were costing the magazine. They just cared about getting their freebies from the designers and goody bags at launch parties. Jo watched Joshua carefully as they offered ideas about reviewing the hip new hotels that were popping up in New York, and plans to go to the Bahamas to shoot the summer fashion spreads. Jo noticed that Joshua didn't say 'no' to any of the concepts, but his eyes didn't sparkle either. Jo could tell that Joshua Garnet no longer wanted *Gloss* to be the best women's magazine in the UK. He wanted it to be the best magazine, full stop. And she was going to come up with some ideas to help him do just that.

June 2003

Six months later Jo fell flat on her face. She'd spent every evening for weeks – and all of her weekends – working on a portfolio of feature-idea mock-ups. Jo got home at ten at night, ate some fish and chips in front of her old TV – that still couldn't pick up Channel Five but was good enough to pick up *The Osbournes* – and then worked on her ideas until two or three in the morning, when her eyes began to blur. Gradually, after filling pages and pages of notebooks, Jo began to form what she believed were fantastic feature ideas – all of which were breathtakingly simple and, most importantly, hadn't been taken from old copies of other magazines. Jo had watched the editorial team for several months and couldn't believe that Madeline Turner hadn't realised that most of the pieces in *Gloss* were regurgitated articles taken from their competitors. As Jo sucked on a pencil thoughtfully, she wondered if Joshua would give her a job above or below Araminta. If it was above, she'd make it a priority to tell her that she knew most of the pieces she had written were near-replicas of what she had seen in some editions of American *Vogue* from 1998. And to make matters worse, they weren't nearly as good as the originals.

In the daytime, when not following Joshua around or making him coffee, Jo paid attention to how the designers worked. She eavesdropped on conversations about different font sizes and photographs, and sat in on a meeting where Madeline explained, in painstaking detail, exactly what she expected of the French art director, who in return stared sullenly at her and ignored everything she said. As she looked over her copy of the minutes from the meeting, Jo began visualising how her feature ideas would look on double-page spreads in *Gloss*. She set about ripping up old issues of the magazine to put together collages of what she thought Joshua and Madeline's concept of *Gloss* was, and when the pages still looked dull she came up with her own version. Joanne Hill's interpretation of *Gloss* was a sparkly mix of fashion, feminism and sophisticated sexual innuendo, wrapped up in a bow of delicious models that looked like they knew about politics as well as pouting. The fashion was erotic and arty, and the articles didn't patronise – they just informed, inspired and more importantly made the reader think she was the cleverest girl in the country for 'getting' the jokes. Jo thought her mocked-up pages were a winner. And now all she had to do was convince Joshua to think the same.

*

'What's this?' Joshua said in a bored tone when Jo nervously went into his office for a meeting. Jo had been Joshua's PA for eight months and she had waited for her appraisal meeting before striking out and showing Joshua that she was not only better than the journalists on the magazine, but on a par with Madeline Turner. She shifted uncomfortably in her deep-red suit from New Look and some spiked heels that she had stolen from the fashion cupboard when everyone had gone home, and she tried not to feel intimidated. She had deliberately chosen to have her meeting on her twenty-first birthday so it would bring her good luck. And judging by Joshua's expression, she was going to need it.

'It's my vision for *Gloss*,' Jo said confidently, passing over the portfolio of all her hard work and thinking that a hundred girls would kill for a one-to-one with the Garnet Publishing proprietor. 'I've five double-page spreads that capture the spirit of *Gloss* as it is, and everything that it should be. And put together, all of these ideas cost less than one current *Gloss* fashion shoot.'

Even though she sounded smooth, Jo's palms began to sweat, and she surreptitiously wiped them on the chair. Joshua picked up her portfolio with interest and flicked through it with a cruel grin.

'Joanne, this is very sweet, but you haven't got the first idea about magazines.'

Jo tried not to let dismay wash across her face. She had been fantasising about this moment for weeks and this wasn't part of the script.

'But I have,' she said, breaking into a smile to show how her lips were cleverly painted the exact same shade as the suit. Joshua need not know it was only Rimmel, and not Chanel. 'I've been listening to you and Madeline in meetings and I think I know exactly what you want. If you just look at the ideas, and the figures attached ...'

Joshua closed the portfolio and looked at Jo with a strange, fond expression.

'I'm sure they're great, Joanne, really, but I think it is best that we leave these types of things to the professionals, don't you agree? Are you after a pay rise? Well, I must say I respect your approach.'

Jo tried not to feel defeated and Joshua watched her with amusement.

'Because you have clearly worked hard at impressing me I'd like to give you a two per cent increase. Why not, you deserve it. And why not have a full hour lunch-break? It can be a special treat just for today.'

Joshua stood up and Jo felt she had no choice but to do the same.

'I'm very happy with your work here, as is everyone else. You don't need to be doing these types of things to further yourself along the career ladder.' Joshua handed Jo back her portfolio and Jo took it, reluctantly. 'You already have the best secretarial job in the company. What more could you want?'

Jo walked aimlessly through Soho and told herself not to give a damn that Garnet had ignored her ideas. Apart from being the biggest magazine publisher in the UK, what did he know anyway? she thought. All he had to do to become the boss was be born into the Garnet family. And rumour had it his father, Harold Garnet – who had taken a back seat to enjoy his yacht – disapproved of how he was handling things. Yes, circulation at *Gloss* was up, but some of the other magazines – the less high-profile ones that were not as glamorous as *Gloss*, yet pulled in four times the advertising – were slowly failing, and there had been talk of redundancies. Jo kicked at an empty can of Coke a tourist had just dropped and yearned to take her heels off. She hadn't mastered walking in them properly, and her feet were killing her. Still, she thought, it took her mind off Joshua Garnet and his stupid closed mind. She was willing to bet that Harold Garnet would have looked at her portfolio. If he was the man she had him pegged as, she knew that Garnet senior would be on the lookout for anything that could save money and pull in more advertising and sponsorship – not like his son, who could only think about how to scrimp on articles while eyeing up the models on the fashion shoots.

'Jo! Joanne!'

Jo heard a familiar voice calling her through her haze and she spun round. She had just spotted a tall, broad man standing in front of her before she was embraced in a big bear-hug.

'I thought it was you,' the man said, speaking into her hair as he held her close to his chest. 'But I wasn't sure – not until I got closer! I didn't think my luck would stretch so far as to bump into you!'

Jo breathed in the familiar scent of musky aftershave and immediately relaxed, enjoying the sensation of William's strong arms enveloping her until she realised that he could feel the rolls of fat on her back underneath her cheap red suit. Jo wriggled out of his embrace, and she shyly looked up at him, taking in how William's dark blond hair had grown longer, how tanned he was from the summer sunshine and how his fitted grey T-shirt didn't quite hide the muscles of his torso. A mixture of emotions swept through her, ranging from pure, utter happiness to insecurity that William should see her looking miserable and dishevelled. She desperately wished she had bothered to refresh her make-up after her disastrous meeting with Garnet, or that she had used some spray to keep her hair in place in the summer breeze. Despite being slightly longer her hair was at the awkward growing-out stage, and it danced across her face at unwieldy angles.

'Look at your hair!' William exclaimed, reaching out a hand to affectionately push the hair from Jo's face. Jo was torn between basking in his affection and not wanting him to touch her because it brought back memories of how close they'd been in Hampshire, and how lonely she was in London. Jo didn't think she could bear remembering what they had been like at the pub the year before, but William didn't seem to notice. 'I barely recognised you,' he said while looking her up and down, and Jo felt her heart sink. She knew it was her extra weight – and not her shorter hair – which wouldn't have made her easily recognisable. As much as she loved seeing William, she didn't like seeing him like this. She imagined she looked like a tomato in her red suit.

'What are you doing in London?' she managed to croak.

William gave her a slow, sexy, disturbing grin. 'I was forced into coming,' he said, and Jo remembered how much he hated the city. 'But if this book is going to end up on the shelves of Waterstone's I have to do what's best for it, and that means meeting with a publisher who happens to have an office in horrible Covent Garden,' he said. 'They're interested in my book.'

Despite her reservations about seeing him again, Jo couldn't stop herself smiling. 'But that's amazing!' she exclaimed, giving William a friendly, awkward punch on the arm. 'You should be so pleased! I'm so proud of you.'

'It's a good start,' he said, modestly. 'But let's not talk about it. It'll jinx it. Look, I have an hour before I need to catch my train, so why don't we go for a drink? Or are you due back at work?'

Jo shook her head and decided she wanted to spend more time with William regardless of how she looked. It was so comforting to see a friendly face, and she wasn't sure she could let him walk away. Not yet. 'I'm allowed extra time today,' she said, trying not to think about the long boozy lunches she knew the editorial team had, and how much of her lunchtimes were spent with spreadsheets and a thin sandwich. 'I know a great little greasy spoon just down the road,' Jo suggested shyly. 'And it's not far from my office. If you have the time we could go there.'

A couple of beautiful girls sauntered past, their arms full of shopping bags, and Jo felt her heart sink. One of them shot William a coy glance, and out of the corner of her eye Jo spotted William blush. As he casually watched them walk away she wanted to drag him into the café as fast as she could. She couldn't bear being in proximity to model-type girls with perfect bodies, and she hated the inevitable comparison William would draw when he looked from them to her.

'So this is your secret home from home, then?' William asked as he held the door of the café open for her. Jo smiled weakly and drank in the nicotine-stained plastic surroundings that were so at odds with the bustle of trendy Covent Garden and the glamorous, gleaming Garnet Tower. No beautiful girls would come in here, she thought. She was safe.

'You could say that,' Jo said, sitting at a small square table opposite William. 'It's one of my favourite places. After The Royal Oak, of course.' She breathed in deeply and took in the smell of frying bacon, cigarette smoke and cheap perfume. Despite all the fashionable coffee houses and tiny, unique cafés that surrounded the office, Jo truly only felt at home in Mattheus's, with its plastic-coated menus and tired-looking Greek waitress. It was a slice of Peckham in Central London and one of the few places where Jo felt she could relax and be herself, away from the bitchy glares of Garnet Publishing.

'It seems it's popular with some of your colleagues, too,' William remarked casually. Jo looked up at him with a jolt, and followed his eyes to where Debbie and Katherine were waving at her with smirks on their faces. They had cups of tea and a shared plate of chips in front of them, and they would clearly be making the chips last so they could watch Jo with her mysterious friend. Jo swore under her breath.

'Er, did you actually want something stronger?' Jo said to William, trying to ignore the girls, who were whispering to each other while laughing at Jo's discomfort. 'There's a great pub just down the road that Chris Evans and Billie Piper sometimes go to …'

William looked around the café and stretched, casually brushing his denim-clad legs against hers. 'This is perfect, and I'm sick of pubs,' he said. 'I'd rather not spend my free time in one when I've managed to escape The Royal Oak.' He ordered them two cups of tea from a bleached-blonde waitress and leant back in his chair.

'Are you sure …?' Jo said, hoping she might be able to change his mind. She was worried about Debbie. She knew she was the type of girl who wouldn't hesitate to come over and make a bitchy comment or two.

William reached across the table and put his hand on Jo's. Out of the corner of her eye she could see Debbie mimicking his action to Katherine but for a sweet, sharp moment she didn't care. Her whole body was suddenly on fire and nobody else mattered. She blushed and took a sip of tea.

'We're OK in here, aren't we?' William said softly, leaning closer to Jo. 'I don't want to embarrass you in front of your friends but we have so little time and I'd rather spend it sitting down chatting than walking around looking for somewhere to go.' He looked at Jo anxiously. 'It's good to see you, you know. Really good. I've missed you.'

Jo smiled at him, and decided not to tell him that Debbie and Katherine weren't exactly her friends. Despite their thrilled expressions at having something new to tease her about, Jo genuinely didn't care what her colleagues were whispering to each other. William's familiar friendly face and relaxed manner were all Jo needed to block out their audience, and she wondered if William had spent the last nine months pining for her like she had for him.

'It's good to see you, too. I'm sorry I've not been in touch,' she began. 'I wanted to talk to you so badly, but I've been busy, and—'

William interrupted her. 'You don't need to apologise. When you left it was hard, I won't deny it. I couldn't stand not knowing where you were, but I got used to it, and I eventually got over it.' He gave a little laugh. 'I mean, it's not like we were ever together, was it. We were just friends then and we're still friends now. Right?'

Jo swallowed hard and concentrated on the chipped por-celain on her mug of tea. Jo had only ever had one true friend – Amelia – and she certainly had never made her feel as William had done late at night in his bedroom. Hearing him say those words was a massive, disappointing blow. 'Right. So do you ... do you have a girlfriend?'

William shrugged easily. 'I've had a few, but nobody seri-ous. Like I said, I had to get used to you not being around and life had to go on. I didn't know if I'd ever see you again. I certainly didn't expect to bump into you in the street!'

'No, nor did I.' Jo didn't know what to say and she felt like she could barely speak – the news that he had had girlfriends ripped straight through her and physically hurt. She felt sick, and she pictured William in his bed with beautiful, toned girls. She was torturing herself but she couldn't help it.

'And speaking of bumping into people, I saw your friend from school the other day – she was shopping in Winchester, and looking a bit stressed about getting her degree results.'

Jo tried to look as normal as possible, and concentrated on ignoring her hurt. 'Amelia! She'll be fine. I spoke to her the other day – she's in line for a first, and from what she said she aced her finals.'

William grinned. 'She seemed a bit strung out when I saw

her, said she was buying new outfits to take her mind off it. She showed me the tiniest pair of shorts ever – I think she may have mixed up Miss Selfridge with a children's shop.'

An irrational image of Amelia flirting with William shot into her head, and Jo downed the last of her tea so she wouldn't have to speak.

'She was full of praise for you, though,' William remarked. 'Kept on telling me about how you've landed an amazing job on one of the best magazines in the country … although she refused to tell me which one it was!'

Jo swallowed. 'It's called *Gloss*,' she said, 'and it's one of those slick women's magazines that feature articles about people's relationships as well as, you know, fashion pieces.'

William raised his eyebrows. 'So you're writing about the best way for a woman to achieve an orgasm while persuading men to strip off for the centrefold?'

Jo blushed scarlet. 'No, no, that's *Cosmo* … I …' Jo trailed off, not wanting to disappoint William by admitting she was only a PA. She swallowed. 'I work alongside the publisher – Joshua Garnet. I assist him on the business side of the magazine as well as providing him with an opinion on editorial ideas. My portfolio has some of the latest ideas for our relaunch …' Jo nodded down to her portfolio, and William looked at it with interest.

'May I?' he said, gesturing down towards it, but Jo caught Debbie's eye.

'Best not. There are some staffers in here who don't know about it, and, well, I'd hate for something to get leaked.'

William leant back in his chair and shot Jo another smile. 'You know, I had reservations about you storming off to the big city to get a job on a magazine, but you've really landed on your feet.' Jo gave him a wide smile, and he continued. 'It seems like things have really worked out for both of us – you have your incredible career with *Gloss*, and I'm finally getting somewhere with the book. You were right – it was worth not getting together after all.'

Jo felt her heart sink, but she forced herself to keep smiling. 'No regrets, then?' she said lightly, and William shook his head.

'Jo, I'll always have regrets about not being with you, but what will be will be,' he said softly, and once again he put his hand on hers. Jo felt the electricity between them, and for a moment she wondered if she could pack in her job and go back to Winchester with him. Why was she sticking around in a job that seemed like a dead end? Joshua Garnet clearly had no interest in helping her develop her career, and she couldn't see a way to make it as a journalist if she stayed there ...

William removed his hand from Jo's, and as soon as he did the spell was broken. Jo felt herself slump a little in her chair, and as William looked at his watch she felt her eyes prickle with tears. There was no way she could give up on her dream, and she had to let William go.

'I hate to say it,' he said, with genuine disappointment in his eyes, 'but I'm going to have to make a move. Look, you must give me your phone number. I'm not losing touch with you again.'

Jo blinked, and without thinking she scribbled her landline number on to an old receipt. As she handed it to him, William stood up and pulled Jo towards him for a kiss on the cheek. Jo blushed, and as she looked away from him, embarrassed, her eye caught Debbie's, who was sitting at her table with an evil grin on her face.

'I'll phone you soon,' William said, holding Jo's hands in his before slowly letting them drop. 'And Jo ... happy birthday.'

Jo smiled in delight, and as she watched him walk down the road she felt carefree. Despite having meaningless girlfriends he'd still remembered her birthday, and he wanted to stay in touch. She rushed into a lift in Garnet Tower, but just as the mirrored doors began to shut, Debbie appeared and stuck her foot out so she could stand next to Jo. She waited until some advertising sales guy got out on the fifth floor before speaking.

'Well, well, well,' she said nastily, and Jo tried to ignore her, hoping Debbie would take the hint that Jo wouldn't rise to the bait. 'Who would have thought that Heifer Hill would have a boyfriend? And such a good-looking one at that!'

Jo focused on the front of the lift and watched the buttons light up as they rose higher up the dark red skyscraper.

'Madeline Turner will be interested to hear that you have a boyfriend, you know,' Debbie said, looking at herself in the mirrors of the lift and preening her hair.

Jo turned to look at her sharply. She could ignore bitchy comments about her weight – she had done all her life – but she couldn't ignore this, not if Debbie was going to talk about her to the editor. 'Madeline Turner doesn't give a fuck about my private life,' Jo said, suddenly furious. She looked at Debbie and decided she didn't have to play nice. 'But then, at least Madeline knows who I am. I'm not some nobody with no brain who spends her days typing up other people's work.'

The doors to the lift opened and both girls got out. As Jo tried to walk away Debbie grabbed her by the arm.

'Oh, she knows who I am, mark my words,' Debbie hissed in a quiet voice, looking at Jo in surprise. She had no idea that Jo could be so sharp. 'But that's to be expected, given that Joshie Garnet once came on to me.' She looked Jo up and down and smirked. 'He likes blondes, you see, and he likes girls who look after themselves. Not like you. Although if you've managed to score yourself such a hot boyfriend you may have some hidden talents that Joshua might like.'

Jo gritted her teeth. 'I don't care if Joshua finds me attractive or not. I wasn't employed for that.'

Debbie laughed. 'You can say that again! His wife only chose you to be his PA because you're the ugliest secretary in the building. She knew there was no chance of him putting his hands on you. Not like he did with me that evening when he cornered me in the filing room.' She shot Jo a triumphant look and grinned.

'Oh, hadn't you worked it out? Madeline Turner's doing her best to make sure Joshua doesn't fuck his assistant. They couldn't bear the risk or the scandal, especially since his last PA got pregnant.'

Suddenly it all made sense, and Jo felt the colour drain from her face. Debbie cackled.

'Can you imagine? A bastard heir to the Garnet billions would never have done, and Harold Garnet would go crazy if he knew, so they sacked the poor girl and gave her a "bonus" to keep quiet and get rid of it. But that's beside the point. I'll leave you to think about this news,' she said, walking backwards and taking in Jo's expression. 'Not that it's news to anyone but yourself, really. Have a good day now, you hear? I'll send your love to the others in my office. They'll be delighted to hear you're getting on so well.'

Chapter Nine

As Jo ran into the ladies' lavatories she felt tears running down her face and she tripped on the cold, school-style tiles before she shut herself into a cubicle, slamming the door behind her. It was like hiding her sobs from the school bullies all over again. Through her tears she managed to lock the door, and she dropped her portfolio and handbag on the floor before putting her head in her hands. How had she ever thought she was good enough to do this? She hadn't even shone as a secretary, and had only been picked to be Garnet's PA because she was fat, ugly and no man wanted to go near her. Jo buried her hands into her growing-out haircut and sobbed, letting self-pity wash over her and wondering if she could afford to leave this job, if she had enough money in her bank account to walk out of Garnet Tower and never come back. Compared to the bullies at school — who strutted around like teenage princesses — Debbie was nothing, a nobody with a head full of split ends, a wardrobe full of clothes fit for a tart and the worst estuary accent she had ever heard. Jo grinned and felt the salty tears drip from her cheeks on to her lips. She had survived Jemima and Dominique and she knew Debbie was no match for her. She wouldn't allow herself to cry any more.

Jo sniffed, and wiped her eyes with the back of her hands, seeing how the mascara left over from her meeting with

Joshua stained her skin black. Going back to her desk would be intolerable but she was determined not to do it with red eyes. Thank God, she thought, nobody would see her in this state. She had to act like she didn't care about Debbie's revelations, and she had to walk back into that editorial office not giving a fuck. Jo shuddered as she imagined how the girls on the editorial team would react if they saw her looking like this. Jo unlocked the door so she could examine the damage in the mirror and put her face back together again, but as she pushed the stone-coloured door open she saw Lucy, one of the girls from *Gloss*, looking at her curiously.

Jo baulked at the sight of her. She was super-slim, effortlessly beautiful and as polished as any model, with long light brown hair, huge grey eyes and an outfit which cost more than everything in Jo's wardrobe put together. There was something about Lucy's lack of haughtiness that meant that as much as she tried, Jo found she couldn't instantly dislike her.

'I just wanted to check you were all right,' Lucy said, looking Jo up and down with concern. 'I couldn't help but overhear you crying ... I was in the cubicle next to you, and ...'

Lucy looked from Jo to the toilet cubicles, and she went into one and pulled the toilet chain so that it flushed. 'I didn't want to disturb you. Or make you feel embarrassed. But I have, haven't I? I'm not very good in these situations, I'm sorry.' Lucy started to turn red and Jo looked at her in amazement. She always thought the journalists on *Gloss* were unflappable ice-queens.

'I'm not doing very well at this, am I? I'll start again. Are you OK?'

Jo nodded and slowly walked to the sinks where she turned on the taps. Despite imagining a wealth of different situations where she spoke to Lucy, or Araminta, or Lizzie, Jo had never expected to be in a position like this. She washed her hands and then ran her fingers under her eyes, rubbing at the panda-bear rings that had formed beneath them.

'I'm OK,' she said, her voice thick with emotion. As much as she was desperate to talk to Lucy about journalism, about *Gloss*, about how she could be a bigger part of the magazine, she just wanted to be left alone. 'I had a bit of a shock, but I'm OK.' She looked Lucy in the eye and wondered if she was in on Debbie's little plan to kick Jo where it hurt. Jo didn't think so – Lucy neither sounded nor looked like the type of girl who would listen to a word of Debbie's bitchy gossip.

Lucy went into the cubicle and pulled out a wad of tissue to give to Jo before leaning awkwardly against a wall. 'When I'm upset I try to think about the last time I was happy. I put myself back into a good mood.' She flicked her mane of long hair behind one shoulder and looked at herself in one of the mirrors. Everything about her – from her large grey eyes to her soft, plump lips – was perfect.

Jo looked down at her shoes and ignored a fresh scuff mark on one of them. 'I was happy this morning, but that seems like a long time ago now.' She leant against the sinks and thought about how she had felt that morning, when she had dressed with the thought that she was going to convince Joshua Garnet to give her a promotion. That – coupled with unexpectedly seeing William, and then being told by Debbie that she had only been made Garnet's PA because she was ugly – made Jo's head spin, and she could feel the beginnings of a headache.

'Do you have any Nurofen?' Jo asked Lucy, and she watched her rummage in her hard-to-get-hold-of Louis Vuitton Murakami, putting samples of make-up on the sinks so she could get to the bottom of the bag.

'Here,' she said, as she handed Jo the cardboard packet. She broke into a wry grin. 'But only take two, mind. Whatever it was that gave you that shock it's not worth overdosing for.'

Jo stared back at Lucy incredulously and then burst out laughing. Lucy's eyebrows shot up.

'What?'

Jo stopped giggling and smiled at her. 'It's nothing. It's just …' Jo took a deep breath and decided to take a chance. 'I've never heard any of the *Gloss* girls crack a joke before.'

Lucy grinned. 'Nor have I. And I've been here nearly a year.'

Lucy leant against the sinks so that they were side by side, but was careful not to let her tight black jeans get wet. 'I sometimes wonder if they even find some of the jokes in the magazine funny. I often catch Madeline's eye and wonder if her face is about to break into a grin, but it never does, which makes me wonder if she's had too much Botox or is just humourless. Who would have thought that working on a women's magazine would be so serious?'

'That's exactly what I was thinking,' Jo said, checking her top for wet spots made by her tears. 'Everyone's undoubtedly glamorous, but …' Jo stopped herself from finishing her sentence and Lucy looked at her.

'It's OK, you know. I won't tell anyone what you think. God, if Minty could hear me saying she didn't have a sense of humour I'd be sacked outright. She thinks I'm after her job as it is. Go on, what were you going to say?'

Jo looked at the floor. 'I was going to say that you'd think there'd be a bit of personality behind everyone's glamorous appearances, but there isn't.'

Lucy smirked. 'Agreed. It's a lot like the magazine, isn't it? All gloss and no substance. Do you think they're robots?'

Jo looked at Lucy in shock. Her mouth dropped open, and Lucy rushed to correct herself.

'I didn't mean it like that, it's just, well … Look, don't tell anyone I said this, OK, but I've never worked with a team of people who take themselves so seriously. They wear the "right" clothes, they say the "right" things, but they only do what *Gloss* dictates, and they're the ones who make it up. They live in their own little universe and they don't seem to realise they're caricatures of themselves.' Lucy shook her head in disbelief at herself, and continued. 'I worked at *Eden* magazine before this and, believe me, *Gloss* is a different world to most magazines.'

'What do you mean?' Jo said, eagerly.

'Well, nowhere else do journalists believe they are on a par with Hollywood actresses. Helena, that junior writer, said to me the other day that she was thinking of phoning up Keira Knightley's manager and telling him she'd be the blonde version. That she didn't think Keira was much cop and she'd be a lot better, especially since most of London knows who she is and people tend to only think Keira is a nobody who got lucky in *Pirates of the Caribbean*.'

Jo giggled. 'You're joking? Helena can't act, can she?'

Lucy smiled. 'I very much doubt it. And to make matters worse, Helena thinks she's prettier than her. Keira, I mean. Thinks she has a "talent". Not that you need talent, but anyway. It's not just that. I mean, every publishing company is cut-throat – that's the nature of the business – but here it seems like everyone is stabbing each other in the back every single day. It's a fucking game, and it's one I hate taking part in, but my mortgage repayments depend on me playing it well. And to make matters worse, there are no definite alliances – your best friend today could be your worst enemy tomorrow, and if you don't fit in then you're nobody. A nothing.'

'I know how that feels.'

Lucy looked at Jo sympathetically. 'I know you get ignored – I see you hovering after meetings and it's like you're invisible, but can you imagine what would happen if I spoke to you? It would be social death to even acknowledge that you existed, because to the other girls, you don't.'

Jo felt like she had been punched in her stomach. She had known all along that people ignored her because of their pack mentality but, after hearing Lucy admit it, Jo wondered if there was any point in trying to befriend anyone on the editorial team. It was just like being at school, only ten times worse, because rather than getting detention for being mean, you seemed to get promoted.

'Please don't take it personally – we probably all think the same thing, but none of us is brave enough to speak to you, or anyone else who isn't part of the "exclusive *Gloss* gang".' Lucy rolled her eyes. 'Unless one of us does something, nobody will ever step out of line. It's that competitive and paranoid.'

Jo sighed. 'I know,' she said in a small voice. 'But I still want to be part of it. I want it so much.'

Lucy looked at her with interest. 'What, you want to be part of the editorial team?'

Jo nodded. 'Desperately. I only took a secretarial job here so I could break in, but Joshua Garnet isn't having any of it.'

'Are you any good?'

'I think I am. But ...' Jo looked down at her portfolio on the floor of the cubicle and picked it up. 'What do you think?' Jo handed her work over to Lucy, and as she flicked through the pages in silence Jo nervously set about putting fresh make-up on, trying not to care that Lucy's opinion mattered to her as much as Joshua Garnet's did.

After ten minutes Lucy looked at Jo in amazement. Her eyes were shining, and she kept on looking from the portfolio to Jo in bewilderment. Lucy couldn't believe that the dumpy, mousy girl in front of her had produced ideas that anyone on the team would be proud to call their own. 'This is fantastic

– I can't believe Josh would tell you otherwise.'

Jo felt herself brimming with pleasure, and she smiled. Coming from one of the editorial team this meant a lot to her. Perhaps her lifetime of hard work and struggle had been worth it after all. 'Do you really think so?'

'Yes, I do. Each of these is the perfect *Gloss* feature – they're funny, smart, sexy – and they look the part too. This is exactly what Madeline Turner tries to make us achieve but we can never seem to. They truly are fucking amazing. I'm impressed.'

Jo felt her smile fading. 'Why didn't Joshua think so?'

Lucy sighed but didn't take her eyes off the portfolio. 'Did he look at these properly?'

Jo shook her head. Joshua had barely even flicked through them.

'Well then. If he had, he would have snapped you up to be a feature writer on the spot. If I was in charge – or a features editor like Araminta at the very least – I would.'

Jo wasn't consoled. 'But how do I make him listen to me? It's like banging my head against a brick wall. He can't see past me being his PA.'

Lucy chewed on her lip and Jo was struck at how such an innocent gesture looked sexy on her. 'I don't know,' she admitted. 'Joshua Garnet is a good publisher if you ask me, but he's not so good at seeing things that aren't obvious. I'd love to have come up with just one of these ideas – if I had I'm willing to bet Joshua would give me a promotion. Or, at the very least, one of those rewarding smouldering smiles he only turns on when we have been good girls.'

Jo laughed. She'd seen that look.

Lucy stared at her with a strange expression. 'But what if I did pitch one of your ideas in the next meeting? How would you feel about that?' Lucy's voice was neutral, and Jo felt her smile suddenly freeze.

'Are you asking for my ideas?'

Lucy shook her head. 'I could say they're from a freelancer I know – someone who lives in America or something so she can't come into the office.'

Jo looked reluctant, but Lucy was insistent. 'Wouldn't you like to know if your ideas really are good enough? Look, you've tried to pitch them and nobody seems to be interested, but what if I tried? What if Joshua just can't see past you to realise what great ideas these are?'

'I suppose it would be OK,' Jo said slowly. 'If you think it will work. But what piece do you think we should go for?'

Lucy flicked through the portfolio and landed on a beautifully designed page.

'How about this one?' she said, with a glint of amusement in her eyes. 'We'd be killing two birds with one stone if Joshua and Madeline gave the thumbs up to this.'

Jo smiled. It was one of her best ideas, and she knew that if Madeline liked this one she'd be able to prove Joshua Garnet wrong. 'Why not?' she said with a smirk, and she gathered up her belongings to go back to her desk.

Lucy grinned. 'I just wonder who will volunteer to be the guinea pig.'

'Lizzie, that's brilliant,' Madeline said in the next editorial conference. As Jo kept the minutes she flicked through the notes from the previous meetings, and realised with a jolt that the script for almost all of them was the same. Lizzie suggested a rubbish fashion idea – normally based around men she wanted to fuck, she noticed – and then when Madeline chided her she came up with a brilliant idea, seemingly off the cuff. Madeline applauded her, Lizzie basked in her innovative brilliance, and then suddenly everyone else piled in, offering their ideas to a now-contented Madeline.

Jo looked up at Lucy and caught her eye. Well, she thought, today would be different.

'And Lucy, what about you?'

Jo sat up slightly straighter and tried not to look directly at Lucy or at Joshua. She kept her head tilted downwards as though she were concentrating on her notes, and hoped she wouldn't blush. If Madeline went for this, she thought, not only would she have confirmation that she was good enough, but she'd have contributed to *Gloss* without Joshua even knowing. Jo's heart pounded.

'Have you all heard the rumour about how Keira Knightley landed the lead in next summer's blockbuster?' Lucy began, as she looked around at the ten or so journalists with her eyes shimmering. She was wearing a dark grey sequinned T-shirt that fell off one shoulder, her trademark black skinny Sass & Bide jeans and red Gucci mules. She commanded the attention and respect of everyone, and Jo was impressed at how she provoked interest in her idea already. Keira Knightley was still the hottest actress in the UK, but Jo knew that there had been too many features about her in the magazines lately. There had been a Keira overkill that *Gloss* had steered away from, but if Lucy pitched this right, there would be a whole new angle to create a fresh feature.

'Apparently she walked straight into the casting agent's office after reading the novel it's based on, and she persuaded him to give her a deal just by smiling at him. She didn't even say a word. He knew he'd be stupid if he didn't give her the part – she's *that* good.'

Madeline Turner looked up at Lucy. 'Is that true?'

Helena interrupted. 'I don't think it is, you know,' she brayed. 'It's just one of those industry rumours. But you have to hand it to the girl; she's managed to get the column inches without having done very much. Why, I could do better myself.'

Jo forced herself not to look at Lucy and struggled to write everything down. She could feel bemusement rippling from where Lucy was sitting and Jo knew that if she caught her eye she'd start laughing. Helena was a tall, horsy-looking girl who produced some of the most mediocre articles Jo had had to type up when she was working with Frieda in the secretarys' office. Keira Knightley had more talent in her little fingernail than Helena had in her whole body, but Helena was one of those self-possessed girls who was over-confident with Daddy's money. She didn't seriously think she could take on Keira and win, did she?

'Which leads me to this article, which has actually been sent in by a friend of mine,' Lucy said smoothly. 'There's definitely something about Keira. She's tall and gangly, but we still can't seem to get enough of her. She's not the best actress, but she's managed to get more column inches than Scarlett Johansson did for *Lost in Translation*. She's hot, but nobody knows why. I think we can safely say that as long as Keira Knightley has that x-factor she'll be successful.'

Joshua interrupted, looking at his steel Officine Panerai watch impatiently. 'So what's the idea?'

Lucy flashed Joshua a smile to placate him. 'We take a girl off the street, condition her into acting like Keira would – you know, she acts sexy, special, full of English-rose charm – and we make her a star. We devote pages on how to get the x-factor, conveniently forgetting of course that it's not something you can buy in a shop, but focus on the fashion, the beauty and the attitude of the x-factor. We turn the girl into a babe, the type of girl who could walk into a casting director's office and get a ten-million-dollar lead part just by giving him a sparkly grin. And most importantly we show our readers that you can change your life without spending hundreds on designer clothes.'

Joshua looked doubtful. 'I doubt our advertisers will like that.'

'But our readers will,' Madeline said, her eyes glowing. 'Lucy, this is a brilliant idea, absolutely fantastic.'

In the corner Jo struggled not to jump for joy.

'Lizzie, scrap your fashion idea about Paris couture, I want you to concentrate on what the high street is offering, and to scour charity shops for bargains. We're going to give the whole magazine an x-factor theme. Araminta, I want to see real-life pieces abut girls with the x-factor, and, Charlotte, make sure the beauty is affordable and in keeping with Keira. Perhaps offer solutions on how to get the look that Keira will sport next without even knowing it. We need someone to be the girl from the street ...'

Madeline's eyes swept over the room, and she lingered briefly on Jo before settling on Helena, who looked fit to burst.

'Helena?' Madeline said, with a hint of amusement in her voice. 'Something tells me you'd like a stab at this?'

Helena beamed at Madeline. 'I think I'd be perfect at it, actually,' she said in her haughty voice. 'I have the looks, I have the body to wear any type of fashion, and, really, how hard can this be?' She leant forward and spoke directly to Madeline. 'I always thought that it would be quite easy to be like Keira Knightley,' she said in a confident voice. 'Why, if the girls made me over properly I could be the blonde version of her.'

Lucy let out a snort of laughter and hid it with a coughing fit. Madeline looked over at her, and Jo wondered if she was trying to grin through the stiff mask of her face. 'Lucy, I need you to co-ordinate this piece with Helena. Helena needs to write it from her perspective, but I need this freelancer to write the lead article, give some background into what the x-factor is ... Who did you say came up with this idea again?'

Lucy caught Jo's eye but remained calm. 'She's called Olivia Windsor,' Lucy said, using the fake name that Jo had suggested to her earlier, 'and I worked on a local paper with her after I left journalism college.'

'Well, I want her in here,' Madeline said.

'She's based in New York at the moment,' Lucy said smoothly. 'She freelances out there. But I'm sure she'd love to come in next time she's in town.'

'Fine,' Madeline said, and she turned back to her notepad. 'Now, Lucy, if you could ask Olivia if she could—'

'Now hang on a minute ...' Joshua interrupted, and Madeline whizzed round in her chair to look at him. 'This is all well and good but you're not thinking straight. Chanel are taking four pages in this issue, and they're not going to like being placed next to bargain-basement fashion.'

Madeline held his gaze. 'But they are going to like the boost in circulation of what I predict will be our bestselling issue. Our readers have lipstick-lesbian crushes on Knightley so I'm going to get her on the cover. With no clothes on. So who wouldn't want to buy it?'

Lucy looked at Jo with wide eyes – she had never seen Madeline so animated about anything.

'And how are you going to do that?' Joshua said easily, looking at his wife. 'Are you going to phone Keira up? Offer her a diamond-encrusted eye-patch she can wear in the next *Pirates* film?'

Madeline shot Joshua a scornful look. 'Of course I'm going to phone her up, don't be ridiculous.' She turned back to the rest of the editorial team. 'We need to get cracking, so everyone come up with your new outlines by the end of the day and present them to me before you leave for the evening. Lucy, it's time we promoted you to joint features editor with Araminta.' Lucy's mouth dropped open, and Araminta shot Madeline a sour look. 'Thanks for the meeting, everyone, well done.'

Jo sat frozen in her chair as the editorial team filtered out of the meeting room. She felt like she was in a dream, and she couldn't believe that one of her ideas, something she had come up with in ten minutes late one evening while surrounded by take-away cartons, was going to alter the whole of the next issue of *Gloss*.

Lucy sat back in her chair and waited until everyone apart from her and Jo had left the room.

'Now do you believe me when I say your ideas are good?'

Jo looked at her, dumbfounded, and didn't know what to say. A small voice in the back of her head told her that she had known she was good enough all along.

September 2003

When the magazine hit the streets the editorial team celebrated the x-factor issue of *Gloss* being an instant hit. Joshua opened bottles of Veuve Clicquot to toast the fact that he'd ordered a reprint of that issue, and Jo overheard Madeline telling someone on the telephone that because of the x-factor theme, circulation had tripled. Even though Jo was used to hearing the advertising sales team embellishing the circulation figures to sell advertising space, Jo knew that Madeline's figures were true. Even Harold Garnet sent an email from his yacht in the Bahamas to congratulate the team on their success. Nobody thought for a moment that the shy, overweight girl in the corner was the brains behind it.

When Jo took a copy of the magazine home with her she sat on her floor and stared at the cover, letting silent, joyful tears gently slide down her face. Without her this issue of *Gloss* wouldn't have an exclusive interview and fashion shoot with Keira Knightley, the hilarious article where Helena unintentionally proved that the x-factor couldn't be faked, and more pages of advertising than any other issue of *Gloss* had carried. Jo bit into a bar of chocolate and tried not to feel glum that it wasn't Jo Hill who had become an instant success at *Gloss*, but Olivia Windsor.

'Try not to think about it,' Lucy said over the phone that night. 'You've made a mark on the magazine and you're well in there now.'

Jo didn't smile. 'But how am I going to get paid?' she asked, 'or what happens if Madeline wants to phone Olivia up, or wants to fly her out to London, or ...' her voice trailed off. She wasn't sure she could be Joshua's PA, write as Olivia Windsor, and keep up the deception at work. She was exhausted.

Lucy's voice sounded triumphant down the phone. 'I've sorted it all out. One, your money is being paid directly to me as Garnet Publishing won't pay invoices in dollars, and apparently "Olivia's" bank in the States won't accept English cheques. Two, Madeline won't need to phone Olivia up, as it's the job of the features editor to do that. And three, Olivia can't be flown out because she's too busy freelancing,' Lucy finished with a flourish.

'Do you really think this will work?' Jo said quietly down the phone.

Lucy laughed. 'Babes, it already is working. Now listen, I need your bank account details as I have a hot two thousand pounds just desperate to be transferred to you, and I also need five feature ideas for the meeting tomorrow morning.'

Jo looked through her notebook and began to smile. She could do this. She was going to do this. 'No problem,' she said breezily.

'Good,' Lucy said. 'And, Jo, make sure they're as good as the last one.'

Chapter Ten

March 2004

'And what has Olivia Windsor got for us today?' Madeline Turner asked Lucy, who was sitting at the meeting table with sheets of paper stacked neatly in front of her. As Lucy read out the list of Jo's ideas in a clear, confident and cut-glass voice, Jo realised just how lucky she was that she could count Lucy as a friend. Lucy's eyes glittered under the palest blue eyeshadow as they skimmed 'Olivia's' list of features, and her lithe body was dressed in a Prada slate-grey shift dress that highlighted her long neck and limbs. Jo turned to Madeline to gauge her reaction to her newest ideas and her heart flipped when she spotted the editor looking impressed. Even though she had been writing for *Gloss* for months it still gave her a buzz to see Madeline nodding in approval.

'Tell Olivia that I'd like to run the piece about women's fashion adopting masculine lines for the July issue, but I'd like the article about DIY fashion for this month, along with the "how women can have it all" piece. Thanks.'

Lucy shot a quick look at Jo, and Jo tried to focus on the minutes she was meant to be keeping. It was hard – her brain was already racing on how she'd compose her pieces.

Jo had been writing as Olivia Windsor for nearly eight months, and her bank account was beginning to look healthier. Lucy suggested that Jo start her own company so that her freelance cheques from *Gloss* could be made out to a company name rather than going through her, and Jo spent most of her next pay packet on an accountant who created Platinum Consulting for her. The finance division of Garnet Publishing duly made out their cheques to Jo's company after 'Olivia' sent them a letter on Platinum Consulting headed paper, and Jo watched her bank balance grow. She transferred what she needed to her current account on a monthly basis, but the rest of the time she imagined the golden pound coins given to her courtesy of *Gloss* multiplying in a vault. For the first time in her life she had over £25,000 in savings, and it felt good.

But not as good as it was every time Jo saw one of her articles in *Gloss*. The first time Jo had seen something she'd written in print she'd actually given a loud whoop of joy, but when Joshua had frowned at her she had forced herself to remain composed, despite her jubilation. Since then Jo had remembered to stay in control of her emotions, but with more and more features appearing in print she was always on a high on publication day, even if the name 'Olivia Windsor' appeared as a byline rather than 'Jo Hill'.

Jo was – on the inside, at least – a different person. Not only was she a published writer at the age of twenty-one, but Olivia Windsor was the envy of everyone at *Gloss*, the talk of all the staff within Garnet Publishing and the hottest new writer to hit the news-stands. Every idea Jo pitched was accepted, and after only a few months her writing dominated the magazine – 'Olivia' was an instant hit, partly because of Jo's writing talent, but also because Jo used her editorial-meeting notes to her advantage. If Madeline mentioned she was interested in a piece on what true love really was, the next day Jo would formulate her pitch. Even though being a PA at *Gloss* was boring as hell, Jo was using it to give her the edge.

As Madeline rounded up the meeting, Jo hurried to make

sure that her minutes summed up everything that had been said, and she rushed through the pages of her notebook checking that everything was correct. Jo was finding it increasingly difficult to stay alert in the daytime, and as she pretended to pay attention to what Madeline was saying about an editorial team-bonding session she accidentally let out a long yawn. Joshua Garnet caught her eye and looked displeased, and Jo spotted Araminta smirking. Shit, Jo thought, as she tried to stifle another one. She had to try to get an early night tonight and leave her feature on why girls loved boy bands for the weekend.

'A word in my office,' Joshua said to Jo sharply after Madeline closed the meeting. Jo froze – had he found out about her moonlighting? She nervously walked into Joshua's exquisite corner office, and forced herself to look at her boss rather than the view of London below.

'I'm slightly concerned about your commitment to the job, Joanne,' Joshua began, gesturing for her to sit and speaking to her in the cold tones she recognised from the meetings he had with the accountants. 'You seem distracted, you're making mistakes, and that yawn in the editorial meeting was, frankly, an embarrassment,' he said to her, looking her up and down with barely concealed distaste. Jo guessed that he would have preferred her to dress like some of the girls on the editorial team, or better still, be a more glamorous PA who was sexy as well as efficient. Jo tried not to feel defensive. She didn't have any free time to lose the extra weight that was piling back on.

'If I was one of those new age human resources types I'd ask if you have something on your mind, if you have personal problems you'd like to share with me.' Joshua stared at Jo intently, but before she could speak he continued. 'But I'm not one of these namby-pamby liberals and the mere thought of your private life bores me. If you have issues outside this office sort them out, because your filing has gone downhill and these letters – the ones I was going to send to the board – are full of mistakes.' Joshua pushed a pile of letters across his smooth walnut desk to Jo and she saw at least five words ringed in red. He'd clearly asked another one of the secretaries to go through her work. She hoped it wasn't Debbie.

'I'm really sorry,' Jo began, but Joshua cut her off.

'In this industry we don't have time for apologies. I expect better from you, Joanne, and frankly I'm disappointed. You were hired to be my assistant, and I expect you to assist me, not cause me more problems. You can be replaced in a flash, and mark my words, if you don't get up to speed you will be.' He let his eyes linger on the damp patches appearing under her armpits, and Jo spotted a small, cruel smile playing on his lips. He was enjoying this.

'Do I make myself clear?' he drawled, and Jo burnt red. If only he knew she was his elusive star writer, she thought, with her fists closed so tightly that her fingernails dug into the palms of her hands. Jo took a deep breath and forced herself to keep her voice under control.

'Yes, sir,' she said, neutrally, and Joshua leant back in his chair and smirked.

'Good. I thought you'd understand. Now, get me a black coffee,' he said, and he paused, thinking something through. 'And while you're there why don't you go and ask everyone on the editorial team if you can make them a drink,' he said. 'Circulation is up, and I think it would be nice if, in future, you helped the team with their creativity by running their errands.'

When Joshua saw the anger flashing in Jo's bright green eyes he laughed, cruelly. 'Well, you did say you wanted to be part of the team.'

*

A week later Jo felt like the living dead. Lucy had told her that Madeline wanted three new features within ten days, and Joshua had increased her workload, telling her that Edward Sampson-Brown, the finance director, needed some urgent filing that meant she had to spend two evenings a week in the accounts office organising spreadsheets. When Jo got home at ten in the evening all she wanted to do was fall asleep, but instead she pulled out her freshly bought laptop and lost herself in making her features sparkle. Other girls would hate having two intense jobs on the go, but to Jo writing in the evenings was a reward, something she craved even when her body cried out for sleep. However, as Madeline's demands on her new writer's productivity increased Jo found that in the daytime her eyes began to blur, and her head pounded. She managed to pull herself together when Joshua was around, but in between tasks she let her eyes shut for a few minutes, only snapping out of her haze when the phone rang.

That morning, Joshua took great delight in telling her that his whole personal filing cabinet needed to be reorganised, and that he wanted Jo to do it while he was in a meeting with an advertiser. Jo looked at him with a heavy heart. She already had to photocopy articles to give to the secretaries, arrange the food for the monthly editors' lunch, and was also in the middle of a difficult phone call with the distributors, who said they had not received a renewed contract from Garnet. As she slowly stood up to walk into his office, Joshua focused on her bottom, and she realised she was past caring if he found her attractive or not. Through her sleep-deprived daze she thought she could hear Joshua chuckling behind her. Jo slowly turned round to face him.

'I think it's time we got you a bit more active in your role here,' he said, laughing and eyeing the rings of flesh round Jo's stomach. 'Maybe get you walking up and down the stairs carrying magazines. We wouldn't want you to break any more chairs, would we?' Joshua was referring to an incident that had happened the week before, when Jo had sat on an already broken chair in the canteen and had crumpled in a heap on the floor. Nobody had helped her up.

Jo looked down at her stomach, knowing that if she opened her mouth to tell Joshua to go fuck himself she would instantly be sacked.

'Oh, and by the way, there's a birthday in my diary and I need you to send a present for me. It's in the top drawer on the right-hand side and it needs to be wrapped. Send it to her by three o'clock, will you?' Joshua turned on his heel and walked off, and Jo set about reorganising his filing cabinet, wondering how it was possible that he could make it so messy so quickly. She had only tidied it last week. As Jo opened Joshua's desk drawer to get out the birthday present, she was slightly put out to see a silky thong on top of Joshua's black diary. Jo sat back in the black leather Eames chair and stared at them. She'd never seen such a sexy pair of knickers before – they were a tiny scrap of coffee-coloured wisps held together by the thinnest threads of silk, and there were glimmering creamy beads dotted around the satin and lace. Jo gulped, and imagined what it would feel like to wear knickers like these.

Jo gingerly pushed the Coco de Mer knickers aside and opened up Joshua's black diary, sighing when she saw his handwriting was worse than ever. Jo rubbed her tired, blurring eyes and found the entry he'd meant – 'M—'s birthday, do not forget.' Jo looked at the knickers again, this time visualising Madeline in them, and grimaced. She'd put the present and card that Joshua had already written in Madeline's pigeonhole by three o'clock, and she hoped that the editor would never know that her husband had made her wrap them up.

At half past three exactly Jo knew that her time at Garnet

Publishing was at an end when Joshua stormed towards her with a red mark on his face from being recently slapped.

'You stupid fucking bitch,' he hissed at her loudly, as Jo's mouth dropped open in surprise. 'What the fuck do you think you're playing at?' Jo shrank back in her chair, and the whole editorial team went silent as they watched Joshua yell at her. His voice had taken on a rough edge and he dropped his 't's – a sure sign that he was furious. Jo glanced at Madeline who was watching the exchange with a hurt expression, and as Joshua pulled her into his office she wondered what she had done wrong.

'Is this some petty revenge for me making jokes about your blubbery body?' Joshua said sharply, as he glared at her before slamming his glass door shut so nobody could hear what they were saying. His chocolate-coloured eyes were glinting with anger. 'Is this meant to be a practical joke that will have everyone in fits of laughter? Because believe me, Joanne,' he spat, 'nobody is laughing.'

Jo tried to think of something she could say that would defuse the situation and failed. She hadn't expected Joshua to find out she was Olivia Windsor … and she certainly didn't think he'd have reacted so badly.

'I should have told you sooner, I'm sorry, I didn't think—'

Joshua interrupted her. 'You didn't think? Oh, I think you thought all right,' he said in a low voice. 'You planned the whole thing so Madeline would receive the knickers meant for Marina. I don't give a damn why you did it, but I want to make sure you don't make things worse so sit here and shut up while I think.' Joshua pulled on the blinds that gave his office complete privacy – something Jo had not seen him do the entire time she had been his PA – and he began pacing around the office muttering to himself.

Jo looked at Joshua curiously, and realised with a rush of adrenaline that she had got to him, that she had riled the man who *Forbes* had called one of the most level-headed business-men in the country. He wasn't annoyed at her for writing under the name of Olivia Windsor – he didn't even know about it – but he was furious that she had accidentally sent his wife some sexy knickers meant for one of his girlfriends. Jo wondered what was in the card he had written, and why he couldn't pass the thong off as a sexy present from husband to wife.

'So the lingerie wasn't meant for Madeline, then?' Jo asked tentatively, and Joshua gave her a hard stare before laughing harshly. He opened his desk drawer and threw his black diary at Jo. It hit her hard on the stomach and she could feel her skin stinging underneath her blouse.

'Can you read, Joanne?' Joshua said quietly, and for the first time Jo could hear menace in his voice. With shaking hands Jo opened up the diary, and she felt her heart sink when she saw that Joshua's entry read: 'Marina's birthday, do not forget.' Jo silently closed the diary and shut her eyes. Shit. She'd been so tired she'd skipped over the name. Joshua took the diary from Jo and tore out the page with the birthday reminder on it, ripping it into tiny pieces that fell to the floor like confetti. He stared at Jo for what felt like the longest time, and then he spoke.

'You are going to apologise to Madeline for your sick practical joke, you are going to do it in front of everyone who works on *Gloss*, and then you are going to walk out of this office and never come back.'

'But it wasn't a practical joke,' Jo began nervously, but Joshua cut her off with a glare.

'You'll say it was or there will be hell to pay. Come on,' he said menacingly, as he took her by the arm again and dragged her into the open-plan editorial office. Everyone watched them curiously, and Jo could see the concern in Lucy's eyes. Joshua made Jo stand in front of Madeline.

'Well? What have you got to say for yourself?' Joshua said, as he turned to Jo impatiently. He rolled his eyes at Madeline, and suddenly Jo felt a flash of anger sear through her body. Yes, she'd made an embarrassing mistake, but it wouldn't have happened if Joshua weren't having the affair in the first place. Jo looked from Madeline to Joshua, and wondered what would happen if she told the truth. Taking a deep breath Jo gathered up all her strength and forced herself to be brave.

'Don't speak to me like that,' Jo said, her voice wobbling slightly. As she concentrated on looking calm she heard gasps from the editorial team – nobody spoke to Joshua with anything less than reverence, as the Garnet name had always commanded respect. Jo refused to play by the rules any more, and she spoke in a low, measured tone. 'You may pay me peanuts to pick up your shirts and do everything but wipe your bottom, but you don't pay me nearly enough to listen to you talking to me like that.'

Joshua burst out laughing, amazed that his fat, mousy PA had such a bite on her. He thought it was all an act and that she would crumble. 'Oh, is that right?' he said in an incredulous tone. 'I'd say we pay you far too much to sit on your fat ass to do nothing but eat.' He looked around the office and was clearly pleased he had an audience. When Madeline had opened the package and card written for Marina – one of London's hottest new models who had just turned seventeen – she'd marched over to Joshua and slapped him, hard, before dropping the knickers on his lap as he looked at her in shock. Joshua was determined to make sure Jo carried the can for this one.

Jo gave Joshua a sly little smile. 'I'd say you pay me far too much to write as Olivia Windsor, certainly, but I don't think all the money in the world could pay me to carry your spunk-covered suits to the dry-cleaner's again.' Jo didn't take her eyes off Joshua, and she was dimly aware of Helena giggling in the background. She thought she could see a small wave of fear wash across his face, but if she had it was gone in an instant, and he grinned at her before turning to Madeline with a smug expression.

'See? I told you she was delusional.' He walked around the office making sure all eyes were on him. 'Now she's pretending that she's Olivia Windsor.' He rolled his eyes and spun on his heels to look at Jo. 'Of course you are, sweetheart. Why on earth couldn't I have guessed that? Your brilliantly worded letters and tantalising minutes from meetings have always had me on the edge of my seat!'

Jo remained rooted to the spot. 'I am Olivia Windsor,' she said firmly, her eyes ablaze with fire. 'And I've written the best features this magazine has ever seen. When you didn't look at my portfolio I decided I'd make my own chance. And I fooled all of you.' Jo surveyed the editorial team, who looked at her doubtfully. She caught Lucy's eye and noticed she suddenly looked very pale. 'Tell them, Lucy,' Jo said confidently, and she watched Lucy shrink down in her seat. She shook her head ever so slightly, and refused to meet Jo's gaze.

'You're sick in the head,' Joshua spat at Jo happily. 'You've made up a pack of lies about being Olivia Windsor, and to get some sort of "revenge" on me for not looking at your GCSE artwork you've sent my wife a sexy pair of knickers and a forged card to make her think I'm having an affair. Well, guess what, Joanne, it hasn't worked.' Tiny beads of sweat had formed on Joshua's brow, and Jo began to realise she had dug a hole for herself and there was no way out.

'I don't know why you have tried to harm my relationship with my husband,' Madeline added, 'or why you're lying about being one of our contributors, but I suggest you get some help,' she said calmly, putting her arm around Joshua. 'I believe my husband, not you.'

Madeline's voice was so cold that Jo felt a chill run down her spine. Without meaning to she had alienated herself from the industry's most powerful couple, and there was nowhere to go but down.

Jo turned back to Joshua, and she began to feel panicked. She had not planned her outburst, and she began to clutch at straws, hoping that Joshua valued his reputation more than anything else. 'I'll go to the press,' Jo whispered, and Joshua grinned at her, clearly not caring what else she said because his wife believed him and not her. 'I'll tell them everything!'

Joshua kissed his wife on the cheek and walked over to a phone. The editorial team watched him in silence, wondering who he was going to ring. 'Do you really think they'd believe your lies any more than we do? Do remember, Joanne, that my family owns most of the press. And don't even think about trying to work for anyone else, because by the time you leave this office I'll have phoned everyone in the industry and told them you're a liar who stupidly tried to fuck with me and failed.' He looked at Jo and grinned, showing his wolf-like teeth. 'The best thing you can do is to stop eating and hope that you rot into something more attractive,' he said with a flourish. 'But mark my words, Joanne, even if you do that you haven't a hope in hell of getting a job on a magazine again.'

Jo felt her heart sink and she saw two security guards hovering by the double doors, waiting for Joshua's command before taking her by the arms. Jo turned to Joshua in the hope that she could have the final word, but as she caught his eye she realised that Joshua had humiliated her so much that there was nothing else she could say.

'Now get the fuck out of my building.'

PART TWO

Chapter Eleven

----- - -- ---- ----- - ---- --- ---.

April 2004

'Sorry to disturb you, but would you like a glass of champagne?' A haughty voice cut through Jo's thoughts and she
opened her eyes. She'd been so busy thinking about Joshua
Garnet that she'd momentarily forgotten she was on a plane,
and she gripped the armrests so tightly her knuckles turned
white. Jo knew she was being desperately unsophisticated
compared to the other passengers in business class, but she
couldn't help it. It was her first-ever flight.

'That would be great, thanks,' Jo said.

The hostess slowly took in how Jo's stomach folded
over her waistband, how her thighs strained against her
jogging bottoms and how her grown-out hair was tatty
at the ends. If Jo hadn't been feeling so out of place and
jumpy she'd have glared back defiantly, openly mocking
the hostess's thick orange foundation and obvious blow-job
lips.

'I'm sorry, but I have to check your passport for proof of
age,' she said with an amused glance, and Jo looked at her
incredulously before digging out her passport, flashing her
year of birth and noticing the smirk that the hostess gave
Jo's passport photo. Jo cringed inwardly and tried not to let
it bother her. The harsh white light of the photo booth had
caught her face at a bad angle and her chins looked treble

their normal size. In her photograph Jo looked like a whale, an enormous, ugly freak.

As the hostess concentrated on pouring a glass of champagne, Jo tried to imagine what Florida would be like, but she couldn't stop thinking about Joshua and everyone back at Garnet Publishing. Jo leant back in her chair and closed her eyes again. For the past ten minutes she'd been fantasising about marching into Garnet Tower and telling everyone that Joshua Garnet had been fucking Marina Stone, who he had clearly seduced when she had recently posed for *DG* magazine. The cover had been *DG*'s most successful as Marina had been photographed on all fours wearing nothing but Swarovski crystals scattered on her honey-coloured skin. Her full breasts hung from her taut, smooth body, her glossy red lips were slightly open, and her eyes were glazed. If the rumours were to be believed Marina always got high for shoots so she could lose her inhibitions, and true to form the cover of the magazine was strictly top shelf.

Joshua had hung a blown-up image of that particular cover in his office, something that seemed an obvious thing for a publisher to do at the time, but was loaded with meaning in retrospect. Jo grinned to herself as she imagined using it as evidence of Joshua's infidelity, but as she imagined what Harold Garnet's reaction would be, her smile faded. The old man would refuse to listen to her despite the evidence she produced – he'd want to think his company was safe in his son's hands, that Joshua was solid, dependable, and had given up chasing jailbait. Harold Garnet would never believe her over his son in a million years.

'Jo, Jo, over here!' Amelia's voice rang out in the air-conditioned airport lounge, and as soon as Jo spotted her she suddenly felt a weight lift from her shoulders. Amelia was toned, brown and gorgeous, with natural blonde highlights streaking hair that had grown so long it skirted the top of her bottom and completely covered her perky breasts. She was wearing tiny denim cut-off shorts and a faded grey vest with no bra. She looked great. In comparison to her friend Jo felt fat, lumpy and pale, but she pushed her distaste about her body to the back of her mind as Amelia ran towards her with a huge smile.

'I thought you were never going to appear! We've been waiting here for absolutely ages, and I was beginning to wonder if I got the time wrong . . .'

As Amelia made small talk she quickly cast her eyes over Jo and tried not to let her surprise show. Jo had regained a lot of her weight and looked drawn – she was a shadow of the sparkling girl she'd seen a year ago, and she looked like she'd been defeated by life. She was wearing saggy-looking jogging bottoms and a tired T-shirt, and Amelia wondered what had happened to the girl who had been the secret star of *Gloss*, the girl who had revelled in being in a glamorous, picture-perfect world. As Jo gave her a warm smile, Amelia resolved to make her shine again. With the Longboat Key sunshine and lack of nightlife, fast pace or anything to do, it wouldn't be that hard – after all, it had done the trick for her, she thought, as images of Charlie rushed through her head without warning. Amelia felt a slight touch on her elbow, and she turned round, banishing her ex-boyfriend from her mind. She grinned at the man standing next to her.

'Jo, this is Jackson,' Amelia said proudly, as the man shook Jo's hand firmly and gave her a flash of exquisite white teeth. He looked like a movie star. 'He's my tennis coach this summer,' Amelia giggled, and as Jackson turned his back to the girls to pick up Jo's scruffy psychedelic Top Shop cases, Jo flashed her an inquisitive look. Amelia merely beamed back. 'Well, I say he's my tennis coach but he's not actually teaching me any tennis. He's coaching this summer at that tennis academy everyone is raving about. Apparently Agassi and Sampras have both played there,' Amelia said proudly, waiting for Jo's impressed reaction. Jo gave her an exhausted, weak smile.

'How was the flight?' Jackson asked Jo as he carried her beat-up luggage to the shiny black SUV parked outside. The heat of the late-afternoon Tampa sun hit Jo at full force and she squinted in the sunshine, breathing in the faint scent of hibiscus and smouldering tarmac. Everything and everyone out here already seemed big, larger than life. Middle-aged women heavier than Jo wandered about the car park fanning themselves, and the cars all seemed to be double the size of the ones in England. Palm trees swayed slightly even in the languid breeze, and boys walked around with their jeans around their knees, hip-hop style. They clutched mobile phones to their ears and gesticulated wildly as they yelled to their friends. They looked all-American, in an Eminem way, and Jo felt as though she'd been airlifted in straight from *EastEnders*.

'It was great,' Jo said nonchalantly, as they began to drive to Longboat Key, the thin ribbon of land where Amelia was staying for the summer. As Jackson and Amelia pointed out tiny wooden houses and areas of deprivation Jo blinked, wondering why these places weren't mentioned in the guidebooks to Florida. Were these really part of the American Dream? They drove past orange trees ripe with fruit, vast shopping malls that Amelia promised they would visit, and just as Jo started to nod off Jackson showed her the impressive white Sunshine Skyway Bridge. As they got closer to Longboat Key, Jo noticed the local beaches were full of skinny teenage girls playing volleyball. They all looked preppy and perky, and Jo grimaced.

'This is home,' Amelia said happily, as the car pulled up outside a small, low block of flats. 'It's actually Granny's holiday condo, but since she only comes out in the winter the folks and I use it in the summer. This year Mummy and Daddy are on safari so I'm here all by myself "practising my tennis".' Amelia shot Jackson a coy, flirtatious look, and Jo looked at the two of them. There was definite chemistry, and Amelia was dressed in what everyone at school had called 'slutty casual'. The idea was that you didn't need to use much imagination to visualise her naked.

'Jackson's got a dinner thing at one of the golf clubs, so it's just you and me tonight.' Amelia looked at Jo slyly. 'I thought we could open a bottle of wine and catch up. I've not told you anything about my split with Charlie, and rumour has it you bumped into William not so long ago.' Amelia had a devilish look in her eye but Jo ignored her, taking in the view as they went in. Outside were spiky bits of dark green grass that led down to a small quay, and there was a lone heron strutting about looking like it didn't have a care in the world. Jo thought back to the pigeons that sat on the stairwell outside her flat and felt a million miles away from home. It felt good.

'So what did happen with Charlie?' Jo said, tearing her eyes away from the quay and focusing on Amelia, who'd poured herself a glass of wine and downed it in one.

'As you know I moved back home after I got my degree and didn't bother to get a job. It was Mummy's idea – she was convinced Charlie was about to propose and she told me that men like him didn't like "career women". But Charlie never seemed to be around. I was thinking about going travelling but Charlie wouldn't come with me – so I just, you know, watched daytime TV and did lots of shopping. One night I decided to drop in at Gigolo as a surprise, and went into a private room to find Charlie fucking two fifteen-year-old bottle-blondes next to a mountain of coke. It was kind of like a back-to-front roasting situation. A Charlie sandwich.'

Amelia's eyes went black as Jo's hands quickly covered her mouth in shock – even though she knew Charlie was a bastard, the mental image of Amelia walking in on him to find that was terrible.

'He tried getting out of it, of course, made some lame excuse about how he loves me and was only fulfilling a basic need, but there's nothing you can really say when you get caught out, is there? Especially if you've got your cock in one girl and another's tits in your mouth.' Amelia sighed. 'It was so common, really. And the galling thing was they weren't even pretty. They looked like girls who wouldn't even be able to be extras on *Hollyoaks* – you know the type – tarty, aspirational footballers' wives without the looks for it. I had to get myself tested for STDs and everything. It was so shameful. All I wanted to do was hide away – to stay in my bed until the pain stopped. I was gutted.' Amelia gave a little laugh and Jo could tell she was trying to hold back the tears. 'But Mummy made me realise that he wasn't worth it, and told me that if Charlie wasn't going to marry me I had to get on with my life. In the end Daddy thought it would be a good idea if I came out here for some rest and relaxation, and I've certainly been getting in the relaxation bit with Jackson. He's the perfect tonic for getting over Charlie, and it's definitely sorted my head out.'

Amelia poured some more wine and turned to Jo. 'And here you are, too. So what's the story?'

Jo took a long gulp from her glass of wine before filling Amelia in on what had happened with Joshua Garnet. As Jo told her how she had accidentally sent Madeline Turner knickers meant for Marina Stone, Amelia's mouth dropped open.

'But that's amazing. You were working for the man screwing London's coolest model since Kate Moss!' Amelia looked incredulous. 'Do you know how incredible that is? How close to the action you have been? It sounds like something out of a film ... Did you ever meet her?'

Jo shrugged. 'She phoned the office a couple of times and she was always a bit of a bitch, to be honest. I got the impression she loves herself.'

'If I looked like Marina Stone I'd love myself too,' Amelia said, looking at the tiny folds of skin on her stomach. Jo laughed at Amelia's frown. She was stunning and she knew it.

'If I looked like you I'd love myself,' Jo said, examining her pale white skin mournfully. 'Because I've been so busy I've not been looking after myself and almost all of my weight has come back, and I hate it, I really fucking hate it. I hate this flab, I hate my ruined career, and to be honest I'm starting to hate myself. I'm not surprised William didn't whisk me off my feet when he bumped into me in London. I look awful.' Jo normally didn't allow herself to wallow in self-pity but just this once she thought she deserved it. She hadn't the energy to be strong. Not tonight, not with her jet lag and alcohol-muddled brain.

Amelia poured Jo another glass of wine. 'Your hair isn't brilliant, I'll give you that,' she said, casting her eyes over Jo's hair, which hadn't been cut in months. 'But you lost all that weight before, and I'm sure it will be easier to do it again.' She fixed her usual, positive smile on her face and tried to make Jo see there was light at the end of the tunnel. 'All the magazines say it's easier to lose weight the second time around.'

Jo laughed. 'Ames, the journalists who write that crap make it all up. I can guarantee that whenever a journalist writes an article about losing weight she has never had to herself. They're all size eight – which is quite handy because that way they can fit into the fashion samples that are sent to the office,' she said, thinking of Araminta, Helena and

Lucy back at *Gloss* with jealous irritation. 'But I do want to get back to how I was before. I can't bear feeling so rubbish about myself.'

'Then come and work out with me. Come roller-blading on the cycle paths, play tennis at the academy, borrow my bicycle and run on the beach. You'll lose the weight in no time, I'm sure of it.'

Jo eyed her stomach and felt the raw band of skin where the waistband of her jogging bottoms was digging in. She knew her love handles were showing through her T-shirt, and she felt several folds of flab underneath her bra. Very soon she'd need to get some underwiring to hold them up, she thought, idly. Jo imagined herself running on the beach and her heart sank. She was exhausted – mentally and physically – from working on her career in London, and the thought of getting up early and working out while she was on holiday filled her with dread. But what did she have to lose by trying? At the very least she'd get a tan from spending so much time outside, and everyone knew that tans were slimming.

Jo sighed and couldn't bear to let Amelia down. 'OK, then. But give me a few days to relax, first – there's no way I'm going to try roller-blading while I have jet lag.'

Amelia hid her self-satisfied smile in her glass of wine.

Jo twisted in front of the full-length mirrored wardrobe in her bedroom and glared at herself. The expensive one-piece swimming costume she'd picked up at the Surf Shack did absolutely nothing for her, but then again, she thought, what skimpy piece of clothing would? Her stomach bulged through the thin black fabric, and the straps of the costume dug into the spongy flesh on top of her shoulders. Jo tried not to look at her ass, but she knew it was impossible to miss the doughy, dimpled mass of fat on top of her large thighs, or her flabby upper arms. Jo grabbed a towel from the pile on her dresser and wrapped it around her body before padding down to the pool. She'd been in Florida for three weeks and had her daily routine completely mapped out, with everything she did a deliberate attempt to either lose weight or relax.

Every morning Jo woke up and sat outside by herself, watching the sun slowly appear over the horizon, and breathing in the warm air that swept in from the Gulf of Mexico. After she'd waved to Harry and Sylvia, the silver-haired couple who lived in a glorious corner condo on the floor above, Jo would make her way down to the communal swimming pool. She swam forty small lengths, thinking of William the whole time, before letting the morning sun dry her lightly tanned skin. Even though her arms ached from breaststroke and her legs were like lead, she felt refreshed. Invigorated.

When Jo was dry she'd eat breakfast with Amelia, taking small mouthfuls of Florida oranges and grapefruits while Amelia feasted on crispy bacon and pancakes. Without fail Jo would eye Amelia's plate hungrily, and even though Amelia told her that a few rashers of bacon wouldn't hurt, Jo was determined to stick to a fat-free diet. It was severe, but the memory of Joshua's taunts and Debbie's catty comments spurred her on. Jo was going to do everything in her power to get down to a size ten — even if she had no control over her career she had control over what she ate, and how she worked out.

After breakfast Jo would jump on Amelia's second-hand bicycle to go to the supermarket. Publix was like any other American store — the aisles were full of brightly packaged, luscious junk food. Enormous bags of crisps sat alongside the largest variety of dips Jo had ever seen, and there were rows and rows of cake mixes, chocolate bars, cookie dough, frozen pizzas and types of pasta. The first time Jo had seen a bag of honey-and-mustard-flavoured sourdough pieces her mouth had actually watered, and to make it worse the smell of delicious store-cooked fried chicken made her stomach rumble loudly. Jo normally spent about twenty minutes every day examining the food, telling herself that the vibrant, shiny packets carried more calories than anyone should eat, but she still wanted it. At night she even dreamt about breaking into Publix and cramming the crisps into her mouth. It wasn't something she was proud of.

To force herself to buy fruit, salad and fish, Jo reminded herself of what she looked like in her swimming costume, and how she'd never be able to stand William seeing her like that. Every time she pictured her body naked but for the Lycra costume her eyes would get hot with prickly tears, and she made herself walk to the vegetable aisle, loading up her basket with corn on the cob, squash and salad.

But despite her weight Jo knew she was nowhere near as large as the majority of obese Americans who ate all their meals at McDonald's or Taco Bell. The first time an over-weight stranger had said hello to her Jo had eyed her suspiciously, but Amelia set her straight, telling her that Longboat Key was a small community where everyone was friendly. Jo compared this to the bitchy magazine world and wondered why she had stuck at it for so long. For the first time since she could remember she was fully relaxed, and although she loathed herself she didn't feel uncomfortable wearing shorts and vests, as ninety-five per cent of Longboat Key was made up of retired Americans who didn't give a damn what Jo looked like. She wondered why she hadn't allowed herself a holiday with her freelance money sooner.

In the afternoons Jo roller-bladed with Amelia, and they whizzed along the cycle paths up to St Armand's Circle, where they looked in the windows of exclusive designer shops for older ladies and laughed at the fashion. Every day they allowed themselves to spend ten dollars on a piece of junk jewellery, and every day they fell about laughing outside the shops, reminding themselves of the sales assistants' enthusiastic comments about how great their new pieces were. Like Amelia said, as she examined her fake Cartier ring over their daily lunch of Caesar salad (with no dressing for Jo), who needed taste when you had money, and who needed money when you could buy knock-off jewels for a couple of dollars?

When Jo and Amelia got back to the condo, Amelia would jump in the car and head down to the tennis academy to help Jackson teach twelve-year-olds, and Jo would cross the road to the beach. Longboat Key was made up of a single main road, with the Gulf of Mexico and the beach on one side, and the quay on the other, and Jo relished being so close to the water. For hours she would lay flat on her back savouring the empty stretch of white sand and the endless blue sky, and if she got bored she would flick through American editions of *Vanity Fair*, *Glamour* and *Cosmopolitan*. Jo idly wondered if it was worth trying to get some work on an American magazine, but she pushed the thought out of her head. She was here to relax, have fun and lose weight. And she was managing to do all three, even though she couldn't see how the weight was falling off her.

A few months later Amelia noticed that Jo's clothes were all too big for her, but Jo didn't want to know.

'You've lost weight, you know,' Amelia said absent-mindedly one evening as they ate a crab and lobster salad by the swimming pool. The stars twinkled over the Gulf of Mexico and Jo realised what a romantic setting it would have been if Amelia had been a man. Jo felt a sharp yearning for William, but she pushed it aside and tried to concentrate on enjoying what she was experiencing rather than wanting something else. Jo digested what Amelia had said and snorted with laughter. Clearly the moonlight had cast a flattering shadow over her body.

'It's sweet of you to say that, but I don't think I have,' Jo said sceptically, as Amelia ate a piece of walnut bread spread liberally with butter. 'I'm enormous.'

Amelia looked at Jo incredulously. 'You are joking, aren't you? Your clothes are pretty much hanging off you.' She leant over and pulled at Jo's light cotton T-shirt. 'What size is this?' she demanded, and Jo felt a flash of anger ripple through her. Why couldn't she relax and enjoy her supper? she thought. Why was Amelia bringing this up now?

'It's an eighteen,' Jo said, sullenly, and glared at Amelia to make a point. 'It's from Evans.'

Amelia looked satisfied and ate some more salad, chewing on a piece of lobster thoughtfully. 'I'd say it's at least two sizes too big for you. I wouldn't be surprised if you were a size sixteen now. Or even a fourteen.'

Jo looked at Amelia distrustfully. 'You can't seriously be suggesting I've dropped two sizes since I've been out here. Is that even possible?'

Amelia shrugged and speared a piece of crab on her fork. 'I don't know, but it looks like you have. I mean, all you do all day is work out or sunbathe, and I don't think a morsel of food has passed your lips unless you have checked that it has less than ten calories. You can't be eating more than a thousand calories a day. If that.'

Jo shook her head. 'I think I'm eating too much,' she said. 'And I feel really lazy – for hours every afternoon I sunbathe, and I could be working out in that time. In fact, I was thinking about joining that new gym in Sarasota. I know we're not here for that much longer but I think it will be worth it. I've got a craving to lift some weights ... it might help me shift some of this lard.'

Amelia rolled her eyes. 'Jo, look at yourself! Can you not see that you've lost loads of weight already?'

Jo shook her head and Amelia looked at her sadly. Jo's

eyes had turned to steel. 'I think you must have forgotten what I look like because I've barely lost any weight at all.' Jo cast her gaze over the swimming pool and tried to control the anger bubbling up inside her. She really didn't want to fall out with her best friend.

Amelia dropped her fork on her plate with a clatter and pushed her chair back away from the table. 'Right, I've had enough. Come with me.'

Amelia led Jo back to the condo and made her stand in front of a mirror, where Jo tried to look at everything but herself. 'Can you see your cheekbones?' Amelia asked pointedly. 'And look here,' she said, yanking down the neck of Jo's T-shirt. 'Look at your collarbone. You couldn't see it a month ago, but you definitely can now.' Amelia started pulling at Jo's clothes, doing a great Trinny and Susannah impression. Jo wondered at what point Amelia was going to cup her breasts and say that she needed a better-fitting bra.

Jo gave in and concentrated on her image in the mirror. She scowled. 'But look at my stomach. It's hanging over my shorts. Look at my legs, and, God, look at my thighs. I'm so ugly.' Jo sat on the bed and tried not to cry. Her hair was messed up from the chlorine in the swimming pool, and she could barely see her eyes, which she believed were still hidden within the fat above her plump cheeks. She felt so disgusted with herself.

Amelia sat down next to her and sighed, awkwardly putting her arm around her friend. 'I've not wanted to share this with you because I didn't want you to become obsessed. But I have a secret.' Despite herself Jo was interested – did she have diet pills? Laxatives? Even though she knew they were bad for her Jo was getting desperate. She absolutely had to lose some weight and maybe this was how Amelia managed to never put on a pound. 'They're in my bathroom. Do you want to see?'

Amelia came back into Jo's bedroom with her hands behind her back, and she produced some expensive-looking electric scales. Jo felt her heart sink — she'd have preferred diet pills, even though she knew William would have been disgusted with her for even thinking that.

'I think it's time we let the scales speak for themselves,' Amelia said, and Jo eyed them warily before burying her head in her hands. She didn't think she could stand the shame of Amelia seeing just how overweight she was. It would be on a par with her friend trying out some bikini wax strips on her — absolutely mortifying.

'I can't do it. I don't think I can bear knowing.'

'Jo, I really think you should,' Amelia said gently, and she put the scales on the floor and felt sympathy flood her body. She had read enough magazines to know that Jo had a distorted image of her body, and she wanted her friend to realise that everyone else could see a slimmer, more toned version of the girl she thought she was. 'How much did you weigh the last time you stood on a pair of these?'

'Sixteen stone,' she said sullenly, and she waited for a disgusted reaction from Amelia that didn't come. Amelia's face remained passive.

'I am willing to bet you have lost at least a stone,' Amelia said. 'And you know me, I'm never wrong. Come on, get on.'

Jo refused for about ten minutes, but when she realised Amelia was not going to leave her alone she slowly kicked off her flip-flops and climbed on to the scales. As well as hating herself she also hated Amelia for making her break her promise — despite her friend's earnest observations she was sure she hadn't lost any weight at all, and Jo didn't think she could bear knowing she hadn't lost a pound. Jo looked at the back of Amelia's head as her friend peered down at the display, and when Amelia didn't say anything she felt animosity run through her body.

'Well?' she said defensively, unable to keep the nervousness from her voice.

'I was wrong, I'm sorry.'

Jo stared at Amelia and felt a sudden hostility towards her. What did Amelia know about humiliation? Jo thought, as she took in the tiny denim hotpants and tight Abercrombie T-shirt that her friend was wearing. Nothing had ever gone wrong for Amelia – apart from the situation with Charlie – and that had only happened because Amelia was so nice and so trusting that Charlie had walked all over her. No, Jo concluded, that couldn't have been that humiliating. And it was nothing on Jo getting all her hopes up about losing weight and finding out she'd not lost any at all.

'You've lost nearly four stone.'

Jo looked up at Amelia in surprise and then looked down at the scales in shock. Without realising it, she'd got down to twelve stone.

Chapter Twelve

September 2004

'I can't believe you're going home. What am I going to do without you?' Jo said through her tears as she gave Amelia another hug.

'Hey, you'll be fine, just you wait and see. I almost wish I could stay, but I have to go. Daddy's already paid the tuition fees for my MA and he'll go mad if I don't go back home.' Amelia struggled out of Jo's grasp and surveyed her friend. In the time they'd spent together Jo had gone down to a size fourteen and was a happier, more confident version of the girl who had walked through arrivals clutching her handbag nervously. She was wearing beat-up Diesel jeans and a close-fitting T-shirt and she looked healthy. Mission accomplished. Amelia was proud of her, even though she had tears dripping down her face.

'I don't care about your dad. Drop out of college and get a job in Kilwin's ice-cream parlour,' Jo said with a pout. 'I'll get a job selling those handbags that people carry tiny dogs in and we can live out here permanently.'

Amelia grimaced. 'What, and face seeing broken-hearted Jackson for the rest of my life? No, thank you.' Amelia thought back to the previous week when she'd gently told Jackson she was going home. Despite him knowing theirs was only a holiday romance he seemed genuinely devastated when she'd told him she wasn't willing to have a long-distance relationship. Amelia hoped he'd get over it – his backhand had gone downhill since then and she couldn't bear it if he lost his job.

Amelia glanced at the TV screen that said her flight was about to board. 'I'm not forsaking my education for anything – not even for Kilwin's fudge-flavoured ice cream.'

'You know, I always wonder how my life would have turned out if I hadn't messed up my A-levels,' Jo said thoughtfully. 'I'd be at journalism college right now. I'd not know about the shady, shallow world of magazines, and I'd probably be having a whale of a time, living in digs and getting pissed every night.'

The girls stared at each other thoughtfully.

'But you know what, I'm glad I didn't go to university, and I'm even happier that I can stay out here for a bit longer while I find a place in Miami. Are you sure your grandmother doesn't mind?'

Amelia shook her head. 'Granny's not coming over until November and she's pleased to have someone staying in the condo when nobody is here. You're welcome to stay until you sort yourself out. Are you sure you're going to stick with Miami? Why don't you move to New York and get a staff job on a magazine? You know you're good enough.'

Jo shook her head. New York would have been too much like London, and after taking a long, hard look at her life Jo knew she needed a break from the rat race. When she finally admitted to herself that she'd lost weight and was on track to being the thin, sparkly Joanne Hill that she'd always wanted to be, she imagined what her life would be like when she got back to London. The thought of going back filled her with dread, and she suddenly realised that apart from wanting to have her revenge on Garnet there was nothing to go back for. She had no friends, and no love life – even though she knew William liked her, he clearly didn't have the feelings he once had for her. She was in love with him – and probably always would be – but he didn't feel the same way, and she just had to accept it somehow. On top of that Jo knew her career in London was finished, and she was damned if she was going to go from being Olivia Windsor, darling free-lancer of *Gloss*, to being another nobody trying to kick-start her career again.

The problem, Jo thought, was that she wasn't a nobody – Joshua Garnet had a personal vendetta against her – and she knew she'd not be able to get any work on a magazine in London if he could help it. Knowing how spiteful Joshua could be, Jo didn't doubt his threat for a second. What she had to do, she decided, was keep a low profile. There was no way she wanted Joshua Garnet keeping tabs on her, as she needed an element of surprise when she finally gave him what he deserved, whatever that might be. New York would have been a difficult place to work as Joshua had contacts crawling all over Manhattan, so Jo decided to live in Miami while trying to freelance for some of the bigger women's glossies. She thought it was time that Olivia Windsor tried making a name for herself in America.

Jo sighed and smiled at Amelia. 'You know, the whole point of freelancing is that you can do it anywhere, so why would I want to leave Florida?' She shot her friend a grin and looked down at herself. 'After all, I do have a tan to keep up.'

Amelia gave Jo another hug, and they both heard the call for the flight back to Heathrow.

'Let me know when you've got a place in Miami sorted,' Amelia said, giving Jo one final hug before picking up her immaculate Gucci hand luggage. She refused Louis Vuitton on the basis that Victoria Beckham and Jordan both used it. She flashed Jo a dazzling grin.

'I'm proud of you, you know,' Amelia said. 'You've come a long way, baby.'

Jo smiled, and she could feel tears pricking at her eyes again.

'I know. And thank you for the wonderful summer.'

Amelia laughed. 'Thank you for coming out to see me! Look, I've got to dash, but good luck.' She started to walk towards the gate, and just before she got there she spun round and beamed at Jo. 'Have a nice day, ya hear?' she said in a perfect American accent.

Jo grinned at her and walked towards the taxi rank to get a car back to Longboat Key. She had an apartment to find and a career to begin.

Jo watched him gulp down a cold can of Coke as he leant against a doorframe. Beads of condensation dripped down the side of the can and Jo smiled to herself. Right in front of her was what appeared to be the original Diet Coke-break man in the flesh – he was the American Dream, with blond hair, piercing green eyes and broad shoulders that tapered down to a tight bottom clad in baggy Levi's. If David Beckham had been raised on a ranch rather than in Essex even he wouldn't be as masculine as this waiter was. He was pure sex. As a customer made a joke he let out a laugh and Jo shivered with pleasure. And even though he hadn't noticed her amongst the bikini-clad blondes and gorgeous tanned guys that were hanging out at Ernie's Famous Deli – a fashionable 1950s-style diner where it was rumoured Britney had ordered three chocolate milkshakes in a row – Jo knew he could feel her eyes on him.

Jo shifted in her seat restlessly and tried to eat her pastrami on rye. It was near impossible – she was on a high from being close to one of the most handsome men she'd ever seen. He wasn't William – he didn't even come close – but when she'd tried to phone William at The Royal Oak to let him know she was staying in America she'd found out he'd moved on. He was out of her life for good, and she didn't know how to deal with that sense of loss. Luckily there were some distractions.

'Not hungry today, huh?'

Jo forced herself to tear her eyes away from the Adonis, and then shivered in disappointment when she saw the Latino-looking waiter standing in front of her with a bemused expression. His black hair curled on to his forehead and, while he was attractive, he had nothing on the blond waiter who had now begun to serve a group of giggling teenage girls. She shook her head and gave him a weak smile.

'Lemme know if I can get you anything else,' he said, and he gave Jo a megawatt grin before sauntering off. Jo followed him with her eyes and shook her head. She had to hand it to the South Beach serving staff – they really knew how to work the customers for their twenty per cent tips.

Jo had been hanging out at Ernie's Famous Deli on Ocean Drive in Miami for the last few days, ostentatiously working on her pitches for *Glamour* and *Seventeen*, but mainly watching the waiter, who she'd first noticed catching rays on the beach. She'd never seen anyone like him outside of a Hollywood blockbuster – he was so good-looking he didn't seem real. When Jo had tried to describe him on the phone to Amelia she could barely get the words out – he was as striking as Owen Wilson but as chiselled as Rob Lowe. He was Action Man, He-Man and Superman all in one. And as he served his customers with a winning smile he always, without fail, made girls blush and the gay guys grin. Nobody was immune to his looks, especially Jo.

Looks aside, Jo could tell he wasn't the brightest man in South Beach. But she didn't care. The intensity of her feelings surprised her – apart from William, Jo had never had a crush before, especially not one so carnal. It was almost as though by losing weight she had unleashed this part of her, and as the feelings swept through her body she surrendered to them. At night Jo imagined him stripping her clothes off and exclaiming that he had never been with a girl so sexy. Jo conveniently forgot about the loose skin and stretch marks on her stomach, that she still had cellulite and that her breasts had sunk low and lost their fullness. When she had the waiter, she thought, she would be somehow perfect. And, she said to herself with a tiny sigh as she heard him talking in his preppy, college-boy voice to a customer, she wouldn't let him speak. They wouldn't need conversation.

As he walked past her table, Jo quickly focused on the magazines in front of her and held her breath. Jo followed his back and bottom as he walked away, and she smelt a faint scent trail behind him as she breathed in. He smelt of expensive, musky aftershave and something else, something deeply masculine. Jo struggled to get a grip. She absolutely had to get some ideas down on paper, but the fluorescent lights on the art deco hotels outside made her head spin with excitement, and the blond waiter inside Ernie's made her knickers fizz. She had lost control, and it was down to being in Miami. She had allowed her emotions and lust to take over, and it felt good. Damn good.

The moment Jo had stepped into Miami International Airport she had felt like she'd arrived home. To her, the horseshoe design of the gleaming airport represented good luck, and as she'd carried her luggage to a cab she couldn't believe downtown Miami was so close, that she had picked the most perfect hotel. The Shore Club – *the* place to stay in Miami Beach – was everything Jo had fantasised about. The hot boutique hotel had a minimalist deco lobby complete with gorgeous, helpful bellboys, and Jo's room had a smooth stone floor, 400 thread-count bedding, a huge powerful shower, Molton Brown products and the fluffiest white towels she'd ever touched. Jo sat on her bed and looked out at the ocean happily, and she phoned for a butler who brought her a raspberry martini. She did everything she could to stop herself fantasising about William sharing the enormous bed with her.

Jo had decided to hang out at the Shore Club for a week while she found somewhere to live, and she emailed Lucy at *Gloss* a short, curt note telling her where she was and suggesting that the magazine would benefit from a hotel review. Lucy had responded with an over-friendly, nervous email asking Jo how she was, but she also added that *Gloss* would love a piece on the hotel with a restaurant review by Olivia Windsor. In return the magazine would pick up the bill, and Jo whooped with pleasure. She had Lucy wrapped round her little finger and was determined to milk her guilt for all it was worth. And if that meant *Gloss* – and more importantly, Joshua Garnet – picked up a $4,500 bill then even better. Jo had grabbed her purse and a copy of the *Miami New Times* and sat on the beach, organising appointments to see apartments on her recently purchased mobile phone.

The first apartment Jo had seen was so stunning she took it straight away without caring that there were roaches in the communal hallway and a tiny kitchen without an oven. The floor-to-ceiling windows had a fabulous view of the Atlantic Ocean, the furniture was low-slung and contemporary and, most importantly, the air-con worked. Jo paid for three months in advance and sat in her red and black living-room watching the sun setting over the Atlantic Ocean. She was, she thought, in heaven. If only the girls who had bullied her at school – especially Dominique – could see her now.

But despite being in a perfect apartment in what seemed to be a perfect city, Jo felt lonely, and she wondered if she'd find some friends to entertain her while she cracked the American freelance market. Getting commissioned on *Gloss* on her first day in Miami was only the start, and Jo was convinced she'd get some work on certain American magazines easily.

The only problem was, she was so exhilarated by Miami life that she couldn't focus, couldn't concentrate. The warm air brushed against her tanned skin like delicate kisses, and the scent of the city – the smell of sweat, sex and fun – made her feel like a carefree twenty-two-year-old, rather than the downtrodden girl who Joshua Garnet had walked over. And because of that she found she wasn't in the mood to work. She wanted to live for the moment, savour the different flavours and sounds of Miami, and find happiness as an all right-look-ing plump British girl. The moment Jo had seen the blond man walking on the beach she knew she was a goner. She absolutely had to meet him, so she followed him to Ernie's Famous Deli and became a regular who always ordered food but never seemed able to eat it because she was too in lust with their star waiter.

'You know, if you eat that sandwich we'll give it to you for free.'

Jo glanced up from her magazines and electricity ran through her as she looked into the green eyes of her blond waiter. She didn't know what to say and could feel the beginning of a blush rising up her neck. He sat down on the stool opposite her and smiled. His teeth were white and perfect.

'Gable,' he said, and Jo, who couldn't stop grinning, nod-ded at him.

'Right,' she said. Gable stared at her for a moment and then raised an eyebrow. Jo wanted to faint.

'And you are ...?'

Jo knew her face was bright red. 'Jo,' she said. 'I'm Jo, and I'm from London.' Jo didn't think she could speak. She couldn't believe the most gorgeous man she had ever seen was in front of her and asking her name. She tried desperately not to swoon – it was like meeting William for the first time all over again.

Gable leant back on his stool and looked so laid-back that Jo wanted to jump on him.

'If you just tried the sandwich you'd love it. Or are you, like, on a kind of diet where you look at food instead of eating it?' Gable looked genuinely confused and Jo wondered if he was joking. She quickly remembered people in Miami were deadly serious about looking good. The South Beach diet had not been named after the area for nothing.

'I want to eat it, but I just can't seem to do it,' Jo said in a squeak, hoping her voice wouldn't crack. 'I'm sure it's perfectly lovely.'

Gable let out a little groan. 'Oh, man, that English accent gets me every time. "Perfectly lovely" – you sound like Liz Hurley. Say something else ...'

Jo felt like she couldn't breathe. 'I ... I don't know what you want me to say.'

Gable burst out laughing. 'Sorry,' he said, clearly enjoying himself, 'I shouldn't laugh at your accent. It's cute.'

Jo gulped.

'You new to the area? You look like you are.'

Jo nodded. 'I've been here for about a fortnight,' she began, before spotting Gable's puzzled expression. 'Two weeks,' she clarified. 'I'm a journalist for a magazine back in London and I'm hoping to start writing for some mags out here.'

'Hey, that's cool. I'm an actor.'

Jo tried not to laugh out loud. Of course he was – he couldn't have been anything else.

'So why aren't you in LA?'

Gable took a long look at Jo before speaking. He seemed uncomfortable. 'I just wanted a change of scene,' he said. 'I lived out there for a while but, like, I wanted to get out of it for a bit. Take some downtime.'

Jo nodded earnestly. 'I know how that feels. I love London, but I need a break from it.' As she eyed Gable's face she felt her heart leap. She couldn't get over how perfect his features were, how sparkling his green eyes were, how every single bit of him complemented every other part. His nose was strong but not over-large, his chin defined, and he had cheekbones that any model would be jealous of. His eyebrows were perfect without looking plucked, his stubble a day old and sexy-looking, and his hair was immaculately tousled. If Jo had a camera with black and white film in it she could have taken a photograph of him that would have been hotter than a Calvin Klein advert. Jo wondered if he knew how good-looking he was, and if he could ever be interested in her.

'Do you—' Jo caught herself quickly, just as she realised she was about to ask him out. Did she dare do it? she thought. Did she have the guts to ask him for a drink? She took a deep breath and decided to give in to her physical reactions, to live a little. She wanted him, and even if he didn't want to get to know her further she had nothing to lose by asking Gable for a drink. Apart, she thought, from her pride.

'Do you want to come and have a drink with me some time?' Jo said quickly, looking down at the Formica table as her cheeks flushed red. When Gable didn't respond instantly she rushed to fill the silence. 'If you don't want to that's fine, I just thought it would be nice, and you're the first person to speak to me since I've been here, and—'

Gable interrupted her. 'Sure, that would be cool. How you fixed tomorrow night?'

Jo looked at him incredulously. He had said yes?

'Yes, tomorrow night is good for me,' she said, trying to keep her voice calm. Jo couldn't get over the fact he had just said yes. He said yes!

'Everyone's hanging at Mynt at the moment – want to go there?'

Jo nodded. 'Yes, sounds good,' she said, hoping she sounded relaxed.

'Cool. Meet me here tomorrow night at about nine and we can grab a cab,' Gable said, and Jo nodded, unable to speak or look at him. She started to gather up her magazines and notepads.

'See you tomorrow,' she said, before quickly glancing at Gable in disbelief. She had a date with the hottest man in Miami, and she didn't know how she'd managed it.

The next twenty-four hours passed in a whirlwind of shopping and make-up experimentation. After leaving Ernie's, Jo rushed back to her apartment to dump her stuff and to look in the mirror. As she assessed herself she couldn't believe she'd snagged a date with such a hot man. How had she succeeded? Her limp brown hair sat on her shoulders now, but it lacked shine, lacked body, and split ends and flyaway hairs stopped it from looking smooth. She needed an appointment at a hair salon, and fast, but she didn't have a clue where a decent place to go was.

As well as the hair issue, Jo realised she didn't have any clothes that fitted her properly. She was definitely a UK size twelve, but she didn't know what American size would fit her. Was she a US ten? A US fourteen? She needed to find a clothes shop that wouldn't baulk at the fact she didn't have silicone breasts, blonde hair extensions and thighs the width of pencils. She needed help, but there was nobody in the whole of Miami she could get advice from. She was on her own.

In a fit of inspiration Jo grabbed her mobile and phoned Sunshine Cars, asking them to take her to the closest and hippest salon the driver knew of. They pulled up outside a place called Mermaid on Lincoln Road and Jo stood at the counter nervously. The salon was painted a deep purple and funky house was pounding from the stereo. The mirrors were all smashed and stuck back together again, and the floor was painted dark silver. The other customers all had immaculate, salon-perfect hair or crazy haircuts Jo hadn't seen the likes of since she was sixteen and had spent the afternoon in Camden. She felt out of her depth and intimidated.

'Er, hello,' she whispered to the receptionist, who looked Jo up and down incredulously. She was probably a size four, Jo thought miserably, realising that even though she had lost loads of weight she still had a long way to go until she was as thin as some of the thinnest girls in Miami. 'I don't have an appointment, but I am having a hair emergency.'

The receptionist eyed Jo's hair disdainfully and smirked. 'Bobby's free,' she said in a New York drawl, and Jo was ushered towards a camp man with pink stripes in his ginger Anna Wintour bob. Jo wasn't sure she wanted Bobby to cut her hair but she didn't feel like she had much of a choice. She was desperate.

Bobby lifted a strand of Jo's hair up and held it towards the light. 'It's a mess, yeah?' he said more as a statement than a question, and Jo nodded, accidentally pulling her hair from Bobby's fingers. 'Where did you get this hair cut before?' Jo could hear a faint Latino accent in Bobby's voice, and she wondered if he had clocked that she was English. It was time to find out.

'Just a cool place in London,' Jo said. 'I've been growing out a style that I got when I was working on a magazine called *Gloss*,' she said, hoping she sounded more confident than she felt.

Bobby nodded knowingly and cracked a smile at her while pushing her into a deep leather chair. 'You want it short?'

Jo shook her head again, more vehemently this time.

'Absolutely not. Just a trim, and a ... a style. And maybe some colour? Some highlights or something?' Jo looked up at Bobby's Bagpuss-style ginger and pink bob and nervously bit her lip. 'Something subtle?'

Bobby stared at Jo's hair for the longest time and then cracked his gum. 'I will give you both highlights and low-lights,' he said, 'and I will not so much cut your hair as shape it. You will look divine.'

Two hours and $300 later Jo had to admit Bobby was right. Her hair had been lightly cut so that it was still long, but it framed her face and brushed against the top of her shoulders rather than just sitting on them. Jo's hair had been streaked with delicate strands of gold, honey and sun-kissed blonde, and then, to make the effect more dramatic, Bobby had added the finest lowlights of chocolate, mahogany and chestnut. Jo couldn't stop staring at her hair. She looked amazing, and her eyes shone a deep, velvety green.

'Oh, my God,' Jo said, as she raised her hand to her mouth in shock. Despite the broken mirror she could tell she looked a hundred times better. She looked almost pretty.

'It ain't bad, huh?' Bobby said proudly, as he gathered some of his colleagues to have a look.

'It's amazing.' Jo couldn't tear her eyes from her reflection. She looked so different.

'If you don't mind the suggestion, I have a friend who does eyebrows ...' Bobby's voice trailed off, and Jo raised her eyes from her reflection up to Bobby's before they both settled on her eyebrows. Jo peered at them carefully, and then saw two faint patches of pink appear on her cheeks. He was right – she did need some work done on her brows. They really were too thick, especially with this beautiful haircut.

'Just tell me where to go ...'

An hour later and Jo was leaning back in a chair while a man named Fred was expertly plucking hairs from Jo's eyebrows.

Her eyes watered as she felt the unfamiliar tingling sensation from Fred's fast, light plucks, but she couldn't wipe them as a woman called Serendipity was giving her a manicure.

'Hold still,' Fred commanded, as he looked at Jo's brows with an intensity that made her feel slightly uncomfortable. 'There, we are done.' Jo sat up and looked in the mirror and was shocked at the difference her new eyebrows made to her face. Somehow, Jo's eyes looked wider and more almond-shaped. The neat, perfectly arched brows made her face seem younger, fresher, and as Jo peered down at her newly painted pink nails and back up to her face she realised there was no other word for it. She looked groomed.

'You'll be the belle of the ball tonight,' Fred said happily, and Jo smiled. When she met Gable tomorrow night she hoped she would be, but she still had a night to get through and then a whole day of clothes shopping before she saw him again.

The next day Jo hit Miami with her guidebooks sitting in her new Mulberry bag. On Collins Avenue she bought Seven jeans at Barney's, glittery turquoise eyeshadow at MAC and some understated Paul Smith tops in Scoop. Jo then headed up to Lincoln Road, where she spent $300 in Chroma. She found a beautiful black sequinned mini-dress by a local designer called Stern, and the most gorgeous shoes she had ever seen. They looked slightly like the gold Manolos Jo had been coveting, but they were black with a rounded toe, 1940s-style straps and the tiniest crystals embedded into the heel. Even though they were $200 Jo couldn't resist them. She could even walk in them.

Jo practically skipped back to her apartment, swinging her bags as she walked and checking out her reflection in the windows of the cafés and shops she passed. If she didn't know who she really was, she thought, she could have passed for a girl on Bond Street or on the King's Road. And the best thing was, she thought, everything she had purchased was in a US size ten. She was a US size ten! Jo grinned to herself and decided that as soon as she got back to her flat she'd cut one of the labels out of her clothes and stick it on the wall. She had never, ever bought anything in a size ten before, and it was something she wanted to savour. But as she cut the label from her dress and pinned it to her noticeboard she suddenly felt her stomach tense. In the exhilaration of shopping she had pretty much forgotten that she had a date with Gable. And as she looked at her old watch nervously, noting that she had to get the strap tightened, she realised she only had four hours in which to get ready.

Jo began with a shower – she washed her hair with Bumble & Bumble and scrubbed her body raw with an exfoliator she had picked up from the Body Shop. Then she shaved, plucked and polished, liberally smoothing coconut moisturiser all over her body. Jo tried not to dwell on the dimples on her thighs, or the way her breasts hung low due to the amount of weight she had lost. She focused on her hair, which she straightened with new GHD tongs, and on her make-up, which she spent almost an hour on, using the turquoise eyeshadow as liner to bring out the colour of her eyes even more.

When Jo squeezed herself into her black sequinned dress and looked in the mirror she gasped. She barely looked like the Jo Hill she knew, and she felt liberated and drunk with possibilities. She was in Miami, nobody knew her, and she had a date with the hottest man in Florida. Jo blew a kiss at herself in the mirror and blushed.

But by the time she'd left Ernie's Famous Deli with Gable, Jo had lost some of her confidence. Gable had done nothing wrong – he'd held the door open for her as they had left the diner, and had helped her into the cab he had hailed to take them to Mynt – but he hadn't done anything right, either.

Apart from commenting on her 'bangs' (which she soon worked out meant her fringe) and her shoes, he had barely looked at her at all. He certainly didn't look at her as though he wanted to ravish her, and Jo couldn't work out what she had done wrong.

'I once had the most amazing conversation with Justin Timberlake in here,' Gable said, as he led Jo past the roped-off queue into Mynt.

Jo started to tell Gable about when she'd interviewed Justin for her school magazine, but he was so busy checking out the crowd that he didn't hear her.

'He was just the coolest. Turns out we knew loads of the same people from LA. Including,' he said, with a knowing wink, 'Cameron.'

Jo blinked and tried hard not to look shocked. Was Gable implying he'd slept with Cameron Diaz? Suddenly she felt stupid in her dress and new shoes. If Gable only spent the night with stunning A-list Hollywood actresses then she hadn't a hope in hell. Being a published journalist from London just didn't have the same kudos, and she knew it.

'Mojito?' Jo took her drink from Gable and looked around the bar. It was cool. The green walls seemed to give off a minty aroma, and deep red lamps hung from the ceilings, casting a decadent light over the beautiful, shiny, perfect clientele. Jo took a sip of her mojito and smiled. It was subtle, like the bar, and she had a fleeting memory of the first time she had seen Gigolo. Miami was laid-back cool, and Mynt captured that attitude. In comparison Gigolo and Winchester seemed like they were trying way too hard.

'Wanna sit?' Gable led Jo to a spare table and gazed at her intently. Jo felt a hit of lust rush to her knickers and she wondered if Gable could feel their sexual attraction too. By the way he was staring at her she couldn't imagine that he wasn't experiencing it. 'So tell me about yourself,' he said.

Jo wondered where to begin. As she filled Gable in on her school-days, on the time she spent at The Royal Oak ('They served partridge? That's a real bird?') and how she had pulled the wool over everyone's eyes at *Gloss* she could sense his enthusiasm for her increase. He slapped his thigh and laughed several times, and Jo grinned. She hadn't realised her life was so funny.

'Man, that sounds like something out of a film,' he said excitedly, and Jo smiled at him. She supposed it did in a way. 'So you're going to go back to London and have revenge on this Joshua?'

Jo nodded and gulped down most of her mojito, trying not to grin at Gable's American-speak. Revenge was definitely the plan, even though she didn't know how she was going to do it yet.

Gable looked her up and down. 'You know, I just can't imagine you as some fat ugly ducking,' he said. 'I mean, you're not beautiful, sure, but you're not *that* bad. Which is something, because everyone knows English girls don't look after themselves properly.'

Jo felt Gable's words hit her violently and her eyes began to sting. Gable didn't think she was beautiful? Anger rose up inside her as she thought about the money that she had spent getting ready for this date, and the time and effort she had put into losing weight. She didn't want to date someone who didn't think she was stunning, did she?

'Yes, it's a shame that us English girls are too intelligent to spend all our time grooming ourselves. Why, if we did we'd nearly look as perfect as you,' she said, sarcastically. Gable didn't hear her deadpan voice, though, and nodded enthusiastically.

'You got it,' he said. 'Looking like this has taken years of work.' Jo looked at his body and tried to work out what he meant. His muscles, defined underneath a tight white T-shirt, weren't that impressive. Compared to William, she thought, they weren't amazing at all, and she felt as though she had been put under a cold shower. The more he spoke, the less attractive he became. 'You wouldn't believe the pain I've gone through.'

Jo looked at Gable – who was technically the most stunning man she had ever seen, even though she preferred William – and she felt disdain at his American slang, his self-centredness and the way he didn't get irony. Jo hadn't realised that men could be bimbos too, and she felt a pang for William, who was rougher around the edges and could have a conversation, too. She forced herself to finish her mojito and went to the bar to get several more for both of them. Once she was drunk she'd find him less irritating.

Four hours later Jo and Gable were wandering home, singing JLo songs at the top of their voices and stumbling into each other. Every time Gable's hip brushed against hers Jo felt waves of lust vibrate through her body and when she could stand it no longer she grabbed hold of Gable's waist, walking with her head against his chin. He smelt salty, masculine, and she told herself to ignore the fact his face was baby soft without his usual designer stubble. She tried not to think about how William's bristles had rubbed her raw when he had kissed her, and how much she had liked it.

'Way over there,' Gable slurred, gesturing at the ocean, 'is England. That's, like, where you're from.' Gable prodded Jo in the stomach and even though she was drunk she still recoiled slightly. She was very aware of the layer of fat that separated her skin from the abdominal muscles she knew she had underneath. 'Don't be fooled by the rocks that you've got, you're still, you're still Jo from the block,' he sang in an off-key voice and Jo smiled. It was true, in a way: despite her glamorous haircut and expensive dress she was still the same old Jo Hill. They stopped to look at the Atlantic Ocean rippling on the beach, and Jo looked up at Gable as he stared at the sea. It was a perfect romantic moment, and Jo knew it was time.

'Gable,' she said softly, as she positioned her body in front of his. Jo pushed her hips against Gable's groin and then she wrapped her arms around him, smiling as Gable hugged her back and drew her into his body to keep her warm. His body was hard against hers, and Jo ached to feel his chest through his T-shirt, to run her hands down his washboard stomach to the top of his jeans. However, the hug was a friendly, platonic gesture, and Jo felt impatience sear angrily through her body. What was up with this man? she thought. Why didn't he get her?

'One day when I'm old I'm going to come back to the beach and stand right here,' Gable said in a husky voice. 'I'm gonna remind myself of how young and ambitious I was, and I'm gonna look back through my life to see how far I have come.'

Jo shut her eyes to prevent them from rolling in exasperation. She supposed Gable was being romantic, was trying to tap into Jo's determined, career-hungry side, but it wasn't having the desired effect. She didn't want American-style romance that sounded like something from a dumbed-down version of *Dawson's Creek* – she wanted sex. She didn't want to be a twenty-two-year-old virgin any more.

'That's sweet,' Jo murmured into Gable's T-shirt, and she wondered if she should just go for it, if she should kiss him rather than waiting for him to kiss her. Jo stepped back and stared at Gable until he moved his focus from the waves to her, and just as he began to look confused Jo moved closer to him, swooping in and placing her lips on his. Before he had a chance to realise what was happening, Jo was kissing him, and in a moment of absolute daring for her she darted her tongue into his warm, mint-flavoured mouth. Through her drunken haze she briefly wondered why she wasn't as turned on kissing Gable as she had been with William, but she forced the thought to one side and began to move her hands from Gable's waist to his bottom, and then to the front of his thighs. She wondered if she would feel his erection through his jeans.

Gable suddenly pulled away, and he stared down at Jo incredulously. 'Jo ...' Gable ran his hands through his hair nervously, as Jo felt her heart sink. He didn't fancy her. He had a girlfriend. He had a wife.

'Oh, man ...' Gable began pacing up and down the deserted road and Jo felt embarrassed. What was wrong with her? Was she still too fat? Too ugly? All of Jo's drunken confidence fell away and she felt vulnerable and exposed. She felt like an idiot.

'Look, I should have told you, I had no idea you felt that way, that you thought this was a date.'

Jo couldn't speak. She could taste bile in her mouth and she wondered if she was going to throw up. Suddenly she felt dizzy. She stared at Gable mutely and burned with embarrassment, and felt stupid for thinking that a man would ever fancy her, and that she could ever pull a man so beautiful as Gable.

Gable moved slowly towards Jo and reached for her hand, raising it to his lips and kissing it gently. Jo felt her heart leap, and she wondered if she had misunderstood him, if maybe she had just come on too strong. What was it that Americans had? Bases? Maybe she had jumped over some bases and scared him off, she thought. Maybe he did like her but she had just been too brash, too British about it.

Jo looked up at Gable hopefully, but she could tell by his discomfort that he definitely didn't fancy her. He looked at her guiltily and tried to crack a grin.

'I'm sorry, babe, but I'm more into men. I'm gay.'

Chapter Thirteen

Jo was people-watching on the beach, comparing the tired, lined bodies of retired domino players to the sleek, nut-brown limbs of roller-bladers. She looked down at her own tanned thighs and wondered why being slimmer than she'd ever been before didn't make her as happy as she'd hoped. She gazed out to the ocean and remembered how unhappy she'd been in London, how lethargic eating junk food had made her, and how miserable she'd been every time she'd dressed in the morning and found her clothes were tighter than they'd been the day before. Jo admitted to herself that she'd finally learnt the value of moderation – that eating one bar of chocolate wouldn't make her fat, but that eating as many as she wanted to in a row would ensure that the pounds piled back on. As if to prove a point to herself Jo bought a small ice cream from a man who was walking around with a cool-bag slung low on his shoulders. As she chose her cone he winked at her, and she smiled. If the wedding ring on his finger was anything to go by, at least he was straight.

Jo's mouth watered as she ripped of the paper on the ice cream – it had been months since she had eaten anything sugary apart from fruit – but just as she stuck her tongue out to scoop up the soft, gooey vanilla cream she suddenly found she had lost her appetite.

Gable was standing over her, his head blocking the sun and his blond hair burning like a halo around his head.

'I've been looking for you since for ever,' he said, slumping down on the white sand and looking at her casually. 'I worried when you ran off the other night, but hey, you're cool, so I'm glad I didn't get search and rescue out.'

Jo wondered if it would be considered rude to just stand up and walk away from him. She decided she didn't care and started to pick up her brand-new Kate Spade.

'Hey, not so fast,' Gable said, the sunlight making his eyes glitter. 'Don't you want to chat about what happened?'

Jo looked down at the sand. 'Gable, look – you're gay, I didn't know at the time, but I do now, so what's there to talk about? Why do you Americans always have to analyse everything? There's nothing to discuss.'

Gable grinned, and he leant back in the sand. He looked relaxed and happy and it maddened Jo. 'There's loads to "discuss",' he said, eyeing a group of twenty-something men who were throwing a frisbee to one another. Jo didn't think any of them were remotely attractive – they all had arms like pipe-cleaners and thin, brittle chests. 'The question is, why are you Brits so uptight when it comes to sharing your feelings?'

Jo's face burned. She supposed she deserved that, but she was still too mortified from trying to kiss him to admit it.

'Even if we did spend a couple of hours analysing every single part of the evening – right up to the point where I threw myself at you – what good would it do either of us? Or do you just want to relish the memory of an English girl who was too thick to know a gay man when she was speaking to one?'

Gable looked out at the ocean for the longest time, and just as Jo was wondering if she had offended him he spoke.

'I apologise for leading you on,' he began, 'if that's what I did, but I'm not going to apologise for playing it straight.' He turned to look Jo in the eyes, and once again Jo was struck by just how gorgeous he was. He was breathtaking, even when he looked sad. 'If I thought you liked me like that I'd never have gone out with you – I thought you were just a lonely English kid who was looking for friends. I had no idea you were nursing a crush on me.'

Jo looked at her melting ice-cream cone and she licked it cautiously. Like much of the food in America it didn't taste of anything – it looked great, but there was no flavour.

'I don't have a crush on you any more,' Jo said, and the moment the words left her ice-cream-covered lips she knew it was true. After spending the evening with Gable her attraction for him had begun to wane, and now, sitting next to him and knowing he was gay, she felt nothing for him at all, just embarrassment at her misjudgement.

Gable grinned. 'So can we be pals now?' he asked her, and Jo thought about it. Since that night, Miami had lost some of its sparkle – it had gone from being a place where you could make all your dreams come true to being just another city, albeit one with palm trees, fantastic beaches, and the coolest laid-back vibe Jo had ever known. As Jo finished her ice cream she realised just how much she would like a friend in the city, and even though Gable wasn't William he did seem like a lot of fun. She had decided that as well as working hard she wanted to start playing hard, too, and Gable would be the perfect partner-in-crime – especially if he knew all the doormen at the hottest bars in South Beach.

'We can,' Jo said, 'but I want you to explain to me why you didn't tell me you were gay to begin with.' Gable eyed her warily and Jo could tell it was a subject he didn't want to talk about. She grinned and decided that if they were going to be friends she needed to know what the score was. 'You can tell me over dinner.'

At Tiger that evening – a new Thai place that had just opened up on the beach – Jo and Gable sat at a table and studiously read their menus. The restaurant had fake tiger-skin walls, and the menus were fur-lined to match. Rainbow-coloured spotlights lit up the dark wooden tables, and even though they were thousands of miles from the jungle, the restaurant had an exotic, humid feel to it. Jo had never seen a restaurant like Tiger before, and she resisted the temptation to stroke the wall behind her. She didn't want to look uncool.

'I'm going to take the beef salad,' Gable said to the waiter, and Jo looked at him in surprise. The menu was full of delicious-sounding dishes, and Jo could barely make up her mind about what she wanted. The meal Gable had chosen – sliced beef with cucumbers and tomato – was possibly the blandest, most low-fat choice on the menu. Jo had a suspicion that it had been included by the chef for stick-thin blondes – the type that were sometimes forced into eating mouthfuls of food by their partners who got sick of paying for plates of food that were only ever played with.

The waiter turned to Jo expectantly. He had a sweet, shy smile and Jo beamed at him.

'I'll have the king prawns with garlic and pepper, the coconut rice, some chicken with lemongrass and a couple of vegetable spring rolls, please.' Jo's mouth began to water, and Gable smiled at her.

'I can't remember the last time I was with a girl who ate a proper meal,' he said ruefully, as Jo was struck again by how beautiful he was, especially with the hot-pink lights catching his face. But despite his Viking features and striking green eyes, Gable began to look uneasy, and Jo realised that underneath his perfect, polished features there was something inconsolable, something that wasn't that attractive. She wondered what was wrong.

'So tell me about LA,' Jo said, as she bit into a complimentary prawn cracker. Almost unexpectedly it tasted of
prawns and chilli, and Jo could feel the slight oiliness of the
cracker on her tongue. She couldn't remember the last time
she had eaten something fried, and it tasted perfect.

As Gable thought about LA his face lit up. 'LA is totally
amazing,' he said, and Jo grinned at his enthusiasm. Maybe he
wasn't in a quiet mood after all. 'It's the shallowest, vainest,
bitchiest place in the entire world and I love it. I dig the attitude, the fact that if you want to be a waiter you have to
pass auditions against other models and actors, the way that
even if you're the hottest up-and-coming actor you're still
treated like a piece of shit by someone higher up than you.
It's dog eat dog and it's great – so long as you play the game
properly.' Gable looked at the basket of prawn crackers with
mild disgust.

'It sounds like hell on earth to me,' Jo remarked.

Gable smirked. 'Oh, it is. It's truly offensive. The first
time I was out there I was eaten alive. It wasn't cute. But I
think I know how to play the game now. I'm heading back
soon and when I do I'm going to be a different person, one
who has the bright lights of Hollywood chasing him rather
than the other way around.'

Gable picked up his knife and fork and began to cut up his
tender grilled beef into tiny pieces. Jo barely noticed him do
this as she marvelled over her prawns – they were possibly
the most delicious things she had ever eaten; they were suc-
culent, juicy and full of flavour.

'But how are you going to do that?' Jo said, thinking of
her own life in London, and how desperate she'd been to get
a job on a magazine.

Gable stopped eating, and after a pause he flicked a small
photograph of a nondescript man across the table and Jo
picked it up. She looked at it with interest.

'That was me when I first moved to LA.'

Jo examined the grainy photograph of a dark-haired man with bad teeth and looked up at Gable. She could see no resemblance between the two — Gable was the complete opposite of the man in the photograph.

'But . . .' she began in disbelief. 'How can this be you?'

Gable toyed with a piece of cucumber on his plate and sighed. 'It's a long story.' He ate the cucumber and then started cutting up an already sliced piece of tomato. He put it in his mouth gingerly and swallowed. 'I used to be called Simon.'

Jo looked at Gable incredulously and he grinned at her, displaying perfect white teeth.

'You remember when we were at Mynt that night and I told you that your life was like a film?' Jo nodded. 'What I meant was that your life was almost as bizarre as mine. You see, when I wasn't washing up dishes in dirty kitchens I was trying to audition. When I say "trying" I mean just that — do you know how hard it is even to get the chance to audition in LA? You get open auditions, where hundreds and hundreds of people go, but most casting people only see people with agents, and getting an agent is practically impossible. Even more so if you're gay and you looked like I did. So I finally got a meeting with an agent — but she told me that I didn't have the looks to be a leading Hollywood actor. She picked up that I was gay and told me I'd never be the next Orlando Bloom, only a Rupert Everett, one without the looks, the accent or the talent. She told me all of this in the nicest possible way, and I was grateful, but it didn't put me off wanting to be an actor, it only made me more determined.'

Gable took a long sip on his mineral water and assessed Jo. 'So far so similar, wouldn't you agree?' he said, and Jo nodded. His life did have some strange parallels with hers.

'I was nursing my wounds and wondering what I was

going to do when a new show – *Nip/Tuck* – came on TV. It was like a sign from God. I decided to move to Miami, get some plastic surgery, and start acting straight. I told myself I'd sort myself out, turn into a heart-throb and move back to LA to start again.' Gable's eyes glittered in the pink light. 'Because, after all, what is the point of being an actor if you can't reinvent yourself?'

The waiter came to take away their plates of cold, uneaten food, and Jo stared at the photograph of Gable in amazement. She didn't know what to say for the longest time, and just as Gable began to look uncomfortable at feeling so vulnerable and exposed, Jo spoke. Her cheeks were flushed.

'You must want to be an actor very much,' she said.

Gable nodded earnestly. 'I do. I really do. And I am so sorry that I didn't tell you I was gay, but nobody out here knows. If I was still Simon then I'd have told you in a flash, but I'm Gable now, and as far as South Beach is concerned Gable is a straight, cute guy who is planning on moving to Hollywood to be an actor.'

Jo smiled. 'So tell me about the surgery.'

Gable nodded and took another sip of his drink. 'I was scouring magazines trying to work out what I wanted to have done, when I came across a photograph of a Swedish soccer player in some tight Calvin Kleins – have you heard of Freddie Ljungberg? Plays for an English soccer team called Arsenal?' Jo nodded – Freddie Ljungberg was gorgeous, and suddenly Jo realised that Gable looked very much like him. 'I ripped the advert out of the magazine and took it to my surgeon, who said that if I wanted to look like him I'd need a lot of work. My chin and nose were first, and then I had my teeth straightened and whitened. After that I had Botox in my forehead, collagen in my lips, and cheekbone implants. I've had my ears pinned back, and I work out at the gym for two hours every day. My hair is professionally done so that you can't tell I'm not a natural blond, and I top up my sunbed tan by spending as much time as I can on the beach.'

Jo recalled the image of Freddie Ljungberg nearly naked in the Calvin Klein advert and looked at Gable – if anything, Gable was better-looking than the footballer. 'Do you think it was worth it?'

Gable nodded at the photograph of him as Simon. 'I'd say so, wouldn't you? I knew that if I wanted to make it I couldn't make it as nerdy little Simon Lynott – I knew I had to look spectacular, and even though it has cost me thousands of dollars on credit and months of pain and bruising I'm happy with the results. I look like the man I feel like I am inside, and now people think I'm straight – as proven by the number of girls at Ernie's who check me out – I feel like I could take on Hollywood and win.'

Jo stared at Gable and could feel the beginning of an idea creeping through her body.

'I wonder if—'

Gable interrupted her. 'If you're thinking about having surgery I wouldn't even go there. Jo, you're a naturally cute girl. Sure, you're not a model, but since when have journalists needed to look that hot? I didn't have a choice – all actors have to be devastating in the looks department – but you do. You don't need surgery.'

Jo thought back to *Gloss*, and how every girl who worked there was stunning, from Rachel on reception to Lucy, who was cool, mysterious and could have been a model with her huge grey eyes and long, lithe limbs.

'I'm willing to bet you could rise up the ladder on a magazine with your talent alone – you have a slender body and an intelligent face, and I'm sure you have more feature ideas in your little finger than any model would have in their entire lifetime. If anything, not being supermodel-hot means you'd be taken more seriously.'

Jo picked up her drink and stared into it. As much as she wanted to believe what Gable was saying, she knew that talent alone didn't cut it in the magazine world, and even though she looked a hundred times better than she had done when she was at *Gloss* she wasn't sure she was pretty enough. She wasn't sure she was sparkly enough.

'Besides,' Gable said, gesturing for the bill. 'Since when have freelancers had to worry about what they look like? I thought the whole point of working from home meant you didn't have to brush your hair or even get out of your pyjamas if you didn't want to.'

Jo grinned. He was right. She ignored the tiny voice inside her head that said that she'd eventually want to work in an office again – running a magazine rather than going on coffee errands – and told herself plastic surgery was out of the question. After all, Madeline Turner hadn't had cosmetic surgery to get where she was, had she? Jo felt a wave of anger rush through her. No, Madeline hadn't needed surgery – she'd married the boss instead.

March 2005

Jo finished the last sentence of the email she was writing and yawned. A quick look at the clock on the laptop told her it was three in the morning and she rubbed her eyes. If it hadn't been for the sound of the surf sliding up the beach or her tiny silver laptop placed on the smoked-glass dining-table, she could almost have imagined she was back in London, frantically thinking up pitches before going to work as Garnet's slave the next morning. Jo quickly reread the email and felt a familiar buzz rush through her body – working for magazines gave her a high better than any drug could have done, and she hadn't realised how much she missed that hit until she started writing again.

For the last six months Jo had been busy establishing herself in the American magazine market, and Gable was busy in Hollywood, where he'd landed an agent and a massive part in a film almost as soon as his plane had hit the tarmac in California. As he waited to find out if he'd got the lead in another big blockbuster, he'd flown back to Miami to see Jo, and she had made sure she made the most of her new best friend being in Miami. He wasn't Amelia, who she could confide anything to, or William, who she still yearned for late at night, but he was a great friend – easy, relaxed and happy in his skin.

'Are you sure about this?' Jo asked him, and Gable nodded. 'You really want me to pitch this idea?'

Jo looked at her email to Lucy at *Gloss* and reread it. During a heavy night at Oblivion for Gable's homecoming, Jo had told him how much *Cosmopolitan* had liked the 'Help! I just came on to a gay man!' piece she'd written as soon as they'd made up. Gable had suggested she write about the culture of plastic surgery in Miami for a magazine back in England as an off-the-cuff remark, but something had clicked in Jo, and she realised there was a whole scene in the city that British magazines would lap up. When Jo said that she was still writing for *Gloss* – small pieces mainly, on fashion trends coming out of America – Gable had asked her if there was any reason that Lucy or Madeline Turner wouldn't want an article highlighting the growing inclination for cosmetic surgery in America. Jo couldn't think of one, and when she'd suggested it in an email, Lucy had, as usual, gushed over her idea. Jo supposed that Lucy was still feeling guilty about how she'd let Jo down, but she didn't care. As much as she hated her, Lucy was still her main contact at *Gloss*, and this was business. One day she'd make sure Lucy apologised properly, but in the meantime Jo had a career to develop, and that meant using whatever contacts she had, regardless of what she thought of them personally.

As a result of Jo's idea, and the fact that 'Olivia Windsor' was now based out there, *Gloss* had decided to do a Miami special, with a large section on plastic surgery. Lucy had asked Jo if she knew of anyone out there who had undertaken surgery to make his or her life better, and after a few drinks Jo had asked Gable, telling him that if he'd like to share his story with *Gloss* readers it would be completely anonymous. Gable had nervously agreed, but now Jo was about to send her pitch over to Lucy he didn't seem so sure.

'What if they find out who I am? My career will be in tatters before my first film comes out. I'll be a laughing-stock!' He walked around Jo's living-room and Jo was struck by how camp he was in private. When they were in public nobody would have guessed that Gable preferred men, but in the privacy of their own homes he could be completely himself – and he was almost a sillier, younger, happier version of the serious, professional man that he became in the top bars in Hollywood.

'Look, I've changed your name, and I've said you based your look on Thierry Henry rather than Freddie Ljungberg—'

'Who?' Gable interrupted Jo.

'He's French. Black. Sexy. He plays for Arsenal too, but—'

'He plays for the same team?' Gable looked at Jo in horror, and she sighed.

'We could change it to Michael Owen if you like.' When Gable looked none the wiser Jo smiled at him. 'Or David Beckham?'

Gable's eyes lit up. 'Ooh, yes, please,' he said, and Jo bit back a laugh. Even though the piece was anonymous Gable was still incredibly vain about it. Jo made the changes and looked at him. Gable was now sitting on the red and black sofa, staring into the distance.

'Once I send this, Lucy will cream herself over it. You do know that, don't you? Once this is in her in-box you'll have to do this interview with me.'

Gable nodded. 'If this helps you out I'm happy to do it,' he said, and Jo looked at him.

'Are you sure?'

Gable stared at Jo and then broke out into a wide grin. 'Of course I am, darling,' he said. 'Send it and let's send your career into orbit.'

Jo pressed 'send', and she imagined Lucy sitting in the office, reading her email and squealing with pleasure. Jo had to admit that the pitch was incredible. She had suggested that she interview a previously unknown Hollywood actor who had landed a leading role in a blockbuster because of his good looks, which were achieved through cosmetic surgery and full-on sessions in the gym. The piece would not disclose who the actor was – Gable's career would have been in shreds if anyone ever guessed he hadn't been born looking like a heart-throb – and in return the actor would give an exclusive interview to *Gloss* about his physical insecurities. It was tantalising stuff. The tabloids would all want to syndicate the article, and the gossip websites such as Hecklerspray and Holy Moly would spend days trying to work out what Hollywood actor had spent $100,000 on surgery. So long as his surgeon never disclosed the work he had done on Gable – and he wouldn't, as he had signed a NDA that would cost him millions if he talked – Jo would have the biggest splash of her career.

'It's gone,' Jo said ominously, and she joined Gable on the sofa, mentally working out the time difference and realising that it was still only the morning in London. 'So how is it all really going in LA? I'm really missing you, you know,' she said, meaning it. Since Gable had gone back to the West Coast, Miami had lost some of its allure. Even though she had a wide circle of friends who hung out at the same clubs every night, without Gable by her side Jo felt a little bit out of place. She had started to think about returning to London, but Jo still didn't know how she was going to get her revenge on Joshua Garnet. Until she knew what she was doing, she thought, she would have to stay in Miami. Jo grinned to herself. Not that it was such a horrible thing to have to do, now she was a UK size ten and the girl she had always wanted to be.

Gable took another slug of his vodka and smiled. 'LA is amazing,' he said, putting his glass down on the floor and curling himself up on the sofa. 'Everyone's talking about me, about how I suddenly appeared and landed the part in the new Cameron Crowe film. Apparently Keanu was devastated,' Gable said. 'He thought the part had been specially written for him.'

Jo shook her head in amazement. She still couldn't believe Gable was about to become a player, that he was name-dropping Keanu Reeves into conversation. 'My agent has been fantastic since the moment I walked into his office. He's got me screen test after screen test, has hooked me up with Violet Compton – you know, that girl who is going to be playing Jessica Alba's little sister in Ang Lee's new picture – and we're quite the celebrity couple,' he said, smugly. 'The paparazzi love us,' he said, and Jo burst out laughing.

'I know!' she said, and she grabbed a copy of *US Weekly* from her dining-table. 'Check you out!' Jo giggled, throwing the magazine to him.

Gable stared at his image in the pulpy magazine and laughed quietly to himself. 'It's a dream come true, you know,' he said. 'All that pain, hard work and cost is starting to pay off. I'm a Hollywood actor,' he said, looking at Jo intently. 'And I'm going to Leonardo di Caprio's wrap party next week. Because he asked me to.'

Gable shook his head in disbelief and Jo gave him a massive hug. Tears began to fill his eyes and Jo couldn't remember ever having felt so proud of anyone else before.

'You've made it,' she said, and she tried not to think about her own career. True, she had enough freelance work to keep her in expensive clothes and a luxury condo, but it still wasn't enough for her. Jo wanted to be at the top of her game, and although she'd been in discussions with the *Guardian* about having her own column in one of their supplements, she didn't want to do it as Olivia Windsor, but as Jo Hill. Unfortunately she had backed herself into a corner, and she knew that the *Guardian* would never believe her if she suddenly said she was Olivia Windsor, and that it was she and not her *nom de plume* that owned Platinum Consulting. Jo knew she had to find a way to break into the magazine world as herself, but she couldn't think of how to do it. Jo knew it was hopeless while Joshua Garnet would still remember who she was.

As Jo went into the kitchenette to fix them more drinks her email bleeped, and after she had poured them both healthy measures of vodka she walked over to her laptop, trying to ignore Gable's eyes boring a hole in her back. She secretly hoped he was admiring her new black Chloé top, too.

'Well?' Gable yelped, both excitedly and nervously all at once. 'Is it that Lucy girl? Does she want my interview?'

Jo sat down and read Lucy's email.

'She says they'd love an interview with you,' Jo read out happily, and she looked at her friend who had turned white under his tan.

'But it will be anonymous, right? It's gotta be anonymous or the deal is off.'

Jo laughed. 'Of course it will be,' she said. 'I'll make you ten years younger, as straight as an arrow, a womaniser, a former soap star and a model all in one. Nobody will ever guess that Gable Blackwood, star of *Fire Crossing* and boy-friend of Violet Compton, is the king of cosmetic surgery.' Jo grinned and turned back to her laptop, and Gable grunted.

'I trust you with my life,' he said, and Jo nodded distract-edly. 'What's up?' he said to her, walking over to the table and picking up his fresh drink. 'Is there a problem?'

Jo shook her head and turned to Gable, biting her lip. As much as she loved Gable she wished Amelia was here.

'I suggested in my pitch that *Gloss* gets a real-life account of someone who has had a breast enlargement to show just how painful it is . . .' Jo began, and when she saw Gable look-ing serious she averted her eyes and continued. 'You know – to balance out all the "surgery is good" stuff. The thing is, though . . . Lucy has asked me if I want to do it. She says she doesn't expect me to want to, but if I do then *Gloss* will pick up the tab. Joshua and Madeline have approved the budget already.'

Jo's eyes shone and for a moment Gable felt nervous at what he saw. The living-room was filled with a tense silence, and Jo took the opportunity to look down at her chest. Were her breasts really that bad? Did she really want to change them? For months Jo had been unhappy with how low her breasts hung. She wore Wonderbras pretty much every day to keep them high, but they seemed almost too soft, too deflated, to be what the media portrayed as 'sexy'. Jo had recently taken to checking out other girls' cleavages in bars, and without fail she always felt a cold chill rush down her spine when she realised that almost every other girl had a pert, full chest, and in comparison she was flat, invisible. Jo was used to being the ugliest girl in a crowd, but the little voice in her head was getting louder. Why shouldn't she have natural-looking breasts rather than the ones she had ruined through her overeating and dramatic weight loss? Just because she wanted to improve an aspect of her physical appearance, she decided, it didn't make her a superficial person. After all, she wasn't thinking about doing it to make her name in the glamour industry or to look like a footballer's wife. She was considering having it done to make her look like she was a normal twenty-two-year-old. And where was the harm in that?

'I'm going to do it,' she said decisively. 'I'm going to get some brand-new breasts and they're going to be my twenty-third birthday present from Joshua Garnet.' She looked out at the moonlit ocean and raised her glass in the direction of England. The idea of changing her body felt powerful, dramatic, and even though she knew it would hurt, and that she was giving in to the idea of 'perfection' promoted by the very magazines that she wrote for, Jo wanted her slender body to be even better. A hint of an idea started to formulate in her brain, and she downed her drink in one, realising what she needed to do to have revenge on her former boss.

'Joshua Garnet is going to rue the day he ever offered Olivia Windsor a breast job,' she murmured, in a voice so filled with venom that Gable looked surprised.

'Gable Blackwood, how would you feel about having a little sister who shares your amazing good looks?'

Gable buried his head in his hands.

Chapter Fourteen

April 2005

Jo stared at a photograph of Kate Moss in a copy of English *Vogue*. She was in a Dior advert and was naked on a chair with her legs pulled up to her chest. On her bare legs were chocolate-brown leather boots that laced up, Victorian style, from the bottom to the top, with sheepskin buckles that gave the boots an aggressive edge. They looked warm, comfortable and were undeniably sexy. Jo looked at them for a moment and wondered how much they cost before returning her gaze to Kate's face. She was stunning. But as well as being the most beautiful woman in the UK, there was something else to her. Yes, she looked like she was in the middle of having an orgasm even when she was doing something as innocuous as pushing her hair back from her face, you could see her hip personality through her doll-like 1960s-style features. Anyone could tell that Kate was edgy, cool and rock and roll – and you knew that from how she looked, how she presented herself. Because Jo had been reading magazines and looking at images of Kate Moss for years she felt like she knew her. The truth was Jo couldn't remember ever reading an interview with her or even hearing her speak. Kate Moss was silent, but through her face you knew exactly who she was. Jo looked in the mirror and wondered what her own face told people.

Even though her hair was no longer mousy-brown, and

was cut into a sleek, bouncy style, Jo wondered what she would look like if she was blonde. Thanks to Bobby at the salon her hair was still impeccable, and she loved her subtle streaks of gold, caramel, butter and mahogany. Her hair looked classy, and her eyebrows – a nondescript shade of light brown – were arched perfectly. Jo remembered how they had been before she had learnt to pluck them and she shuddered with embarrassment. She wondered if the girls at school had ever called her Liam Gallagher behind her back, and she realised they probably had. She raised her eyebrows and looked at her reflection in the mirror. When they were half a centimetre higher on her face she looked prettier, she thought.

Jo turned her attention to her lips, which were pale, thin and cracked from drinking the night before with a group of girls in the Ammo Rooms. She quickly glanced at Kate Moss's pouting lips – which were soft, plump and juicy – and looked at hers again, feeling miserable. Kate's lips weren't blow-job lips – Kate wasn't so obvious to have lips like that, and besides, they would have distracted people from her amazing, sex-glazed eyes – but they were lickable. Chewable. Jo pushed her lips out as far as she could without looking like she was pulling a face and marvelled at what a difference slightly bigger lips made to her expression. If she had cheekbones, slightly plumper lips and maybe her eyebrows positioned higher up so she didn't look like she was frowning all the time, she could be pretty, she thought. And if her nose was slightly more button-shaped, like Kate's, then she could even be beautiful. At the moment her nose looked like it belonged to Paris Hilton. Which was fine for Paris – who was all long lines and haughty angles – but not for Jo Hill.

Jo stared at herself in the mirror and felt depressed. Her insecurities were rearing their ugly head again, and this time all the make-up in the world could do nothing to change how

Jo felt about her face. It was only the thought of Gable, and how he had transformed himself from being boring and dull Simon into the stunningly attractive man he was today, that gave her some hope. She phoned him.

'You know when you decided to get your face done so you looked less like Simon Lynott and more like Freddie Ljungberg?' she began nervously. 'Well, in percentages, how sure were you that you wanted to get it done?'

'One hundred per cent,' he said firmly, before pausing for a second. He was on set in the Grand Canyon, and although he'd been shooting for a couple of days and was dressed as a cowboy, Gable couldn't get Jo – and her plans – out of his mind. He was worried sick, and felt responsible for telling her about his own surgery and possibly encouraging her into doing the same thing.

'Well, maybe not one hundred per cent, but I couldn't see any other way of being the man I wanted to be ... Look, do you really believe that you'll never be happy looking the way you do?' he asked her, and Jo didn't know what to say. She'd always thought that when she had reached the elusive size ten she'd wake up one morning and be happy, but it hadn't happened. Every day she felt as though she was still the frumpy Joanne Hill who nobody liked or took seriously. She wanted to wipe her childhood away from her memory so she could start her life again, but she couldn't.

'Listen to me,' Gable said. 'You're a cute girl, and when you go back to England you'll look amazing compared to all those dowdy girls in London, just like everyone else who's groomed and looks after themself.'

Jo shut her eyes. Gable hadn't a clue that most of the girls who worked in the media in London looked like models.

'You know,' she said, 'maybe it's looking like everyone else that is part of the problem. For years I was either ignored or mocked because of my weight – my blubber made me stand out, and even though I hated it, it was all I knew. But now I blend in, I feel it's for all the wrong reasons. I don't want to be just an average-looking girl who happens to be a great writer and has a famous actor for a friend. I want to be a hot-looking girl who happens to run the best magazine in the country.'

As she began pacing around her condo Jo realised she didn't need to talk about it any more – she was just going to do it.

'Forget about percentages and me not knowing if I should get more surgery,' Jo said, her voice sounding stronger than Gable had ever heard before. 'I'm going to use all my pay cheques from *Gloss* to get surgery, and I'm going to get it done. I'm one hundred per cent.'

'But are you sure about this? It all seems so rash, so sudden ...' The sun pounded down on him and he could feel sweat prickling at his thick foundation.

Jo spoke into her mobile. 'Yes, I wasn't absolutely convinced it was a good idea, but now I've spoken to you I think it is. OK, so I admit I'd had too much to drink when Lucy's email came in the other week, but I really don't see anything wrong in doing this – hundreds of girls get plastic surgery every day. Why shouldn't I?'

Gable was silent for a moment. 'But you're not just talking about breast implants, are you? You've been saying you want the works – chin, nose, cheeks ...' He lowered his voice. 'You said you were going to have more surgery than I did, and you were going to come out looking just like me! A girl-me! So you can be my "little sister"!'

Jo bit her lip. 'Look, I know you hate the idea of me getting surgery, but I see this as a chance to improve myself, to finally be the woman I always wanted to become. What harm can this do?'

'Lots, if you've not thought about it properly,' Gable

muttered almost inaudibly. 'I just don't see why you need to do this. I changed the way I look because I'm an actor – because nobody would give me the time of day unless I looked like a Hollywood star. The last time I checked, magazine editors didn't need to look like models.'

Jo laughed. 'They don't need to, no, but they tend to – especially at Garnet, and that's where I want to work as a "talented but also stunning editor". What's so wrong with that?'

Gable knew it would be hypocritical to try to talk Jo out of it, and chose not to answer her. 'Have you spoken to my surgeon about your rash plans to become my "little sister"?'

'Yes,' Jo said patiently. 'And he's happy for me to go ahead with this. He could hardly say no when I said you recommended him, could he?'

Gable tried not to sigh. 'I just want to make sure you really have thought this through. Once you're in the operating theatre there's no going back, you know.'

Jo knew – it was all she could think about ever since she'd received Lucy's email. A small voice in her head asked if she needed to take such severe measures, but Jo knew she'd never be beautiful without a helping hand, and that if changing her appearance meant she could become a magazine editor – a player – then she had no choice.

Jo opened her eyes and wondered if she was dying. She was in a small, clean, private room in the hospital where Gable's surgeon worked, and even though she could make out the bandages around her chest she had a sudden fear that the surgery had gone wrong, that she was having a heart attack. Jo had never experienced such a tight feeling in her chest before and she felt like she was about to explode from within her skin. She hurt so much, and despite the fear running through her veins she couldn't shake off her drowsiness. It scared the shit out of her.

'Hey, you're OK. You're OK,' Jo heard Gable say, and she felt his hand stroking her hair. She tried to relax. 'The surgery went well, there were no complications, and you're now the proud owner of two C-cup breasts.' Gable eyed Jo's face, which remained scared and confused. 'How are you feeling?'

Jo tried to shake her head. She didn't think she could speak.

'It hurts,' she whispered.

'I'll go and tell a nurse that you're awake, see if we can get you some painkillers,' Gable said, looking quickly at the clock on the wall behind the bed. 'I'll be back in five minutes.'

Jo felt hot tears dripping down her face and she suddenly felt like a fool. Was she really so shallow and ambitious that she would put herself in this much pain?

For the next eight weeks the ache in Jo's breasts ranged from complete agony to merely very uncomfortable. When she was released from hospital, Gable gently put her into a cab from Sunshine Cars and went home with her, sitting her up in her bed and holding an ice-pack to her chest. Jo wanted to angrily brush it aside, but Gable persevered, telling her the swelling could last for months and that the more they held the ice-pack to the area, the better she would feel in the long run. Jo wasn't sure this was a scientific fact, but she took his word for it, and drifted in and out of sleep feeling sick and wondering what she had ever done so right to deserve such a good friend as Gable.

When she could, Jo slowly walked around the condo experiencing pain that was so excruciating she sometimes thought she'd no longer be able to bear it. Gable had two weeks between films, and he spent them with Jo – brushing her teeth when she couldn't raise her arms, dressing her in baggy jogging bottoms and oversized T-shirts, and driving her to his surgeon to get her bandages changed. Even though she was warned that it would be the case, she felt alarmed when she realised her nipples were still numb, and she tried not to look at the bruising that was on her chest. She felt sick to think that she had chosen to put herself through such an experience.

Gradually, though, the swelling became less noticeable, and the pain began to disappear. Jo started sleeping on her back rather than in an upright position, and even though she knew she couldn't bend or strain, the tightness in her chest seemed like a distant memory. Jo's breasts began to feel smaller, and softer, and the surgeon was pleased with the results. On the twelve-week anniversary of her surgery Jo was happy too.

The first time Jo stepped out of her apartment she felt incredibly self-conscious. She knew she couldn't hide out in the condo for ever, but as she walked along the street to the beach she realised her new breasts were constantly in her eye-line, and it surprised her that they were always 'there'. Jo had decided that she needed to top up her tan – it had faded from the months she'd spent indoors recovering – and she couldn't wait to relax in the sunshine. But as she lay on South Beach Jo realised that her bikini top made her new breasts look even bigger. She'd forgotten to replace the top half with a larger size, and she looked ridiculous.

Jo was making sure her bikini covered her properly when she became aware of men staring at her as they strolled past. Other girls – ones with natural breasts that were nowhere near as perky or as full – gave her dirty looks as they briskly walked past, and Jo couldn't work out what she'd done wrong. It was only when a man came up to her and proposed – in utter seriousness – that Jo realised that people were staring because they thought she was sexy. For the first time in her life Jo felt sexually attractive, and it spurred her on to start her second lot of surgery as soon as possible.

The first procedure Jo had was an implant put over the front of her jawline to give definition to her chin. At the same time, Jo had a nose job to balance out her face; the low tip of her nose was corrected with added cartilage; and her nostrils were brought closer together. Jo had always hated the way her nostrils flared from underneath her long, straight nose, and she remembered a phase in her childhood where she had spent days walking around flaring and then tightening her nostrils in the hope that they would correct themselves. Unfortunately, Jo thought, as she calculated that the cost of her nose job alone was $7,000, her pre-teen attempts to slim her nose by herself hadn't worked.

After she'd recovered from her chin and nose surgery, Jo had cheek implants, where an incision was made on the inside of her upper lip and implants were inserted directly on to Jo's cheekbones. When she'd fully recovered from this she then undertook the final part of her transformation – lip injections where fat taken from her own body was inserted into her lips, giving her a fuller, more juicy pout, just like Gable's.

Over the course of the six months of surgery and recovery, Jo experienced pain on a level that she'd never thought possible. Like he had done when Jo had her breast implants, Gable made sure she took her painkillers; he held dry ice-packs to her face, and stroked her hair, telling her in a soft, comforting voice that it would all be worth it. Jo hurt so much she wasn't convinced.

When Gable took her to see the surgeon Jo was forced to look in the mirror. Without her dressings – and the splint that she imagined was holding her nose in place – Jo thought she looked like a monster. As well as being swollen and bruised, Jo no longer recognised herself. It was a sensation that she couldn't find the words to describe, but she felt as though she had walked into a black and white horror movie. Her world seemed devoid of colour and, to make matters worse, Jo found she often couldn't sleep for the pain, even though she had been prescribed sleeping pills. When Jo did manage to drift off she had nightmares about her face never recovering from the invasive surgery. She dreamt that when she woke up her face would be a mask of patchwork skin, crudely put together with large, black stitches. When Jo woke up in a cold sweat Gable would hold her hand, but nothing he did helped her sleep. In the darkness and haze of her medication she sometimes thought he was Joshua Garnet, silently mocking her. Jo yearned for William's touch.

Slowly, though, the swelling began to subside, and the deep purple bruises faded to green, and then yellow. Jo's face began to settle, and even though she had mild discomfort and swollen lips for five days after her lip injections, she began to see the results she had been hoping for. When her lips stopped being swollen, Jo cracked a smile at herself in the mirror, and even though she wasn't officially allowed to laugh for a week on her surgeon's orders in case she stretched her lips, she couldn't help herself.

She looked unrecognisable, like a woman who people would stare at as she walked down the street with a stylish gait, her expensive handbag swinging from her arm with carefree abandon. For hours Jo sat in front of her mirror and stared at herself, coming to terms with how she now looked. The Jo Hill who'd been bullied at school and had worked at The Royal Oak had been erased, and a butterfly had emerged from the chrysalis that she'd been cocooned in while in Miami. There were no other words for it: she was beautiful.

*

'Have you worked out what you're going to do next?' Gable asked her one evening, while Jo was gazing at the sun setting over the ocean. She had a bit of a headache, but even her throbbing head didn't distract her from wondering what William – if she ever saw him again – would think of her new face. She turned to Gable.

'I've finished all my surgery—' Jo started to say, but Gable shook his head, cutting her off.

'And you look stunning – unnervingly like me! No, I mean what are your plans work-wise?'

'I'm going to be your little sister,' Jo said simply, and when Gable looked confused she smiled. Once again Gable was struck by how stunning Jo was. Her freshly highlighted hair made her green eyes shine, and her face, now that it was no longer bruised or swollen, was exquisite. Her chin was defined so that it was perky rather than weak or strong, and Jo's nose, formerly plain and slightly wide, was almost aristocratic. It was slender and tapered away at the tip, and was an exact replica of Gable's. Under her nose her plump, juicy lips begged to be kissed, and Jo's new razor-sharp cheekbones gave her face the impression that she was a Scandinavian ice-maiden. Her eyes – her familiar green eyes – softened the overall effect of the paint-by-numbers beauty, and when she grinned her whole face lit up. She was gorgeous.

'I know I've always said that I wanted to be successful as "Jo Hill", but so long as Joshua Garnet remembers me – and he will, Gable, he'll never forget me – everything will be a hundred times more difficult. I probably wouldn't even be able to pitch to a magazine as myself, let alone actually write something. So I've decided to put both Jo Hill and Olivia Windsor to bed, and re-emerge as your little sister – just as I've been planning. Why not? I'm unrecognisable as the girl I used to be so I may as well use it to my advantage.'

Gable looked at Jo curiously. 'Sounds like you've really worked this all out.'

Jo nodded. 'I came up with the idea the night Lucy sent that email offering me a breast job, and I've been formulating it ever since. I'm going to email the best magazines in America and tell them that Gable Blackwood's little sister has joined Platinum Consulting alongside Olivia Windsor, and I'm going to pitch my newest story ideas as her. I'm bound to be a hit — who wouldn't want an article from the sister of the hottest Hollywood star since Johnny Depp?'

Gable grinned. 'Damn right,' he said. 'But how is that going to help you get a job at Garnet Publishing in the UK?'

'Once your little sister is American media property in her own right, Joshua Garnet will be desperate to give her — me — a job. He salivates over pretty girls, and with some celebrity sparkle added into the mix he won't be able to resist.'

Gable laughed, but then his face froze. 'But you don't sound American . . .' he trailed off.

Jo shrugged. 'Your little sister got sent to an English boarding school when she was five,' she said simply. 'You ended up at a day school in America. We were separated because we were incredibly naughty when together.'

'Hmm, it could work,' Gable said. 'And what if someone asks why I never mentioned you before?'

Jo tried not to roll her eyes. 'Gable, why would you have done? Really, it will be cool, trust me. Hollywood stars are supposed to be incredibly quiet about their personal lives.'

Gable took a sip of his mineral water and encouraged Jo to do the same — it was good for the elasticity in her skin.

'So what's your new name going to be, Miss Blackwood?' he asked her, and Jo blinked. She'd been so distracted by her new face and her plans for her career that she'd not even thought about it.

Jo looked out of the window for inspiration and started to run a list of names through her head. The sky was turning to a beautiful violet from the deep red, and as Jo watched the sun disappear in the horizon a glittering plane caught her eye. It was preparing to land, and, suddenly preoccupied again by her future, Jo imagined packing up her belongings and heading back to the horseshoe-shaped airport with Joanne Hill's passport in her hands. The assistants at check-in would not believe that the slim, beautiful woman in front of them was the same dumpy, ugly girl in the passport photo, and Jo smiled. From the moment she stepped on to the plane and away from Miami it would be the beginning of her new life. Miami had been the making of her, and as Jo remembered the airport's nickname – MIA for Miami International Airport – she knew what she had to be called.

'I'm going to be Mia Blackwood,' Jo said, as she turned back to Gable. 'It has a nice ring to it, don't you think?'

PART THREE

Chapter   Fifteen
------- ---------------------------

December 2005

Mia stood in the arrivals area of Heathrow and tried not to let her tiredness show through her polished, haughty exterior. Even though she'd not been in England for nearly two years she'd been looking forward to coming back, but the harsh British weather made her suddenly yearn for the warm breeze of Miami. Outside, the sky was a cold, slate grey and all around her were pale, miserable people who were rushing around looking poor, malnourished and stressed. Mia adjusted her vintage Gucci sunglasses on top of her $500 blonde highlights and surveyed the crowds of people waiting excitedly for their friends and family. As everyone's eyes flickered on everyone else, Mia tried not to feel self-conscious as men openly looked her up and down in front of their girlfriends and wives. In comparison to the perfectly groomed girls of Miami, most of the women in the airport looked frazzled and grey, with split ends, badly fitting clothes, and skin that was either so pale they looked like ghosts or so orange they looked cheap. Standing in the corner of the airport Mia looked as though she was bathed in sunshine – no part of her appearance had not been tended to, and she lit up the arrivals lounge in a flawless glow. She knew people were nudging each other and trying to work out if she was famous.

'How about I buy you a coffee?' a male voice murmured into Mia's ear, and she whizzed round to see an attractive forty-something man in a well-cut navy suit. He had an American accent and even though he had a baby face there was something unnerving in his arrogant, over-the-top masculine demeanour. 'My driver's not here yet and I'm always partial to some female company.' He looked directly at Mia's breasts. 'Especially if she's as gorgeous as you are, baby.'

Mia stared at the man for a moment, and without saying a word she walked away from him, feeling his eyes on her Diane von Furstenberg-clad bottom as she pulled her luggage behind her. It had been the same on the plane. During the flight four different men had tried to engage her in conversation, and even though a part of her loved it that she was now deemed attractive enough to be hit on, Mia didn't know how to handle the attention.

As she sat down on a hard plastic bench, Mia pulled out a tiny mirror that she kept in her handbag. Despite the long-haul flight her eyes were still sparkling white, and even though she was now back in London she looked as good as she had done when she had left Miami. Her mobile rang, and Mia dropped the mirror in search of it, being careful not to snag her newly manicured nails.

'Where are you?' Amelia's question came through the phone in a mock-accusing tone. 'I can't find you anywhere and I've been here for absolutely ages.' Mia felt herself relax as she heard her friend's familiar perky voice. It was good to be home.

'I'm near the exit,' Mia said. 'Want me to meet you there?'

As Mia approached the automatic doors she spotted Amelia. Her friend had barely changed, although her hair was longer, more tangled, and she looked as though she had lost a few pounds. She was wearing grey skinny jeans, black ballet slippers and a grey waistcoat over a white T-shirt.

Mia stopped and stared at her for a moment, and she held her breath as she realised just how beautiful her friend was. Amelia was writing a text message on her phone, and she had a look of concentration on her face. Even when she was frowning she still managed to look incredible. She possessed a cool, intelligent beauty that no amount of money or surgery could buy.

'Hey,' Mia said, in a fake American accent, and Amelia looked up at her blankly.

'Do you know where I can get a cab?' Mia asked, struggling with her accent as she tried not to laugh. Amelia restrained herself from rolling her eyes and assessed her coolly.

'I think there's a help-desk over there,' she said, with a barely perceptible nod towards an escalator, and she looked back down at her phone and finished writing her text message. As she put her mobile into her pocket she looked up again, and was surprised to see the stunning blonde was still standing in front of her. Just then the girl's phone beeped, and Amelia watched her dig her tiny silver mobile out of her Celine Boogie bag. She'd wanted one of those bags for months, but Selfridges had a waiting list of for ever. What with her expensive bag and the oversized vintage Gucci sunglasses on top of her head, this girl looked and acted like a celebrity. Amelia stared at her contemptuously. Who did this girl think she was? Nicole Richie?

'Hurry up, there's an American model who keeps staring at me and has just tried to chat me up,' Mia said, reading the text message that Amelia had just sent her out loud in her fake American accent. Just as Amelia turned white, Mia burst out laughing. She had really had no idea that her best friend wouldn't have recognised her.

'Ames, it's me,' Mia said gently, as she watched her friend look her up and down in shock.

'But you're ...' Amelia began, and she found she couldn't

finish her sentence. Mia was the most attractive girl Amelia had ever seen, and her mouth dropped open.

'Oh, my fucking God!' Amelia shrieked, and Mia hastily ushered her out of the airport. 'You look amazing. Ohmigod ohmigod ohmigod! Look at your hair! Look at your nose!' Amelia peered closely at Jo's face. 'I can't believe it's you!'

'Let's go to the car.' Mia grinned back, and Amelia led them to the Beetle, gushing all the way.

'I never would have believed you're Jo – your face is immaculate. I was expecting tiny scars, but there's nothing, it's incredible!'

Mia smiled. 'Thank you. But as you know, it took months of agony to look like this.'

Amelia beamed. 'No pain no gain, I say. Wow! Now, do I call you Jo, or Mia, or what?'

'It's Mia now,' she said, biting her lip. 'It's odd, I know, but you'll get used to it. I've stopped thinking of myself as Jo Hill, and you will too ... Do you really think I look that different?' Mia asked, and before Amelia could say anything she answered her own question. 'I do, don't I? But I really thought you would recognise me – you know me so well that ...' Mia trailed off. She was so jet-lagged, and so overwhelmed at being back in London that she struggled to articulate herself. 'It's quite weird, you know, because I'm exactly the same on the inside, but look completely different on the outside.'

Mia pulled out her mirror and stared at herself again. 'I keep on forgetting I don't look like plain, fat Joanne Hill any more. I look just like Gable's little sister, though, don't I?'

Amelia nodded as she remembered a recent cover of *DG* magazine where Gable had looked moody and arresting in a black suit and an open white shirt. Mia was the female version of him, a Scandinavian-style ice-cool blonde with a warm personality that radiated through her perfect features.

'You're absolutely stunning,' she said, her eyes sweeping over her friend again. 'And you look so completely different.'

Mia gave her friend a wry grin and clasped her hand mirror shut. 'That was the idea,' she said, and she told Amelia every gory detail of her surgery on the drive to London.

Amelia pulled up on a road in Hampstead and gently woke Mia, who had fallen asleep when they'd got stuck in traffic on the M4. 'We're here,' she said quietly, and Mia opened her eyes, allowing the shock at being in London to melt away before she looked at her new home. From the outside the cottage appeared to be perfect. Set two roads down from Hampstead High Street on a wide, quiet avenue with horse-chestnut trees and a cobbled pavement, the house nestled between other detached Victorian cottages, each with large sash windows and shiny front doors. As Mia got out of the car she stared up at the house. This would be where she started her London life again, she thought, and she buried her chin into a cashmere scarf that Amelia had lent her.

'Have you got the keys? It's bloody freezing,' Amelia complained, and Mia rummaged around in her handbag until she found the envelope that the letting agents had left for her at Heathrow. Mia opened the door, punched the combination into the alarm, and looked around the hallway that led into her new home. Amazingly, the original Victorian floor had been preserved, and Mia gingerly walked over the red and cobalt-blue decorative tiles into a living-room that was filled with comfortable stone-coloured sofas and cream mohair throws on stripped wooden floorboards.

'It's not too bad for a serviced house, is it?' Amelia commented, as she fingered the heavy cream curtains. 'How much did you say you were paying for this a month?'

Mia grimaced. 'You don't want to know,' she said, but as her eyes flickered across the room she realised that the price was definitely worth it. Subtle abstract oil paintings hung from the walls, and Booker Prize-winning novels sat on the mahogany shelves that were built into the recesses on each side of the original Victorian fireplace. Mia could picture herself watching the state-of-the-art television as she tried to relax after a day at work, and she instantly knew she'd made a good choice when she'd found this house on the internet.

The pair explored the rest of the house. Next to the living-room was a small dining-room that was perfect for intimate dinner parties, and in the kitchen, stainless-steel appliances sat on top of silver-coloured work surfaces. Upstairs was a large bedroom with an en suite, a guest bedroom – just the thing for both Amelia and Gable, Mia planned – and a small study complete with wi-fi and a large glass-topped desk. Mia thought the cottage was great.

'It's amazing,' she said to Amelia, as she stood in her new bedroom, charmed by the views of the city and yearning to take her boots off so she could feel the luxurious cream carpet between her toes. The bed was made of oak that had been stained a dark brown, and the crisp white sheets and crystal chandelier dangling over it gave the room a touch of elegance. Mia cast her mind back to the flat she had grown up in. She never could have imagined living in a place like this in London.

'I can't picture Gable Blackwood's little sister living in anything less,' Amelia commented, and they went down to the kitchen, where Amelia opened up a bottle of complimentary champagne while Mia sat at the table. Mia looked at her carefully – she looked as though she was on the verge of saying something, but was holding back.

'What's up?' Mia asked her, as she took a sip of champagne. Amelia wondered how to phrase what had been on her mind since she'd picked Mia up from the airport.

'I know that you're planning on trying to get a job at

Gloss, but aren't you a bit worried that this Garnet man – or someone else – will recognise you?' she asked, hoping that her friend wouldn't mind the subject being raised.

'You didn't.' Mia smiled. 'I'm being myself with you, but when I'm with Joshua I'll play out the first rule of magazines, and I'll give my audience what they want. To Joshua I'll be sexy, beautiful and funny, but I'll also be smart, savvy and brilliant at boosting circulation and stealing advertising from his competitors. He never knew Jo to be like that – he thought I was a timid, naïve mouse – so he'll never guess in a million years.'

Amelia fiddled with the foil on the neck of the champagne bottle and gazed at Mia. 'But now that I know you're really Jo I can see the old you mixed in with your new face. It's your eyes, you see, they totally give you away. And if I recognise you, who's to say Joshua won't?'

'Ames, I'm telling you, he won't know it's me. Sure, if he found out that dumpy old Joanne Hill had surgery then he might put two and two together, but it's not going to happen.'

Amelia exhaled slowly. 'I'm just really worried about what he would do to you if he found out,' she said. When she spotted Mia's confused face she hurried to explain what she meant. 'I'm not talking hit-men or anything like that, but from what you've told me this Garnet guy is pretty powerful, and he could crush your career before you know what's happened. He's done it to you once before,' she said. 'And I wouldn't put it past him doing it again.'

Mia drank some of her champagne and thought about what Amelia was saying. She had a point.

'Look, why don't you go and test your new look on someone else first, and see if they recognise you ...?' Amelia paused, and dug out a copy of *Time Out* from her bag. 'And while we're on the subject, have you seen this?'

Mia wordlessly took the magazine from Amelia and stared at the cover. Steve Coogan was whispering into Rob Brydon's ear on a white background, but over their faces were black straplines previewing the fifty cultural highlights of 2006. The name 'William Denning' jumped out at Mia immediately, and she flicked through the pages frantically.

'Seems he's written a hit novel that's being published next year,' Amelia remarked. Mia looked up at her.

'Good for him,' she said as lightly as possible, hoping her voice didn't belie her true feelings. Her heart was thudding, and as soon as she spotted the tiny photograph of William she felt her face flush. William looked as gorgeous as ever, and Mia wondered how she'd found the strength to walk away from him all those years ago.

'Do you think one of those American magazines you write for would be interested in an interview?' Amelia asked.

Mia stared at her friend in surprise. Mentally she'd already written the pitch.

January 2006

Mia examined herself in the mirror and wondered if she'd made enough effort. Her blonde hair hung like a waterfall down her back, and her make-up was impeccable. The cosmetics she'd already applied – from Crème de la Mer moisturiser to Chanel Glossimer lip colour – made her look polished, poised and expensive. Her clothes – knee-length Versace boots, a leather mini-skirt and a tight black T-shirt – were sexy but understated, and she'd added a flash of colour with a hot-pink Marc Jacobs 'Angela' bag. So far so perfect, she thought.

Mia peered at her face again, and swept some Brigitte Bardot-style eyeliner across her lids. A quick spray of Lolita Lempicka perfume made her feel feminine and demure, and when she smiled she liked how her shimmering lips caught the light as they curled. Mia was aiming for 'professional sex kitten', and she hoped she'd done enough to look more gorgeous than she'd ever looked before. She wanted William to be spellbound as soon as he met her – and then, when he'd fallen in love with her looks and she'd proved that she was unrecognisable, Mia planned to tell him who she really was.

With a deep breath Mia left the toilets of the Charlotte Street Hotel and walked into the foyer, once again struck by how busy the hotel was. In the Oscar bar and restaurant trendy media types were chatting on their tiny mobile phones, and serving staff supplied cocktails, placing drinks on tables without waiting for acknowledgement or thanks. Of all the smart venues in London, the Charlotte Street Hotel was currently the one where the most important people in the media industry cut deals, and Mia felt flustered and out of place until she remembered that she no longer looked like plain old Jo Hill.

'Mia Blackwood for William Denning,' Mia said to a passing girl, who had been showing some men wearing Jarvis Cocker-style glasses into a private room. 'Could you point me to the drawing-room, where I'm meeting him?'

The girl glanced at her notes, but didn't stop to read them. 'Are you the one from American *Vanity Fair*?' she asked, and Mia nodded, impressed – this girl had clearly memorised the day's schedule. 'Follow me,' she said briskly, and Mia followed her through to a drawing-room, the girl's steel stiletto heels clattering on the wooden floor.

The drawing-room was what Mia had come to expect from the best hotels in London. There was a roaring fire, creamy white sofas and chairs, and oil paintings created by the local Bloomsbury set hung from the walls. However, Mia paid no attention to them, for sitting in an armchair near the fire was William. Mia felt her heart race as she watched him tug at his expensive-looking suit, and she ran her eyes over him, greedily drinking in every detail.

William's blond hair looked as though it had been recently trimmed, and his face – which had rarely seen a razor when he lived in the Hampshire countryside – was free of the dark blond stubble she was used to. Mia didn't think she'd ever seen William clean-shaven before, and his smooth skin made his jawline appear even stronger: it was incredibly masculine, and Mia wondered what it would be like to run her tongue over his chin. William's eyes still shone the electric blue that Mia remembered, but his lips – his kissable, touchable lips – were scowling. On any other man his expression would look childlike and petulant, but it just made William look dark and brooding. William had always been the sexiest man Mia had ever seen, but the new, more sophisticated William took her breath away. He was gorgeous. And Mia didn't know how she would be able to control her emotions in front of him.

'Mr Denning, Mia Blackwood from *Vanity Fair* is here to see you,' the girl said, and she walked off, leaving William staring at Mia with an unreadable expression. Mia quickly wondered if William recognised her, but when he stood and looked her up and down he didn't seem to realise who she was. Neither did he appear to find her attractive, which Mia found unnerving. She was used to making an impact on men immediately.

'How do you do,' William said formally, and he offered Mia his hand. Mia held her breath and as her hand slipped into his, she felt a spark of electricity blast through her body. She tried not to blush, and she gazed up at William through lowered eyelids. If he'd felt anything between them it certainly wasn't showing on his face.

'I'm sorry I'm late,' Mia said, her voice wobbling slightly. 'I couldn't get a cab for ages.'

William looked down at her. Again, Mia couldn't tell what he was thinking. 'It's fine,' he said kindly. 'But let's get on with it, shall we? I have interviews all afternoon and I don't want to run behind.' Mia thought she heard well-masked irritation in William's voice, and she wondered why he didn't seemed charmed by her beauty like every other man was. She quickly took her dictaphone from her handbag and put it on the small round table between them.

'Um, why don't we begin by you telling me what your book is about,' Mia said with a smile. She had been so wrapped up in working out what to wear, and wondering if William would recognise her, that she hadn't prepared any interview questions. It was unprofessional and absolutely unlike her. William sighed heavily, his broad shoulders slouching slightly.

'I'd rather not, if it's all the same,' he said. 'My publicist should have sent you the notes beforehand, but I've got a spare set here if you want.' William leant down and produced a scruffy-looking rucksack from behind the chair. In comparison to his expensive suit and the opulence of the room it looked out of place, and it reminded Mia sharply of the William she'd fallen in love with, not of the shaved and polished version in front of her.

'Thanks, that's very kind,' Mia said, before tentatively wondering what her next question should be. 'What inspired you to write *Caviar Society*?' she asked finally, and after a long pause in which William tried not to roll his eyes, he spoke. His voice was gentle, but there was a slight patronising edge to it.

'If you know anything about the book you'll know it's a pastiche of society in London. I mostly grew up in the country, but I sometimes had to visit the city with my father when he did business. I immediately noticed how shallow people were in London compared to those who lived in the country, and it seemed like a natural idea to write about. They say "write about what you know", and I did just that.'

Mia swallowed. She imagined William writing the book at The Royal Oak, and memories of his bedroom – and how his bed had smelt deliciously of him – flooded her mind. Mia yearned to tell William who she was, to touch him, but she knew she couldn't. She needed to get a grip.

'What is it specifically about London that you don't like?' Mia asked, hoping her voice sounded neutral. She settled further back into her chair, and didn't realise that her already short skirt had slid up her thighs. William ignored Mia's tanned, toned legs and looked around the room. He seemed to be amused.

'Why, all of it. What's to like? London has such a fascinating history, but the people who live here make a mockery of it, creating pastiches of what they think the city should be like. Look at those watering cans, for example, he remarked, gesturing at some silver watering cans with leafy plants growing out of them. 'They're ridiculous, and probably cost hundreds of pounds. Why on earth would anyone think that this urban version of gardening would be appropriate for a drawing-room in a hotel? And who would spend a stupid amount of money on something so crude?'

'Some would say that they're in here because they look nice,' Mia commented, and William laughed.

'And existing because "they look nice" sums up London good and proper, doesn't it?' he said, sparring with her. 'My editor goes on about London having the best of everything – restaurants, museums, architecture – but if you scratch beneath the surface you'll see that there's nothing actually there. Everything in middle-class London looks nice, but really, it's meaningless beauty. And that statement includes the women,' he said, pointedly.

Mia shrank back from his gaze. 'I'm sorry?' she asked in a small voice. She thought they had been getting on so well, but now, rather than chatting like they used to, William had just insulted her. She almost wished William knew who she really was so he would scoop her up in his arms like he once had. She wasn't sure she liked being on the wrong side of him.

'Miss Blackwood, if you'd read one of the hundreds of preview copies of *Caviar Society* that were sent out, you'd know that a large section of it sends up London's painted ladies. Of course, prostitutes in London are nothing new, but there's a new breed of women in the city who think that the world is their oyster just because they were born with bright eyes, impeccable features and cupid-bow lips. Truly, the way they whore themselves about the city is disgusting. They say they're career women – "working" in PR, journalism, fashion – but really they're just on the lookout for either a man who is rich or one who is famous. They don't want real love, they just want to be worshipped, and *Caviar Society* captures that growing trend.'

William stopped talking and took a glug of his whisky. He refused to meet Mia's eyes. 'Let's take you, for example,' he said. 'You're the fourth journalist I've met today, and just like you, the three other girls who came to interview me dressed up, pouted, and didn't know what my book was about. Of course, you're by far the prettiest, but when did magazines stop sending real journalists on assignment? When did beauty overtake talent in many of London's key professions? I read an article in the paper today about City men who get their eyebrows waxed to get ahead. It's ludicrous. And I resent that every facet of London society has to be perfectly groomed.'

Mia didn't know what to say. She felt physically sick that William didn't respect her, but she needed to hold her own, despite her eyes stinging with tears. 'You're just seeing one side of London,' she said, after managing to control her emotions. 'You're assuming that because you find me attractive I must be dumb, that because the media industry employs girls with pretty faces as well as brains, we're shallow, and that because a few London hotels are stylish, the city doesn't have any depth. Surely you're the one who is superficial by making these presumptions.'

William stared at Mia, he wasn't used to fawning journalists standing up to him. 'Maybe I am,' he said, downing the rest of his whisky. 'But maybe I'm just sick of being interviewed by people who don't know the first thing about me, as well. Look, no offence, you seem like a perfectly nice girl, but I'm going to have to end this interview. I'm here on sufferance because the publishing company thinks I should get some media exposure to boost sales, but I've had enough of it for one day.'

Mia leant forward and turned her dictaphone off. Part of her wanted to stop the charade, to tell William who she really was, but another part wanted to leave too. If William ever knew who she really was he would no doubt be disgusted by her for changing how she looked, for being so superficial.

'Fair enough,' Mia said as flippantly as she could, and she bit her lip hard, desperately hoping she wouldn't start crying. 'I'll tell the magazine that you changed your mind.'

William nodded as he pulled off his smart shoes and replaced them with heavy walking boots that were at odds with his suit. They were very him. 'You do that,' he said, and he glanced at her with a smile. 'Look, don't take anything I said to heart and don't be upset,' he remarked, and he gave her a friendly look that made her want to confide in him, that made her want to tell him the truth. But before Mia could say or do anything, William walked out of the drawing-room, leaving his smart black shoes behind.

Mia sat back down again and stared at them until the tears that welled up in her eyes blurred her focus. Even though Mia had never really had William, she realised that by having surgery she had lost him for ever.

-- -- -- ¬-- -- -- -- -- -- -- -- -- -- -- -- -

Chapter Sixteen

The moment Mia walked through her front door her phone began to ring. She picked it up when it was obvious Amelia wasn't going to be content with leaving a voicemail message.

'So ...?' Amelia asked, without bothering to say hello.

'He didn't recognise me,' Mia said bluntly so that her voice wouldn't wobble. 'I was a bit disappointed, but ultimately I'm pleased. If William doesn't recognise me then Joshua Garnet won't either. So it's good. It's great. Perfect.'

'But how was it seeing him again? Did you connect?'

'Not really, no.'

Amelia was silent, wondering what had gone wrong. 'Are you OK?'

Mia forced a smile, hoping it would make her voice sound happier. 'Great, never better,' she said briskly. 'I'm in the middle of working out how to get a meeting at *Gloss* next week, in fact.'

'Jo—' Amelia began.

'It's Mia,' she interrupted. 'I'm never going to be Jo again. Never. Meeting William proved that much to me.'

Amelia sighed. 'Don't you think you deserve a bit of a break? You've had months of intense surgery, and you're flinging yourself into your career here ... do you fancy going to Italy or something? Just for a long weekend?'

Mia briefly considered it, but then pushed the thought

away. 'I'd love to, Ames, really I would, but I'm in London for a reason, and I need to get on with things.' Her eyes flashed in anger, and, for the first time in hours, a real smile spread on her face. 'I can't wait to see Joshua Garnet again.'

Mia sat in the reception area of *Gloss* and marvelled at how, in the space of a few years, nothing seemed to have changed. Even though a beautiful, ice-blonde Russian called Natalia had replaced Rachel, the hostility that Mia could feel prickling over the reception desk remained unchanged. As the receptionist stared at her spitefully, Mia wondered if it had been written into her hand-over notes that she had to be as rude as possible to other girls. Mia grinned back at her, and shifted slightly on the red suede sofa so that her skirt rose slightly on her slender tanned thighs. Despite the chill in the winter air Mia couldn't resist showing off her Miami tan, and even though she had some misgivings about not wearing tights to a job interview she knew that Joshua Garnet would appreciate the look. When Natalia's expression changed from one of dislike to that of utter hate, Mia knew she looked more than good. She just hoped that looking hot would distract Joshua from realising that she was Joanne Hill.

'Mia Blackwood? Lucy Davenport. It's so lovely to finally meet you.' Mia stood up and smiled at Lucy, and the girls shook hands and assessed each other quickly. Lucy had let her light-brown hair grow even longer so that it brushed past her nipples, and she was wearing a dark grey shirt-dress that was buckled tightly at her tiny waist. It fitted her perfectly. To complement the outfit she was wearing some purple crocodile-skin Dior boots – ones that Mia had been coveting ever since she had seen the winter collections in the magazines. Mia beamed at Lucy brightly, and hoped she didn't come across as nervous.

'I know I'm not sitting in on this interview, but I absolutely had to come and meet you to say hello. Joshua's PA asked me to let you know that our finance directors are in our boardroom all day, so the interview is going to take place in Joshua Garnet's office. It's at the back of the editorial room so you'll get to see the layout of the place,' Lucy said, as she led Jo through the familiar corridor towards *Gloss*. 'Madeline Turner is off work at the moment – I'm sure Joshua will fill you in on that – so it's just going to be you and him in the interview. I hope that's OK?'

Lucy shot Mia a quick glance as they paused outside the double doors that opened into the office. 'I know that having a one-on-one with the man who runs the whole publishing group is quite daunting, but I'm sure you'll be fine,' Lucy said. As she quickly cast her eyes over Mia's poker-straight expression she wondered if there was any point in trying to reassure her – she didn't look at all concerned about being left alone with Joshua Garnet. 'Everyone at *Gloss* is really friendly, and we've all been dying to put a face to the famous Mia Blackwood for ages.'

Lucy pushed the doors open and Mia remembered how overwhelmed she'd been when she'd first seen the editorial office at *Gloss*. Now, though, she looked at the girls behind the desks coolly. They were still elegant, still dressed impeccably in black, but they no longer intimidated her. Mia knew most of them inside out, and she was going to use it to her advantage, as she had done as Olivia Windsor with Madeline Turner. Very soon, she thought, the girls who used to boss her about would be answering to her.

'Madeline's office is just down there, and over here is Joshua's office.' Lucy led Mia towards the glass-fronted office at the back of the room, and as they got closer towards it Mia stared at his PA. Debbie, the girl who had spent most of her time bullying her when she was Jo Hill, was now Joshua's assistant. Debbie must have replaced her as soon as she had been sacked, and Mia wondered why Madeline had agreed to it. As far as Mia knew, Debbie had never been promoted to Joshua's PA before because of her tendency to flirt with him.

'Debbie, this is Mia Blackwood who is here for the features editor job. Is Joshua going to be long?'

Debbie looked Mia up and down, and Mia stared at her defiantly. Her blonde hair still looked unhealthy and brittle, and she was wearing heavy orange foundation to try to disguise her bad skin. Even though she'd lost some weight, Debbie's Top Shop designer copies didn't fit her body properly, and, most interestingly, her left hand was free of an engagement ring. Debbie shot Mia a sour look and casually tapped something into her computer.

'He's in a meeting with design so he probably won't be too late,' Debbie said, her estuary accent more pronounced than ever. She gave a melodramatic sigh. 'I'll go and get him, though,' she said, as if she was extremely put out at leaving her seat. 'He has an important meeting later so he can't be running behind. In case you're wondering, your interview shouldn't take too long,' Debbie remarked pointedly, and she slowly got up from her desk and walked away.

'She's not the friendliest PA, admittedly, but Joshua likes her,' Lucy said quietly. 'She's not a patch on his previous assistant, though.' Mia felt the hairs on the back of her neck stand on end, and she forced herself to smile at Lucy. 'Look, here he comes – grab me afterwards and maybe we can go for a coffee,' Lucy said, but Mia didn't hear her. She couldn't stop staring at Joshua as he swept past her while concentrating on entering something into his Blackberry.

Mia felt her heart thudding. She had dreamt about this moment for years, and now it had finally come: she was here, standing in front of her nemesis, and she was about to do battle. While Joshua frowned at his Blackberry and jabbed at its tiny keys with his fingers, Mia surreptitiously examined him from under her long eyelashes. How could she have forgotten how attractive he was? Mia drank in his dark hair – with only a hint of grey sprinkled through it – his long Roman nose, his strong chin and dark brown eyes. He had the remains of a tan from a recent holiday, and his shirt stretched across his broad shoulders. Compared to Gable he looked positively beefy. Mia noticed that despite her impending job interview Joshua wasn't wearing a tie, and she could see the faintest smattering of coarse curly hair by his shirt buttons. He was aggressively masculine, and coupled with the power he had and the respect he commanded, Mia could easily see why she'd let him walk all over her when she'd worked as his PA. She wasn't going to let him do it again, she thought, as Joshua looked up at her and caught her eye. When he grinned at her, Mia swallowed hard and she realised her palms were sweaty.

At Joshua's command Mia walked into his office, giving Debbie a cool, neutral smile when she whispered a staged, sarcastic 'good luck' to her just in Joshua's earshot. Mia knew she didn't need luck – she just needed to be herself, she thought, as she took a seat at Joshua's circular meeting table, which was already laid with crystal glasses of water, notepads and pens. Mia spotted that one of the pens had bite marks around the top of it, and she quickly shot a disdainful look at Debbie through the glass partition.

'Lucy has already provided me with your cuttings, so there's no need to go over old ground,' Joshua said efficiently, shutting the glass door behind Debbie's retreating short skirt and knee-length boots combination, and settling back down behind his desk. 'And Madeline Turner has already granted approval for you to be features editor so long as you make the grade with me. Not normal for an editor, I know, but Madeline is currently busy with some personal issues outside of work, and she trusts my judgement implicitly.' He stared at Mia coolly and tried not to look surprised. He hadn't seen a girl this hot – and with brains – for a long time. She vaguely reminded him of how Madeline used to be before he married her. But Madeline Turner had never been this beautiful, and had never had such a knock-out body.

'Tell me about your brother,' Joshua directed, and as he settled back in his Eames chair his eyes wandered over Mia's sheer, silky top, her perfectly cut Chanel suit and her blonde hair.

'Gable's currently in Russia filming a classic black and white comedy with Uma Thurman,' Mia said confidently, re-membering a conversation she'd had with Gable before he'd flown out to Moscow. 'He's playing the part of a man who works as a postman but is secretly a KGB spy. One day he de-livers a letter to a woman who he needs to gather information on, and he accidentally falls in love with her. Gable's looking forward to shooting the sex scenes, apparently, although he's slightly worried Uma will fall in love with him.' Gable raised his eyebrows at this information, and Mia could tell he was lapping up the Hollywood gossip. 'Of course, as much as Gable finds Uma attractive he's still going steady with Violet Compton, who, I believe, featured in your most recent issue of *DG* magazine.' Mia expertly led the conversation back to magazines, and Joshua nodded.

'She didn't push sales like Marina Stone did,' he said, ges-turing at the blown-up copy of *DG*'s cover that was still up on his office wall, 'but she did well. Our UK readers are tired of the normal British babes – even Jordan is going the way of Abi Titmuss since she hooked up with Peter Andre – so someone hot and exotic like Violet was just what we needed. Do tell her thanks again for me next time you speak to her – she didn't respond to my handwritten note but I imagine she's a busy girl.'

Mia nodded brightly, and she noticed Joshua looking at her hungrily. She tried not to blush.

'I'm assuming you know people in Hollywood other than your brother,' Joshua said bluntly, and Mia obediently ran off a register of the Hollywood A-listers who Gable was friends with. Mia may not have actually met them, but she had access to them through Gable, and that was the most important thing. Both she and Joshua realised that having Lindsay Lohan's personal cell phone number was like having a hotline to the prime minister, something that no amount of money could buy, especially if Lindsay was rumoured to have a new part and her agent and PRs refused to take media calls.

Joshua leant forward and rubbed his hands together. He looked genuinely excited. '*Gloss* is keen – extremely keen, I must say – to introduce more celebrities like that into the fold. The UK public is already bored of the Shayne Ward-type people of yesterday, and they want to identify with proper Hollywood glamour. Anyone can be Shayne or that Anthony who won *Big Brother*, which was rather the point, I must say, but being someone like Uma Thurman or Scarlett Johansson is quite exceptional. They're the ultimate in aspiration, and they represent *Gloss*'s ideology far better than a pasty soap actress laden with puppy fat and bad skin ever could.' Both Joshua and Mia involuntarily looked at Debbie for a second, and then back at each other. Mia smiled.

'I shouldn't think talking to any of these people would be a problem, Mr Garnet,' she said lightly. 'Like I said in my original letter to you, my contacts, combined with my feature ideas, are absolute dynamite. What I can bring to the magazine is something tremendously special,' she said, leaning forward so that a hint of tanned cleavage was showing. 'Mainly because nobody else is me, has my ideas, or can bring my expertise to your publishing company.'

Joshua stared at her for a second, and he raised his eyebrows. Mia could tell that she had him, but he was still going to try to make her work for it. She looked forward to it.

'What I want to know, Miss Blackwood,' Joshua said, changing the tone of the interview so that he was dominating again, 'is what you are worth without your Hollywood contacts. Let's pretend for a moment that you're not Gable Blackwood's little sister,' he thought out loud, as Mia bit her lip to stop herself from laughing at the fact that she actually wasn't, 'and that you're just a normal girl who wants to be one of *Gloss*'s features editors. Why should I employ you?'

Mia leant back in her chair and held Joshua's gaze. If she didn't know the magazine inside out she'd have been nervous. 'Because I am the girl every *Gloss* reader wants to be – I am famous, but I have not had to do a thing to gain even moderate celebrity status. I am beautiful, without being a bitch with it, and I am the smartest woman who has ever walked into your office. I could double *Gloss*'s circulation in six months without even breaking into a sweat, purely by changing the tone of your articles so that they appeal to me, and not Araminta. I'm assuming it was her judgement that contributed to a drop in circulation over the last six months.' Mia saw a flicker of annoyance wash over Joshua's face and she knew she was right.

'And just how would you boost my circulation?' Mia raised one eyebrow at Joshua, and as she let out a dirty laugh he clocked his *double entendre*. 'My mistake,' he drawled. 'How would you boost the circulation of my magazine?'

Mia grinned. 'The same way that I would send the blood pumping around your body. I'd spend some time looking into what had let the libido drop, and then I'd begin with a quick, sharp shock before slowly letting things reach a climax.' Mia shifted in her chair and turned from being a sex kitten into a magazine professional. Although he didn't show it, Joshua was impressed.

'I estimate that your issue last month probably represented the biggest drop in your circulation figures yet. You may not have the numbers, but I'm willing to bet an awful lot of money that an issue featuring "how to give him the best sex of his life" and "what your diet says about you" wouldn't have shifted as many magazines as the April edition from last year, which contained a guide to the different fashion trends coming out of all the major cities in England and a piece about how to deal with affairs that take a turn for the worse. Quite simply, your readers don't want to be told who they are in such overt, obvious ways any more. They can form their personal identification by reading between the lines, picking and mixing the different voices that come out of the editorial so that each reader feels unique in who they are, separate to the girl who is sitting on the Tube reading the same issue. And articles such as "what to wear to that crucial job interview" just don't cut it in 2006.'

Joshua looked at Mia with a neutral expression on his face, and Mia continued. 'It may surprise you, but girls already know what to wear to job interviews. And on behalf of every reader of *Gloss* who is sick to the back teeth of being told what to wear, I'm telling you this so she never has to read that article again. Are you paying attention, Mr Garner?' Mia asked flirtatiously, and as Joshua nodded – wondering how such a firecracker had found her way into his office – Mia crossed her legs. Joshua ached to look under the table to see if her skirt had inched up her thighs, but he was far too smooth to do that.

'Your average *Gloss* reader doesn't want to be told that a pencil skirt and a cute cardigan will get her the job, but she does want to know how she can dress to encompass all the things she knows she is and can be in a new job. She wants to dress so that she stands out from the crowd without the interviewer knowing why. She wants to tap into the subconscious of the man asking her the questions, and she want to leave with him trailing his eyes on her bottom as she walks out of the interview room. She wants to look like she sparkles.'

'So you would recommend an expensive Chanel suit,' Joshua began slowly, 'and a silk shirt flimsy enough so that the interviewer can tell that your nipples are dark pink?' Joshua didn't take his eyes from Mia's face, and she let a pause hang in the air between them before softly chiding Joshua.

'I wouldn't recommend wearing any one outfit, Joshua,' she said, quietly, with amusement rippling through her voice. 'And I certainly wouldn't suggest that a *Gloss* reader dresses like me. She wouldn't have the salary to afford it, or breasts that are so perky that they don't need a bra. But since you've been listening to me intently you would already know that.'

Mia grinned a devilish, sexy smile at Joshua, and then tore her gaze away from him, trying not to blush at the fact he could see through her shirt, or worry that she had disagreed with him. She knew nobody ever told Joshua Garnet off.

'I'd give the reader a selection of clothes, a pick-and-mix capsule wardrobe with the psychology behind each selection, and how various high-flying employers rate each outfit. I'd interview the designers from behind the high-street labels to find out what inspired certain lines, and I'd ask celebrities – proper ones, not the D-list – to explain what they would choose to wear to portray various aspects of their character. You could almost run a whole issue based around the psychology of what to wear for a job interview, but you would have to conclude, in the end, that it's never what you wear but how you wear it, and that not even *Gloss* could help with that.'

Mia took a sip of water, and as she put the glass back on the table she could feel Debbie's stare blazing through the glass partition. She had been in this interview for a long time – longer than the time she suspected she had been allocated – but Joshua didn't seem to care. He appeared to be genuinely fascinated by her, which had been the idea. It felt good to know she had Joshua standing to attention to listen to her, when a few years ago he had ignored her ideas due to how she looked.

'But why work for me?' Joshua said. 'You could take your pick of magazines to work for, from *Vogue* to *Cosmopolitan* to *Glamour*. So why *Gloss*?'

Mia shrugged, but inside her stomach was turning somersaults – Joshua thinking that she was good enough for *Vogue* was a compliment she never thought she'd hear.

'*Gloss* used to be my favourite magazine a few years ago, but I feel that recently it's lost its way. Whether that is down to Araminta or because of Madeline Turner, I cannot say, but of all the magazines I could work on I feel *Gloss* needs the injection of energy I could provide. It's been lacking for a couple of years – apart from the Miami special you did – but really, the magazine needs to be brought back to how it was when I was younger. My favourite issue of *Gloss* was the one where it explained exactly how to get the x-factor like Keira Knightley. It was about more than just fashion or beauty, it was about attitude, an attitude that anyone can have. I liked that issue because it would have struck a chord with every girl in the UK. It certainly interested me, and I thought it was a triumph in terms of magazine journalism.'

'That was our bestselling issue of the year,' Garnet admitted, looking at Mia with admiration. 'But if you'd done your research properly – and I assume you have – you would know that already.'

Mia laughed. 'Yes, I admit that I do, but the whole issue was inspiring. It was genius.' Mia silently applauded herself again on a terrific issue of *Gloss*.

'Thank you,' Joshua said. 'I take credit for that issue, it certainly wouldn't have happened without me.' Mia felt any jubilation about how well her interview was going drain away from her, and her whole body clenched in anger. How dare he take credit for her work? she thought, as Joshua continued to smile. Mia inwardly fumed, and she struggled to remain composed.

'But I'm confused,' Joshua began, his eyes narrowing as if he had just thought of something that there couldn't be a feasible answer to. 'I can't understand why a woman like you would be so interested in reading articles about getting the x-factor in *Gloss*.' Mia froze, and she felt a cold chill run down her body. 'Articles like that are aimed at women who will, frankly, never have the x-factor purely because they have to read about it to find out about it. Take, for example, my old PA. I'm sure she was sweet, but she was so desperate to be a journalist that it literally oozed from every enlarged pore on her blubbery body. It really was quite revolting. I used to catch her rereading that particular issue so many times that I used to imagine she was committing every bit of it to memory. Eventually the issue she kept on her desk became so dog-eared that I had to ask the cleaners myself to remove it. The greasy fingerprints on the glossy pages were extremely off-putting. I wondered if Jo was planning on eating the magazine next.'

Mia thought she was going to faint. She suddenly felt light-headed, and she wondered if Joshua was on to her, if he was testing her. She gripped her glass of water, and desperately tried to force a smile on her face. Breathe, she thought to herself, as Joshua looked at her curiously.

'She certainly sounds quite the character,' Mia said diplomatically, and Joshua nodded.

'And she was the type of girl who loves *Gloss* because it is everything she wants to be but never can be,' Joshua said. 'Fundamentally our readers are lazy — they need to be told what to wear to job interviews because, to be honest, they haven't a fucking clue. But I do agree with you that they need to feel like they are the ones in charge. You're right – we should offer advice, but we shouldn't dictate things to them like our competitors do. We should state that what we say is merely being offered as the *Gloss* opinion – from people who know what they are talking about.' Joshua stared at Mia, who he thought looked slightly bored, but he was on a high from her ideas.

'Rather than being told what they should do, *Gloss* readers want to have a conversation with a person who they want to be, someone it would be impossible for them to have access to in their daily lives, and even if they did, they'd never have the courage to ask for advice. Miss Blackwood, you genius, they want to be having that conversation with you.'

Mia put her glass back down on to the meeting table and shot Joshua a megawatt smile.

'I mean, look at you,' Joshua said, as he ran his eyes slowly and suggestively across her body. Mia could feel his gaze stripping her naked, but she felt neither offended nor turned on as relief that he hadn't caught her out flooded through her. 'You are possibly the sexiest woman I've ever met,' Joshua said. 'You are not the most beautiful, and nor are you the cleverest, but you are disgustingly sexy and smart. You are everything that a *Gloss* reader aspires to be, but you are also so much more. So, so much more.'

Despite herself Mia grinned. She had Joshua Garnet right where she wanted him, and it felt fantastic.

'But even though you are all that, I have decided that I don't want you to be features editor on *Gloss* after all,' Joshua began, and Mia felt her grin freeze on her face. She didn't understand what was suddenly happening, but she had a gut feeling that something hadn't gone to plan.

'If I could just—' Mia began, but Joshua cut her off.

'I'll admit that you strike me as special, Miss Blackwood, but Garnet Publishing doesn't just give jobs to pretty girls willy-nilly,' he said, raising an eyebrow and smirking. 'And I think the board may have a problem with your age ... Especially as I'd prefer you to be our deputy editor, rather than in charge of features.'

Mia allowed herself to blush – deputy editor was more than she had dreamed of.

'If it makes a difference I'm nearly twenty-four, and I've got years of writing experience.' Mia paused and decided to bring out her secret weapon. 'I was speaking to my friend Paris Hilton just the other week about my meeting here, and she said she'd love to do an interview with me for *Gloss* ... so long as she got the cover.' Mia tried not to look smug, and made a mental note to thank Gable for promising her a meeting with the hotel heiress. Paris Hilton covers always sold magazines, and Joshua knew it.

'Let me talk to the others, and then come back to see us in a week. If you can convince them then I'm sold ... and Mia ...' Joshua slowly looked Mia up and down. 'When you come back, impress them like you've impressed me today.'

As Mia walked out of his office she felt Joshua's eyes on her bottom.

Chapter Seventeen

April 2006

'Lucy, what are your ideas?' Mia asked as she led the weekly editorial conference in the meeting room. As Lucy spoke Mia watched her, impressed with how cool and composed she remained while reading out her feature plans. Araminta had gone on maternity leave, meaning Lucy was in sole charge of managing all the freelancers, and she was clearly doing a great job. Despite wanting to hate her, Mia found she couldn't. She understood why Lucy hadn't spoken up when Joshua had sacked her – nothing she could have said would have saved Jo from the chop – and enough time had passed for Mia to realise it. Lucy was now Mia's number one, and the magazine was flourishing with both of them in management positions.

As Lucy outlined a feature idea involving a man who'd set up a clinic for models who got depressed when retiring aged twenty-five, Mia checked out the rest of the team. Lizzie was still in charge of the fashion desk – with Tally, Imogen and Rosebud all covering the shows – and Helena, who used to be junior writer, had stuck it out long enough to be the main staff writer on the magazine. Mia briefly wondered why Madeline had kept her on, but decided Helena could write the small pieces that freelancers refused since there weren't enough words to make it worth their while. Hayley still looked after the picture desk, Hannah was the travel editor, and the same faceless men were in charge of design. Despite not having worked at *Gloss* for two years, nothing much seemed to have changed. Mia looked at all of them as she watched them focusing on Lucy and she tried not laugh as the realisation hit her. At only twenty-three she was the youngest of them all – yet she was in charge.

Everyone knew how old Mia was, of course, and when she'd first joined as deputy editor, gossip about her had run wild throughout Garnet Tower, with the boys from *Lewd* magazine coming downstairs to check her out, and various journalists from *DG*, *Honey* and even *Cycling Monthly* looking at her with curiosity in the canteen. Nobody thought for a moment that Mia could be as good as she said she was – after all, how could she be? She was only twenty-three, a baby. Mia overheard several of the girls in the toilets suggesting that she had only been given the job because she was Gable Blackwood's little sister, and one afternoon Mia caught Debbie bitching to Katherine by the smoking room, saying that Mia had been employed because Joshua fancied her. Mia shot her a look of absolute blankness as she walked past the pair, and Debbie froze, unsure if Mia had overheard her or not. As Mia stepped into the lift she smiled to herself. Debbie's time was nearly up, she thought.

As the weeks went on, however, Mia had worked her magic so well on the magazine that the editorial team grudgingly had to admit that she *was* good. A month after she had begun, the team put the finishing touches to the first issue Mia had controlled, and they confessed it was killer – it was a breath of fresh air that incorporated the *Gloss* brand but took it to dizzying new heights. Word on the street was that *Cosmopolitan*, *Marie Claire* and *Glamour* had all managed to get hold of Mia's dummy copy of the magazine, and that they were all having crisis meetings to discuss how to get the edge back into their publications. Although it pleased her to find out that she was panicking her competitors, Mia found the girl who had sent the dummy issues to the rival publishing groups and sacked her in front of everyone. As the security guard led the sobbing girl out into the bustle of Covent Garden, Mia surveyed the room silently. She had their respect, and it had only taken four weeks to get it.

Although Mia was one hundred per cent focused on *Gloss* she also kept an eye on Madeline Turner. The editor only spent a few days a week in her office in Garnet Tower, and Mia was unsure of what she did the rest of the time. Whatever it was it must have been exhausting, as Madeline now seemed like half the woman she used to be – her thick black hair no longer gleamed, and she was pale and withdrawn, with dark circular shadows under her almond-shaped eyes. When Mia first 'met', Madeline Turner she was shocked at how tired she appeared to be. Her husband, on the other hand, was more energetic than ever, enjoying the ripples that Mia was causing in the industry.

'Everyone at *Marie Claire* is quaking in their boots,' Joshua said with evident satisfaction, as the pair had lunch at Petrus one afternoon. Mia and Joshua were sitting near one of the abacuses with blown-glass beads, and before they had ordered Mia had run her hands over the claret leather chairs and crisp white linen tablecloths, feeling tiny ripples of pleasure rush through her body. Being able to grab a quick working lunch in the Berkley's restaurant definitely proved she was a player, and other people obviously felt she was too, judging by the number of diners who had appeared at their table to introduce themselves.

Mia grinned, and she speared a piece of roasted Scottish lobster on to her fork. Even though she was as busy as she had been the last time she was at *Gloss*, at least she had the money and the spare time in the evenings to ensure that she ate properly. She hadn't put on a single pound since she had been back in the UK, and that was the way she liked it.

'I told you they would. We pretty much sold out last month's edition, despite the larger print run, and *Gloss* is hot again. We ran a few focus groups, and it seems we're now appealing to a slightly younger AB1 woman. Eva in commercial has told me about a thirty-two per cent surge in advertising because of it, and we're allocating more pages to ads next month.'

'So would you say you're on track with your promise to double circulation by the summer?' Joshua asked, and Mia nodded.

'I'd say so – we've signed a deal with a book publisher to include two summer bonkbusters with the June issue, but not only that, we have a secret weapon for July – it's never been done before.'

Joshua stopped eating his breast of Gressingham duck and sighed. 'What is it, then?' he asked, sounding bored despite his eyes lighting up. Mia could tell he was desperate to find out what she had in store but he couldn't bear for her to know it.

Mia took a sip of her mineral water, and then, sensing Joshua's impatience, she ate another mouthful of her meal – she had ordered lobster with scallops, followed by salmon and lobster ravioli and it was the best seafood she had ever eaten. As much as she wanted to rhapsodise about it she noticed that Joshua ate his meal with minimal interest, not even looking as though he was enjoying it. However, Joshua certainly appeared to be interested in her, and his eyes were flashing as he waited to hear what she had planned. She loved watching her boss get hot under the collar.

'Ever heard of disposable MP3 players? They're the latest thing to come out of Japan, and they're incredibly cool. They hold up to a hundred tracks, but the difference between these

MP3 players and all others is that they're so cheaply made that once you're done with them you just throw them in the bin – perfect for taking on to the beach if you're scared your iPod is going to be ruined by sand.'

'How much?' Joshua asked.

'They're retailing in Japan for the equivalent of ten pounds, but we've been talking to the manufacturer and have managed to get enough to mount 900,000 for the July issue at a pound a pop. What the manufacturer doesn't realise is that Eva managed to sell them five adverts across our other properties – *DG* is taking two ads, *Lewd* is taking one plus an advertorial, and *Honey* is taking one as well – and that these are covering the cost of the MP3 mount on *Gloss* as well as bringing in a tidy profit.' Mia looked at Joshua triumphantly, but rather than looking impressed he looked pissed off.

'And on whose authority did you do that? Only editors can create initiatives like that, and even then individual publishers can only OK cross-advertising once they have spoken to me.'

Mia stared at Joshua. 'I'm pretty much running *Gloss* now, and I just thought—'

Joshua interrupted her. 'Do bear in mind that you are only deputy editor of *Gloss*, and therefore anything like this not only needs to be run past me, but also past Madeline.'

'It's a bit difficult when Madeline's hardly in the office,' Mia said sullenly, and she kicked herself. She'd let her guard down, and Joshua's eyes flashed in anger. It was the first time Mia had overstepped the mark.

'Madeline is certainly there long enough for you to brief her on your plans for the magazine. She told me last night that she feels pushed out of her own title, and even though you're bringing in results I want you to spend more time filling her in.'

Mia quietly ate the rest of her meal, and when she'd

finished she cautiously arranged her cutlery on her plate.

'I apologise,' she said. 'I should have discussed it with both of you. It won't happen again.'

Joshua shot her an easy, relaxed smile from across the table. 'That's better,' he said, and Mia felt herself tense up. She hated it when he patronised her. 'Don't do it again, and if you're finding it hard to work with Madeline tell me. It's what I'm here for.'

Mia took a sip of water. 'I do have to admit that my relationship with Madeline is struggling somewhat. I'd be happy for some advice, if you have the time.'

Joshua indicated for a waiter to take their plates away, and then he gestured for Mia to continue.

'Madeline seems ... she seems disinterested. I know that she loves the magazine, and that she wants to stay involved, but I do find it difficult when emails asking for her opinion go unanswered. There is only so much chasing I can do, and when a deadline approaches I have to make the final call, normally because she isn't here. It's difficult to be sympathetic to what she is going through,' Mia said carefully, 'when I don't know what it is that is keeping her occupied.'

Joshua stared at Mia for a few moments, and then he lowered his voice.

'Can I be personal with you?' he asked, and Mia nodded. She had been hoping that her relationship with Joshua would move from the professional to the private, and it looked as though it was finally going to happen. The more information she had on him, the easier it would be to fuck him over, Mia thought.

'Madeline is ... well. How old would you say Madeline is?'

Mia shrugged. 'Thirty?' she guessed.

Joshua let out a callous laugh. 'Just goes to show those expensive creams I buy her are doing the trick. No,

Madeline's approaching forty, and like most women her biological clock is ticking away. As you know, it's in the family interest for me to have an heir, and although Madeline is keen for a son she is struggling to provide me with one. We've been trying for years, but Madeline may have left it too late. The stupid bitch should never have lied to me about her age.'

Mia tried not to look at Joshua in shock as she digested his insensitive language about his wife, and she hastily reminded herself of who he really was. Nothing he did, she thought, should surprise her any more, and she recalled how much of a bastard he'd been when she had accidentally sent Madeline the knickers meant for Marina Stone. Mia told herself to remember why she was here in the first place. She had been having such a great time running *Gloss* and working with Joshua that she had almost forgotten she was only there to wreak her revenge. It was time to play the game.

'It must be difficult,' Mia said, reaching over to Joshua's hand and putting her own on top of it. 'No wonder poor Madeline is looking exhausted.'

Joshua let out a bark of laughter again. 'I don't see what's so exhausting about IVF, I must say – and the company is paying for her to have the best treatment on Harley Street. No, Madeline only has herself to blame for this; she should have told me her real age from the start so she could have got pregnant sooner, but she's one of those "career women",' he said, disgust prickling at his voice. 'She's not like you, playing in magazines until she finds a rich husband to take her away from all of it. She actually meant it when she said she wanted to be the most powerful woman in magazines! Shame she was never much cop at it . . .'

Joshua drained his post-lunch brandy, and looked around the dining-room. Most of the businessmen had gone back to their offices, and the only people who remained were women who were dressed in designer clothes and had an air of being drugged on whatever painkiller was in fashion. Joshua ran his eyes over their bodies disinterestedly.

'Do try to keep Madeline in the loop, though, please. The last thing I want is for her to go running to my father moaning about how she's feeling undermined. Father has a soft spot for her – well, I suppose he would given she's my wife – but really, I think the sooner she is pregnant and unable to work, the better.'

Mia stared at Joshua incredulously – did he really believe that all Madeline was good for was to be a baby machine for him? Despite experiencing a wave of pity for Madeline, Mia felt her heart leap. If Madeline could get pregnant Mia would have full control of the magazine, she thought. The IVF couldn't work soon enough.

'And if Madeline doesn't manage to get pregnant, then, well, something is going to have to be done,' Joshua said ominously, and he stared intently at Mia until she began to feel uncomfortable. Trouble was definitely brewing for Mrs Garnet.

October 2006

'So you're happy with that features list?' Lucy said, sitting on a chair next to Mia's desk and swinging her legs. She was dressed completely in black – spike knee-high boots, opaque black tights and a black baby-doll dress – and the only colour on her was a deep red slash on her lips. Her skin was lightly tanned, and her hair gleamed under the fluorescent lights of the office. 'I wasn't sure about the "divorce interview" with Britney, to be honest, but Jessie claims it will be an exclusive.'

Mia smiled at her features editor. 'It all sounds good – just make sure Jessie takes more than one dictaphone, and that the lawyers legal everything before and after it's passed on to the subs.'

'Will do. Now what's this I hear about the *Media Guardian* phoning up earlier for a quote from you?' Lucy said cheekily. 'Are you doing an interview?'

Mia shook her head. 'I'm not quite sure what that was about, to be honest. They were asking questions about Madeline, mainly – maybe they're doing a profile on her.'

'What sort of questions?'

Mia thought for a moment. 'They asked what it was like working for her, and if the success of *Gloss* was down to Madeline overdoing it.'

Lucy laughed. 'Overdoing it? She's hardly ever here.'

Mia grinned. 'That's what I said, and then I asked them to scrap that comment. I suppose they wanted a quote or two about our run of success recently – it was nothing very interesting.'

'What isn't very interesting?' Joshua Garnet asked, as he walked past Mia and Lucy on his way to his office. He was dressed in a dark blue Savile Row suit and he looked fantastic. Even though she hated him, Mia had to admit he was incredibly attractive, despite looking nothing like William.

'Oh, the *Media Guardian* phoned up Mia to ask what it was like working for Madeline,' Lucy said.

Joshua looked at Mia sharply. 'Did they ask anything else?'

'Not really,' she replied. 'They wanted to know what it was like working on a thriving magazine, that kind of thing. I gave them bland, inoffensive answers, don't worry.'

Joshua grimaced. 'Bloody journalists have been sniffing around us recently – I had to sack one of our newer cleaners for speaking to them. I think they're trying to do a hatchet job on us. Why they persist in hating everything Garnet Publishing does I'll never know ...'

'Jealous of our achievements, I expect,' Mia said smoothly. For once Joshua's poker-straight face looked worried, and it gave her a tiny thrill. Little did he know, she thought, that when the time was right, he was going to be the subject of her revenge – and it was going to hurt more than a newspaper running a negative article about him.

Mia watched him sweep back to his office, and just as she began to imagine Joshua begging her for forgiveness, Lucy interrupted her. She was staring at Mia with interest.

'A penny for your thoughts?' she asked, but Mia merely shook her head at her features editor, and tried to push her emotions out of harm's way. She smiled brightly, and sensing that it wasn't the right time to probe any deeper, Lucy summarised the meeting and returned back to her desk. It had been bugging her for a while now, but after her exchange with Joshua she couldn't ignore the feeling in her gut that something about Mia wasn't quite right. Lucy put on her mirrored Gucci sunglasses – something everyone did in the office when they had a hangover – and stared at Mia directly. She reminded her strongly of someone, but much to Lucy's annoyance, she couldn't quite work out who it was.

Mia was working late on a dummy copy of a relaunched version of *Gloss* when she heard Madeline's extension ringing incessantly. It wouldn't stop, and it was distracting Mia from her report on a selection of revamped logos. Sighing, Mia went into Madeline's office to turn the ringer off, but as she leant over the desk she jolted the mouse, which, in turn, woke the computer from hibernation. Mia glanced at the screen and saw Madeline's email was open, and unable to resist, she sat down at the editor's desk and stared at the inbox. The newest three emails were all from a journalist at the *Media Guardian*, and they all asked the same questions – why Madeline was ignoring their phone calls, and if the rumours were true: that Joshua was preparing to sack her from *Gloss* to make way for Mia, and that he was going to divorce her for not providing him with an heir.

Mia looked around the deserted office and felt her heart thudding. Although she quite liked Madeline – or what she knew of her – Mia recognised that she was the one obstacle to achieving her dream: to become editor of *Gloss*. If Madeline got pregnant Mia knew she'd become editor by default, but the IVF wasn't working, and as a result Mia had to remain as deputy editor. It wasn't enough – she wanted to be officially in charge, and she wanted Joshua to come to a decision about the editorship now, and not in a year's time when he decided enough was enough.

Trying not to feel guilty, Mia clicked open the first email and read it in full. The journalist's questions were personal and invasive, and Mia wondered how Madeline was coping under the pressure of trying to please her husband in both the office and at home. Judging by the number of ignored emails in her in-box Madeline wasn't coping professionally at all, and Mia wondered briefly if she ever regretted marrying into the Garnet dynasty. She was certainly paying for it now. Without pausing to think, Mia quickly typed out a response to the journalist as Madeline and pressed 'send'. As she walked back to her desk Mia reasoned that the sooner Madeline was put out of her misery, the better it would be for everyone. And then, she thought with a smile, *Gloss* would be hers.

Mia was taking her first sip of her Starbucks skinny latte when she froze. She'd taken the *Media Guardian* out of the main newspaper when she'd spotted the cover – a photograph of Joshua and Madeline on their wedding day. Mia quickly turned the page over and found what she was looking for – an exclusive article with a reproduction of an email that claimed Joshua Garnet insisted on sleeping with all the *Gloss* cover girls. The email had been sent, according to the story, from Madeline three days before and it said, quite clearly, that Joshua was a philanderer who abused his position of publisher.

Mia allowed herself a small smile before drinking the rest of her coffee. Joshua would be forced to sack his wife now, she thought, and Mia briefly wondered what the scene would be like at the Garnets' home. She was willing to bet it wasn't pretty. Mia turned the page over to see what other industry news there was, when the colour drained from her face. The next headline asked 'Has Madeline Gone Mad?' and the accompanying article detailed Madeline's 'breakdown' in a double-page spread.

To accompany the article, the newspaper had printed several photographs of Madeline. The first showed her triumphant as she won the Editor of the Year Award, but the second was a paparazzi shot of how she was now – tired, frail and seemingly more interested in shopping in Selfridges than taking control of her magazine. In the image Madeline was looking at baby clothes longingly, and Mia felt guilt consume her – it had never occurred to her that by sending an email as Madeline she'd be giving the journalists even more ammunition to do a character assassination on her. To distract herself from the image of Madeline cutting a lonely, pathetic figure, Mia finished reading the article, which suggested that Joshua Garnet was not only going to sack, but also divorce his wife for making up rumours and being incompetent.

Mia suddenly felt ashamed of herself; after all, what had Madeline ever done to her? She'd given Jo Hill her first break as Joshua's PA, and even when she'd sent Madeline the knickers picked out for Marina Stone she'd never been mean to her – she'd just chosen to believe her husband over her. And, Mia thought glumly, what wife wouldn't? Mia wondered what Madeline's reaction would be to the article detailing her breakdown, and worried that she'd helped Joshua push her over the edge. As the guilt firmly began to set in, Mia looked up from her desk, spotting some of the editorial team whispering to each other in shock while holding the newspaper. A couple of the designers were talking to Helena, wondering if Joshua really would sack Madeline, and they concluded that he most probably would have to, that there was no way he could condone Madeline's talking to the press and saying such explosive stuff.

By the end of the day Mia was sick of everyone talking about the situation, and her head pounded, despite the Nurofen she'd swallowed. Debbie had tartly told her that both Joshua and Madeline would be working from home that day, and Mia had fended off all types of intrusive questions about what was going to happen from her team, from other magazines within the group, and from the press. Although she hated Debbie with a passion, she felt a tiny twinge of sympathy that the girl had had to answer the phone all day to the media. If she had been Joshua's PA she'd have probably burst into tears, but Debbie had remained calm, telling every journalist that phoned up that Garnet Publishing had 'no comment', and that a statement would be released at some point during the week. Mia noted that Debbie enjoyed feeling important, and she wondered if she knew more than she was letting on.

Of course, it was entirely possible that Joshua would issue a press release explaining that Madeline had been under a lot of stress and that she was sorry for the email she had sent, before allowing the situation to die down and putting Madeline back in her office as normal. Mia wondered if Joshua's silence on the situation was indicative of that, and as minutes ticked away the tension headache that had wound itself around her head pulled tighter. An hour before she was due to go home Mia picked up her bag and caught the Tube back to Hampstead, where she allowed herself to bite her nails and feel as insecure as she had done when she had been overweight and called Jo Hill. Even a bar of chocolate did nothing to ease the pressure.

That evening Mia had just sunk on to her sofa to watch *EastEnders* when Joshua phoned her mobile. As she had predicted he sounded fucked off and tired, and Mia reminded herself to sound sympathetic and not anxious to know what had been happening. She knew how much Joshua hated the appearance of desperation in anybody, and she was determined to play it cool.

'It's been a hell of a day, but I've managed to speak to the board and we now have closure. Madeline has "resigned", but before we issue a statement to the press, my father and I would like you to confirm that you'll be editor of *Gloss*. Before you say yes we need you to agree with two conditions.'

Mia stared at her phone incredulously – she was so excited that she wasn't sure if she could breathe. This was the most amazing phone call of her life; she could feel her tension easing away and her head feeling light. Just before Mia floated away – or fainted – Joshua continued.

'Number one, we need to get some decent press about Garnet Publishing into the media asap,' Joshua began, and as he spoke Mia realised she'd never heard him sound so efficient before. She wondered if Harold Garnet was in the room with him, and where Madeline Turner was. Were they in Joshua's living-room while Madeline was in the bedroom? Or had Joshua decamped to a hotel, desperate to leave the marital home? 'As soon as you sign on the dotted line we're going to want to do some intensive PR with you. You're going to be the youngest women's glossy magazine editor in history, but you're also the little sister of a major Hollywood star, so the company is going to want to capitalise on that. Although many people already know who you are, by becoming editor of *Gloss* you are going to be A-list. Everyone will know your name, and everyone will be watching your every move.'

Mia remembered how she had seen Joshua and Madeline entering Chantez a few years earlier, and how awe-inspiring they had been. Mia was younger, prettier and skinnier than Madeline Turner had ever been, and she instantly realised that by committing herself to a career of editing *Gloss* she was agreeing to become a serious player, one who was talked about as much as her magazine was. It was the stuff dreams were made of.

'And what's the second condition?' Mia asked neutrally, not wanting to give her excitement away.

'Number two, you have dinner at my house tomorrow night so we can discuss this, and our relationship, in more detail.'

Mia remained silent for a moment as she thought about what Joshua was implying. Mia knew that he had only married so that he could demonstrate to his father that he had given up his playboy ways, and that marrying Madeline was proof enough to Harold Garnet that his son was ready to control Garnet Publishing. Now that his wife had disgraced the company so dreadfully, Mia realised that there could be an opening for Madeline's other position within the Garnet empire. The thought of it excited and disgusted her all at once, but Mia now realised just how powerful she could become if she did end up being Joshua Garnet's second wife. If Madeline hadn't been able to get pregnant, Mia was sure that the family would see her as surplus to requirements, leaving Mia shining so brightly as Garnet Publishing's new golden girl that nobody would see Madeline lurking in the shadows.

'Let me think about what you have just said, and I'll let you know my thoughts about this at dinner tomorrow night,' Mia said, after some consideration. She had briefly toyed with the idea of announcing to Joshua that he had just offered Joanne Hill a job as editor of his most popular magazine, but Mia knew that if she bided her time, her declaration would be even more spectacular.

Joshua agreed. 'A car will pick you up from your house at eight tomorrow night,' he said, and Mia felt a shiver of excitement run down her spine as she remembered that one of the perks of being an editor at Garnet Publishing meant you were automatically assigned a gleaming dark red Mercedes complete with driver. 'Dress up, Miss Blackwood,' Joshua said softly, and without saying another word he hung up, leaving Mia speechless that she had just been offered the job of controlling *Gloss*. It took a moment, but she suddenly realised that she was so close to having her revenge on Garnet that she could almost smell it. The thought of finally treating Joshua Garnet as he had treated her was exhilarating, and all night she tossed and turned in bed, guiltily imagining herself encased in Madeline Turner's office, but also wondering what she should wear to dinner the following night.

Chapter Eighteen

Mia was standing by her window when she noticed the dark red Garnet Mercedes discreetly pull up outside her house. She skipped over to her full-length mirror and checked her reflection one final time. She looked like Cinderella, she thought, as she remembered how she had loved the old Disney film as a child. A man named Pedro at Vidal Sassoon had spun her blonde hair into an intricate bun earlier in the afternoon, and as Mia twisted in front of the mirror she noticed that the gems on the tiny combs that held her hair in place sparkled in the light. Mia's dress was a cloud of peacock blue, with hand-sewn crystals twinkling on a bodice that pushed her full breasts higher and made her already small waist look even tinier. At her hips a full skirt flared into a waterfall of silk that cascaded down to her delicate silver heels, and as Mia walked over to her bed to pick up her silver Prada handbag the skirt moved with her, making Mia look as though she were gliding across her bedroom carpet. She had never looked lovelier, and she couldn't wait to present herself to Joshua. He would want to ravish her, she thought, as she sprayed herself lightly with Ralph Lauren Romance. And the best bit was that she'd never, ever sleep with him. She only wanted to tempt him, to make him crazy about her.

The car left Hampstead, eventually pulling up outside a tall Georgian house in Connaught Square, and Mia tried not to let her eyes widen in disbelief. Was this really where Joshua and Madeline lived? It was so grown up, so expensive, so exclusive. Her surprise was answered soon enough, as Joshua pulled open the heavy black door and grinned at her from inside his house, which, despite looking cold and imposing on the outside, appeared to be warm and inviting on the inside. Joshua was wearing a navy Turnbull & Asser suit and a white shirt from Haines & Bonner, and Mia could see a shadow of stubble on his chin. Despite the stress of the Madeline situation he still managed to look attractive.

'Glad you made it,' Joshua said, drinking in Mia's appearance as she walked up the path to his house. The press would love her, he thought, as his gaze swept over her breasts, her waist and her hips. Just looking at her turned him on, and it made him grin. Working even closer with Mia when she was formally editor of *Gloss* would be a lot of fun.

'I was beginning to think old John here had got lost,' Joshua remarked as he nodded curtly at the driver, and he shut the front door firmly on Mia's chauffeur, refusing to tip a Garnet driver when — in his opinion — they were paid well enough. Mia stood in Joshua's hallway, but before she had the chance to take in her surroundings he led her into one of his sitting-rooms. Mia looked around nervously, hoping there'd be no personal items of Madeline's lying around. She didn't think she'd be able to cope with seeing a more human and intimate side to the woman she'd pushed over the edge.

'Have a seat,' Joshua gestured, as Mia took in the room. Cream rugs were thrown across the oak floor, and four large chocolate-brown leather sofas formed a square formation around a huge glass coffee table. A plasma television screen dominated one of the white-painted walls, and gold-framed mirrors hung from the others. Joshua clearly liked looking at himself, and thankfully there were no photos or traces of Madeline's personality dotted around — it was as though she'd been erased. Mia perched gingerly on one of the sofas and she looked up at Joshua, who was staring at her with a mixture of pride and lust so intense that she could feel herself involuntarily squirming under his gaze. To distract herself Mia concentrated on the leather beneath her hands. It was soft and buttery, and without warning she remembered the feeling of William's skin. She couldn't shake the memory of him, no matter how much she wanted to.

'I adore your house,' Mia said, as she tried to stop staring at what looked like an original Vettriano hanging on a wall. 'It's beautiful.'

'It's not too bad,' Joshua said, brushing the compliment aside. 'I'm sure the price has devalued since that politician and his awful wife bought the one down the road, but there wasn't much I could do to stop him from getting it. There's an actor who lives here too, terrible riff-raff. To be honest, I'm thinking about moving out, getting a place in Mayfair.'

Mia gulped. Although she'd always read about the Garnets' enviable wealth she'd never imagined stepping into Joshua's life and experiencing it for herself. A memory of an article about Joshua running baths of Veuve Clicquot Grande Dame for former kiss-and-tell lovers flashed through her mind. She'd always thought that the Garnets' wealth was more urban myth than fact, but sitting here, in one of Joshua's opulent sitting-rooms, Mia could tell Joshua Garnet had never needed to work in the equivalent of The Royal Oak. It intimidated her, and she had to remind herself that she was good enough to be Joshua's companion for the evening. Mia had earned her position by working up the ladder and being cunning. It was more than Joshua Garnet had ever had to do.

'Drink?' Joshua asked, as he leant against his original Georgian mantelpiece. 'Have you ever had a Louis XIII cocktail?' Mia shook her head, and Joshua looked pleased. 'Women love them. Marina Stone, the model, is a dear friend of mine, and she once had one at the Piano Bar at the

Sheraton Park Hotel. I managed to persuade the head man there to make two for us to celebrate your editorship. They were delivered ten minutes ago. Let me get my girl to bring them in.'

Joshua pressed a subtle panel in the wall and murmured something quietly into it. Within a minute a girl in a French maid's uniform placed a silver tray with two cocktails on the coffee table, and before Mia could thank her she slipped back out of the room. Mia wanted to laugh. Of course Joshua would have servants, and of course they would be dressed in French maids' uniforms that, if made of latex, wouldn't have looked out of place in a sex shop in Soho. Joshua raised his eyebrows at Mia, as if he could tell what was on her mind, and passed her the drink.

'I don't fuck her, if that's what you're thinking,' Joshua said, startling Mia with his frankness. He changed the subject. 'Now, before you taste this, let me tell you exactly how it is made,' he said. 'Knowing how expensive it is will make it taste even better. A shot of Rémy Martin Louis XIII – the finest cognac in the world, I must add – is poured into this crystal martini glass. A sugar cube is then added, along with two drops of angostura bitters, and then it is finished off with Charles Heidsieck champagne.' Joshua stared at the liquid in the crystal glass and then looked at Mia. 'But look closer. Can you see any other ingredient?'

Mia peered at her cocktail, and, in shock, she realised there was a diamond nestling at the bottom of the glass. It had to be a whole carat. Her mouth dropped open and Joshua laughed.

'That's four thousand pounds' worth of cocktail in your hands, Mia. It's a special cocktail for a special girl, and I couldn't think of anything finer to toast your promotion with.' He raised his glass and Mia copied him, still grinning in disbelief at the cost of the drink in her hands. 'Congratulations, Mia Blackwood, and welcome to your editorship of *Gloss*.'

Joshua took a sip of his drink, and Mia followed suit. It was one of the most delicious drinks she had ever tasted, and even though she was impressed that Joshua had gone to the trouble of getting them, a tiny voice in her head asked if she wouldn't be more at home with a gin and tonic. Mia ignored the voice and smiled. She would just have to get used to such extravagance. She was editor of *Gloss*, after all. She had a lifestyle to keep up.

'Joshua, it's superb, thank you so much,' Mia said, and she took another sip. 'I can see why Marina Stone likes this cocktail so much.' Mia wondered if Joshua would mention that he and Marina were lovers. Would he ever be that honest with her?

Joshua laughed. 'Marina likes extremes, and this drink takes "ice with a slice" to a whole new level. Unfortunately Marina also likes to powder her nose a little too much, so I've not seen her in a while. She's at a place in America at the moment cleaning up. I have to admit I miss her – she's a good friend, even if her nose is falling to bits.'

'Joshua . . .' Mia began hesitantly. 'May I ask where Madeline is?' The moment Mia asked the question she instantly regretted it. Joshua's face turned to thunder, and Mia could tell that the subject of his wife was a sore point. Best stick to mistresses, Mia reminded herself as she took another sip of her drink. She had to admit it was exquisite.

Joshua sat next to Mia and sighed. For a moment she thought she could see real pain in his face, but the closer Mia looked, the more she realised that Joshua was putting on an act. He didn't give a fuck about Madeline Turner, and Mia knew it.

'She's gone,' Joshua said melodramatically, and Mia wondered if he stretched to fake tears. 'Our marriage has been unhappy for a long time, and unfortunately Madeline became so preoccupied with trying to have a baby that our relationship floundered. I don't believe Madeline is well, so she is spending some time in a hospital while I file for divorce.'

Mia put her martini glass on the coffee table carefully and turned to look at Joshua. Was she hearing him correctly? 'A hospital?'

Joshua nodded. 'I'm afraid to say Madeline isn't quite right in the head, so we persuaded her some time in a little clinic would do her good,' he said, sighing again. Mia could see an amused glint in his eye, yet she played along. Lying was what working in the media was all about.

'The newspaper piece was the final straw to be honest. Anyone could see that Madeline was not well, and my father and I realised we had to do something about it. The poor woman was quite delusional and refused to admit she had spoken to the *Media Guardian*, but we phoned them up and they forwarded a copy of the email she originally sent them. I think they thought we were going to sue, but Madeline's health was our main priority. We were rather shocked – we didn't think that Madeline was this bad.'

Mia bit her lip and felt ashamed of herself. Poor Madeline.

'But let's not talk about my soon-to-be ex-wife any more,' Joshua announced, the mood in the sitting-room lightening instantly. 'And let's talk about you. I must say that I knew it was only a matter of time before we handed the magazine over to you. What you have done with *Gloss* is marvellous,' he said, brushing her arm with his. 'And now that you are formally editor the sky is the limit with what you can achieve ... with my help, of course. I hope you don't mind but I thought we'd run through the salary increase and the flat when we're back at the office.' For a moment Joshua looked a little uncertain, and Mia stared at him. She could guess what was coming as he cleared his throat and turned on his charming smile, reserved only for women he wanted to fuck.

He spoke softly. 'I really want to use this evening to get to know you, Mia. I think you're one of the most beautiful women I have ever met, and, if you don't object, I want to forget about the Mia who I work with in the office and get to find out more about what drives you, what turns you on. You fascinate me, Miss Blackwood, and I want to discover the real you.'

Mia tried not to laugh. If Joshua knew who the real Mia Blackwood was he would have made her regurgitate his £4,000 cocktail back into the glass before throwing her out into the street. Imagining his fury when he found out who she really was pleased her, and she gave Joshua a slow, sexy smile. If she could get Joshua to fall in love with her, revenge would taste even sweeter.

'I'd like that,' Mia said tenderly, and as she put her hand into Joshua's she could feel him squeezing it gently. Even though she could see past all of Joshua's bullshit there was something about him that was quite sexy in an obvious way. She let Joshua lead her into the dining-room, and she didn't even mind that his eyes never left hers the entire time.

'Tell me you didn't fuck him,' Amelia said on the phone to her best friend the next day. 'Please tell me that even you wouldn't fuck Joshua Garnet. You hate him!'

Mia lay on her bed and giggled as she remembered the evening. Joshua's private chef – who used to work at the Ivy, no less – had served up a meal of her favourite foods: tender sirloins of steak, crispy fries and a soufflé that oozed a river of dark, bitter chocolate the moment her spoon broke the surface. After dinner Joshua had tried to tempt her with Paxton & Whitfield cheeses, Rozes Port Red Reserve and Pierre Marcolini chocolate truffles, but Mia was too high on the conversation with Joshua to eat another bite. She knew Joshua was trying to seduce her with food, and she appreciated his attention to detail. To her surprise, Joshua was brilliant company, full of funny stories and amusing anecdotes, and above all else he knew the magazine industry as well as she did. It was wonderful to have a sparring partner, and even though Mia hated him she allowed herself to ignore her vendetta for one evening so she could enjoy a side of Joshua Garnet she had never experienced before.

'It's all part of my plan, Ames,' Mia said, ignoring her question. 'If I can get him to fall in love with me, it will make the realisation that I am Jo Hill hurt all the more.'

'You did, didn't you,' Amelia said bluntly, and there was a pause at the other end of the phone.

'I won't say it didn't cross my mind,' Mia admitted, 'but no, I didn't. When it comes down to it I'm old-fashioned about my virginity, and I don't want to lose it to the person I hate more than anyone else.'

Amelia let out a sigh of relief.

'Besides,' Mia said, 'if I refuse to sleep with him he may even propose just to get me into bed. Imagine Joshua Garnet getting down on one knee to Joanne Hill and how he'd feel once he knew what he'd done.'

April 2007

Six months later Joshua sat in on the editorial meeting. As Mia gave a presentation about her vision for the future of *Gloss*, Joshua let his eyes wander over her. Although she was dressed sedately for spring in a pink Ballantyne cashmere jumper and soft grey trousers from Joseph, Joshua thought Mia was still incredibly sexy. With her high, firm breasts almost jutting out of the cashmere every time she made a point, and her juicy, round bottom being hugged deliciously by the wool of her trousers, Mia was scandalously sexy. She may have acted like butter wouldn't melt, but Joshua knew that underneath that sweet exterior there was something a lot dirtier than most people would think. She had a devious side, and there was something in the steel in her eyes that made Joshua realise that she was a lot like him: cunning, manipulative and accustomed to getting what she wanted. However, Joshua thought, as he shifted in his seat to try to hide his erection, if you didn't know her, Mia could almost have passed for a virgin. There was something about her that reminded him of a schoolgirl desperate to lose her virginity, and it turned him on even more.

Yet the more she spoke, the more Joshua realised that there was more to Mia than just a knockout body and a face that Cameron Diaz would be jealous of. Mia truly was a brilliant editor, and it looked as though his instinct about her was right. She would not only be a credit to the company – selling hundreds of thousands of magazines and bringing in enough advertising revenue to wipe his ass on – but also to his family. If she just spread her legs – and Joshua was sure that she would, as no woman had ever said no to him – then the Garnet heirs would be beautiful children.

Joshua tried to concentrate on Mia's sales forecast, but gave up. He let his gaze lazily wander over Mia's body again, and he could feel his balls beginning to ache. Mia was a distraction, a horny, beautiful and lithe distraction, and Joshua loved women who played hard to get. Girls who threw themselves at him were a turn-off – they were only after a slice of the Garnet fortune, and Joshua wanted a woman who already had money. If they were poor they couldn't possibly be able to afford to look after their bodies properly, and a flabby twenty-something with badly applied fake tan and cellulite didn't do it for him. Mia did. And however much Mia pretended she didn't want him, Joshua knew that when the time was right she would pour herself out of whatever designer dress she was wearing for his exclusive benefit, and would allow herself to submit to him. It was only a matter of time, and even though Joshua was nearing thirty-five, there was still all the time in the world for Mia to realise she was going to marry him and have his child. But if Mia thought he was going to propose without a taster of what she was like in bed, she had another thing coming. There was no question that Joshua was going to try her out first and make sure she was up to scratch at sex. He had made that error with Madeline, and he wasn't about to make the same mistake twice.

As Mia rounded up the meeting and her editorial team filed out of the room, her eyes caught Joshua's. She blushed.

'Great meeting,' Joshua said, and as he walked past Mia to leave he lightly brushed past her breasts. Mia blushed even harder, and Joshua laughed softly to himself. He wouldn't have to wait much longer, he thought to himself. Mia Blackwood was very nearly his.

'Have you seen this?' Lucy asked, waving a newspaper at Mia as she rushed into *Gloss* first thing on Monday morning. Mia was drinking a strong Starbucks latte in her office in the hope that it would wake her up, and she glanced at her features editor wearily. So long as it didn't involve her, Mia wasn't interested in whatever exploits the tabloids were banging on about – she had better things to be thinking of. Mia had spent most of the early hours on the phone to Gable, hitting him for his opinion on how she could get away with not losing her virginity to Joshua. Although she loved her fictitious brother, she loathed the time difference between London and Hollywood, as it meant that one of them – usually Mia, because she was the one whose mind raced as soon as she climbed into bed – missed out on sleep because of it.

Gable had spent nearly four hours on the phone to her

that night, and after finding out that Joshua was desperate to sleep with her, he'd concluded that what Mia really needed was a boyfriend. Gable didn't think Mia would ever be able to forgive herself if she ended up having sex for the first time with the person she hated most.

'What about that William guy?' Gable had asked as Mia yawned down the phone and watched the sun beginning to rise. The sky above London was a bright pink, and Mia reminded herself that red sky in the morning was the shepherd's warning. She sighed. Even nature was telling her not to go near Garnet.

'William? When I came back to London, Amelia was desperate for me to "test" my face on someone, so I pretended to interview him,' she said quietly. 'He didn't realise who I was and I don't think he liked me very much.' Mia tried not to sound sad. The thought of William's reaction to the beautiful Mia Blackwood still hurt, and she wondered why William hadn't recognised her when Amelia eventually had.

'Yeah, but he adored you once, right?' Gable hadn't the patience to even try to be subtle. He had a supper coming up and he had to start to think about getting ready for it. 'Why don't you just give him a ring and ask him to go for a drink?'

Mia had laughed down the phone. William was the only person who she had ever loved, the only man who had appreciated her for who she was rather than what she looked like. It had merely been her insecurities about her body that had prevented them from taking their relationship further, but despite Mia now being confident about how she looked she couldn't see William liking her any time soon. To him she represented 'shallow London', his number-one subject of loathing.

After Mia had hung up she looked at her mobile. It was nearly six in the morning, half an hour before her alarm was supposed to wake her up. Sighing, Mia turned the alarm off and padded into her kitchen to make herself the first of what she estimated would be many coffees.

As she switched her espresso machine on she stared at her kitchen in amazement. Even though she'd lived in her Garnet penthouse apartment overlooking the Thames for nearly six months, she still couldn't get over the fact that it was hers for a minimal rent. As well as a doorman, a swimming pool and an insulated media/cinema room on the floor below, Mia's penthouse had been refurbished to the tune of almost £4 million – with no expense spared on the specification.

In addition to the pool and cinema, Mia had three big bedrooms – all complete with large en suites and wet rooms where the shower cascaded as though it were hot, tropical rain – a wood-panelled walk-in wardrobe bigger than her first flat, a glass-fronted wine cellar, a humidity-controlled cigar suite (which, Mia had laughed down the phone to Amelia, would come in handy if she knew what she was meant to do with it) and a fingerprint-access strong-room where Mia stored her jewellery, including the diamond and garnet necklace Cartier had sent to congratulate her on her promotion.

The eat-in kitchen contained shiny red units and brushed-steel appliances, and the dining-room – which was perfect for hosting Mia's media gatherings – was bedecked in metallics, with delicate gold-leaf wallpaper and a chandelier that glinted over the long silver and glass dining-table.

In Mia's main sitting-room there was a grand piano, and the roof terrace – which contained imported Japanese trees and fragrant roses – overlooked the Thames, allowing her a view of Big Ben to the left, and Canary Wharf to the far right.

Mia thought her penthouse was beautiful, but she spent most of her time in the comparatively tiny television room that contained a large squishy sofa and a medium-size plasma television screen. It was the one room that Mia truly felt comfortable in, because every time she walked through her apartment she felt guilty that she'd stolen the editorship of *Gloss* from Madeline. It was there that she sat now as she sipped her coffee and looked at a text message that had been sent to her two days ago. If she played it right, Mia thought, she could make amends to Madeline after all.

'Mia, seriously, wake up and check this out!' Lucy snapped Mia out of her thoughts and flung the copy of the newspaper on to her desk. Mia sighed and put thoughts about her virginity out of her mind as she reached for the paper and saw that rather than it being the *Sun*, it was the *Media Guardian*, and that she was on the cover of the supplement. Although she'd done the interview only two weeks before she had forgotten that her profile was coming out, and her stomach fizzed in excitement.

'What do you think?' Lucy asked excitedly, and Mia stared at her photo on the front of the paper and tried to remain calm. If anything confirmed how far she'd come, it was this; her photo on the country's leading media supplement, and a double-page feature all about her. The article inside made it clear that Mia was the rising star of 2007, but ... but it wasn't really her on the cover; it was a fabricated woman who had taken the industry by storm in a cloud of deceit, cosmetic surgery and designer clothes.

Mia stared at the stunning blonde woman on the front of the supplement, and she felt all the excitement drain from her body. Quite without warning she yearned to look like she used to, when she had brown hair, a natural body and face, and a naïve sparkle in her eyes when she thought about her future and everything she could achieve.

Mia put the newspaper on her desk and slowly ran her fingers over her face, feeling her cheekbone implants, her enlarged lips and her sculpted nose. If she had not had cosmetic surgery, she thought, there was no way she'd have ended up on the front of this supplement, or as Joshua Garnet's prospective new girlfriend. Doors had only opened for her because of how she looked, and even though she had the talent to make sure her career progressed quickly, what she could do professionally seemed to take second place to the fact she was sexually attractive. In a way, Mia was just as she had been when she was overweight – she was still trying to prove to people that despite how she looked she had the ability to do great things.

Mia held the supplement up against one of her office walls and considered framing and hanging it as her first piece of PR, but the more she looked at her image grinning back at her, the more a sour taste began to rise in her mouth. Seeing herself like that was a reminder that the world she was in was so shallow that it didn't allow overweight people to be part of it, and that, rather than trying to take a stand and fight for who she was, she'd buckled under the pressure and changed the way she looked.

'You look great, right?' Lucy said, and Mia turned to her, startled. She'd forgotten that Lucy was still in her office, and that she'd been watching her reaction. Lucy was staring at her intently, and Mia didn't like the knowing look on Lucy's face.

'Right,' Mia said abruptly, and she reminded herself that she had to play the game – most people would be delighted at such brilliant personal coverage of themselves in the press. Mia forced a bright smile and beamed at Lucy, before turning her gaze back to the photograph of herself. 'Do you think my arms look fat, though?'

Lucy laughed, and then she sat down on the chair on the other side of Mia's desk. 'They're nowhere near as large as they used to be, Jo,' she said quietly, and Mia froze.

'How long have you known?' Mia whispered, watching her hands shake so much that she had to put the paper down.

'A while,' Lucy admitted, and she reached over and touched Mia's hand. 'As I got to know you, I realised that even though you looked different you hadn't changed that much. OK, so you sometimes speak with a hint of an American accent, and you still act like you're unsure of just how gorgeous you are, but you're pretty much how you used to be, just a happier, more confident version,' she remarked.

'Why didn't you say anything?' Mia asked, and she watched Lucy lower her eyes to the floor.

'I didn't think you would ever forgive me for not standing up for you,' Lucy said, and both of them remembered that fateful day. 'I've been over that day so many times in my head, and if I could go back in time I would have told Joshua that you were his star writer, but I can't, and there's nothing I can do to make it up to you.'

Mia sighed. 'I forgave you a long time ago, you know,' she said, as she remembered how pleased she had been when Lucy got *Gloss* to pay for her stay in the Shore Club in Miami. 'And the fact that you've known I am Jo all this time and have not said anything ... well ...'

Lucy gave Mia a rueful smile. 'Even now I still feel really bad,' she said.

Mia brushed her comment away. 'Don't,' she said. 'I know how hard it is to stand up and be different in the media, and who knows, if our roles had been reversed maybe I'd have done the same. What matters now, though, is that Joshua doesn't find out who I am,' she said, and Lucy stood up to give Mia a hug.

'I'll never tell,' she whispered into Mia's ear, and just then Joshua appeared in the doorway.

'Loving the lesbian action almost as much as I loved the *Media Guardian* piece,' he said casually, without saying hello or asking how either of the women were. Lucy left them to it, and Joshua eyed Mia's tight indigo shirt that was left open to show the top of her breasts, wondering how hard Mia liked her nipples to be pinched. 'Fancy dinner tonight at my house to celebrate?'

Mia looked at Joshua and realised that if Lucy knew who she really was, it was possible that it would only be a matter of time before Joshua guessed, too. It was time to crank up her revenge mission, she thought, and it meant making Joshua want her so much he couldn't concentrate on anything else.

Mia gave Joshua a coy smile and looked at him from under her eyelashes. 'Josh, I'd love to, but it's the UK Magazine Awards tomorrow night,' she said sweetly, 'and I need to get some sleep because I plan to be the last person to leave the after-party.' Joshua struggled to maintain a disinterested expression, but he failed.

'The weekend, then,' Joshua said.

Mia nodded. 'Perhaps,' she said, and she walked away from him, knowing that Joshua had never experienced a woman playing hard to get before, and that it made him want her even more. Mia grinned as she flipped open her mobile and started writing a text message. Everything was going to plan.

Chapter Nineteen

Lee Stockhead, editor of *Lewd* magazine, took one look at Mia walking into the reception area of the UK Magazine Awards and let his mouth drop open.

'Babes,' he said cockily, leering at Mia's cleavage, which was popping out of her Christian Dior couture dress, 'you look hot as hell.'

Mia shot a goofy grin at Lee, and then quickly reminded herself that she was supposed to be acting demure. She was wearing a strapless pale grey gown that pushed her breasts up to extraordinary heights before dropping to the floor dramatically, and the silk clung to the shape of Mia's slender body like a second skin. To accessorise, Mia had dressed in the first diamonds she had ever bought herself. A platinum Chopard necklace dripped princess-cut diamonds around her neck, and a matching bracelet dangled from her wrist, making her already slender arms look even slimmer. Mia's freshly highlighted blonde hair was pinned up at the back of her head, and she had arrogantly kept her make-up simple – she was wearing just a touch of blush and a slick of mascara. Most of the women in the ballroom were in their thirties and Mia could feel their glares pricking at her skin. She was pleased – she wanted them to be jealous of her and her youth.

'Please tell me you're sitting next to me,' Lee whined in

his cockney accent. Like Mia, at only twenty-eight he was younger than most of the other editors, but Mia felt as though she was a world away from him and his beer, football and tits lifestyle. 'If I have to sit next to that fucking bore Nigel from *Cycling Monthly* like I did last year I think I'll fucking top myself.' Lee dragged his eyes away from Mia and checked the table plan before letting out a little groan. 'Fuck's sake, I am as well. Do you think the organisers hate me or something?'

Mia said nothing; she'd heard the story about Lee pissing against the ice sculpture the year before and was surprised that he had been allowed back this year, despite his magazine being up for an award.

'You'd better sit on my lap later to cheer me up,' he said, leaning towards Mia unsteadily. Mia laughed and walked away to check another table plan, noting she was sitting on a table full of *Gloss* staffers. She let out a sigh of relief. If she had to sit next to Nigel she probably would have bribed the organisers to poison his meal. He was a good editor, but was a bit too obsessed with the Tour de France.

The UK Magazine Awards was the most important award ceremony in the magazine industry, and true to form the ballroom of the Savoy was decked out accordingly. Swathes of burnished gold hung from the walls, and each circular table, laid with crisp white linen tablecloths, lit up the room with tiny tea-lights in midnight blue. The stage had been set with a podium, and behind it was a table laden with awards, each glittering under the rainbow spotlights. Traditionally dressed serving staff hurried around serving the most important people in the business glasses of champagne, and when the guests weren't clocking each other's outfits, they looked at the sumptuous menu in disbelief, feeling their stomachs rumble appreciatively. The UK Magazine Awards' organisers had outdone themselves this year.

'You look nice,' Helen said bluntly as Mia approached the *Gloss* table and sat down next to Lucy. Helena was wearing a gathered silk Chloé halterneck dress that, despite its price tag, managed to make her look slutty rather than sexy.

'You look more than nice,' Lucy said, hurrying to cover Helena's overt jealousy. 'You look terrific. Is that Dior?'

Mia nodded, and Lucy cast her eyes over Mia's dress approvingly. 'It suits you,' she said. Lucy had kept it simple in a white Armani dress and a single ruby that dangled from a silver chain round her neck. 'Is Joshua coming this evening?' she asked Mia innocently, and Mia gazed into Lucy's eyes before answering. She'd not told Lucy that she was planning on playing with Joshua's lust for her, but uncannily, Lucy was on the ball yet again.

'Of course,' Mia said lightly. 'He's sitting over there.' Mia gestured to a table full of what she had nicknamed 'the suits' from Garnet Publishing. Joshua was wrapped up in a conversation with Edward Sampson-Brown, the finance director, but when he felt Mia's gaze on him he looked up and shot her a private, sexual look. Unfortunately both Lucy and Helena spotted it, and Mia quickly changed the subject.

'Who do you think is going to win?' Mia asked, hoping Lucy would follow the conversation and stick to safe territory. Lucy considered the question.

'*Lewd* for Magazine of the Year, *Cycling Monthly* for Fucking Boring Magazine of the Year, and Hannah winning Travel Writer of the Year for us.' Lucy ran off a list of magazines on her fingers, critiquing each one and explaining why she didn't think many of the big names – such as *Cosmopolitan*, *Marie Claire* and *Heat* – were going to win anything. Mia listened quietly while sipping her champagne, and she marvelled at how astute Lucy was. Perhaps it was time for her to be promoted to deputy editor, she thought, but only if they could poach a decent features editor – such as Holly Morrison – to replace her.

Mia sighed. She desperately wanted *Gloss* to win Magazine of the Year, but she knew that they didn't really stand a chance. When the judging period had started, *Gloss* had still been the publication that Madeline was ignoring while concentrating on her ovulation charts, and even though Mia had turned it around in the last few months, she knew that the magazines were judged on the whole year and that every single month counted, rather than just the ones that she had been in control of.

'I think you're right,' Mia agreed. 'But I do hope Lee stops drinking. Joshua will be fucked off if he makes a scene.'

Lucy laughed. 'Lee thinks he's the new James Brown, and he will do whatever it takes to piss off *Loaded* and *FHM*. If making a scene at an awards ceremony gets him and the magazine in the "Bizarre" and "3 A.M." columns tomorrow, you can count on him doing something. I'd put fifty pounds on Lee pretending to fuck one of those ice sculptures,' Lucy said, nodding at one of the many ice-carved angels that twinkled in the light.

'Or perhaps throwing his food at Mark Frith from *Heat*,' Mia murmured, as she watched Lee trying to start a food fight with one of his competitors in the Magazine of the Year category. As *Heat*'s pristine white tablecloth was splattered with the starter of light-pink salmon mousse, Mia watched a discreet security guard have a word with Lee, who sat down sulking. Mia and Lucy laughed softly to themselves, only stopping when the main course was served.

Even though Mia was used to eating in expensive restaurants, she didn't think she had ever experienced a meal that tasted so good. The food was simple – spring lamb with green vegetables and roast potatoes, but Mia had never enjoyed a meal so much. The lamb was cooked perfectly and melted in the mouth, and the vegetables were snappy and full of flavour, so unlike the ones Mia bought from Planet Organic in the hope that they would taste of something. The roast potatoes were ones that Mia had always hoped to make herself but had never managed. They were crisp from goose fat on the outside, and so fluffy on the inside that Mia felt as though she had died and gone to heaven. As Mia devoured every one she declared them the best she had ever eaten, only realising that Helena was staring at her with a sour expression when she had finished chewing.

'You shouldn't eat carbs, you know,' she said, cutting up her lamb delicately and wrinkling up her nose at Mia. 'You'll get fat.'

'Oh, come on, Helena,' Lucy said, with a hint of irritation. 'The Atkins Diet died a death years ago – do catch up.'

Helena looked smug. 'It's not Atkins, it's GI, and roast potatoes have a high GI and are therefore bad. The lamb is OK, but I'm not sure about these vegetables. Don't eat them if you don't want to bloat out, Mia,' Helena said in a sinister voice, prodding at the sugar-snap peas on her plate with a knife. Mia wondered what her problem was.

Lucy rolled her eyes at the staff writer. 'Keira Knightley eats roast potatoes,' she said sharply, and despite herself Helena looked slightly abashed. Nobody had forgotten how Helena had desperately wanted to be Keira – she had never lived down the article in *Gloss* where she tried emulating her. 'Besides, I can't see Mia ever getting fat, can you?' As soon as Lucy asked the question she knew that half the girls around the table were gleefully imagining what Mia would look like if she was overweight. Mia ignored them and ate another roast potato from Lucy's plate while trying not to laugh. If they were picturing her as the size she was when she was Joanne Hill they were close to finding out her secret, she thought. Not that they would ever realise it.

As Mia slowly enjoyed every mouthful of the dark choco-late mousse that was served for dessert, she kept a close eye on Helena. Her staff writer was shooting daggers at her from across the table, and Mia wondered what she had done to deserve the evil eye. None of Helena's pieces for the next issue of the magazine had been edited that much, so she couldn't have been offended by Mia's article cuts, and even Lucy had begrudgingly admitted that Helena was becom-ing a better writer with every piece she submitted. Helena – a Jewish princess who had three credit cards in Daddy's name – was steadily becoming more professional as the months went by, and as Mia licked her spoon she wondered if Helena's parents had finally put their feet down and insisted that their daughter pay her own rent. Mia looked at Helena carefully. If her staff writer was hoping for a promotion and a pay rise she was definitely going the wrong way about it.

'They're about to start!' whispered Lizzie excitedly, cut-ting into Mia's thoughts as the rest of the room watched Damien Jay swagger on to the stage in an overdone macho walk. Mia turned to look at him. His baggy jeans hung low off his ass, and he wore a baseball hat tilted to one side, which was appropriate if you were presenting imported American programmes to hungover teenagers on Sunday mornings like Damien did, but not for handing over important industry awards to a room full of egotistical and cut-throat journalists in black tie. Even though he had been a male model before tak-ing to television, Damien appeared to be nervous and jittery at standing in front of the cream of the magazine industry. His eyes darted from table to table, and Mia recognised the telltale signs of cocaine. As Damien began to stutter through the first few awards – mainly for business publications that nobody was interested in – some of the journalists sitting near the front of the stage began to heckle. They could smell blood, and their sport was in going for the kill. Mia didn't join in – she was full of sympathy for him. Damien reminded Mia of herself before she had undertaken surgery, and she couldn't understand why a man who was model-handsome could be so insecure.

When Damien had managed to award seven glittering statues without being booed off the stage entirely, he turned his attention to presenting the award for Magazine of the Year. As he ran through each title in a bored, monotone drawl, Mia felt her heart leap when the name *Gloss* was read out. She had done so well that the magazine had been nominated, and even though she knew it wasn't possible to win, the fact that her magazine was recognised as good enough to be considered gave her a thrill. She would win next year, Mia thought, as Damien methodically told the audience about each consumer title. It was good enough for her that they were the only women's glossy to be nominated, and that in itself spoke volumes about how they were perceived compared to their competitors.

As the drum-roll vibrated quietly in the background, and a spotlight shone on their table, Mia thought of Gable, and how he would feel if he was nominated for an Oscar for one of his roles. Would it be as amazing as this? Would he feel like everyone was watching every small facial movement he made, hoping to see if he was nervous, confident or blasé? Mia stuck out her chin defiantly, and as she did she could feel Joshua gazing at her. For a split second Mia caught his eye and grinned nervously, forgetting to play it cool, and she spotted Helena scowling at her. Lucy grabbed her hand under the table, and Mia felt the tension in the room mount as her mouth went dry. Magazine of the Year was probably the most important award presented in the industry, and even though she kept on telling herself that *Lewd* would win, Mia still held her breath in anticipation as she watched Damien

Jay fumble with the envelope containing the name of the winning magazine.

The drum-roll got louder, and finally, after what seemed like hours, Damien opened the envelope. He smiled cheekily to the crowd, and any sympathy Mia had for him vanished. She wanted to hit him.

'And the winner is ... *Lewd* magazine from Garnet Publishing!' A round of applause rang out in the ballroom, and Mia tried desperately hard to maintain her smile. Don't be disappointed, she told herself, clapping mechanically as Lee Stockhead bounded on to the stage and raised the award above his head. Lucy shot her a sympathetic look, and even though they were all clapping wildly and wolf-whistling the *Lewd* editorial team, she could feel everyone from *Gloss* slump in their chairs. Mia knew she had to perform too, and she loudly told her team how brilliant it was that a Garnet title had won Magazine of the Year, how fantastic it was to have been nominated. Everyone looked at her with dull eyes, and nodded in agreement. They had all wanted it so much.

When Lee had finished making his sexist and non-PC speech, Mia decided she'd had enough for one evening. She was just thinking of excuses to make to her team when Damien Jay took to the stage for a final time. Mia looked at him in confusion. Wasn't Magazine of the Year the final award? Damien opened another envelope – this time more deftly – and Mia stared at the stage. As much as she had had a good evening, she just wanted to go home to get an early night. She had to plan a year's worth of killer material so that *Gloss* would win the Magazine of the Year title hands down next year. She didn't think she could stand the thought of Lee Stockhead lording it over her, thinking he was the better magazine editor.

'And now for our final award,' Damien said, his voice

taking on slightly more confidence now that he could see an end to his evening, 'Editor of the Year.'

Mia and Lucy stared at each other, and Mia looked back at the stage. Was it possible? Could it be possible?

Before Mia could even begin to consider that she might have been nominated for the most covetable award that any one person could have in the industry, Damien swiftly opened the gold envelope in his hands and shot the crowd a dazzling smile. Unlike the rest of the evening, everyone was completely still and silent. Every single editor in the room could feel their heart beating, and each crossed their fingers in the hope that their name might be on the card in the television presenter's hands. With every eye in the room trained on him with such intensity, Damien began to get nervous again, and before the heckling could start he blurted out the name of the winner.

'Mia Blackwood for *Gloss* from Garnet Publishing!'

The spotlight flashed to the *Gloss* table, and Mia froze, unable to take in what she had just heard. A roar rang out loud enough to disturb the rich Americans eating their supper in the dining-room next door, and surrounding competitors rushed to pat her on the back, offering Mia their congratulations. Mia barely heard them. It was like she was encased in cotton wool; as if everything was in slow motion and she was on the outside looking in. Was this really happening to her? Was it possible that at the age of nearly twenty-five, Mia was Editor of the Year? Mia watched her team rise to their feet excitedly, and as they clapped wildly and beamed at her, she was jolted out of her astonishment and stood up, smoothing her dress down against her body and looking up at the stage.

Damien Jay's gaze had followed the spotlight to their table, and all eyes were on her – the editor of *Gloss*. Mia slowly wound her way through the tables of magazine journalists, editors and publishers, and as she stepped up on to the stage the claps got louder. Mia was deafened – all her senses were trained on the thunderous sound of her heartbeat racing in her ears, the clapping, cheering and wolf-whistles. Mia accepted the spear of crystal rising from a brushed-steel base from Damien, and she stood on the stage looking out at the sea of faces. Everyone was giving her a standing ovation, and Mia felt tears welling up in her eyes. Stop crying, she thought, as she felt tears running down her face. Just fucking stop crying. Flashing cameras took her picture, and Mia was struck by how she was not only the Editor of the Year, but a news story in herself. She would be on all the front pages tomorrow as the impossibly young Editor of the Year who looked like a gorgeous actress on the red carpet, and Mia wondered if it got any better than this.

Mia glanced down at her award, and she was startled to see her name had already been engraved on the glass, along with the title of the award and the year. And even though she didn't show it through her professionally maintained beam, Mia felt her heart break. The award had been made out to Mia Blackwood, and she would have given anything to have seen the name 'Joanne Hill' engraved on it instead.

May 2007

Mia sat in Gordon Ramsay at Claridge's feeling uncomfortable. Joshua had insisted on taking her out for dinner to celebrate her success of winning Editor of the Year, and even though Mia had managed to make up a week's worth of excuses, citing deadlines and dinner parties as explanations for her full calendar, Joshua had finally cornered her late one evening in the office, refusing to take no for an answer until Mia agreed to dinner. When Joshua had told Mia that Debbie had booked the best table at Gordon Ramsay, Mia's heart sank. She knew he had chosen the spot to see and be seen rather than to experience the food, and after his public display of affection after the awards ceremony – when he had kissed her full on the lips and let a hand linger on her bottom in front of all the *Gloss* team – Mia had no doubt in her mind that he would act in the same way tonight. Joshua was treating Mia as his new girlfriend, and their relationship was the talk of Garnet Tower, especially when Helena had burst into tears after seeing Joshua kiss Mia for the first time. It had turned out that the poor girl had been nursing a crush on Joshua for years, and her suspicions about her publisher pursuing her editor had been confirmed – particularly when she had read about it in the gossip magazines.

As Mia picked at her poached poulet de Bresse and confit de foie gras, Joshua congratulated her again by raising a glass of vintage Bollinger and toasting her and the magazine. Mia felt miserable, despite her superb starter. All around them were company directors, film actors, publishing barons and the cream of London society, and even though everyone was far too polite to stare directly at them, Mia knew that she and Joshua had an audience. Joshua grabbed Mia's hand despite her trying to eat, and he looked like he wanted to ravish her. Mia wanted to throw up.

'You look beautiful tonight, darling,' Joshua said across the starched cream linen draped on their table. He eyed Mia's silver Balenciaga dress and the garnet and diamond necklace approvingly, and Mia could feel her skin prickle with distaste as his eyes roved over her body hungrily. Memories of how cruel Joshua had been to her when she was his PA taunted her as she tried to swallow her starter, and when she remembered Joshua's lips on hers at the awards ceremony she could feel herself begin to cringe. Play the game, she thought to herself, as she managed to swallow her foie gras. She smiled brightly at Joshua, and squeezed his hand in what she hoped was a friendly, non-sexual way. Her plan to make him want her had worked too well – he wouldn't leave her alone and she was out of her depth.

'Thank you, Joshua,' Mia murmured. She looked around the restaurant and pretended to admire the lavish art deco design while surreptitiously checking to see if anyone was watching them. She wondered if Claridge's was really the best place to tell Joshua that she wasn't interested in a personal relationship with him, and she decided she didn't care. If one of the other diners was unrefined enough to go running to the press reporting that they had had a spat, it wasn't her problem, she thought. At least it would show Joshua that she meant business.

'It's a beautiful restaurant, isn't it?' Joshua commented, dipping his spoon into his smoked eel and celeriac soup and eating it without really tasting it. Mia quickly glanced at the high ceilings, the high-backed purple chairs, the geometric design of the carpet and the heavy deep-red curtains. Even though the overall effect of the room was impressive, Mia didn't care for it, preferring the simplicity of her local Italian on Gabriel's Wharf.

'If you like this sort of thing, I suppose it is,' Mia said sullenly, and he looked at her in concern. Mia stared back at him, willing him to be the Joshua she had known when she had begun hating him, the Joshua that she knew he really was deep down. Despising Joshua when he was acting like such a wet blanket made her feel like a bitch, and Mia hated that. She had to remind herself that Joshua was the bastard, not her, and that he was only being nice because he wanted her to be his trophy wife.

'But do you like the food?' Joshua asked worriedly. Mia sighed.

'Yes. It's fine. But I'm not a fucking restaurant reviewer like Charles Campion, so please stop quizzing me,' she snapped.

Joshua looked around the room quietly. Nobody, not even Madeline, dared to speak to him out of line, and Joshua's eyes narrowed before resuming their troubled expression. Mia was so busy glaring at the table that she missed the flash of Garnet supremacy under the façade.

'Mia,' Joshua began, 'is something wrong?'

A waiter served their main courses – baked baby sea bass with aubergine caviar, and fillet of monkfish wrapped in Parma ham – and Mia took a deep breath. She was letting her real feelings ruin her performance, and she knew that she had to let Joshua down gently. He was her boss, after all.

'Look, I've been thinking,' Mia began. 'As much as I like you I don't think I'm ready for a relationship, certainly not a full-time one.' She gave Joshua the sweetest smile she could, and ignored the lines of confusion that were appearing on his forehead. 'I want *Gloss* to win Magazine of the Year next year, and I owe it to the company to put the magazine first. I can't do that if I'm involved in a relationship, and working alongside you makes it so very difficult for me to concentrate in the office.'

Mia delicately began to slice up her monkfish. She didn't dare look at Joshua's expression, but she thought she had pitched their 'break-up' well. Every man wanted to think he was so sexy that no woman could concentrate on anything but him.

'Oh, darling, I had no idea you were finding it hard juggling everything. You should have said,' Joshua said in a soft voice. Mia looked up at him in surprise. 'I know how much you like running *Gloss*, but I'm sure Lucy would be able to take over the magazine. You have to think about what's important, and now that you've won Editor of the Year – which, in my opinion, is better than Magazine of the Year – it might be time for you to concentrate on other things.'

Mia balanced her knife and fork on her plate and watched

Joshua eat a large mouthful of sea bass. She couldn't decide if he was being deliberately obtuse or if he simply had not heard her correctly.

'Joshua, I don't want to give up *Gloss*. There's so much more work that needs to be done on it – such as getting the website off the ground – and besides, I enjoy it.'

Joshua grinned at her. 'I know you do, but you're my girl-friend now. And really, what's more important at the end of the day? A silly little job running a magazine, or being a wife and mother?' Mia felt her temper bubbling under the surface. He was maddening. If he thought she was going to become the second Mrs Joshua Garnet and give up her career to pop out mini-Joshuas he had another thing coming.

'Joshua, for fuck's sake, I'm not even twenty-five yet. I've only just begun my career and I don't intend to give the magazine up,' she hissed. She should never have put herself in this position, she thought.

Joshua laughed, and several people turned their heads to look at him. He spoke quietly. 'Don't forget, darling, that my family owns *Gloss*. If you don't think you can have a relationship with me while running the magazine I won't hesitate in asking you to resign. I have to put the magazine's best interests first.'

Mia stared at him. Suddenly, through all the tender glances and softly spoken words, Mia could see the glint of steel in Joshua's eyes. She was back on familiar territory, but it un-nerved her.

'And if I want to put the magazine's interests first rather than your personal ones . . . ?' Mia asked.

'Then I shall fire you.' Joshua had nearly finished his plate of food, and he curled up his mouth in amusement. 'You have to remember, darling, that not only do I own the magazine, but I also own you. And if you won't have a relationship with me I will see to it that not only do you not work on a

Garnet magazine ever again, but that every other publishing company knows that you are such a power-hungry bitch that you forged an email from Madeline and sent it to the *Media Guardian* to get her sacked.'

Mia went white. She had no idea that Joshua had known she was behind that.

'It suited me at the time because Madeline was a lame duck who couldn't run the magazine or get pregnant to save her fucking life, but if you're not going to play fair then neither am I.'

Joshua finished his meal and looked at Mia's nearly untouched plate.

'Not hungry, darling?' he said, in his gentle, caring-boyfriend voice. Mia shook her head. 'Then why don't we go back to your flat? I have a proposition I would like to discuss with you. I had rather hoped we would be able to talk about it in here, but I can see that this restaurant is making you grouchy. I'd much prefer you were in comfortable surroundings before I ask you the most important question of your life.'

Mia held Joshua's gaze for what felt like minutes. Yet once more he had taunted her with the threat that if she crossed him she would never be able to work in the magazine business in the UK again, and it made her seethe. The last time Joshua had spoken to her like that she'd run away to Florida – but this time, well ... Mia wasn't a little girl any more, and she wasn't going to let him think he could treat her like that again.

Joshua offered Mia his arm, and as she took it she looked up at him and gave him a dazzling smile. Joshua interpreted it as Mia guessing that he was about to propose, and as he led Mia out of Claridge's foyer he felt the small Asprey box in his jacket pocket. He knew that Mia was only making a scene about giving up work because he hadn't offered her a ring, and now that he was about to he could see Mia's silly tantrum about wanting to work full-time fading away. If she was a good girl, he thought, he would let her be a consultant on *Gloss*. Why, she could be editor-at-large for as long as she wanted provided she got pregnant. He shot Mia a tender smile, and was relieved to see her smiling back at him.

As her Jimmy Choos clicked against the black and white tiled floor of the foyer, Mia realised that for the past few years her life had been like a game of chess. She had plotted and planned so much that with every step forward and back she had let herself get caught up in the tactics of playing rather than concentrating on winning the game itself. Mia pulled her soft grey cashmere shrug over her shoulders to keep herself warm, and as she did so she realised she had almost forgotten her aim – to take down the king and acquire control of the board. Mia smiled to herself as they crossed the foyer and walked into the crisp night air. It was the right moment, she thought, to tell Joshua exactly who he had fallen in love with.

Chapter   Twenty

Joshua was going to go nuclear, Mia thought, as she sashayed seductively across her living-room to hand him a whisky. As she leant down to pass him the Tiffany cut-crystal tumbler, she caught sight of herself in the darkness of her floor-to-ceiling window. She paused slightly as she once again acknowledged just how beautiful she was. Her long limbs were lightly tanned, her make-up was as fresh as it had been when she'd applied it earlier in the evening, and her cheeks were flushed with anticipation.

Mia smiled softly at Joshua and then walked over to the antique mirror to scrutinise herself properly. Yes, she was stunning, but there was something about her reflection that made her feel uncomfortable: she was too perfect. Mia remembered how she used to look, and rather than disliking the memory of her former appearance, she was haunted by an image of a happier, more carefree girl. As much as she loved her Balenciaga gown, the Cartier garnet and diamond necklace that sparkled against her neck, and her expensive gold-spun highlights, she'd have been happier in jeans and a sloppy T-shirt. She wanted to be herself again.

Across the river Big Ben began to chime midnight, and Mia suppressed a tiny smile. It was so apt. This was the moment when Cinderella turned from the mysterious woman who stole Prince Charming's heart back into the put-upon scullery maid, and Mia was about to do the same.

In the mirror Mia could see Joshua walking over to her with a fond expression on his face, and as he turned round he produced a small Asprey jewellery box and got down on one knee. Mia tried not to look pleased. Joshua really believed that she would accept his proposal and give up running *Gloss* magazine.

'Mia Blackwood,' he announced theatrically in his booming voice, 'will you marry me?'

It was one of those chick-flick moments that Joshua was so keen on, and as if on cue he flipped the lid on the box to expose the largest pink princess-cut diamond Mia had ever seen. She tried not to laugh. She'd always known that Joshua traded in magazine clichés, but this was ridiculously over the top, even for him. His divorce hadn't even come through yet.

'Oh, Josh,' Mia said with a sigh, glancing at the platinum ring with minimal interest. 'What if I told you that at midnight I turn from being the beautiful princess into one of the ugly sisters? Would you still love me then?' Mia scrutinised Joshua's face while keeping hers as emotionless as possible. She sounded like she was in a play, but she knew it fitted the situation perfectly.

Joshua laughed patronisingly, and scooped Mia up into his arms.

'You and your fairy stories,' he said, kissing Mia's nose affectionately. Mia slithered from his grip in a quiet rage and took a deep breath. She was going in for the kill.

'Joshua, I'm serious.' Mia's eyes glinted with steely determination. 'You sit in your gilded office and think you know everyone and everything, but how much do you really know about me? I'm willing to bet you haven't a clue about the secret in my past.'

Joshua burst out laughing. '"Secret in your past"? Why

the melodrama, darling, and what on earth are you talking about?' Joshua took Mia's hands in his and smiled. 'Did you once make a porn movie in Hollywood when you were helping your brother start his career? Might I have seen it?' Joshua's tone was light, but Mia knew he was worried. He couldn't have a wife with any skeletons in her closet. 'Because I'd rather like to watch you having sex … especially considering you've been making me wait all this time.'

Mia's green eyes narrowed and her voice turned to ice. 'Don't be stupid,' she snapped, and Joshua stopped laughing as he saw how serious the beautiful woman in front of him was. 'Take a closer look at me, Josh,' she said with slight menace in her tone. 'Don't you remember me? Because after all this time I never forgot you.'

Mia took a deep breath, and as the memories of her childhood, her time as Joshua's PA, the pain of the surgery in Miami and, finally, winning Editor of the Year consumed her, she knew it was time to say those cruel little words that would crush him.

'I'm Joanne Hill, sweetheart.' Mia's voice broke and suddenly her icy tones sounded bitter. 'You know … the fat girl who was so desperate to write for one of your magazines that she let you bully her when she worked as your PA? You remember who I am, don't you? I think your exact words when you sacked me were that you'd make sure nobody else would employ me, and that I should "stop eating and hope that I rot into something more attractive".'

Mia let out a little laugh as she realised her voice had taken on the cold tones she had heard Joshua use so often in meetings, and as she stared at her boss she was pleased to note he was pale.

'So no, Mr Garnet, I don't think I will marry you. Unless, that is, you still want to marry me.'

Joshua let the small velvet box fall to the floor. His white face suddenly gleamed with a fine layer of perspiration, and Mia marvelled at how panicked he looked. She had never seen Joshua as anything but calm and collected, and she realised, with pleasure, that she had finally got to him. Game, set and match, she thought triumphantly.

'You're lying,' Joshua spluttered, as he forced himself to look at the woman who he had thought was going to produce the Garnet heir. 'You're Gable Blackwood's little sister, not that fat bitch who used to be my PA.'

Mia laughed cruelly. 'You don't sound so sure,' she said, taunting him.

'Is this some fucking joke?' He took Mia's arms roughly, pulling her closely towards him so he could stare at her face. Mia could smell the whisky on his breath and she was glad it hadn't dulled his reaction to her announcement. 'There's no way you're Joanne Hill,' he finally announced, and Mia heard the tension in his voice. 'She could never have turned into a woman like you.'

Mia removed his hands from her arms and took a step backwards, pleased that Garnet Publishing had thought to put panic buttons in every room of the flat. Even though she was sure Joshua wasn't going to do anything to hurt her, she had never seen him so agitated, so angry. Mia took a deep breath and resolved to lower the imaginary guillotine even closer to his neck.

'Look at my eyes, Joshua,' she said softly. 'Look deep into them and tell me they're different to the ones that would have haunted you if only you had some morals. Don't you remember them? Don't you recall how they used to look at you adoringly right up until you told me I was worthless? How they turned to hate when you refused to give me a chance?'

Joshua stared at Mia for what felt like hours, and just as she began to feel worried about what he would do next he gave her a twisted, acidic smile. Through his narrowed eyes he picked out some of Joanne's features on Mia's face, and even though he could barely believe it, he could see traces of the girl who had formerly been his PA. Although Joanne had thinned down, Joshua could see that the shape of her face was the same, and that her nose – although slimmer – was roughly the same shape as he remembered. But it was Mia's eyes that disturbed him the most. As she looked directly at him, he wondered how he had ever failed to see that they were the same murky green that used to irritate him, especially when Jo had dared to look him in the eye as he chastised her. He couldn't believe that he had fallen so hard for Mia that he had never noticed that her raw sex appeal barely hid the same characteristics of his mousy PA. Joshua felt his whole body tense up in fury.

Joshua stared at Mia with the iciest glare she had ever seen, and finally, he spoke. 'So it's true,' he spat angrily. 'Well, Joanne, top marks for reinventing yourself. But I'm curious – what did you do to raise the money for surgery? Whore your body to men who like to fuck fat girls?'

Mia laughed. Nothing he could say would ever hurt her again.

'You paid for it, darling. Olivia Windsor thanks you from the bottom of her cold, black heart. It's just as well you didn't believe me when I told you I was writing for *Gloss* using that pseudonym, or I'd have needed to take out a loan. But am I to take it that the engagement is off? It's a pity because I would have liked to give birth to your treasured little Garnet heirs. It would have given me great pleasure to see dumpy little versions of Joanne Hill running your magazine company – the greatest revenge ever.'

Joshua crossed his arms against his chest defensively, and Mia could see that her words stung.

'You think you're so clever, don't you, Joanne,' Joshua

said harshly, and Mia grinned at him. She was on a high from revealing her secret, and Joshua knew it. 'But with one little phone call to my friends at the *Guardian*, I can ruin you. I can tell the journalists exactly what you told me, and within twenty-four hours they will have gathered enough research on you – medical records, birth certificates, bank accounts – to have an exclusive front-page story that will shock the world. I can see the headline now: "Mia Blackwood Committed ID Fraud for Petty Revenge." Sounds good, don't you think?'

'Hardly,' Mia laughed. Not only was she thousands of steps ahead of him, but she also loved every minute of seeing Joshua scrabble about desperately for some ammunition. His threats didn't scare her, and nor did his mock-up of a headline. 'Stick to the day job, Joshie. Although it's lucky you're a publisher and not a sub-editor, isn't it? If you were a junior sub on *Gloss* I'd have sacked you for coming up with a crap headline like that.'

Joshua took his tiny black mobile phone from his pocket and flipped it open.

'Keep laughing, Joanne, because as soon as I dial the number you're history.'

Mia sighed dramatically, and walked over to her glass coffee table. On top of the sparkling surface lay some proofs of a magazine, and it was only when Mia handed them to Joshua that he realised that they weren't for *Gloss*.

'A four-page spread in the next *Vanity Fair* about how I changed my image and name to make it in the shallow world of magazines,' Mia explained, as Joshua's fingers gripped the inky proofs tightly in anger. 'Gable – who isn't really my brother, although I'm sure you've realised that by now, darling – gives his insight into why he pretended to be related to me, and Jessie, the journalist who did the piece, cleverly weaves my life story in with the horrid reality of the cosmetic surgery I undertook. I must say, it's a great article.

You might want to consider Jessie as a freelance for *Gloss*.'

Mia leant over the proofs, brushing her breast against Joshua's arm, and pointed out some of the photos. 'Look, here's me at my last day at school – don't I look miserable? – and here's some photos from a shoot I did a couple of weeks ago. It's a bit like playing spot the difference, isn't it?' she said, conversationally. 'Only it's more "guess what work Jo had done on her body and where".' Joshua looked up from the proofs with such rage that Mia suddenly wondered if she was going too far.

'You fucking bitch,' Joshua said to her abrasively, and even though she was slightly scared, Mia gave Joshua another brilliant grin.

'The magazine is out next week, but I wanted to tell you about it myself before someone at the printers leaked the story to the *News of the World*. If you like you can keep these proofs. I don't need them any more,' Mia said, but straight away Joshua ripped them up and let the pieces of shiny paper drop to the floor. He glared at her for the longest time, and then, quite without warning, a smile spread on his face, and Joshua suddenly looked pleased with himself.

'There's still the matter of the fraudulent email that you sent to the *Media Guardian* – the one that resulted in my having to sack Madeline,' Joshua said, slowly walking around the room. She hadn't considered that, he thought, triumphantly. He was going to nail the bitch if it was the last thing he did. When Mia didn't speak instantly Joshua spun round, and was surprised to see Mia still looked calm.

'Ah, yes. That,' Mia said matter of factly. 'Well, that's covered too, I'm afraid. I've spoken to Madeline and she knows all about it. She was a bit shocked at first, I have to admit, but when I explained why I had to do it she eventually came round. She even admitted that if the roles had been reversed she'd have considered doing it too. We had quite a little reunion, you know,' Mia said, her voice taking on an amused tone. 'And what surprised me most of all was how little Madeline knew about you and your sham of a marriage. But don't you worry – I filled her in on the gaps.'

Joshua narrowed his eyes. She was bluffing, he thought. She had to be. 'You "filled her in"? Really, Joanne, I do sometimes forget that you're just a kid. You can be so tiresome when you're trying to be dramatic. Spit it out.'

Mia took a deep breath. 'Fine. I told Madeline that you only married her so you could control Garnet Publishing,' Mia said, raising her eyebrows and watching Joshua's lack of expression with interest. His face remained poker-straight from years of business experience. 'She didn't believe me at first, but once I told her everything I knew about you, she realised just how naïve she had been. The truth hurt, but she needed to understand just why you discarded her like a piece of shit. I mean, she always knew you had an eye for the ladies – which was why she asked me to be your PA in the first place – but she really didn't think you were so stupid to start having affairs again.' Mia watched Joshua's eyes widen. 'When Madeline came round to the fact that I was telling the truth, she told me more about you and your home life. I never knew, Joshua, that your father really believed that Madeline was mentally ill. And I certainly didn't realise that for the whole time you were married, your father believed you were faithful to your wife. Really,' Mia continued, with a wink, 'I'd have thought that it would be a Garnet tradition to have mistresses, but it sounds as though your father is quite the moral, family man. I wonder how he would feel if his former beloved daughter-in-law phoned him up to tell him that not only was she sent to a clinic when she was actually mentally fit, but also that his son had an awful lot of affairs when he was supposed to be concentrating on producing heirs and building the family business up.'

Joshua scowled. 'You have no proof,' he said, crossing his arms and walking around the room again.

'Wrong again, darling,' Mia said. 'When I was your PA I had access to your email in-box. Well, I very cleverly made copies of all your emails to Marina, as well as to Jasmine, Natasha and Serena, and not only that, I took the liberty of photocopying your diary one night, too.' Mia laughed quietly to herself as Joshua stopped pacing and stood deadly still. 'All those nights you made me work late really paid off.'

'The media wouldn't dare to run any of these stories,' Joshua said angrily. 'Rupert Murdoch is a good friend of mine, and as for the Barclay brothers and Lord Rother-mere—'

Mia interrupted him. 'But stories like this *sell*, Joshie. You and I both know that. Can you imagine opening the *Sun* and seeing Debbie in some tarty red lingerie? If she was offered a couple of quid she'd do it in a second – it would be her big break and before you knew it she would be a contestant on *Celebrity Big Brother*, crying her eyes out about how badly she's been treated. Or how about a hand-wringing piece in the *Guardian* about how bosses always take advantage of their employees? This is a story that even the most discreet of newspaper proprietors wouldn't worry about running. Especially if you add in the fact that you got your perfectly sane wife sent to a private hospital just to get her out of your life.'

'Madeline would never do that to me.'

'Oh, you're so wrong. Madeline and I have grown rather close recently – well, we do have a lot in common – and she is perfectly prepared to go to any number of magazines or newspapers so that the whole world knows the truth about you. She'd prefer to break the news to your father in person, considering how decent he was to her when you were married, but other than that she'd be happy to go to the press. She needs the money, you see. Madeline and I both agree that it's time she gets what she's owed. And while we're sorting out what she rightly deserves, I need some hush money too.'

Joshua looked at Mia blankly. Ordinarily he thrived on negotiations, but Mia had him backed so far into a corner that he was willing to give her whatever she wanted to shut her up. If he lost his reputation, he thought, he would lose everything – his position within the company, the respect of the industry and his pride. 'What do you want?' he said emotionlessly.

Mia sat down on her sofa and crossed her legs. Her silver dress rose slightly up her tanned thighs, and even though she looked like a model, she spoke like a confident business-woman who knew she'd won a bloody battle. 'Ten million pounds each. Call it severance pay, and neither Madeline or I will ever go to the press with our story.'

Joshua stared at Mia, and his mouth dropped open. 'I don't have a spare twenty million sitting around. And if I don't have it, you can't have it.'

Mia laughed. 'You may not have it, Joshua, but your publishing company does,' she said, while smiling lazily. 'I asked Debbie to get the latest finance figures from Edward Sampson-Brown, and it seems Garnet Publishing is doing rather well. Ten million pounds each is small change to the company, and the figure is – at the very least – what we're worth. After all,' she said, 'what price would you put on your reputation?'

Joshua didn't speak for a minute as he assessed the situation. It would be worth spending £20 million just to get Joanne Hill and his stupid ex-wife out of his life, he thought. Just so long as they never darkened his door again.

'You will both sign a statement saying you will never speak about any of the things mentioned tonight,' Joshua said, menacingly. 'Because if a word of this gets out, you will not only be liable to give me back every single penny, but I will sue you so hard for breach of contract that you will have to beg your surgeon to take back your breasts in order to raise the money you'll owe me.'

Mia grinned. She didn't have a problem with his terms at all. 'Get the contracts to us within twelve hours and you have a deal,' she said, glancing at her clock. It was nearly one in the morning, and twelve hours was plenty of time for Joshua to call his lawyers to an emergency meeting. 'If you don't, I won't be held responsible if Madeline happens to phone up her cousin in tears. Do you remember her cousin, Joshua? The one who writes for *The Times*?'

Joshua shot Mia the most malicious glare she had ever received, and without saying a word he swept out of the penthouse and on to the rain-sodden streets of London's South Bank. As soon as he left, Mia slumped on her sofa, and it wasn't until she noticed the pink diamond ring glittering on her living-room floor that she realised she'd won: she'd taken on Joshua Garnet and beaten him. All the nervous energy that had built up soon drained from her body, and Mia felt only calm, soothing relief that quickly gave way to pure, ecstatic exhilaration. Even though she knew she could phone Amelia, Gable, Lucy or Madeline to fill them in on what had happened, Mia realised there was only one person in the world that she really wanted to celebrate with, and that was William.

Chapter Twenty - One

May 2008

A year later Jo was composing an email on her computer when Madeline walked into her office. Jo looked at the older woman carefully, and realised, sharply, that her business partner was beaming at her – something she'd never done when she'd worked at Garnet Publishing. When Madeline smiled, Jo thought, her whole face relaxed, and despite being in her forties, Madeline looked ten years younger than she really was. Motherhood suited her, Jo realised with a jolt, and she recalled how Madeline and her new partner, Dan, had summoned her to the hospital to meet Alfie Turner when he was only three hours old. Madeline had gazed down at her son with such tenderness that Jo had felt a pang of regret about how badly she'd treated Madeline in the past.

'Lucy phoned, and she says that Joshua has just called a crisis meeting,' Madeline said happily, as she sat down on a cow-print chair in Jo's large glass-fronted office. Framed covers of *Cerise* – their first women's glossy magazine – hung on the hot-pink walls, and in pride of place on Jo's desk was a photograph taken on a recent trip to Thailand. In the photo Lucy and Amelia were hugging each other, and Jo was being carried, piggyback style, by Gable. She was beaming directly at the camera. Jo knew that without the support of her friends she would never have been able to get through the intense weeks of media coverage about her surgery and deception, so she had treated them all to a luxurious few weeks on a remote Thai island.

Jo leant back in her indigo leather chair and laughed. Her natural brown hair fanned out on her shoulders, and even though she'd put on half a stone and wasn't wearing any make-up, she still looked as beautiful as she had done when she was pretending to be Gable's little sister. 'So he's finally realised that *Cerise* is going to shut him down,' she commented, and Madeline nodded as she smoothed out a wrinkle in her white Prada suit. In it she looked more like Bianca Jagger than ever.

'Lucy says that the staff have been whispering about *Gloss* folding and people being made redundant,' Madeline added. 'However, Lucy's certain she'll be offered a position on one of the other Garnet magazines. Apparently Joshua is still so sucked in by Lucy's simpering routine that he told her he "values her editorship skills". Really, he hasn't a clue that she's actually employed by us to ruin *Gloss* from the inside.'

'Good,' Jo said with satisfaction. 'But until *Gloss* goes under, Lucy is going to have to keep on pretending – we've worked too hard for anything to go wrong now.'

When Jo – or Mia, as she'd been known at the time – had decided to launch her own magazine to rival *Gloss*, the first person she'd phoned was Madeline. Over a lunch of chicken Caesar salad and mineral water at Soho House, Madeline had agreed to partner up with Jo and form Platinum Publishing, a consumer magazine publishing company that would specialise in high-end magazines as well as web properties that complimented their brands. They funded the company with the hush money they had received from Joshua Garnet, and within a fortnight they'd rented a large office in Soho and employed a receptionist, a research team, an art director and an advertising sales team. For six months both Jo and Madeline worked fourteen-hour days and planned every aspect of their first launch. *Cerise* magazine, they had decided, was going to be aimed at women who were sick of being dictated to by shiny women's magazines like *Gloss* and *Cosmopolitan*, and even though the ideology behind *Cerise* defied convention, Jo knew that the magazine would be an instant success.

When Jo was growing up, she had always wanted to tell magazine readers which clothes from the catwalk would be the season's hottest trends. Now, however, the internet had changed all that, and even though magazines could still dictate, their messages were falling on deaf ears because women preferred the instant accessibility of the internet to magazines that were out of date because they only came out monthly. Jo's research team discovered that women now visited and created websites that helped them carve out and define their individuality, and in doing so they stopped buying the magazines that said, rather sinisterly, that if they didn't wear tulip skirts or Sienna Miller-style leggings they were committing fashion death. Jo saw that *Cerise* would never work if they preached to women in the same way that *Gloss* did, and instead she focused on the pick-and-mix ethos of the blogs she was reading; the online diaries where women could publish what they really liked, rather than pretending to rate the same fashion and trends that magazines told them to buy.

Jo watched the internet intently during those six months of planning. For so many years she had viewed magazines as her knowledgeable older sisters, and when Jo had been at school, magazines were her best friends – they were what she turned to when she was feeling insecure and believed she didn't know any of the answers to life. Even though the magazines couldn't help her lose weight or make friends, Jo drew comfort from knowing the best way to apply liquid eyeliner, or who the hottest new Brazilian model was. What Jo didn't realise was that the magazine makers weren't trying to make Jo feel better about herself, but were in fact hoping they would make her feel worse by subliminally saying, 'You don't know this, but we do, so therefore you need us because you're as worthless as you think you are.' Now she was older, Jo believed that women's magazines sold unhappiness and insecurity, and what she wanted to do with *Cerise* was sell happiness instead. Jo didn't want people to feel dissatisfied with their lives when they were reading *Cerise*, and she hoped they would feel normal for not fitting into a magazine-produced stereotype of who they had to be, what they had to buy and say, and – most importantly – what they had to look like.

As Jo had planned the launch of the magazine and accompanying website, she'd realised that not only was she breaking down the messages that all other women's magazines were sending out, but she was also destroying the media-produced stereotype of what a beautiful girl should look like. With hindsight, Jo now realised that she too had subscribed to the magazine ideal of beauty, and that it was magazines she had turned to when she was planning her cosmetic surgery. Rather than just envying the pretty girls in the magazines like so many other readers had, Jo had taken it to an extreme and bought herself that near-unobtainable beauty so she could have a career in the media. Jo felt ashamed as she realised how shallow she had been, and she set about trying to transform herself back into a version of the girl she had been before she had surgery.

The first step was to rid herself of her golden hair and to become a brunette again. When the hairdresser at Charles Worthington had removed the towel from around her head, Jo's eyes had filled with tears on seeing her newly dyed hair. With shiny mahogany hair, Jo looked like the slimmer, prettier version of the lumpy girl she could remember being as a teenager, and as she admired herself a quiet rage formed within her, spurring her on to make sure that *Cerise* was the best women's magazine in the UK. Jo knew she couldn't blame *Gloss* entirely for the media-construct of women – where all girls were supposed to be beautiful, slender and highly sexualised – but she did know that her magazine would never be held responsible for making any girl who was slightly plump or plain feel bad about themselves again. But as well as making her readers feel more secure about who they really were, she also wanted to entertain them and make them laugh, and she formulated *Cerise* to be everything she had ever wanted in a magazine herself. When Jo and Madeline looked at their first dummy copy before sending it to the printers they both agreed that they had never seen anything like it. They both thought it was the best magazine in the world.

The first issue launched as a package of showbiz gossip, paparazzi photographs that showed what celebrities really looked like without airbrushing, and real-life stories that all women could identify with. Instead of employing a fashion director who was a slave to what men wanted women to look like, Jo employed a team of girls who were so hungry to be part of the industry that they had previously set up edgy fashion websites that reported on the trends on the street. In *Cerise*, each fashion journalist described real-life fashion that they saw in London, New York and Milan, and on top of that the magazine invited readers to email in high-resolution photographs of themselves in their favourite outfits. The mix of real fashion combined with straight-talking reportage of the catwalk shows was a hit with women who didn't have the money to copy what the fashion houses were churning out, and Jo and Madeline toasted their success. They had combined citizen journalism with celebrity glamour, and the readers were lapping it up. So much so that Lucy, who was now editing *Gloss*, reported a forty per cent drop in the

Garnet title's circulation soon after they had launched. Jo remembered their conversation exactly.

'Joshua is beside himself,' Lucy had said quietly down the phone, after she'd spotted Joshua throwing a copy of *Cerise* magazine at Debbie in a rage. 'He's asked me to think of ideas for *Gloss* that will get our circulation rising again. What do you think I should do?'

Jo had laughed. 'Put a stick-thin blonde on the cover and make sure that your fashion pieces are even more commanding than usual,' Jo had said. 'Oh, and find a Hollywood anorexic and write an editorial saying now women aren't sexy if they're not as thin as her.'

Lucy hadn't spoken for a moment. 'I get what you're saying, but isn't that a little irresponsible?' she'd asked. 'I mean, *Gloss* still has some readers, and I'd hate to think of them starving themselves because we've declared size zero the coolest body shape for the year.'

Jo's smile had frozen. She had been so intent on destroying *Gloss* that she hadn't thought about their readers. 'You're right,' she'd said seriously. 'Why don't you take the most extreme outfits you can find from the catwalk and tell your readers that they won't look sexy unless they copy them completely? You know, full-blown Gautier sailor costumes for the office, and Betty Jackson gothic ball-gowns for nights out on the pull. Rather than looking fashionable your readers will just look silly instead. And hopefully they won't resort to throwing up to lose a drastic amount of weight.'

Lucy had chuckled down the phone. 'You got it,' she'd said, and the next issue of *Gloss* followed Jo's advice perfectly. Circulation dropped even more, and as a result Joshua closed *Cycling Monthly* and spent their budget on redesigning and marketing *Gloss*. When he did so, circulation fell further, and it was then that Jo had realised that it was only a matter of time before *Gloss* went out of business.

'Joshua *has* to be shutting *Gloss* down, he's run out of options,' Madeline said, as she crossed her legs and leant back in her chair. Her white Dior sandals, crusted with crystals, sparkled in the sunlight that beamed into the office. 'I've thought about what else he can do to salvage *Gloss*'s brand, but really, nothing can be done. It's dead, and he knows it.'

Jo smirked, and as she did Madeline was struck by how fresh-faced Jo was, despite working to deadline the night before. Her simple navy blue Chloé wrap-dress showed off her size-twelve curves, and the diamond solitaire necklace that hung from her neck nestled on top of her lightly tanned cleavage. Despite everything Jo had gone through in the last year she still looked stunning, and as she thought about *Gloss* shutting down her cheeks flushed excitedly. 'I bet it hurts for him to realise it, too. Not only have we put one of Joshua's most successful magazines out of business, we have also done it with his money. That's got to be painful.'

Madeline smiled. 'He deserves it.' She sighed and looked out of the window that overlooked Soho Square. Outside people were enjoying the early summer sunshine on the grass, and Madeline itched to be at home with her baby. The sooner *Gloss* folded, the sooner they could employ Lucy to run *Cerise*, meaning that she could take the maternity leave she desperately craved. Madeline tried to stop thinking about her son and work, and changed the subject. 'Now, while we're waiting, tell me what you thought about Jake. He certainly liked you – he's already sent me an email asking if you'd appreciate a phone call.'

Jo recalled the weekend before, when she had attended one of Madeline's dinner parties. Although the food had been excellent – Madeline had asked her local Thai to deliver as she didn't have time to cook – Jo had been set up with Jake Pritchard, an investment banker who kept Porsches and visited New York for long weekends. The moment Jo had seen him she'd admired his choppy light-brown hair, his impressive broad shoulders, and the way his eyes twinkled when he gave her an easy, relaxed smile, but there was something about Jake that just didn't feel right. There was no spark.

'Jake was lovely,' Jo began slowly, hoping she wouldn't hurt Madeline's feelings, 'but ...'

Madeline raised her eyebrows. Jake was one of many men she had set Jo up with, and yet again, he didn't fit the bill despite being one of London's most eligible bachelors and clearly having a thing for Jo.

'But he's not right for you,' Madeline concluded with an exasperated sigh. 'You do know you're going to have to get over this mythical William fellow at some point, don't you?' she asked gently, and at the mention of William's name she saw Jo flinch.

'There's nothing to get over,' Jo said lightly, forcing a smile. 'William Denning and I were never "together", and to be honest ...' Jo trailed off when she saw that Lucy had appeared in the doorway to her office, and in a flash all thoughts of William disappeared. Lucy stared at Jo and Madeline with a grave expression, and for a moment neither partners of Platinum Publishing felt as though they could breathe. Lucy clearly had news, but it didn't look good.

'Well?' Madeline whispered, as Lucy looked down at the floor. Jo looked from one woman to the other, and before she could stop herself she felt her heart sink. *Gloss* hadn't folded, she thought. Somehow Joshua had weaseled out of the inevitable yet again and had managed to keep it going. Just as Jo felt disappointment run through her body she saw a tiny flicker of laughter appear at the corners of Lucy's mouth, and in that moment she knew they had done it.

'It's over, isn't it?' Jo yelled, and despite hoping to keep her face poker-straight for as long as possible, Lucy gave her the biggest grin Jo had ever received and nodded happily. Jo let out a massive whoop, and she leapt over to Madeline and flung her arms around her. 'We've shut down *Gloss*! We've shut down *Gloss*!' The three women hugged each other and started bouncing around the office, and as they congratulated each other the editorial team watched them through the glass divider that separated Jo's office from the open-plan editorial floor. All three were crying tears of happiness, and even though nobody else knew what they had done, the industry press would soon be reporting how *Gloss* had shut down after experiencing a ninety-three per cent drop in circulation.

'Where the fuck are you? You're late,' Lucy barked down the phone to Jo two weeks later. 'This is our celebration dinner and we can't order until you get here, so jump in a fucking cab and get here now.'

Jo tried not to laugh and turned off her computer. In the two weeks since Garnet Publishing had announced that *Gloss* would be folding, Jo had pushed herself even harder to make sure that *Cerise* would win Magazine of the Year at the UK Magazine Awards. Although there was no doubt in her mind that the magazine would definitely be shortlisted, Jo knew that if she made the next issue even better *Cerise*'s circulation would go through the roof, setting a record in women's magazines and making Platinum Publishing's turnover the largest in the country. Jo wanted it all, and she wasn't scared of working hard to get it.

But despite being on a constant high because her magazine was doing so well, Jo still went to bed every night feeling like something was missing from her life. As she hailed a black cab and told the driver to take her to Hakkasan, Jo thought about her friends. Amelia – who was travelling around India sourcing material for the interior design company she had set up with her mother – was sending coy emails about a man she had met. Madeline had Dan and their baby son, and even Gable, who was still officially in a relationship with Violet Compton, had found a discreet boyfriend who was happy to spend time with him out of the limelight. Only Lucy was still single, but, unlike her, Jo now wanted to share her success with someone she loved. Despite having a bestselling magazine and an enviable mortgage-free home in Primrose Hill, Jo found that her life still felt empty, and it was when she was eating supper alone in her kitchen late at night that she wished she had someone to go home to. She wished she had a boyfriend. She wished she had William.

As the cab pulled up outside the restaurant, Jo checked her reflection one final time. Her brunette hair had grown so long that it nearly touched her waist, and despite putting on weight, Jo was comfortable with her size-twelve body. She looked healthy, she thought, as she remembered how she had struggled to get down to a size ten. And not only that, she looked happy, too. Tonight she was wearing a peacock-blue Yves Saint Laurent chiffon dress, and to co-ordinate she was in the silver Jimmy Choos she had been wearing when she had told Joshua Garnet who she really was. They were fitting heels for a fitting evening – one where she and her friends would celebrate running the best magazine in the country and toasting the end of *Gloss*.

Jo walked past the bouncer and down the red-lit stairs into Hakkasan, and she wove herself around the carved oriental screens until she reached the table where her friends were sitting. As she did so she could feel the eyes of some of the other diners on her, and she heard faint whispers of her name. For a second she heard the name 'Mia Blackwood' said in hushed tones, and she smiled to herself. She was still Mia Blackwood, just as she had never stopped being Joanne Hill, and even though she now wanted to be known just as Jo, she didn't mind being called Mia. That name would always be part of her, and it was part of her history.

'We thought you'd never get here,' Madeline said wryly, her face solemn in the midnight-blue lighting of the restaurant. Madeline was in one of her black Chanel suits, and she looked every inch the publishing magnate. Jo felt ridiculously girlie when she compared her outfit to Madeline's, but she remembered that she wasn't quite twenty-six and she didn't need to be as grown-up as Madeline was. 'I'm assuming everything is falling apart now that I'm on my delayed maternity leave?'

Jo laughed as she struggled to hear Madeline speak above the music and loud chatter of the other diners. 'As much as I'd love to tell you that we're not coping, I'm afraid that we are. Lucy's fitted in well, as I'm sure she has told you countless times already.'

'Oh, yes,' Lucy laughed. 'I always knew I was a better editor than Madeline was.' Lucy was dressed in a tight dark grey Ungaro dress and she had a red bow in her hair. As always, she looked incredibly stylish. She shot Madeline a pretend dirty look, and grinned. 'Especially considering how well I did with *Gloss*.'

'And if you shut down *Cerise* like you did *Gloss* I will have to kill you,' Jo said happily. As publisher, Jo had final say on everything that happened with the magazine, but everything Lucy had done in the past two weeks had been brilliant.

'You may want to kill me instead when you find out what I've done,' Madeline said, and Jo looked at her business partner curiously.

'Now, I know how much you hate not being in the office,' Madeline began, as the rest of the table – made up of Madeline's partner Dan, Lucy and a couple of girls from the magazine – fell quiet, 'but I have a present for you that you absolutely have to accept, and it will involve not coming into work for a bit. When I first met you, Jo, I think it's fair to say that I didn't have any time for you. I admit now that I was wrong to judge you on your looks, and because of everything that we've both been through in the last few years, I think it is also fair to say that you gave as good as you got.'

Lucy laughed, and Madeline smiled as they both remembered their parts in Jo's climb to power.

'You have been more of a friend to me than I'd ever thought possible,' Madeline continued. 'Without you I never would have seen my bastard ex-husband run his most popular magazine into the ground, and without you I may never have clawed my way out of the black pit of depression I found myself in when Joshua left me.'

Madeline looked down at the table then, and Jo reached over and held her hand. Nobody could ever know what it had felt like to be treated so badly by their husband, and Jo knew that Madeline had gone through some dark times following Jo's promotion to editor of *Gloss*.

'Because you have been such a good friend to me, I have got you the one present that I know you've hankered after for all these years.' Madeline reached into her black Mulberry handbag and pulled out a cream envelope. Jo couldn't think what Madeline could have bought her, but when Jo opened the envelope she saw there were two plane tickets for a month-long holiday in Barbados, with a hotel reservation at the Sandy Lane Hotel. In a million years Jo had never imagined that Madeline would give her a present so extravagant, and she blushed a deep scarlet.

'I don't know what to say,' Jo began, wondering why Madeline thought she had always wanted to go to the Caribbean. Before Jo could say anything else Madeline silenced her.

'There's one condition that comes as part of this present, but I'm not sure how you're going to react when you find out what it is.'

Jo gazed at Madeline, and a thousand ideas ran through her head. Did Madeline want to buy her out of the company? Jo wondered. Or did she want Jo to buy her out? Jo's brain was buzzing with excitement and panic, but luckily Madeline pulled Jo away from her thoughts with a tiny cough.

'The condition is that you have to go on holiday with one of my friends,' Madeline said lightly, and when Jo looked even more confused, Madeline decided to put her out of her misery. 'He's sitting at that table over there.'

Jo followed Madeline's eyes with her own, and despite the blue lights of the room there was no mistaking the man who was sitting alone at a table nearby. His dark blond hair was touching the collar of his navy blue jacket, and despite being the type of man who was more comfortable being in a local country pub, he looked completely at ease sitting alone in a Michelin-starred restaurant while surrounded by celebrities. His eyes penetrated Jo's, and for a moment Jo felt as though a shot of pure happiness had been fired at her from an imaginary Cupid. William.

'Aren't you going to introduce us, then?' Lucy said casually, breaking the silence with her inquisitiveness, but before Jo could say anything William had approached her and scooped her up in his arms. Jo felt as though every nerve-ending she had was on fire, and as she leant against William's chest she felt as though she couldn't breathe – it was actually him, there, in the flesh. William had hardly changed, and – if Jo was reading it right – his feelings for her hadn't changed either. Jo put her arms around William's back and pulled him closer towards her, and he looked down at her tenderly.

'Will someone bloody tell me what's going on?' Lucy said indignantly as she stared at Jo with her mouth open, but neither Jo nor William heard her as they were completely and utterly lost in each other.

Madeline cleared her throat. 'Lucy, this is William Denning,' she said. 'He's the bestselling author of two novels, and his latest one, *Fighting for Fame*, has been at the top of the bestsellers' list for the past three weeks.'

Lucy rolled her eyes. 'Yes, I know *who* he is, but how does he know Jo?' she asked. 'And why are they hugging each other like that?'

William and Jo pulled apart, and Jo was unable to look any of her friends in the eye.

'William's an old friend,' she began, glancing quickly at a beaming Madeline before looking down at the floor so she'd not have to catch anyone's eye. 'We worked together in a pub years ago, and, well ...' Jo trailed off and looked at William. The last time she had seen him had been in the Charlotte Street Hotel, and the memory of him insulting how she looked still stung. She wondered if William still felt the same way, and almost instinctively, he knew what Jo was thinking and cleared his throat.

'The last time I saw Jo I have to admit I wasn't particularly nice,' he said, looking ashamed. 'I was in a hotel being interviewed by a gorgeous, glamorous blonde, and I was hating every minute of it. I was so blinded by my dislike of being interviewed that I failed to see just who Mia really was,' he said, and he turned to Jo and took her hand.

'If I'd known that Mia Blackwood was you I never would have walked out of that hotel,' William said. 'But despite writing about how awful London was, I still had to be there to promote my book. You can see why I couldn't stand talking to magazines that day, can't you?' he said ruefully, and Jo felt her heart thudding.

'I thought it was all about me,' she whispered. 'I thought you despised Mia Blackwood for being a glamorous London journalist, and even though I wanted to tell you who I was, I thought that if you'd known I'd had surgery you'd have hated me even more,' she whispered, and William shook his head vehemently.

'I could never hate you,' he said gently, 'but I do want to get to know you again. It seems like you've been to hell and back in the last few years, and I've missed out on an awful lot.' Jo nodded silently, and prayed that the tears that threatened wouldn't spill on to her face.

'Let's start right now,' she whispered to him, and Lucy clapped her hands together in glee.

'If you'll excuse us,' William began, 'we have several years of catching up to do, and I think it's probably better if we do it in private ... especially considering the number of journalists sitting at this table,' he joked. He turned to Jo and gently touched her face. 'Is that OK with you?'

Jo nodded and grinned at her friends, and William led her out of the restaurant, refusing to waste any time. At the top of the stairs he turned to her, and he leant towards her in the seedy, run-down street. The sound of police sirens on Tottenham Court Road whizzed past, and William waited until there was only the quiet sound of nearby traffic before speaking.

'Before we catch up I need to ask you something,' William said nervously, and Jo had a sudden flashback to a conversation they'd had when she had admitted to being a virgin. She had told William then that she needed to be happy in herself before she could embark on a relationship with him, but this time Jo knew there was nothing else in her life that she wanted to achieve. Apart from William, she had everything she'd ever wanted.

'Once upon a time you told me that you had three dreams,' William began, holding Jo tenderly. 'The first was that you wanted to run the best women's magazine in the country, and the second was that you wanted to be thin. Now, I've been following your career since your exposé in *Vanity Fair*, and there is no question that *Cerise* is the biggest women's magazine in the country. Dream two – to be thin – has undoubtedly been achieved, because, Joanne, I have never seen a girl as exquisite as you in my life.' William let his eyes run over Jo's stunning face, her long, softly waved brown hair and her dramatic burlesque-style curves. William thought lustily about what Jo looked like under her expensive dress, and he took a deep breath and stared into her eyes in order to compose himself. They were still the same vibrant green that he remembered.

'But what was my third dream?' Jo asked, as William raised her hand up to his lips and kissed it so softly that Jo's heart began to thud underneath the chiffon of her dress.

'You wanted to fall in love with someone who loved you back,' William said softly, and as he brushed a tendril of hair away from Jo's face, he realised that even after all this time he loved her as much as he had always done. 'If you'll have me, I'd like to make your final dream come true,' he said, and Jo began to sob with happiness.

'I never planned to ask you this on a street in London, but . . .' Before Jo could realise what was happening, William produced a rectangular velvet-lined box that opened to reveal tear-drop-shaped diamonds that hung delicately from a white-gold chain.

'Joanne Hill, will you spend the rest of your life with me?' William asked nervously, and as Jo looked at the diamonds she knew that they mirrored the tears of jubilation that were currently falling from her face.

'Only if you don't demand that I change the way I look,' Jo joked, and William stood and scooped her up in his arms.

'I will always love you just the way you are,' William said seriously, and as Jo began to kiss the man of her dreams she realised she'd found her happy ending.